Reap What You Sow

Seasons of Man – Book Two

S.M. Anderson

Other Books by S.M Anderson - and reading order:
All titles are available on Amazon and enrolled in Kindle Unlimited. Audio versions for all books in both series are being produced by Podium Audio and are available on Audible.

<u>**The Eden Chronicles:**</u>
Book One: "**A Bright Shore**"
Book Two: "**Come and Take It**"
Book Three: "**New Shores**"
Book Four: forthcoming (2020)

<u>**Seasons of Man:**</u>
Book One: "**End of Summer**"
Book Two: "***Reap What You Sow***"
Book Three: forthcoming

Chapter 1

Virginia

"Gunny? We got a situation."

Marine Gunnery Sergeant John Edwin Bruce had been sure that he'd be able to get some real sleep tonight. Nine months, two weeks, and four days of evidence to the contrary, tonight was to have been the night when he'd sleep for more than a couple of hours at a time. He was nothing if not an optimist. He had to be; after nine-plus months of hiding underground while nearly everyone on the surface died, optimism was all he had left.

"Gunny!" He could tell it was Corporal Hanson's voice shouting from his open doorway. "Farmer" wouldn't be disturbing him on a whim.

"What is it? What'ya got?"

"Sorry to bother your sleep, Gunnery Sergeant." Hanson was a polite, squared-away kid from some farm town in Washington State. A solid Marine and the closest thing to a friend he had left down here. Which meant anywhere.

"The El Tee is acting up again."

He swung his feet off his bunk and pivoted in one fluid movement. His socked feet landed in the accordioned pile of BDU pants. Elbows resting on his thighs, he was still unsure of whether "acting up" required his presence. With all due respect to Lieutenant Benoit, that bar had been raised several times. Once those boots came on, he knew he'd be awake for another day. Well, not exactly awake, but functioning on autopilot. It was the best any of them had left.

"Quoting from the book of Revelations, acting up? Or something new?"

"Gunny . . ." He could see Hanson's head hanging low and shaking back and forth in the backlit doorway.

"Lucas, just tell me."

"He's dry humping the airlock door, Gunny. He's not doing well."

Hanson spoke in a whispered rush as if trying to keep secret the fact that the El Tee's mind had cracked around the six-month mark.

"I was just gonna let him wear down, but he's different. He's freaking the guys out. 'Poy' isn't handling it well."

The surviving members of his Marine recon squad were stacked on this side of the thick ballistic glass of the sliding door separating the airlock room from the hallway. They were watching their commander through the glass when he rounded the corner of the final hallway. He sensed the issue before he saw it. His guys were armed, and standing ready behind the glass.

"He's got a sidearm, Gunny." Corporal Tommy Salguero looked back at him as he approached.

He wanted to scream; somebody had fucked up. They hadn't let the lieutenant have access to more than a plastic spork for months. He did a quick head count and came up with seven, including himself and Lieutenant Benoit.

"Where's Elliot?"

His guys all pulled the momentary, standard military "who, me?" reflex look of confusion at the man standing next to them before they all realized Private First-Class Elliot wasn't with them.

"Shit!" Salguero spit out. "I'm on it."

He nodded in thanks as Salguero rushed past him, providing his first sight of Lieutenant Benoit. The El Tee's back was to them; he was leaning up against the covered control lectern that controlled the airlock. On the other side of the forty-ton blast door was the elevator that had deposited them down here for what was supposed to have been a two-week rotation. They'd been a squad of twelve plus one sane, squared-away lieutenant at the time. Five suicides had reduced their number, and they'd been damn lucky that Lieutenant Benoit had managed to stop Lance Corporal Kearney before he could finish setting off the explosives that would have killed them all. Taking out one of his own men had been the beginning of whatever had snapped in the lieutenant. He pulled his own sidearm, knowing he might have to do the same.

"Open the door."

"Gunny, just let him cry it out."

Nathans was a cold bastard, but that didn't make him wrong.

"He cocks up that control panel, we *will* be trapped. Open the door, close it once I'm through."

The lieutenant gave no indication he heard the hydraulic-powered door cycling behind him. He crept in, holding his gun up. Gunnery sergeant or not, he was no different from any of his guys. He wanted out of here in the worst way. The oppressive weight of "The Hole" had become ever present. Beyond the tons of rock between them and the surface, the constant hum of the air-cycling units was starting to feel like a beehive in his head. Over the months, the smell of the place had gone from hospital-flavored sterile to a funky mash-up of new paint, engine oil, and genuine Marine boot funk.

He'd already made the unannounced decision that if no one showed up with the proper authorization code, he was going to pop the lid at the one-year mark. The virus might still be active on the surface, but at least they would die under the open sky. Their commanding officer was now in a position to screw that up.

"That you, Gunny?"

"Yes, sir."

Benoit shifted his weight but otherwise didn't move. "John, I can't see. My eyes . . . I've gone blind."

"Sir, if you lose the sidearm, we can check that out."

"I can't do this, John." Benoit sucked in a massive breath like a kid who'd been crying. "Not anymore."

"Sir, come with me. We'll get your eyes checked out. You just need some rest."

"You've got this, Gunny. I've . . . I know I've had a poor effect on the command, I can't . . . I'm turning command over to you."

"Sir?"

"Gunny!" The lieutenant's command bark almost brought him to attention out of reflex and eighteen years of programming.

"I wanted out so bad, Gunny." Benoit's free hand looked like he was reaching out and touching something, or someone. "Can't you see? I've made it. I'm going to stay right where I am."

Lt. Benoit never turned to face him, didn't make him do what he feared doing the most. The lieutenant's dangling hand holding the sidearm just flashed upward. A heartbeat later, the top of Benoit's head erupted, as the sound of the strangely muffled gunshot reverberated around the steel box of the control room.

He opened his eyes to see the lieutenant's body in front of him, the blood starting to pool. He knew jealousy was a fucked-up thing to be feeling right now, but there it was. He turned to look back through the glass at his remaining men; they were all looking at him—the one remaining person in their vast underground prison who could open the door and let them out.

*

Chapter 2

"It's a start." Daniel surveyed the former soccer fields that had been plowed and planted with every kind of vegetable he could imagine. They'd planted some of everything they had seeds for.

"Come July, if half of it's alive." Michelle was shaking her head. "That'll be a start."

"Given we don't have a bloody idea of what we're doing, it doesn't look too bad." Rachel shed her work gloves and swatted them against her pants.

"He's having the time of his life, isn't he?" Daniel asked the question, and everyone knew who he meant. One the far side of the plowed field, Pro was driving the small tractor like the rental it was. The teenager had discovered the hand brake that locked up the rear tires and was entertaining himself in the graveled parking lot adjacent to the former soccer fields.

"Somebody should be," Michelle answered.

Rachel knew what Michelle meant. She and the other people who had decided to stay together following the change in ownership at the mall had been working nonstop for the last two months. Their numbers had dropped sharply following the events that led to their takeover of the mall and hotel. A lot of people, given the first freedom they'd had in a while, just disappeared as singletons or in small groups. Many had stayed close and watched what became of the place and had begun filtering back in, usually bringing other local survivors with them. They were over 450 people at the moment, and Michelle had been running herself ragged, keeping everyone busy and pulling in the same direction.

Some of the returnees had traveled farther afield and returned with horror stories of ravaging looter gangs. Others had come back out of a need for some basic food security. Most places had been picked clean of shelf food that hadn't gone bad. Feeding oneself or a group off the leftovers of civilization was a lot more difficult than it had been, and it was only going to get harder. Jason was convinced people would start banding together out of necessity, either to build something through hard work or to be able to take from others. She hadn't liked the way he'd assumed the latter would be easier.

She hoped Jason was alright. He'd made a pretense of caring about getting crops planted and more people trained up to defend what they were building, but it had lasted only until he had fully gotten his legs back. Then he was gone. Like he couldn't wait to get out from under the responsibility and authority that everyone had seemed more than ready to saddle him with. Her greatest fear was that it was her. What she'd assumed they might have had, had only been more pressure laid on his shoulders.

Whatever the reason, he'd left three days ago with very little in terms of a goodbye. He was out there alone. Looking for threats - "patrolling," he'd called it. In her gut, it felt like he'd run away. It had been all she could do to keep Pro from going after him; staying put herself hadn't been any easier. Everyone else's confidence aside, especially Michelle's, she wasn't convinced Jason would come back at all.

"I need a drink!" Michelle announced as she moved through the small group until she threw an arm around her shoulders and pulled her into a one-armed hug.

"So do you, I think," Michelle whispered.

"Am I that obvious?"

"He'll be back, girl."

*

Jason was a long way from Tysons. He'd started out with the intention of getting out to the Shenandoah Valley and checking out the farm property that Howard Dagman had left directions to. It was something that he'd wanted to do since discovering the directions during his first night in Dagman's house. That had been his excuse. The real reason was a host of shit he needed to sort out.

His world had died, and he'd made peace with that fact. He'd survived and stayed true to his promise to Sam—he'd helped. His ordered existence since the suck had almost made sense to him. He'd treated it like a mission that would have an ending. He'd thought he'd found that end, only to regain consciousness surrounded by people he had to admit he cared about. More than cared, in the case of some. That was where and when this feeling of impending doom had come down on him like a rainstorm that wouldn't let up.

He knew Rachel thought it was all her fault. He hadn't been able to find the words to tell her that it had been Elsa's sobbing hug of relief, that had almost crushed him. The little girl had already lost her real father. The pressure he'd felt to somehow step up and be a replacement had run head first into the wall of low expectation that he'd built up around himself and for future. He was self-aware enough to know it for the defensive mechanism it was. He was scared of caring again. It was far too easy to remember what he'd been thinking as he'd walked into the mall a few months past. If he was honest with himself, he'd been running from Rachel, Pro, and Elsa as much as he'd been trying to protect them.

He tried to tell himself he wasn't running away now, but he knew that for a lie, even if he did have every intention of going back. He'd let Reed and Daniel know he wouldn't be gone long. He'd been too chickenshit to have that same conversation with Rachel. The coward in him hoped she'd build some walls of her own.

Traveling at night, he'd made it out to Leesburg. Near as he could tell, the old city and surrounding suburbs were empty. He was sure there were survivors somewhere close. The shelves of homes and businesses had been picked clean. He'd seen firsthand the efficiency with which Bauman's crews had looted, and Leesburg reflected that same wholesale approach. Anything of future use was gone, yet the town was dead. On a hunch, he drove out of town, parked the old Land Rover, and hiked to within binocular range of the resort at Lansdowne, fearing another hotel-based gang of lunatics.

The place had been empty, at least of the living. He'd spent the rest of the daylight hours exploring nearby neighborhoods for any sign of life. Like Leesburg proper, it was as if whoever had looted the place had taken the survivors with them. At dark, he'd headed south on 15. With the scanner running, he started picking up scattered radio traffic. What started as squelch breaks, became scattered words the further he traveled south towards I-66. The interstate was the main artery running west out of the Washington metro area, and in different times, it was the route he would have taken out to the Shenandoah Valley.

Near Haymarket, the radio traffic became heavier. He made it underneath I-66 and pulled into the parking lot of a Bass Pro in the hopes of trying to break out what he was hearing. Two minutes after stopping, he watched as a large convoy of vehicles went past on 29/15 headed south. There were over twenty vehicles, including a few military castoff Humvees and two tractor trailers. They blew by, doing close to fifty miles an hour. That meant two things to him; whoever they were, they already knew the road ahead of them was clear. They'd have to at that speed. They were also going too fast to be looking for anyone, or maybe they just didn't care who saw them or their headlights.

None of that added up to anything that made him feel any better. He sat there, sweating with tension, long enough to confirm the radio chatter he'd been listening in on belonged to the mysterious convoy. By the time the signal started to degrade, he was rolling out onto the road behind them. He drove for an hour, using his night vision goggles to see by.

It had taken him the rest of the night to locate what he thought was their base in a gated community just outside of Culpepper, further south on Highway 15. He couldn't have been more wrong; it was their next target. In professional terms, it wasn't the cleanest attack he'd ever seen, but it clearly had military leadership. The neighborhood was hit from multiple directions at once. He'd watched as one team of attackers passed within twenty yards of where he'd set up to observe the "community." It was well past midnight, and the people in the houses had been asleep, except for a few guards who were killed outright or quickly taken prisoner.

Someone dropped a single mortar round into the community center, which was either a lucky shot or an indication that someone knew what they were doing. It seemed delivered as a more of a message than part of the actual attack. Whoever these guys were, two things were evident. One, they weren't military personnel. They just moved wrong, and their weapons were a wild mix of military castoffs and looted civilian gear. The same could be said of their vehicles. Two, they worked well as a group, showed some coordination, and most alarmingly, it was clear they'd done this before.

If he had to guess, somebody had been training them and had them on a tight leash. He was too distant to hear the shouted commands the attackers delivered from the front yards of the houses they'd surrounded, but in most cases, whatever was said resulted in people coming out with their hands up. The attackers, mostly men but more than a few women, moved in and relieved those surrendering of their weapons, before rounding them up and getting them loaded into the vehicles that had streamed into the neighborhood following the assault.

He wasn't sure what he was watching. Many of the survivors were allowed to go back into their homes to retrieve duffel bags or suitcases before they were loaded up. No one was shot, or seemed to be mistreated beyond the two guards he'd seen taken out. There was no culling of the elderly that he'd been half expecting, and there didn't seem to be any separation of the sexes. It was just a quick, matter-of-fact group abduction. More than a few people clearly didn't want to go, but raised rifles and a few shouts got them moving.

He sat still, in the tall grass of his hill overlooking the neighborhood. The vehicles holding the abductees began pulling out; a mix of big family-sized SUVs and school buses. He'd already decided he was going to follow and had just started to move when two tractor trailers rolled in and disgorged a large team of armed foragers. He couldn't help but be impressed with their technique. They moved quickly and worked as a team, emptying the houses and garages of anything of value. He could follow the tractor trailers more safely than he could the cars and trucks that had already departed.

He was even more cautious during the hike back out to where he'd hidden the Land Rover than he had been on the way in. The whole operation had been run like a forced relocation of an Afghan village that lay in the path of some impending operation. If he'd been planning what he'd just seen, he would have detailed a group of slow trailers to watch the area for a day or two.

Whoever these guys were, wherever they were headed, his trip out to Dagman's farm would have to wait.

*

Chapter 3

Newport News, VA

Pavel Eduardovich Volkov looked down at the sleeping form of Captain Naylor. He'd almost been surprised when the captain had reappeared on the deck of his submarine before it dove for the last time. The American Navy captain had finally dispensed of his responsibility to his ship, without letting go completely. Captain Naylor had, unlike so many others, decided to live. In Pavel's mind, it entitled the man to some uninterrupted sleep.

The fishing trawler with which they'd followed the *Boise* to deep water rode through the waves with a rocking motion that the submarine had not had. When he'd vomited over the side during the first day, he'd felt it a small victory that there had been anything in his stomach to void. They were going to live. None of them feared the virus any longer, not even Dr. Mandel. They'd lost one of the American Antarctic researchers in Cuba, but to insanity, not the virus. The woman had refused to get back on the submarine and wandered away into the hills above their beach.

The *Boise* had brought them to the famed American Newport News naval port before dropping off most of its passengers and returning to the sea for one last voyage. Colonel Skirjanek had remained ashore with the rest of their people, "to try and get organized," while he had accompanied some of the Navy crew on the trawler. The same trawler was just now motoring across some invisible barrier where the dark blue of the ocean took on a muddier green color that reminded him of the Sea of Azov and the waters around Rostov na Donu, where he'd grown up.

He took that as a sign. This place wasn't home, but nor was it Chechnya, Syria or Libya, and his new companions seemed like decent people. To his genuine surprise, he found that he liked Colonel Skirjanek. He didn't yet know if the man was worthy of being followed for the long term. To date, the colonel had been nothing but fair in his treatment of him and his fellow Russians. Time would tell. For the moment, he was grateful for the suddenly smoother ride of the fishing boat and very anxious to have his feet on solid ground again.

"You look like a man with a lot on his mind."

Pavel looked behind him to be certain there was not someone else in the wheelhouse besides Captain Naylor, who was still asleep on the couch. There was only the *Boise*'s executive officer, Hoyt Sweet, driving the ship and looking at him sideways.

"I am anxious to get to land."

"I hear that." Sweet was older than his captain by a good ten years, perhaps in his early fifties. His hair was gray, his face weathered from worry and a lifetime at sea. Pavel knew the type; this man had given his life to service. The Navy personnel on *his* submarine would have been like his children. Pavel thought the big man could have passed for a Russian until he opened his mouth to speak.

"How long, Mr. Sweet?"

"Another ninety minutes in this tub. It's just Hoyt, by the way. I figure my Navy days are just about over."

"What means your name, Hoyt?"

"Doesn't mean anything beyond the fact that it was my grandfather's name."

"I see."

"Meant a lot to me and the others that you were ready to go after the captain, pull him out." Hoyt spoke softly with a glance back at his sleeping captain.

He shrugged. He'd given Skirjanek his word that he would do his best to make certain Captain Naylor did not take the same path as his ship.

"He saved us; he is owed."

"He wouldn't see it that way," Hoyt whispered. "Still . . . thank you."

He didn't know what to say. No one should have to thank anyone for doing their duty. He was going to have to get used to these Americans and their practiced politeness.

Hoyt motioned out the window with his chin. "Given how far you are from home, it seems a shitty thing to say, but I grew up around here. It's going to be strange to see the place with no people."

"Will you remain with Colonel Skirjanek?"

"I suppose I will," Hoyt answered after a moment. The man let out a short bark of a laugh. "Not like I have anything else to do."

"Will all your people feel the same way?"

Hoyt shook his head. "You saw them when we made port. I'd be surprised if half the people we landed with are still there."

He hadn't noticed. He'd just assumed they'd all stay with the colonel. "Would the colonel just let them go? He is in command, no?"

Hoyt just gave him a strange look. "In command of what? The boat is gone, country's gone, no more Navy. I figure whatever his plans are, it's going to be a volunteer effort."

"I would think people would know there is safety in numbers."

"I don't think a lot of our people care, Mr. Volkov."

"Just Pavel, please, or Pavel Eduardovich."

Hoyt barked his laugh again and nodded his head knowingly. "Pavel it is."

"What would these people do if they leave?" He couldn't see the logic in wandering around a dead America, any more than what he imagined for himself had he been able to get to Russia.

"Try to get back to wherever they came from. If they don't die getting there, they'll probably just find that anybody they cared about is dead."

"They should stay."

"No doubt." Hoyt nodded out the window. "That said, first thing I'm going to do is go check on my brother's family in Norfolk. I won't be following anybody until I know for certain. They'd be the only people I have left."

"That is understandable," Pavel lied. The man had to know his family was almost certainly dead. For him, it was easy to think so; he'd had no family left when he'd volunteered for a two-year rotation at Vostok Base.

"And you?" Hoyt asked him. "The colonel seems to talk to you as much as anyone. Do you know what he has planned?"

"I do not." Which was another lie, but an allowable one. He could see the acceptance in Hoyt's face. "He has mentioned he has a location in mind."

"I'd figured your people would try to find a serviceable boat and get across the pond to Europe."

He thought about what Hoyt had said; that many of the Americans would leave their party. He hadn't even considered whether some of his countrymen would feel the same way.

"It would be foolish," he answered. "If they survived the trip, everyone is as dead there as they are here."

He could only make out half a dozen figures on the concrete wharf as the trawler passed the massive dry dock holding the rusting carcass of a half-finished aircraft carrier. Pavel thought he could make out Skirjanek's smaller athletic frame standing next to Antwan Sikes and Chief Petty Officer Cruz, who both towered over him. Behind them, he could make out Dr. Mandel and several of his fellow Russians.

As the trawler neared, he could see a larger group in the shade of an open warehouse door. It was late May, and already the oppressive heat and humidity he'd been warned about had arrived. After their recent experience on the ice pack, Pavel welcomed it.

He watched with interest as Hoyt's Navy crew threw ropes ashore to their comrades. He could not pretend to understand most things nautical, but even to his unpracticed eye, the trawler was tied up with what he considered a bare minimum of care or professionalism. Captain Naylor's emergence from the pilothouse and down the makeshift gangplank was met with a few cheers and more than a few salutes. Naylor seemed to be a different person since awaking. He thought Hoyt had put it correctly when the XO had told his captain that "he still looked like shit, but a lot better than he had."

The Navy captain had actually smiled in response.

The trawler emptied quickly until he was the last one to cross over to the quay. Skirjanek seemed to have been waiting for him.

"I've never been one for speeches," he began. "Having to give them is even worse than having to listen to them. That said, Captain Naylor, we all owe you our thanks." Skirjanek nodded towards the captain of the *Boise*. "It seems somehow small to just thank you, when we all owe you our lives. You certainly don't need me standing here telling you that your duty is done. You know that in your bones. We all do.

"For everyone still here, your participation would be very much appreciated, but it is not expected. Many of our survivors have already elected to strike out on their own. They have my blessings and prayers. In the event they change their minds, I told them we will wait here for one week. You all need to make that same choice, take the same time to refit and regain some strength.

"Anyone who comes with me needs to know that I can't tell you what we will find out there, only that I'm personally going to hang on to my mission. Not because of my last orders, but because I believe it's going to need to be done. Navy personnel and any of our other service members are free from any obligation. I've discussed this with Dr. Mandel; the same holds for our Russian friends. The world has moved on. We each deserve to start anew in the manner of our own choosing."

"What is that mission, Colonel?" Hoyt asked from where he stood next to his former captain.

"I only have a goal," Skirjanek said without a pause. "Create an environment that is safe, somewhere the survivors can recover, rebuild. We've all seen what's happening with the survivors—this place won't be any different than Cuba, just far better armed. I don't have a clue what we'll find. I do know it will need to be done, and it won't be easy."

Skirjanek paused and seemed to nod to himself. "As I said, that's the goal. As far as an immediate mission goes? It's to get healthy and organized. That is going to have to suffice for the moment. I don't want anyone to join me who isn't committed to the goal I outlined, so take the week, think on it, and decide."

*

Chapter 4

Charlottesville, VA

Jason didn't know what to think of Charlottesville, or maybe he needed to think of it as the campus of UVA; other than the one overriding fact that had been echoing in his head for the last hour as he observed the armed camp that had established itself across the University of Virginia campus. *These people have their shit together.*

He'd followed the tractor trailers back here, expecting them to roll up to a camp of armed goons. They'd instead backed into a package-handling facility on the edge of the campus, and started unloading just as another pair of trucks were departing with a convoy of six SUVs. He'd watched as nearly a hundred people—men, women, even a few teenagers, almost all of them armed—unloaded the trucks in the dark. He moved on to a different part of the campus, moving slow and staying hidden within the forested greenbelt, angling towards the area of the campus that was lit.

It had rained all day, but the evening was clear and warm. The common area, lying south of Jefferson's famous Rotunda in the middle of campus, was swarming with people. It looked like a giant swap market. It was by far the single largest concentration of people he'd seen since before the die-off, and as opposed to Bauman and the feudal freak show he'd had going in Tysons Corner, all of these people seemed armed. There wasn't any divide he could see between soldiers and sheep. No one seemed to be guarding anyone, *and* they'd managed to keep the lights running. The whole picture stood in sharp contrast to the activities he'd seen outside Culpepper.

He sat up from where he hid, atop a thick carpet of rain-slick rotting leaves left over from last autumn. He could see a glow of light over a row of dorm housing, across and behind the large lawn running south of the Rotunda. He backed off through the greenbelt and had started moving westward when he came across a wide strip of cultivated land. He couldn't tell what crop had been planted, but the wooden sign in front of him reading "4th Hole, Par 5—468 yds" was just one more piece of evidence that someone here was thinking for the long term.

Twenty minutes later, he'd successfully skirted the western edge of the campus, past the golf course; all what he'd seen had been plowed and planted. The glow of light was coming from the football stadium. His cover gave out as he approached the edge of the stadium's parking lot, and he was forced to stop. He spotted the guards around the place right away. Again, there was a mix of men and women; they all seemed very much awake and attentive as they guarded the tunnel entrances to the stadium. Each of the entrances had two static guards and a chain-link gate backed with plastic tarp, blocking any view within. A single light tower atop the lip of the stadium bowl was lit, and it had only one row of lights burning. Someone had adjusted the big lights to cover the whole stadium.

He was trying to figure out if the guards were there to keep people out or if there were people being held within, when an SUV and short transit bus rolled into the parking lot from the far end and drove slowly around the stadium to the main gate. Unarmed prisoners, subdued to the point that a couple of them were nearly carrying what looked like wounded, were unloaded from the two vehicles and directed at gunpoint down the tunnel. He had his binoculars up and was watching when the covered chain-link gate swung open. He caught a glimpse through the open gate of tent tops and a few figures who stood in the foreground, watching the newcomers come through the tunnel.

Shouts brought his attention back around to the bus. He watched as the guards shouted warnings and pointed their rifles at one teenager or young man who was running for all he was worth away from the stadium.

"Stop! Or we will shoot!"

A second later, two guards opened up and dropped the fleeing prisoner, shooting him in the back as he ran for the woods. The procession of the other prisoners, almost two dozen in all, including a couple of small children, paused for a moment until they were waved on into the stadium.

The gate swung shut, and he lost his view of everything but the guards on the outside, who simply went back to their posts. The drivers of the two vehicles collected the body and threw it into the back of the SUV. The stadium guards waved at the drivers of the two vehicles as they rolled back out the way they had come. Within a minute, the scene looked just like it had before they'd rolled up. There was a practiced routine to the process that left him wondering how long this place had been up and running.

He stayed where he was, kneeling behind a stand of trees and wondering what the hell he had just seen. When the stadium's PA system blared to life, it caused him to almost jump out of his skin. Five minutes later, when the looped recording started over, the hair on the back of his neck and arms was standing out with goose bumps.

"Welcome to the New People's Republic . . . We are the safety and new beginning you have been seeking. Together, we will rebuild and make new, a society that we can be proud of . . ." And on it went. It sounded a lot like somebody's wet dream of a socialist nirvana. Like any other religion, the recorded message hit all the required points of faith, common humanity, sacrifice, and zeal. What was lacking was any room for choice, free will, and most pointedly, any other religion. On that particular point, the suck and the die-off were offered up as evidence that God didn't exist, and never had.

"Those who put their faith in such lies brought us to this point.

Those who remain will not survive to share our new world, nor will any who resist. Others collect the castoffs of the old world. We collect people, the survivors, the builders of all that will be." The message played twice in the baritone voice of someone used to public speaking. It was as well done as he could imagine anything like it being done in the here and now. Background music accompanying the presentation left him wondering if he was just hearing the audio from a video running inside the stadium.

The false dawn was less than two hours away. He'd seen and heard enough to scare the shit out of him. He had started backing off the way he'd come, through the front nine of the former golf course, when the message started up again, this time in a woman's voice. He paused long enough to listen for anything new, but there wasn't; different voice, same message. He felt for the people held within the stadium. If the loop played all night, people were probably agreeing to anything just to be free of the place. Allowed the security of weapons, and fed, housed, and protected by the numbers of the place, why wouldn't they sign up?

He'd seen how they collected people, and it didn't mesh very well with the collectivist message of hope and justice that he could still catch pieces of as he moved farther away from the stadium. He imagined their sales pitch had held a lot more appeal last winter. Many people had still been in shock and a lot more vulnerable than the average survivor was at this point in time. He'd seen that himself. Those still alive at this point, at least the people he'd had contact with in Tysons, were a lot harder and in many cases a lot more self-sufficient than the average survivor had been early on. Judging by the new arrivals at the mall, they didn't strike him as the type to buy into this kind of con. Then again, the group he'd watched get taken in Culpepper hadn't exactly been volunteers, and they were in all likelihood inside that stadium at the moment, listening to Big Brother and Sister.

He shook his head, trying to come to terms with what he'd heard. Hadn't the world had enough of the political bullshit? As a species, mankind was hanging by a thread, and already, assholes were dredging up failed ideologies to better control people. It scared him, because he knew how alluring the message was, like any good lie. Starvation was a great motivator. Fear, chaos, and trauma were the ultimate recruitment tools. Add in the idea of acting for the supposed benefit of all, and there was very little that people wouldn't be able to justify doing. The analyst in him could appreciate the brilliance behind the idea. The former soldier in him could recognize the appeal of numbers; *"we collect people."*

He skirted around what he could recognize as the golf course's clubhouse and noted the two rows of large plastic-skinned greenhouses that had been erected on what the signs said had been the driving range. Another indicator that whoever was running this place was squared away. They might be selling a pipe dream to motivate their people and using thugs to recruit more, but it functioned—and they were probably eating salad with dinner. Michelle had only gotten around to expanding Bauman's greenhouse in the last month.

Before he'd crossed the campus to find the stadium, there'd been a nineteenth - century-looking mansion behind the Rotunda that still had its lights on. He made his way back east across the northern edge of the campus. In the early morning hours, the only people he had to dodge were the occasional security patrol, roaming around in golf carts that they'd repurposed.

As he approached, he realized the lights didn't all emanate from the mansion. There was a sunken field behind the mansion, ringed with what looked like newly constructed floodlights. The sunken area looked like an old football field from the time when the helmets had been leather. In his imagination, he could almost picture Model T Fords parked around the perimeter, shining their headlights down onto the field for a night game.

In the here and now, the field was lined with military equipment. It looked like these people had raided a National Guard armory. There were almost a dozen Bradley infantry fighting vehicles that he was more than familiar with, and two Black Hawk helicopters. The rest of the yard that he could see was filled with a motley collection of beat-to-shit Humvees and probably a dozen or more newer Joint Light Tactical utility vehicles or JLTVs.

He slowly worked his way around the north end of the sunken field, through the parking lots of a couple of abandoned frat or sorority houses. He could only recognize a few of the Greek letters, and he figured the number of pledges rushing a frat this fall was going to be way down. It was there, kneeling behind the wooden staircase that ran up the outside of a frat house, that he realized he'd wandered into the midst of foot patrols.

As opposed to the stadium, whatever was in the field and the mansion at the far end was being actively protected, and he'd just blundered inside the patrol pattern outside the fence line. He cursed himself, knowing that it had been blind-ass luck and nothing more that had saved him from being spotted. It took him a moment to realize why he was so angry. He'd been thinking about the people he needed to get back to, to warn. If he got blown up sneaking around this place, they'd never know. Rachel would never know . . .

Fuck! Get your head right! He would have slapped himself if the guard he could see through his NVD monocle hadn't already stopped and was now looking around between the houses, heading in his general direction. The BDU wearing guard might have looked military, but the way he carried his M4 like a lunch pail militated against that. These were civilians playing at it, he thought. They'd been coached, maybe even trained by somebody, but they were civilians.

He wanted to get closer to the mansion at the far end of the field without anybody knowing he'd been here. Right now, that didn't look like it was going to happen. The guard he'd been focused on took his time turning back towards the fence line. He took out his binoculars and focused on the top floors of what looked like a four-story brick colonial. He could clearly see the profile of a woman standing between open curtains on the top floor and looking out the window, a drink in her hand.

Three o'clock in the morning . . . must be the politburo building, he thought. From just her profile and the backlight of the room she was in, she looked attractive. The asshole running this place probably lived by the "everyone is equal, some are more equal than others" mantra. He imagined the woman was part of the benefits package that went along with running the show. He scanned the other windows; the lights were on, but there was no one else in view.

He slowly came up on his knees, and was peeking around the base of the staircase when he got a horrible idea. He was already climbing the stairs by the time the image of guard dogs and flashlights surrounding him on the ground popped into his head. He climbed to the top of the landing and went prone, getting a much better view of the equipment yard. The chill that passed through him was real. He didn't linger. He checked the position of the patrol at the fence, took a mental picture of the parking lot, and started back down.

These people weren't playing. They had the power to enforce whatever people's paradise they were selling. The image was seared into his brain; two Abrams tanks sat like massive bookends at the far end of the line of Bradleys. He'd been jealous of the cultivated golf course and the size of the greenhouse. There was enough hardware down there to take the mall and the entire Tysons population in as little time as it would take to get the equipment in place. Who were these people?

Driven by the need to get home and deliver a warning, he took a lot more care getting back to the "beast" than he had sneaking in. And it was *home* he thought of. The realization hit him hard. Not the Ritz, not Tysons or Dagman's house; it was Rachel. Rachel, Pro, and Elsa were home. He realized it with a suddenness that punched him in the gut. Everything that he wanted to protect had a face.

*

"You like looking at our toys?"

His voice was one of the few things she had to admit she admired about him. She supposed it was a product of all those years of commanding soldiers. A command presence, reinforced with the traditional patriarchal structure of the military. She understood the concept very well. It was how she had recognized she needed him, and still did.

In truth, Lisa Cooper, former UVA professor of sociology, was looking out the window at *her* toys, not *their* toys. It wasn't the hunks of metal Steven seemed to worship that she valued. It was the soldiers, her people. Men and women who'd step in front of one his silly machines if it meant protecting what she had built here, and by extension, her.

She spoke over her shoulder. "I admit, the more I see, the more I like."

"We'll get more, I guarantee it."

She heard him getting up from the couch. She knew what was coming. This was one of the things she didn't like, even if at times she allowed herself to enjoy it, to a point. She still needed him, and manipulating his infatuation had been easy. In her mind, what was about to happen was her burden, her sacrifice for the movement. A leader unwilling to share the burdens of her people wasn't worthy of the title.

His hands slowly crept up her back, onto her shoulders.

"When are you going to let me use them?" His voice almost purred in her ear. General Steven Marks was her ace in the hole, her most important convert, and her biggest ongoing challenge. She kept her gaze out the window, looking past the tools of his trade in the field below. Her eyes fell on the dorm buildings in the distance. Her tools lived, breathed, and worked. They were the foundation of the world she was building.

She let her head roll back against his for a moment before turning around and leading him away from the window. "It's still too soon." There were tools, she thought; and then there were tools. Even the ones on two legs needed to be kept sharp.

*

Chapter 5

The Hole

"Today, *the* day? Gunnery Sergeant?" Nathans's voice startled him but he was too numb to let it show. He'd thought the canteen was empty. The place had been dark until the moment he walked in and the motion sensors closed the circuits and the fluorescent lights flickered to life. Which meant Nathans had been sitting in here, without moving, for some time. Trey Nathans was the top sniper in the company; disappearing was his stock in trade. Maybe the man had just been practicing.

There was no surprise and very little expectation of good news in the question. Nathans had greeted him with the same query every morning for months. In the week since Lt. Benoit had removed himself from the chain of command, the daily question had taken on an added edge.

"Not unless you know something I don't, Corporal." He pulled a clean mug from the dishwasher and popped a plastic cartridge into the coffee machine before he turned to look at the man behind him. From the look on Nathans's face, he'd fallen asleep at the table atop his own arms and hadn't been lying in wait for him.

"You sleep in here?" He almost asked how that worked. He was willing to try anything at this point.

Nathans rubbed at his face and nodded. "I guess I did."

"You want a cup?"

Nathans grunted an affirmative. "The hiss of the vent in my room was driving me nuts. It's quieter in here."

He knew exactly what Nathans was talking about; he'd tried the gym, he'd tried switching rooms, he'd even buttoned himself up in one of the Bradleys parked two stories below for a night. Nothing had worked. He was beginning to think he had a minor case of claustrophobia or something similar. Minor; no one with a bad case would have lasted a week in the massive underground facility.

He handed Nathans his cup of coffee and sat down. "Does it sound like bees buzzing to you? Like there's a wasp nest behind the wall?"

Nathans gave his head a slow shake. "For me, it's that sad-ass wind you hear out in the middle of the desert. The one that makes you feel like you're alone, the last person in the world."

"Oh."

Nathans cracked a grin. "Don't worry about me, Gunny. I'm just pissed off; I'm not losing it."

"Glad to hear that. Pissed off . . . I get."

Nathans sipped at his coffee. "So, not today?"

"No." He shook his head. "How's the betting going?"

"Farmer and I are holding out for the one-year mark. Poy has eighteen months, but I swear, unless the PlayStation, Xbox, or one of the training simulators breaks, I don't think he really minds it down here. Tommy has the end of the week, every week."

"Elliot?"

"PFC Elliot doesn't play, Gunny. He's gung ho. He thinks you'd be right to let us die down here, waiting for someone to show up and pop the lid."

"That isn't going to happen. I just figure the longer we wait, the better our chances to survive."

"But not today." Nathans accepted.

"Not today."

"Uwasi loses again."

"He had today?"

"He has today, every day. The guy's a glutton for punishment."

Nothing seemed to bother PFC Uwasi. The newest Marine in the detachment was the third in a line of brothers native to Nigeria to join the Marines. Uwasi had been able to maintain e-mail contact with one of his brothers stationed out in Pendleton for a good bit into the suck. At some point, the comms had cut out. But Uwasi had gone on believing that he and his brother might just be the only two family members left alive, anywhere.

It was a nice story and something to believe in. If it helped keep one of his guys stable, he was all for it. He wished they all had something similar to hang on to. The rest of them had managed to get a notification or had just accepted their loved ones were gone. They'd all had e-mail, dutifully censored by Lt. Benoit, until whomever they'd been writing just stopped. They'd had television until the broadcasters topside had died and quit going to work. They'd watched and listened in, as their world died. Then they'd started offing themselves.

He was fairly certain he wasn't going to lose any more of the guys before his self-imposed one-year mark came around. Up until a few moments ago, Nathans had been his biggest worry. Having an actual one-on-one conversation had helped, and he knew it was something he needed to do more of. He kicked himself for dropping that particular ball inside the self-imposed shell he'd built around himself. He was suffering right along with the rest of them.

"I think we all need a little punishment today." He felt himself grin.

"Come on, Gunny, I thought we were having a moment here. Why you gotta go all Marine on us?"

"Sump Run, full loadout." The facility was basically living quarters on the top floor, armory and technical spaces on the two floors below that, and acres of parked equipment and gear for the next six floors below. A matching pair of spiral roadways cut out of the living rock of the place connected the parking decks at opposite ends. Beneath it all, way beneath, was the sump chamber. Down the roadway, across the length of each deck, down a roadway—rinse and repeat—all the way to the sump chamber and then back up was a 4.1-mile circuit. The hole was basically the world's largest parking garage buried three hundred feet in solid rock as old as the world. Sump runs had always been two laps.

"Go, let the guys know we'll kick off in thirty."

"Why me?"

"You still a Marine, Corporal?"

"Not sure, Gunny. The Corp is no more, command authority is rotting, the country is gone." He knew it was just Nathans being his typical caustic self. The man had a lot of ammunition in that regard.

"The Corps is eternal, Corporal. Consider this professional development, and how good it'll look on your next fit rep."

Nathans slammed the coffee back and stood. "Wow, threatening me with a bad fit rep. I thought you were better than that, Gunny."

"Nope."

Nathans gave him a firm nod. "I'm on it."

He was left alone for a few minutes before he heard the bitching start farther down the hall as the word spread. He'd been a Marine long enough to know it for the good sign it was. If they didn't want to embrace the suck, any one of them could have joined the Peace Corps.

The levels were labeled one through nine; the top level was one, the bottom equipment deck was nine. Below that, the Sump didn't deserve a number, just the name. They were in full battle rattle, stacked up at the junction of level two and the green roadway. The spiral roadway at the opposite end was painted red.

"OK, I've decided whoever finishes closest behind Farmer gets an extra mint on his pillow tonight."

Corporal Lucas "Farmer" Hanson was a freak of nature. Today's run would be a rest day compared to the workouts he put himself through on a daily basis. They all, with the exception of Poy, worked out regularly; There was precious little else for them to do. They all knew it helped to keep them sane. His friend Lucas just took it to the next level.

"Chocolate covered, Gunny?" Corporal Salguero asked. "Or those shitty chalk things they put in bowls at the 'all you can eats'?"

They were laughing. It was going to be a good day. No one was going to lose it today, and they could all recognize it.

A rolling yellow light started up overhead. He stared at it for a moment in silence; they all did. He glanced back down the narrowing corridor of level two's armory section. There was a string of similar lights stretching off into the distance—all rolling.

"Park? You been playing with the exterior cameras again?"

"No, Gunny." Poy would 'tinker' with anything electronic he could get his hands on.

"Proximity alert," he breathed. Probably deer. The two times it had gone off before, there had been deer; but . . . did he dare to hope?

All seven of them—as far as they knew, the only remaining Marines on the planet—just stared at him.

"Probably deer." He felt he needed to warn against the inevitable letdown. "Everyone, back up to one. We're already dressed. Alert positions. Let's move!"

Norfolk, VA

Captain Naylor shook his head at the empty armory. "I know I'm just a boat driver, but this isn't good, is it?"

The weapons lockers inside the warehouse had been raided, and the ammo bunker outside looked to have been professionally breached. The twelve feet of dirt piled atop the bunker had been scraped away by a bulldozer that still sat next to it, and the concrete walls had been taken apart by what he guessed was a combination of high explosives and jackhammers. Colonel Andrew "Drew" Skirjanek had expected looting, but this was something different. The small Army depot at Fort

Eustis had been professionally picked clean.

"Shows some level of organization," he agreed.

"That a good thing?" asked Chief Hoyt.

He looked between Naylor and the acerbic naval chief. "That's the question."

He checked his watch; it was almost the top of the hour. He turned his radio on for the planned check. They were down to their last set of rechargeable batteries on their radios, and unless they scrounged up some more solar panels or gasoline for their generator, they were soon going to be relying on smoke signals.

"Pavel—Skirjanek."

"Yes, Colonel." Pavel's slow and measured English, accent included, was easier to understand on the radio than the speech of some of his other team members.

"Any movement?" Pavel was atop the short, squat air traffic tower overlooking the acres of the base with a scoped .308 hunting rifle. Between what he'd managed to bring out of McMurdo and scavenge from Guantanamo and the *Boise*, they had assault rifles for the sixty-two people who had decided to stay with him. What they lacked was sufficient ammunition or any specialized equipment. He knew where there were literal tons of both, but he'd wanted to check Ft. Eustis for some walking-around firepower.

"No movement, Colonel. We appear to be alone."

Thank God for that. "Alright, work your team back to the vehicle, check the warehouse behind the admin building on your way, Cruz can show you where that is. Skirjanek out." He turned the radio off to conserve power.

"Was this part of your plan?" Naylor was jerking a thumb towards the bare concrete of the warehouse.

"No," he answered. "But it would have been nice to pick up some gear to hold us over. Let's get back to the vehicles."

Vehicles? They'd found a school bus and a small collection of pickup trucks that they were able to get running. Fuel was the problem.

They'd been scavenging all they could, but some of the supplies sitting in tanks had already started to age and separate. It was a real problem that was only going to get worse. Much of what they found was used to run the generator that Hoyt's people had rigged up at their temporary base, which was nothing more than a dockside warehouse in Norfolk. They'd been collecting solar panels off of roofs and had found hundreds of the things, but they didn't plan on being there long enough to set them up. It was time to move.

Pavel's two-truck team caught up with them by the time they made it back to their temporary home. Preparations were well underway for loading everything into the backs of trucks and trailers. Everyone was working—or at least everyone who had decided to remain. Thirty-seven people had left during the week he had given them. They'd scattered to all points of the compass, seeking whatever home they dreamed they still had. He wished them well, but he didn't want to think about the trips they had in front of them. He was left with sixty-two people, slightly more than half of them women. A higher proportion of the women had elected to stay rather than risk a trip into the unknown, across whatever was left of the country.

The gender mix wasn't the issue; their collective backgrounds were. Most of the civilians had been support staff or researchers who had been working in Antarctica. Pure brainpower he had in spades. People with actual military experience made a grand total of twenty-six, the majority of which were crewmen from the *Boise*. When he tried to figure out how many of those had actually seen some form of combat, he had quickly stopped counting before depression set in.

His story that he knew where they were headed was wearing thin. The truth was a little more complicated. He desperately wanted to make sure The Hole was operationally viable before he let on that their supply problems might have a solution. That, and he hadn't wanted to say anything to the larger group, mostly former civilians, until those who had planned to leave were well and truly gone.

He glanced at Pavel's empty truck bed as it pulled up. That made

Ft. Eustis a complete bust. Same as Norfolk, same as Langley Air Force Base, same as Little Creek, same as, same as. They'd all been picked clean. What hadn't been removed had been disabled. He was experienced enough to think in terms of logistics; random scavengers could take what they could carry. Someone had possessed the logistical capacity to pack off everything of immediate use. Two-hundred-million-dollar F-22s sat in their bunkers, next to one-hundred-million-dollar F-35s, collecting dust.

At Langley AFB alone, they'd seen three C-141s and one C-5 parked on the apron, sitting on flat tires, surrounded by dozens of Bradley infantry fighting vehicles, Humvees, JLTVs, and transport trucks whose engines had been professionally sabotaged. The empty bags of sand still lying atop the engine blocks had been all the evidence he needed that someone was purposely limiting the military capability of anyone else scavenging for gear. Depending on who was behind it, it was either a very good thing or his worst-case scenario. Anything resembling small arms, ammunition for the same, supplies, food—it was all gone. Where to, was the question.

"We are prepared, Colonel."

Dr. Mandel's voice caught him off guard. He looked up to find the Russian scientist standing next to Captain Naylor.

He spread out the map on the tailgate of the truck and dropped a finger on a site he had circled. "I need you two to get everyone to this campground off of Highway 17. It's a mile past the Virginia Motor Speedway, a big racetrack. I'll be taking Pavel, Hoyt, Antwan, and Cruz to a facility a little further down the road that isn't on any map. Staff Sergeant Mason and his fire team will be going with you. If he and his team are needed, listen to him."

He had a moment of consternation with splitting up like this. Kent Mason was a retired Marine, one of the members of McMurdo's contractor security team who had decided to remain behind with him. He had no worries regarding Mason's experience or his skill set. The Marine had spent six years of his career as a drill instructor at Lejeune.

He seemed the natural pick to take on the task of training up what he thought of as a fire team, utilizing members of Naylor's submarine crew, Seabees from McMurdo, and assorted former researchers, both American and Russian. So far, the results had been as mixed as the raw material Mason had to work with.

"Is it wise to split up?" Naylor asked.

He didn't mind the question. Hell, he needed someone to bounce shit off of, and he'd made it very clear to Naylor that he wanted and needed his input.

"The facility should be manned. If they're alive, they'll have been sealed up since before the suck. I don't want to roll up on them looking like the gypsy caravan we are. You should make the campground within two hours. We'll get word back to you, or rejoin you as soon as we can."

"Is it beyond radio range?" Cruz asked. The Navy chief was one-half of the team along with Army Sergeant Antwan Sikes, whom he'd come to rely on at McMurdo.

"Possibly, but I want to enforce strict radio silence from this point forward in all but an emergency. We'll switch on the radios every two hours." He checked his watch. "Starting at 2100 hours. I want to avoid any and all radio traffic excepting an emergency."

"You're thinking about whoever raided the bases." Naylor hadn't phrased it as a question.

"They might be playing on the blue team." He shrugged.

"They might not." Cruz pointed out the obvious.

"I assume the opponents are the red team?" Dr. Mandel asked.

"Old habits," he answered.

Naylor held out his hand. "We'll be waiting for you. We don't have the fuel to go much further."

"Colonel?" Dr. Mandel had a single finger aligned with his chin. It usually meant the Russian scientist was in pontification mode. He didn't mind; the guy usually knew what he was talking about. If he was surrounded by a bunch of Mensa-qualified professors, Dr. Mandel would have easily qualified as the Grand High potentate. The Russian scientist was scary smart. He'd played some chess with the man on the *Boise* during their trip, and he'd quickly learned that when Yefrem Ilyaevich said, "I will checkmate you in six moves," he meant it.

"These men you seek, if they have been sequestered since before the virus, you should take care. There are likely to be . . . complications arising from their isolation."

No shit . . . He nodded politely. "Noted."

Chapter 6

Tysons Corner, Northern Virginia

Rachel watched the small group approach. Something about them set her on edge, which was ridiculous. Pro and nearly a dozen others with rifles had the six strangers covered from hidden positions within the building behind her.

"Lot better equipped than most," Reed said, standing next to her.

"Might just mean they're smarter than most," Michelle added. Rachel almost smiled at the comment. The women who called Tysons home were probably the most habitually armed group in their community. They'd learned a lesson that they weren't going to forget. For Michelle, her weapons were almost religious talismans, her daily target practice a catechism of sorts. Rachel didn't think she was in the same category, but when she thought about it, she couldn't remember the last time she'd missed one of the self-defense sessions.

"Smart or not, looks like they want to talk." Reed turned to Daniel; they all did.

Daniel knew they were all looking at him. He could almost wish some of them still thought of him as "Sleepy." He'd buried the name in all but memory. It didn't stop Michelle from using it when her claws were out and she was trying to get him to do something. She had that look on her face right now.

The group of strangers was made up of three men, one elderly and moving slow; two women, one about Rachel's age, the other mid-forties; and one young boy of five or six years old. The boy fell into a demographic that they hadn't seen much of. He was young enough that he had to have been found by a surviving adult early on.

"OK," Daniel relented. "We've done this before. They pass muster? We'll separate them, get their stories, and compare notes in a couple of days."

Daniel stepped out from behind the barricade of cars they'd set up at the intersection of Dolly Madison and International. He signaled the rest of them to step out into the clear as well. He wanted the new arrivals to see how well armed they were. Then again, these people should know that already; it wasn't like they hadn't done their own investigation.

He walked the twenty yards to where they stood, alone. In one of those post-suck ironies, he could recall Bauman doing this dozens of times, all smiles and courtesy.

"Where you all from?"

"All over," the older woman answered almost immediately. She had a rugged, solid look to her, no nonsense. "For myself, and this little guy here, we've been together since the beginning. The rest of us been together since the big snowstorm, except Ray. We found each other in Winchester. My name's Carla." She gave a gentle nudge to the young boy, who stood in front of her. "Say hello, Samuel."

The young boy wasn't having any of it, and he kept his eyes firmly on the ground, a few paces from his own feet.

"He goes by Sammy," the older woman explained with a shrug.

On the surface, the story made sense. A lot of people had "found" each other during the winter's big snowstorm. For survivors, footprints in the snow had been proof that they weren't alone. Those same footprints had been used by people like Bauman to gather in sheep.

"The rest of you?"

The old man took a step forward. "Name's Charles Dubois, this is my granddaughter, Tina. My boy's child, my real granddaughter. We hail from outside Winchester."

He felt his eyebrows rise in surprise. Simple probability explained it, but it was the first time any of them had met anyone with an actual blood relation who had survived the virus.

"These two hard cases," the old man continued, "are Thomas and Ray. Thomas has been with me since last fall. We came across Ray a few months past." Of the two men, only Ray looked anything like a hard case to him. About forty years old, he could have been on either side of the marker. The man was bald headed and had calm eyes that seemed to take in everything. He just nodded politely at the mention of his name.

To Daniel, there was a sense of ease about the way he held his gun. The man's attention wasn't so much on him as it was on the others standing behind him and on the windows of the building above him.

"Where you from, Ray?"

"Started outside of Cincinnati, been walking to Georgia since the die-off. Got held up with some trouble in Lexington, Kentucky."

"What kind of trouble?"

Ray glanced at the young boy for just a moment before looking back at him and giving his head a slight shake. Against his better judgment, Daniel thought the man's reticence spoke well of him. "The bad kind."

Daniel turned his attention to the young man, mid-twenties, maybe a little older. He wondered if that was just the road mileage showing.

"And you?"

"Thomas Cairn, just Tom. I was a grad student at Virginia Tech."

It was Daniel's alma mater. He figured there'd be time to test that particular story later.

"What were you studying?"

"Veterinary science, equine medicine to be exact."

"He's a horse doctor," the young boy blurted out, "but he fixed Ray's arm."

He gave the kid a smile and then looked up towards Ray. "What happened to your arm?"

"I'd been shot," Ray answered, after sharing a friendly smile with the young boy.

Daniel waited a moment for more of the story, but it was clear Ray had already moved on.

"Alright, what do you need?" he asked. "We've got a few supplies we can hand out. It's not much, but it'll help you on your way."

"We can't stay?" the young woman, Tina, asked in a tone that screamed exhaustion.

"Why would you want to?"

"'Cause your womenfolk are armed to the teeth," the older woman, Carla, answered for her group. "We've been watching y'all for a day or two. You seem like decent people."

The group of newcomers had scouted them for exactly four days. Pro and his scouts had watched the group's approach down Route 7 and had kept tabs on them since. He couldn't fault the small lie; he'd have played it the same way. Anyone with a shred of common sense would have. He figured those without common sense were already dead or living in places like Tysons had been, or maybe like Lexington was.

"I saw them fields you planted," the old man interjected. "A lot of your rows are too close together, unless it was all wheat or rye."

"You a farmer?"

"Not since my younger days, but I remember a fair bit."

"Can you use a doctor?" the young woman, Tina, asked and pointed at Tom.

"I'm just a vet," the man corrected, "or would have been."

Carla spoke in his defense. "He's a good doctor. Mister, if you aren't taking in newcomers, at least let us stay a few days and rest up. We'll give up our weapons, if you promise us, we'll get them back."

Michelle turned to Rachel at the older woman's last words. "Nuh-uh, no freaking way. I don't trust them." Rachel hoped Michelle's harsh whisper went unheard.

"I'll just be moving on, then." Ray was shaking his head and looking at Carla, who was clearly in charge of the group. "I'm not giving up my gun."

"Now, that makes sense," Michelle whispered again. She and Daniel were on the same wavelength.

"You can keep your guns." Daniel nodded. "We aren't about to ask anyone to go unarmed. We've had some experience with that; it doesn't work. But you'll be watched closely. Everybody works. If it doesn't work out for us, for any reason. . . you'll be asked to leave."

"Sounds fair to us," Carla answered.

*

"I'm telling you, they're not right." Pro had watched the group through his scope for days, and he wasn't holding back. "The old lady runs the group—"

"She's not an old lady," Michelle broke in and dared Pro to argue the point. "You're right, though. She is in charge, and it should be that Ray guy—something's fishy."

"The bald guy?" Pro shook his head. "No way. He's barely part of their group. The geek doesn't like him, probably 'cause he's got the hots for the young lady. I don't think the old . . . sorry, Carla lady likes him much either. The little boy seems to be the only one who really talks to him."

It was all good intel, as Jason would have called it. But Daniel had to hide his exasperated smile behind his hands at Pro's unvarnished report.

"First off, he's a vet," Daniel said. "Which probably makes him at least as close to a doctor as what we have now with Doc Adams. So not a geek."

Pro rolled his eyes and held up a hand. "Sorry, and I know I shouldn't say he had the hots. I just meant that the gee . . . the vet acts like he's worried baldy is going to move in on his girlfriend."

Reed shook his head. "All I know is the old man has forgotten more about farming than anybody we have around here knows. He's already been a huge help."

The group had been with them for three days, during which they'd acted like anyone who knew they were being watched. They'd all been on good behavior, and had worked hard. Daniel and Reed had been working with Ray and the old man all day, raiding fertilizer from every garden store, nursery, and home improvement center they could find. The old man, Charles, had been a font of knowledge, but pessimistic regarding what he referred to as the "piss-poor" clay soil of the area.

Ray had been quiet, but had worked hard. Daniel was more convinced than ever that Ray was hiding something, but he was the last person in the world to hold that against anyone.

"How about the girl?" Reed turned to Rachel. "She really the old man's granddaughter?"

"As far as I can tell." Rachel nodded. "One thing's for certain; she's quite smitten with the young doctor."

"Well, yeah." Michelle laughed. "A doctor! What young girl doesn't want to hook a doctor? Can't you imagine the private schools for their kids, the big house, the parties? She'll never have to work a day in her life."

"That last part is true," Rachel added as soon as the laughter died down.

"Which part?" Daniel asked.

"Girl is a complete sluggard, lazy all day long, and she carries that gun for show. Says she's never fired it. I know it sounds odd, but it's as if she has some sort of entitlement thing going because of the young horse doctor. How does she get that in such a small group? On the road?"

The road scavengers were relentless. The small bands of a half dozen or so were the worst; they were next to impossible to pin down and track. All they'd been able to do throughout the spring was harass them enough to drive them out further into the suburbs. The point being, they all knew how dangerous it was to travel. How would anyone get from Winchester to Tysons on foot without fighting? They all knew it and wondered how anybody could have survived as long as the group had without fighting.

Michelle stood up from the table, signaling the meeting was over. "Like I've been saying, something's not right with these people."

"Has there been a road group you did feel good about?" Daniel asked.

The look she shot back . . . yep, they'd argue again tonight.

*

No one had asked him, but Ray Hoover could not have agreed more. He had no idea he and the others of his group were under discussion, but he would have understood the concerns. He'd agreed to accompany Carla and her group out of a lingering obligation he felt for the pet store antibiotics that had probably saved his life. The gunshot wound had been a grazer, but it had never fully healed. He'd been delirious with fever when Carla and her group had found him. He now knew it had been Sammy who had found him shivering with fever from infection in the back of a car. He didn't have a doubt that without the young boy's concern, Carla would have forced the rest of them to just keep walking.

His choice had been simple; he'd stayed with them because they were headed east and were armed. Five guns wasn't a target that every jackass with a rifle would take on. He'd planned on getting to the 95 corridor, turning right, and heading back to the small town in Northern Georgia that he hadn't seen since leaving home after high school. Now, he wasn't so sure.

This place had potential, and not for the mall, or the hotel bed he'd slept in the last few nights. The location of the place seemed beyond stupid to him. It may have made sense to FEMA when they thought this was just a bad flu pandemic, but now? Now it was just a giant, nearly indefensible target surrounded by high ground in the form of office buildings, and the crops they'd planted were in unprotected fields two miles away.

It wasn't their fault; they were smack-dab in the middle of paved-over suburbia. But if he had a say, he'd move this whole group someplace a lot more rural. These people's real strength was their numbers. They seemed like a cohesive group and were well set up to make a go of it. This was by the far the largest group of survivors he'd seen that wasn't run like a slave plantation. No one had asked him though, and these people had no reason to trust him.

His own group; after having saved their asses a number of times during skirmishes on the road should trust him. But they didn't, or at least Carla didn't, and hers was the only opinion that mattered. What bothered him the most was that he couldn't figure out whatever was going on between Carla and the young doctor. Whatever it was, his gut told him it had everything to do with why they didn't trust him. He'd been trying to figure it out since he'd joined them. Watching quietly was his thing, and he knew it wasn't physical between the two. The doc had the airhead to fill that need, and Carla's energy was focused on something he couldn't put his finger on. It certainly wasn't Sammy. The woman treated the child like luggage.

Ray held up his gnawed-on chicken leg. "Not my mom's, but that was damned good."

His minder, Mitch, seemed like a good guy. The guy was nearly as quiet as he was and hadn't complained when he took his lunch plate out from the hotel to eat outside. It was a nice day; the humidity wasn't as bad as it had been the day before or as close to the evil it would be in another few weeks. The real reason he'd wanted to be outside was that was where Carla, Tom, Tina, and Sammy had gone in the company of their own minder.

They seemed to be enjoying the weather as well, but as soon as Sammy had involved Tina and their minder in a game of three-way catch, he noticed Carla and Tom with their heads bowed in conversation. It was clear Carla was doing the talking and Tom was just nodding in agreement. It was the same strange shit he'd watched for weeks. The two of them used every second they had alone to confer on something they didn't want anyone else knowing.

"You got a friend, there."

Mitch's voice caught him off guard. "Sorry?" Mitch was pointing to Sammy with his plastic fork.

Sammy was holding up the tiny rubber football and waving at him to join them.

"You mind?" he asked.

"Knock yourself out. Time's the one thing we have plenty of."

He knew why Mitch's words set a hook in him. He would have liked arguing the point, but held off. These people didn't need his baggage to add to their worry.

*

Chapter 7

"There!" Corporal Cameron "Poy" Park pointed at the monitor. "We got some tourists, Gunny." Poy's 300 pounds vibrated in his seat, and his Hawaiian-flavored pidgin accent nearly disappeared.

He could see that for himself. The entire approach to The Hole's entrance and the surrounding no man's land was littered with signs warning people to stay away. Several of the signposts had camera lenses expertly embedded in them, and he had a clear shot at the five armed men who had already made it halfway across the cleared ground between The Hole and the tree line. The men weren't in uniform except the boots and digicam pants. They all carried matching M4s.

He was desperate to know who these guys were. If he was being honest with himself, he knew that stemmed from the chance that one of those men was read in on the facility and possessed the proper authentication code to let them the hell out. The first hurdle looked to be a foregone conclusion as the group beelined to the inner perimeter. Even if one of them had the authorization code, he wondered if they were immune or had outlasted the virus somewhere. If they were merely immune and the virus was still active, their freedom would probably be measured in the week it took to die.

"They in the minefield, Gunny."

"Copy that—do not arm," he replied. "Do not."

"No freakin' way, Gunny. We gonna see sum sunshine!"

Poy's pidgin was back. They were all keyed up and wanted out of this place. He'd already come to terms with the virus. If it was still live and a threat, he'd rather die under an open sky than cross the finish line into insanity down here. He wasn't alone in that sentiment. They all wanted out.

He'd sent the rest of the squad down the hall to get out of his hair. They'd been pressed up against the window of the security center's window like kids at a pet store window before he'd ordered them down the hall to take up positions outside the air lock. Poy's excitement was more than enough to deal with.

"One step at a time, Poy."

"They headed right for the ramp, Gunny! What else could it be?"

"Somebody involved in stocking this place? A fucking contractor who put in the plumbing? I'm guessing hundreds of people know about it. Only a few have the authorization code."

"All them others gotta be dead though, right?"

"Lance Corporal Park."

"Yeah, yeah, Gunny?"

"Stop talking and settle the fuck down, or I'm putting you outside."

"OORAH, Gunny."

Hoyt Sweet whistled as they stood at the edge of the old two-hundred-foot-deep quarry, complete with a large pond filling half the bottom. "When you said it was called 'The Hole', I pictured an old barn with a hidden elevator."

He'd let them know where they were headed an hour ago as they had broken camp and started off with the rising sun. There was a wide road cut into the perimeter of the quarry site. It went around three sides of the rectangular-shaped hole in a gradual downward incline until it terminated in a large cleared space at the pond's edge. There was an ancient looking, rusted-out bucket crane parked down there. Next to it was a slightly newer bulldozer; same rust and missing its blade. It was the bulldozer that held the key to this place.

"Good *maskirovka*," Pavel said with approval.

"Good what?" Antwan asked loudly. Antwan had been spending the most time with Pavel and his burgeoning English vocabulary.

"Means camouflage," Skirjanek answered. "Sort of, with a little deception or misdirection thrown in."

"Like as in no fences, no guards?" Cruz asked. "Tricky, I like it."

"Exactly," he answered. Drew didn't feel the need to mention that they'd just walked across a minefield.

"Guys." He circled them up. "I want your opinions. For the sake of argument; Say you've been holed up down there since before the suck. You've been waiting for someone authorized to come along and let you out. Is it better for me to go alone, or do we all go down together?"

"I can't believe anybody would wait that long," Antwan said. "Even if they are scared the virus would get them."

"They're Marines," he added. "They understood the importance of the mission."

"Shit." Hoyt spit over the edge of the quarry. "Marines . . . God help us. Colonel, is there any way you can open the door and let them come to us? Maybe they'll be tired by the time they get to the top."

"The phone and your secret elevator are at the bottom of the pit."

"Together," Pavel said. "We have nothing to hide. We are their relief, yes?"

He'd been thinking the same thing.

"Alright, let's go. I assume we are on closed-circuit video."

There was an ancient intercom box attached to the rear of the bulldozer. The handset's cord had long ago been eaten or had rotted away. He pulled at the mounted box and was almost surprised by the ease with which it popped off, revealing a modern computer terminal underneath, complete with its own telephone handset.

He entered his social security number, followed by his date of birth at the blinking cursor, and the phone's carrier tone activated. He almost started laughing at the surreal irony of the standard ringing from the other end. He didn't have to wait long.

"Gunnery Sergeant John Bruce speaking. Who am I speaking to?"

He could almost see the checklist the voice on the other end of the phone was reading from. It would be the standard Department of Defense, eight-by-eleven-inch laminated orange- or blue-trimmed document.

"Gunnery Sergeant Bruce, I was told there would be a lieutenant in charge down there."

"Who am I speaking to?"

"This is US Army Colonel Andrew Skirjanek. I have the authorization codes given to me by command authority. Is your commanding officer available to speak?"

"No, sir, Lieutenant Benoit died from wounds obtained while inspecting a faulty weapon. I am the ranking Marine at this post."

"Understood, Gunny." If his own experience at McMurdo was any guide, he doubted if the Marine lieutenant was the only one to have had an accident with a faulty weapon.

"Long story short, Gunny, I am sorry it has taken so long to get here, but we started in Antarctica. The good news is the virus has abated, and I am ready to transmit the authorization codes upon your request."

The excited shouting at the other end of the phone was loud enough, he immediately thought there was problem. He heard the phone drop and slam into something before sounds of a scuffle came through. A sharp bang was loud enough that his whole party heard it via the tiny speaker in his handset.

"Gunny!" he yelled, as he could feel the odds of survival drop precipitously for everyone who had decided to come with him.

"Apologies, sir." The gunny came back on the phone, breathing a little hard. "There was a little bit of excitement at our end. I had to remove one of my guys. We're all good, sir."

"Anything to worry about, Gunny?"

"No, sir! Just a three-hundred-pound Hawaiian who hasn't seen the sun in a long while. He was just celebrating your announcement."

"Understood. Where were we?"

"Sir, if you'll bear with me a moment; can you confirm that you are using the Lima Alpha Tango dash 8 dash 3401 tactical landline?"

"Unless there is another phone down here at the bottom of this pit, attached to a bulldozer, let's assume I am."

"I'm sorry, sir, I am. I'm reading off the playbook for outside authorization, and it says at the top, in big, bold letters, that each step must be followed in strict order. Sir, I really can't afford to fuck this up, sir."

He mentally sighed with relief. The gunny sounded a little squirrely, but in balance; he couldn't imagine anyone in the man's position who wouldn't be climbing at the walls. He was still a Marine, though. "Agreed, Gunny, run your checklist."

"Number Two." He could hear the tension in the voice on the other end of the phone. "Is the person I'm speaking to a member of the United States Armed Forces, in good standing, duly authorized to . . . WHAT THE FUCK? I'm sorry, sir, going to skip that one."

It was nearly ten minutes later when he heard the words he'd been waiting for. "Sir, you should have a live keyboard at your end. You are to enter the pass phrase, and press enter."

He typed out a code he'd never forget. He'd been allowed to choose the pass phrase himself before he'd boarded the plane to McMurdo. "Stacy01-21-72Stef08-03-2002" At the time, he'd thought that his wife's and daughter's birthdays were a nice touch. Now it just pissed him off.

"Code authenticated, sir." The relief in Gunny Bruce's voice was evident. "The outer access personnel door should be opening."

"I can confirm that, Gunny." A small door-sized, rock-walled access panel was sliding into a recess, revealing a large stainless-steel elevator lobby within the sheer rock wall of the quarry. "We'll be down to you momentarily."

"No fu—" The gunny caught himself in mid-shout. "Apologies, sir. I strongly suggest we come up to you."

"That sounds like a plan, Gunny. See you topside. Skirjanek, out."

He hung up the phone and smiled to himself. He should have suggested that from the get-go. Hoyt Sweet was shaking his head, laughing to himself.

"What?"

"Just remembering a MEU float in my younger days." The Navy chief pointed at the elevator lobby. "Back in the mid-'90s, we had warning orders, a typhoon and no dock space. It kept us out to sea for six weeks longer than we'd planned. By the time we tied up in Hong Kong, the Marines we had onboard were chewing the anchor chain, sir. We'd been at sea for nearly ninety days, and they had daily runs and PT on the *Iwo*'s flight deck. They were at each other's throats. These guys have been in a tin can for a lot longer than that."

"It's a big tin can." He nodded. "But you're absolutely right. We'll give them some space."

He didn't know what to expect from the Marines. Given what these men had been sitting on for ten months, he'd half expected some type of paranoid suspicion. Mr. Sweet's prediction had been spot-on. The elevator doors had opened with a chime, followed by a rush of bodies that came together at the rock-lined doorway, jammed tight amid flying elbows, curses, and verbal threats. Inertia overcame friction, and the mass of men popped out like a champagne cork.

Gunny Bruce hadn't been joking about the three-hundred-pound Hawaiian. The man looked Samoan to him, and he'd been the primary cork in the bottle, with smaller, unluckier Marines trapped between him and the walls of the narrow entrance on either side. The behemoth shot forward, landing on his gut with a cry of joy. He was on his feet in a flash, sprinting up the road to the surface. He was followed in a rush by two more Marines who quickly overtook him.

He looked back as three more Marines emerged, carrying their assault rifles, followed by a fourth, a very tired-looking gunnery sergeant with the name tag of Bruce.

Their salute was picture-perfect.

"You are relieved, Gunnery Sergeant Bruce."

"I stand relieved." The Marine dropped his salute. The gunnery sergeant was a lifer, older than he'd expected from their phone conversation.

"I've got a very good idea of what you've all been through, Gunny. Why don't you and your men take a break for the night? When you are comfortable with the idea, I'd like a tour of the facility."

"Thank you, sir." The gunny pointed at the ramp road; two of his men had reached the first turn and were still burning for the top. The Hawaiian was lagging well behind but still moving steadily. "I considered standing them for inspection, but . . ."

"Never give an order you know won't be obeyed?" he finished for the man.

"Yes, sir. Thank you for understanding, sir."

*

Chapter 8

Northern Virginia

Pro felt a little bit guilty. Not because he and Rachel were sneaking around following the newcomers, but because Michelle had asked them to do it without telling Daniel or Reed. After a week of good behavior, Daniel and Reed had decided to let the new folks in, officially. That meant they were trusted, sort of. Michelle had argued with both of them, but had lost. Reed had basically said, people had too much other shit to do to babysit folks who seemed as harmless as they were helpful. Daniel had agreed. He and Rachel had been in the room, and he'd been surprised when Daniel asked him what he thought.

Reed had laughed at his comment that he didn't trust anybody who wasn't in the room with them. He of course would add Jason to that list; he'd trust Jason far above anyone else. It wasn't until after the meeting was over that he realized they had all thought he'd been joking. He hadn't been.

Rachel was still in the weird, moody funk they'd all been dealing with since Jason had left. Pro knew she was only half listening to the conversation going on around her. He'd been mad at Jason for not taking him along, but he'd gotten over it in a day or so. Rachel was worried about the simple fact he'd left, and she seemed to get worse every day.

Michelle had grabbed the two of them following the meeting and given them the mission to keep tabs on Carla, Tom, and Ray. None of them were worried about Sammy; the kid had been pretty much adopted by the whole community. The old man was, in his mind, just really old. Besides, he'd been sick the last couple of days and was holed up in his room. They'd promised Michelle they would do as they were told.

The meeting over, he and Rachel had headed back to the house in Great Falls. Elsa was staying with a friend at the hotel, and Reed spent most nights there as well. They'd been in the kitchen when Michelle's voice popped over the radio—the tactical radio. Jason had pretty much put an end to using the hotel's big transmitter. He'd described it as a giant neon sign advertising where they were.

Michelle relayed the message she'd gotten from the guards. Tom, the veterinarian, had left to go and collect the gear that his group had stashed before approaching the mall.

"Why the hell would he do that at night?" Even over the radio, it was clear Michelle was fired up.

"Because he'll be working all day tomorrow?" Rachel was on edge too. Pro thought she looked exhausted.

"Ask Pro if he knows where they camped before they moved in."

He did remember; he'd watched them use the megachurch on Route 7 as a base for a couple of days. He was nodding yes at Rachel as he overheard Michelle's question.

He was there now. Michelle had said Tom was on foot. He'd ridden his mountain bike, and was set up on the top floor of the giant church's parking garage twenty minutes before he spotted the veterinarian's skinny frame trudging up the edge of the Route 7 from the toll road. He'd convinced Rachel to stay behind and get some sleep. She'd argued, sort of, but had relented when he'd explained he'd watched them at the church for days and knew where to go so he wouldn't be seen. In the end, it wasn't anything he hadn't done alone, countless times. Michelle had made him promise he wouldn't do anything other than keep an eye on Tom.

He might not have trusted anyone outside his close group, but Tom seemed harmless to him. The gangly veterinarian struck him as absentminded; maybe that was why he was an animal doctor and not a real doctor. He picked up the movement through his rifle scope and made out Tom's profile approaching along the edge of Leesburg Pike. He didn't have a round in the chamber, but this still beat the hell out of playing video games or reading one of the books from the pile that Daniel had assigned him. He was slowly working his way through the reading list, not because he enjoyed it, but because Jason had told him that if he wanted to live with him, he was going to continue his education.

He'd tried to argue; what the hell was the point in learning crap that he'd never need to know? He could remember the argument and had looked to Rachel for some help. She'd betrayed him in an instant and sided with Jason. Of course she had; she'd already finished school. Daniel's tailored home study program was better than sitting in class with some of the younger kids at the hotel or doing the math homework that used to give him such fits, but sneaking around watching somebody through a rifle scope was going to win hands down all day, every day. Besides, if Michelle wanted something done, she only had to ask, and he was going to do it.

It was a warm, humid night, and the bugs were out in force. None of them, least of all him, had realized how effective the spraying the county had done in previous years had been. Almost a year after the virus, the mosquitos seemed to be the big winner. Along with coyotes, turkey buzzards, rats, stray dogs, and birds of prey, the planet belonged to them. He'd layered up, just as they'd all learned to do since earlier in the spring. It was uncomfortable as hell in the heat, but it was better than being eaten alive. There was enough moisture in the air that the view through his scope was a little bit foggy. Tom was still coming on.

He watched as his target crossed the road and then disappeared behind a bank of foliage from the line of trees that fronted the church's property. He got on his radio and reported in. He wasn't sure if Rachel would be listening in or not, but he could picture Michelle pacing back and forth on the roof of the hotel, worried about him. She was always worrying.

"Copy that," Michelle answered. It was hard to tell over the radio, but she sounded disappointed that Tom had ended up where he had said he was going. "Stay put. Remember, you're just there to watch. Let me know when he leaves."

"I know." It was his turn to be disappointed. He wasn't going to see shit from the top level of the garage beyond watching Tom approach and leave. He was standing up now, no more visible to Tom through the foliage than Tom was to him. He was listening for the sound of the doors being pulled open. A minute or so later, he was rewarded. The beam from a bright flashlight was easily visible, shining through the colored glass of the small round windows that lined the parlor area in the front of the auditorium-sized chapel. Tom was inside, doing what he'd said he was going to do.

He scanned behind him across the expanse of his nearly empty parking level, and the flat expanse of the church's roof across the narrow gap before him. Nothing. He leaned against the waist-high wall of the parking deck and slid down behind it, wondering if one could read a book in the dark with night vision goggles. He should have brought one with him and given it a try. He knew he'd hear the door open when Tom left; then he could head back home.

It was nearly ten minutes later when he heard the door. It wasn't the jerking open that he'd heard before, it was the softer click of it shutting. He came to his feet and laid the rifle across the top of the wall. It would be a few minutes before Tom would appear from behind the trees. He found himself wondering if Michelle was going to be relieved or even more suspicious that he hadn't caught Tom doing anything.

A door crashed open on the roof of the auditorium across from him. Tom was there, having just emerged from what looked like a small shed planted in the middle of the roof. The man was only about sixty feet away from him and waving his flashlight around. Lessons from Jason kicked in, and he ducked down slowly out of sight and crawled fifteen feet to his right before peeking back up.

It was pitch-black, and there was no way Tom was going to see him unless the beam of the man's flashlight outlined him. That didn't seem to be a worry. He could see via his NVG monocle that the veterinarian was focused on the big microwave dishes on the roof and digging around in the bag he was now carrying. A bag he hadn't had when he'd approached the church.

The church! What had he just heard at the main door? He glanced down and could see another weak beam of light playing within the church through the colored windows. There was someone else inside, on the ground floor. He swiveled his rifle and slowly jacked in a round. He loved the .270 that Jason had fitted out for him. It didn't have close to the power or effective range of Rachel's .338 Lapua, but he had gotten to the point where he could almost drive nails with the gun out to 150 yards and kill a pie plate out to three hundred. Tom had moved away from him towards the satellite dishes, but he was still easily within fifty yards.

He adjusted the focus of his scope and watched as Tom pulled a spool of wire from his bag and started stringing it between the two microwave dishes. He couldn't make out the wire through his monocle, but he could see the spool. The process looked like something Tom had done many times. Even in the dark, the veterinarian worked fast. Within a minute, he saw Tom pull a radio out from his bag and then a big battery. He'd watched this group for days, but he'd never seen them use this kind of radio. Then again, he'd been set up behind a house across Leesburg Pike—he hadn't had a line of sight to the microwave dishes on the roof.

Pro knew exactly what he had to do; he didn't hesitate. He focused on the radio, and put a round right through the middle of it. He was rewarded with a flash of sparks. By the time he ejected the round, he saw Tom sprawling on his ass, trying to scurry further from the radio.

He chambered another round and tracked his target as Tom managed to find his feet and make it into an ungainly bear crawl towards the roof's access door.

A second later, the man's mad scramble became a full-out run. Pro wasn't nearly as certain what to do with Tom as he had been with the radio. He thought Jason would want to know who Tom had been trying to contact. He caught himself; Jason wasn't here. Michelle and Daniel would want to know just as badly. He held off firing and watched Tom struggle with the door in the dark and then finally disappear behind it.

Jason's mantra rang in his head; *shoot, move, communicate.* He dropped back down behind the wall and frog-walked to the corner of the parking deck closest to the front of the church. It wasn't far from where he'd originally set up.

"Michelle, you there?"

"Did you just shoot? What's going on?"

*

Ray had been kicking himself for his paranoid stupidity ever since he'd started following Tom. Earlier in the afternoon, he'd overheard Tom ask the guards if he could go out and collect the rest of their gear that evening. Carla had been standing off to the side, all casual-like and far too interested in the answer. He'd traveled with these people; if they had any shit worth going back for, he hadn't seen it. It had been easy to sneak out. He'd just watched Tom leave, waited ten minutes, and then approached the same guard Tom had on his way out of the mall.

The guard hadn't even blinked, just pointed after Tom and told him he'd probably be able to catch his buddy. Buddy? Tom was a squirrely milquetoast son of a bitch if he'd ever met one. The vet student had a handshake that felt like a dead fish, but it was the guy's slavish devotion to Carla that just struck him as wrong. He knew he'd probably get in trouble; his plan was just to say he'd heard they had permission to collect their gear.

These people might even kick him out. He'd be fine with that. He really did just want to get back to Georgia. The idea of living in a place like these people had set up struck him as crazy. Why try to rebuild what was dead and gone? It just made you a target for assholes like the ones he'd escaped from in Lexington. It wasn't for him. Civilization hadn't really been his thing even before the suck. He'd walked out of his parents' home at eighteen with four thousand dollars. It had paid for a semester of trade school, where he'd learned welding.

Three years later, he was a novice undersea welder and living on an oil rig in the Gulf of Mexico. Over the next ten years, he had worked in places all over the world, but they'd all had the cocoon of his diving helmet in common, and he had loved it. It was the perfect job for a loner. He'd had the bad luck to be in Ohio attending a mandatory training class when the suck had shut down the airports and people had started dropping dead. The months that had followed had been nightmarish and left him with a healthy mistrust of anyone not named Raymond Hoover. He should have left Carla and her so-called "new family" a long time ago. If it hadn't been for Sammy, he would have.

He was putting a lot at risk by following Tom. He'd been half-surprised the veterinarian had been able to find his way back to the church. The guy was as clueless as he was book smart and rarely had an idea that didn't start in Carla's head. Standing at the back of the immense auditorium-style church, that thought brought him full circle. What the hell was so important to Carla that she'd send Tom to do it, alone?

He listened in the dark for a moment before clicking on the flashlight and letting its beam play across the backs of empty seats and far wall. When they'd stayed here before, they hadn't come in here much; they'd used the lobby area. There'd been couches, and easy access to several exits. He'd passed by the pile of "supplies" that Tom had said he'd come to collect. The cold-weather coats, sleeping bags, and a few half-used steel bottles of camping fuel were still sitting there where they'd left them. None of it was worth coming back for.

Where is the creepy horse doctor? He shut off his flashlight and just tried to listen. The cocoon of darkness reminded him of being deep underwater without lights. The diving bell he and two other insane idiots had lived in on the bottom of the Norwegian Sea for a week had lost its power once. There'd been a temporary problem on the surface with their minder boat. The darkness in the auditorium was nearly as complete, and there was a silence to the world that he would have craved a year ago. Now, it was just a reminder of how truly alone he was. The auditorium felt empty.

The boom of a rifle shot was still echoing through the walls by the time he realized he'd thrown himself to the floor. He stayed where he was, on his stomach in the aisle behind the back row of seats. He was no expert, but he'd been shot at enough in the last year to know the rifle had been very close. He could hear muted pounding on the roof coming through the ceiling and getting farther away. There was a crash of a door slamming, and then a string of pounding footsteps somewhere within the church. It was somebody running down a set of metal stairs.

He pulled out the Glock that had seen him away from Lexington and sat up enough to look into the darkness towards the auditorium's stage, between the backs of the seats he could feel in front of him. Another door crashed open somewhere behind the stage, and he could see a bloom of light from a flashlight. The flashlight appeared on stage and flashed in hurried jerks all over the chapel. He couldn't make out the face of who was behind the light, but he was pretty certain it was Tom's skinny ass holding it. The figure jumped to the floor and started running up the center aisle towards the back.

"Tom!" he yelled. "That you?"

Whoever it was gave a yelp of surprise and started firing by way of an answer.

Ray ducked back down; he was a section of seats away from the aisle Tom was in, and none of the shots came anywhere close.

"Ray!" Tom shouted in that nasally whining voice. "You have no idea who you're fucking with!"

He was about to reply that it hadn't been him, when Tom fired three more shots. These had been aimed in the direction of his voice and came a lot closer. One round impacted the back of a seat, ten yards from him.

He crawled on his stomach along the back of the auditorium, towards the top of the aisle Tom had been running up. Once he made it, he peeked around the corner and could see Tom hunched over on one knee, a flashlight burning on the floor as he struggled to put a new magazine in his gun.

Ray popped to his feet and ran forward with his own gun held out. "Tom, it's Ray. I didn't shoot at you!"

Tom froze and just looked down at the gun and magazine in his hands. He shook his head slowly back and forth. "It doesn't matter if it was them or you. You can't stand against what's coming. None of you can."

"Who's them?"

"Our guests, the idiots who let us in."

Ray watched as Tom woodenly inserted the fresh magazine. He raised both his own gun and the flashlight in response until Tom was framed in the beam. The slide of Tom's handgun was still locked back.

"I don't want to shoot you, Tom. But I will. Put the gun down."

Tom gave a short laugh. "New beginnings have a price to be paid in blood."

"What!?" Tom was losing it, that was the only thing that made sense to him.

"You stupid redneck." Tom was smiling now, trying to squint past the light shining at him. "You don't get it. You can't understand something bigger than yourself."

"Explain it to me then, mister horse doctor."

Tom paused a moment before looking down at his gun. "You'll see . . . you'll all see the new beginning, the 'New Republic.'"

Tom moved more quickly than he would have credited. The slide release slammed forward as Tom's arm moved. Ray fired three times, point-blank into the chest of the man who had saved his life two months earlier.

Stunned, he stood there a moment, realizing what he had just done. There would be no going back to the mall, not now. Georgia was waiting, again. He took a step, then another, on legs that didn't want to work. By the time he reached the lobby doors, he was almost running. He ignored the leftover supplies, cut through the breadth of the lobby, and punched his way out through an emergency exit door on the side. The first thing his brain registered when his feet hit the pavement of the parking lot was a figure with a rifle, spinning around in surprise.

He'd fired twice before he really even saw the man. He hit him at least once and surged past, still running. He made it as far as the corner of the parking garage complex before turning around to check his results. There'd been a rifle, and he'd sure as shit be needing one. The figure wasn't moving, and he went back with his gun held level, ready to fire again if he had to.

It was the kid from the mall looking up at him, blinking in surprise and trying to bring the rifle that lay next to him closer. The same kid who spent a lot of time with Daniel and Reed. Pro . . . What the hell was he supposed to do now?

"Jesus! I'm sorry, kid." He took the rifle away from him and set it aside. He sat his own gun down and moved Pro's other hand away from where he held it over his shoulder.

"Why . . .?" Pro struggled to speak.

"I didn't mean to . . . What the hell are you doing out here?"

He felt around under the kid's collar and realized his 9mm had punched right through the kid's collarbone, just inside the shoulder, and exited out the back. Great! And he'd just killed the closest thing to a doctor these people had.

Christ, the kid was really bleeding, but it appeared to be coming from all the torn tissue, not an artery. "You got a first-aid kit? Or something?"

"My . . . bike." The kid lifted his good hand and pointed at the garage.

Pro had passed out by the time he got back. He slapped him until he came back around. "You gotta stay awake! You hear me?"

"Help . . . coming," Pro slurred.

Maybe for you, he thought. Ray tried to work as fast as he could; he'd had a battery of first-aid training over the course of his career. Almost all of it had dealt with the prolific dangers of his profession; hypoxia, crushing wounds, electrocution, the bends, burns, and hypothermia. All the shit he and his colleagues worried about on a daily basis. Gunshot wounds had never been part of the conversation. He'd had a crash course over the last year.

He plugged the entry wound with a tampon from the bag and packed the back side tight with all the sterile wrapping the kid had with him. He'd just finished wrapping it all tight under Pro's armpit with an elastic ankle wrap when two Humvees roared up the road to the church. They bounced and plowed their way across the median and disappeared, hidden by the church. He could hear their tires squealing to a stop. For the briefest of moments, he considered making a break for the bushes that lined the parking lot. These were good people, he told himself. He grabbed the flashlight off of Pro's belt and shined it at the corner of the building.

"Over here!"

"Is he . . .?" Rachel couldn't bring herself to ask.

Michelle got up from her chair and hugged her. "Doc Adams thinks he's going to be alright. Pumping him full of blood and IV fluids right now."

"Can I see him?"

"He's out of it, Rachel. Maybe in the morning."

"I meant the piece of shit who shot him."

Michelle gripped her by the shoulders and gave her a shake. "That same piece of shit saved his life."

She should have been there with him. She knew it, even if no one else was going to say it.

Reed joined them. "It was Ray. He could have run. He stayed and did what he could. Tom's body was inside the church; Ray said he did that too."

Rachel didn't know what to say. Ray had been the outlier, the loner from the new group. None of them had thought he'd had it in for someone he'd been traveling with.

Michelle filled them both in on what Pro had reported to her before getting shot.

"Who the hell was Tom trying to contact?" Reed asked what they were all thinking.

"Why was Ray even there?" Rachel added.

Reed shook his head, "Daniel's talking to him right now."

*

Daniel had gotten Ray's story, twice. It hadn't changed one iota. The guy had a straightforward way about him that almost made him wonder if the man was capable of subterfuge. On the other hand, Ray had admitted to following Tom because he'd felt for some time that something "weird" was up between Carla and Tom.

Daniel reached for the bag he'd come in with and sat the remains of a shortwave radio on the tabletop between them. "You ever seen this before?"

"Never."

"Tom was getting ready to use it when Pro shot it. We're guessing that's the first shot you heard."

Ray shook his head. "No way they were traveling with that, I would have seen it."

"They could have kept it hidden."

Ray smiled and gave his head a shake. "Haven't you ever traveled in a group? I mean been on the road, since the suck?"

"No," he admitted. "I guess you could say I'm a local."

"It isn't easy. You spend half your time thanking God you're in a group, praying it's big enough to scare off scavengers. The other half of the time, you're worried the people next to you are going to kill you in your sleep and steal your shit. The stuff people carry takes on value like you can't imagine. You always know who's carrying the most water, the most food, the lighter, whatever. Always," Ray repeated. "Just in case."

"In case you need to kill them?"

Ray just looked back at him without flinching. "It wasn't like that tonight, but in simple terms, yes."

Daniel was almost ashamed that what Ray was saying made sense.

"It had a car battery with it." Daniel pointed at the radio.

"No way they traveled with that, or the radio."

Which meant it had been there waiting for them to use, put there by someone else. Daniel chewed on that for the half second it took to realize the implications of that fact were far worse than the presence of the radio itself.

"What exactly did Tom say to you?"

"I've already told you." Ray set his handcuffed hands on the tabletop. "It's not going to make any more sense if I tell you again."

"Try me."

Ray's story didn't change.

"You hear him or any of the others in your group mention this New Republic before?"

"Never." Ray shook his head. "Look, you have to understand, Tom doesn't wipe his own ass without Carla's say-so. If you can hide what happened with me and Pro tonight, just watch her close. She'll be going apeshit wondering what happened to her puppet. Just get the boy away from her. Trust me, Sammy won't mind a bit, and if Carla does; it'll be an act."

Nothing Ray had said made as much of an impact as his concern for Sammy had. "What am I supposed to do with you?"

"You said Pro's going to make it?"

"So I'm told."

"He'll tell you what happened between us. Just let me go. Carla knows I'm headed to Georgia anyway."

Daniel shook his head. "You can't be gone the same night Tom disappeared."

Ray rubbed at his face for a moment. "I can't argue with that."

"You'll stay here, right here." Daniel pointed at the table. "Until we get Pro's story. If what you say checks out, and I have a feeling it will, I'll ask you to stay on a week or so. I'll have you set up with a motorcycle, and supplies. If you still want to head to Georgia, you can be on your way. For my part, if you *are* telling the truth, I hope you'll stay."

"I can't stay. I just shot your people's mascot."

Daniel had to smile at Ray's understanding of his situation. Pro *was* a mascot to many people. To others, he was a lot more. He could only imagine the fight he'd have with Michelle if he pushed for releasing Ray. Then again, it had been Michelle who had sent Pro to follow Tom in the first place. That wasn't fair, he knew. Pro was the best scout they had, regardless of his age. It would have been safer to have Pro out there than anyone else, except Jason or maybe Reed. At the end of the day, Michelle had been right; something wasn't right with this group. He just didn't believe Ray was part of it.

Looking across the table, Ray seemed resigned to whatever fate had in store for him. For Daniel's part, he couldn't imagine a scenario in which Ray wasn't telling the truth. The man had stayed and, in all likelihood, saved Pro's life. He'd admitted to killing Tom. His story tracked with what Pro had reported over the radio.

"If you're being honest, you don't have anything to worry about."

"Even her?"

"Her who?" Daniel followed Ray's pointing chin and turned around to see Rachel watching them through the porthole window of the hotel kitchen's door.

He turned back around. "She'll listen to what Pro says." He said it with a lot more confidence than he felt. *She sure as hell won't listen to me.*

Chapter 9

Charlottesville, Virginia, UVA Campus

"Kids! Today, we have a special guest. Our leader, Miss Cooper herself."

Lisa watched the children's reaction as she was introduced by name. The teacher had done a good job in getting the kids, orphans every one, ready for her. Hearing the introduction, she was forced to admit that Steven might be right; she needed an official title. Miss Cooper, or "Professor Cooper" as some of the general's men called her, didn't encompass what she was, and didn't come close to describing or crediting her for what she'd managed to build. She'd have to admit he was right, accept his help. Maybe get him to start a grassroots movement in the ranks that would see her awarded a title commensurate with the power she wielded.

What would it be? "President" was overdone and just carried a shit ton of baggage she'd rather not have to deal with. "Commissar" or "General Secretary" would satisfy her personally, but either title would carry a negative connotation for many of the people under her sway, or at least for many of the soldiers she knew her control relied upon. She'd gone with the name New Republic for the same reason; it was *new* and could be as different as she needed it to be. It wasn't going to be defined by the name—her title couldn't be either.

"Thank you, Maggie," she whispered to the retreating teacher amid the burst of applause from the children. She walked to the front of the classroom, aware that all of the kids looking at her, all between the ages of six and fourteen, had lost their real parents to the virus. That fact didn't distinguish them from anyone left alive. They were all orphans. These kids, though, were two-time losers.

Each of these children had lost the adoptive adults they'd been found with. Either to the fight that had accompanied their joining the New Republic, or to the pigheaded inability of their post-virus guardians to accept the hospitality with which they'd been welcomed. She had never held the illusion that her vision for the future wouldn't need to be enforced from the top. The quiet, hidden graves behind the golf course were a testament to that fact. These two-time orphans would be the ones who could drive her dream from the bottom, from within the ranks and for years into the future. She'd gotten to them in time. She could see that in the way they looked at her.

"The New Republic provides." She could feel the power in the words. "No more want, no more fear. We are all equal before our laws. We all have a responsibility to share what we have and the privilege to take what we need."

The applause broke out spontaneously. She clasped her hands in front of her face and smiled back at them. She raised her voice. "Who do we help?"

"EVERYONE!" the class shouted back at her.

"Who can stop us?"

"NO ONE!"

She paused a moment to let the applause die down of its own accord.

"I'm so proud of all of you!" she beamed. "I understand I have some awards to hand out . . ."

*

Outskirts of Richmond, Virginia (the next day...)

"We're ready." Lisa didn't think she'd seen this side of her general before. It was something like macho confidence with an edge of expectation, maybe even nervousness thrown in. Steven Marks had retired from the Army after twenty-two years as a major. He'd been the commanding officer of the ROTC detachment at Virginia Tech and had been leading a group of a hundred or so survivors when they'd found her and her group in Charlottesville.

She'd recognized straight away the opportunity and advantages Steven had offered her. Legitimacy from a dead world, paired with the ability to lead men and women in violent acts that, by then, she'd known would be a permanent fixture of the world going forward. Seducing him had been easy; she'd had professors in grad school who had been more of a challenge in that regard. Converting him to her vision of what they could build had taken more effort, but she'd succeeded there as well. "General" Steven Marks had received his stars from her.

"The advance team?" she asked, far more concerned about the survival of her group of spies that had infiltrated Richmond months ago than she was about the potential losses among her soldiers. Cannon fodder could be replaced. The spies were true believers, her people.

"They report they are ready. If they're smart, they'll hole up and wait for the shitstorm to pass."

"They'll do their duty."

"They've done it," Marks replied, waving at the map spread out on the table within the tent. "Time for intelligence collection has passed. We're spread out on a rough semicircle from the northwest to the southeast, along the freeway and these secondary highways. We're going to drive to the south and southwest, towards the river. They won't have anywhere to go."

"We're starting so far away; won't they hear and see us coming?"

"It's a wider net than I'd use against a trained force. But these survivors? I'd love for them to get organized a bit before facing us. They probably won't, but if we beat them en masse, they'll throw down their guns that much quicker."

"Our soldiers know we are here to help these people, right?"

"They do, but we both know that will have to come after they're defeated."

She knew that to be true. Even then, there'd be hard-core holdouts who would need to be dealt with later. There always were; there were two ways to leave the stadium.

"I'm not second-guessing you, General. I just worry for our soldiers." She said the last loud enough that his people around him in the tent could hear. *I'm also worried that you're a little too excited to play soldier, and we both know you aren't a real general.*

Steven jerked his chin toward the back of the tent. "Here's where I politely ask you to get in the truck and move back a few miles before we roll out."

She couldn't tell if his request indicated sincere concern for her safety or a desire to be left alone to do what needed doing. The only thing that mattered was the fact it had been a request. He was learning.

"I'd like to remain here with you, if you'll allow it." Part of her wished she could be riding in the tank that she knew was going to play a central role in the attack. She'd be as safe as could be and would be able to claim she'd shared the risks with her people. Steven had shot down that idea earlier the same morning, and she hadn't been able to sway him.

"As you wish." He nodded back at her, speaking loudly enough that his people could hear him clearly. "When I go forward, you'll remain here?" He waved an arm, taking in the rest of the command tent. "You've got the map and the radio people here. You'll be able to monitor everything."

"Sounds like a plan," she agreed. She had no desire to steal any of his glory. She knew that like most men in her life, he needed a bone thrown his way from time to time. As long as he never came to doubt who was doing the throwing.

She watched him as he bent over the map yet again before turning to the three radio operators behind him. "All units ready?"

The two women and man gave thumbs-ups from their seats next to their radios. Steven picked up his own radio. "All units, all units . . . Execute go, repeat, execute go."

*

"Go get the colonel." Marine Private First-Class Cameron Park was flying the drone from a ruggedized laptop and shouted at the person nearest him.

It happened to be his fellow Marine, Private Elliot.

"What's up, Poy?" Elliot just stared back at him.

"Elliot, why you always gotta do that? Go! Get! The colonel!"

Park made sure Elliot was moving before looking back at his controls and making a few adjustments. He'd always been good at video games, and the collection of gaming platforms and virtual reality training suites in The Hole had helped keep him sane during the months underground—that and the endless supply of food. He'd always been a big guy, but there was no denying that he'd ballooned in the last ten months. The guys had given him a hard time, but they were easy to ignore.

It wasn't like they didn't all have some crutch that they'd used to stay sane. Nathans had his old-time '90s grunge music and that creepy Nordic heavy metal. Gunny had his stupid books. Farmer had the weight room. Uwasi had his Bible. Tommy had his drawing. He had to smile at that thought. If anyone with "real" authority ever made it to lower levels of The Hole, they'd be met with some of Salguero's artwork on the walls and probably start looking for the Section Eight paperwork.

Then there was Elliot; in his opinion, his fellow private was too stupid to have needed a diversion. Mama Park's eldest boy of Hilo, Hawaii, had survived, even if he knew he'd probably come dangerously close to eating himself to death. He could see himself reflected in the looks the colonel's people threw his way. They'd all known people who had starved to death, and here he was sporting 80 pounds he hadn't had when he'd gone down The Hole.

Captain Naylor had asked him to "volunteer" for extra physical training since being released from their underground post, and he had. It had been a week, and he was already seeing results. The downside was that he was so sore, he could hardly move. It was the main reason he'd volunteered to fly the drone, with a laptop controller, from a camp chair in the shade. Take away the scenery, add a bowl of rice, some Spam, and a soda, and it wouldn't have been much different than how he'd spent the last ten months.

They had set up what the colonel referred to as an armed gypsy camp in the woods, less than a mile from the quarry that held the entrance to The Hole. Skirjanek had directed them to pull some hardware out of The Hole, and a small part of that had been the kitchen-table-sized tactical drone that he'd been flying all morning, looking for what the colonel had referred to as "anything that looks like it could hurt us."

If the stories of Cuba, Miami, Hampton Roads, and Norfolk coming out of Skirjanek's people were real, and he had no reason to believe they weren't, he didn't figure on seeing anyone who would be dumb enough to mess with the unit Skirjanek was putting together—and for the first few hours of his flight, he hadn't.

There had been nothing to see in the immediate area beyond a seemingly endless expanse of overgrown, abandoned green fields going to weeds and corrals full of dead farm animals that had starved long ago. The whole area, from the perspective of the drone's camera, was laced with secondary state roads connecting empty houses, quiet residential subdivisions with an occasional school or strip mall characterized by empty parking lots. Some of those lots had been used to collect the dead before nearly everyone had died.

Even from his high altitude, he could see the burial mounds were a gathering place of sorts for the local wildlife that seemed to have been taken over by rats, wild dogs, and carrion birds. Once he'd been certain there wasn't any enemy force close by, he'd climbed higher and flown the drone westward for twelve miles towards the I-95/I-64 corridor. A black column of smoke coming from the northern edge of Richmond had stood out, and he'd climbed again to the bottom of the low-lying cloud cover at about three thousand feet and moved the drone in for a closer look.

He'd had a lot of practice with the drone while in The Hole; they all had. The drone training simulator, complete with 3D headsets, had been one of the most popular "games" down there; an endless panorama, open horizons, and most importantly, no off-yellow paint on the walls or dark green floors. Controlling the actual bird was easier than the simulator, and much more boring. This actual drone wasn't capable of carrying any weapons. It did have a good camera with an even better telephoto lens.

At the moment, he had no problem making out the line of vehicles, supported by hundreds of infantry on the northern outskirts of Richmond. Just before yelling for the colonel, he'd spotted two Bradley infantry fighting vehicles in the line, slowly encircling the city.

"What do you have, Mr. Park?" Skirjanek asked as he approached, coming around the cold firepit. The way Skirjanek looked and moved reminded him of a wolf from one of those nature channel shows. Not a big guy by any means, the colonel's face was all sharp angles and looked like it had been chiseled out of ice.

"I think this counts as a threat, sir."

The colonel watched over his shoulder in silence for less than a minute before he pointed at the edge of the screen. "Can you pan back northward?"

The colonel's finger danced above another line of vehicles moving in on the city from the northwest. "Tell me that isn't an Abrams, Private."

"Can't do, sir. That is definitely a tank."

He watched Skirjanek pull his radio out and then pause. "How much loiter time do you have left?"

"Just over an hour, sir. I spent a couple of hours close in to us. This thing is just a regiment-level artillery drone; it's nothing like a Raptor or the big Global Hawks." He pointed at the ground to his side. "Though I do think we have a Raptor or two somewhere in the basement."

"Good work, Mr. Park." Skirjanek clapped a hand on his shoulder and moved a few feet away.

"Eagle One, for Wolf One. Eagle One, for Wolf One." So much for radio silence, he thought. Park kept his eyes glued to the screen as he listened in. The colonel was calling the gunny and that quiet Russian cat.

"This is Wolf One." It was the Russian's voice coming back over the radio, and he wondered immediately why Gunny Bruce wasn't "Wolf One."

Cam listened in to their whole conversation and was looking up at Skirjanek as the colonel dropped his radio to his belt and just stared at him for a moment. "You really checked out on a Raptor?"

"Ah, hell no, I mean, no, sir."

"Relax, Mr. Park, this isn't the Marine Corps."

They were all struggling to get used to Colonel Skirjanek and Captain Naylor going super lax on the whole military thing. The gunny had explained it as the need to integrate the civilians they had with them, even as they trained them up. Gunny Bruce had also shared that the colonel felt it was important that their group of gypsies developed something more than just duty to hold them together. He wasn't sure what he thought about all that, or the reasons behind it, but he liked the idea of keeping the laid-back way that had developed while they'd been in The Hole. They'd all known the El Tee was in charge, until he wasn't. Then it had fallen to Gunny Bruce, and now it was Colonel Skirjanek.

"Sir, I just meant I spent a lot of time playing with the flight simulator; we all did. It killed some hours, sir. I don't think any of us are like officially checked out on most of the stuff down there. We're Marines, sir. Everybody knows we don't get new gear until you Army guys wear it out."

The colonel smiled at the old joke, but he could tell the man's mind was far away.

"You think they're friendly, sir?"

"I think friendly is probably a stretch, Mr. Park. From the few survivors we've come across, trust has been an issue. The question will be; are they somebody we can work with or somebody we can't?"

"Got it, sir. I'll shout if I see anything new?"

The colonel nodded at him and then, as an afterthought, turned fully to face him. "Well done, Mr. Park. I'm glad I've got people like you to rely on."

"Yes, sir. My pleasure, sir." This guy was pretty cool. For an officer.

"Captain Naylor tells me your PT program is progressing well; you certainly are looking better. Stick with it. I'll be running with your group this afternoon as long as Wolf Team stays out of trouble."

"Yes, sir." *Freaking officers, just when you think they're chill, it's the old sugar-then-spice sneak attack.* "I'll be there, sir."

The presence of the Russian soldier speaking to him was still throwing Gunny Bruce curveballs. He'd heard the story of Skirjanek's experience in the Antarctic from the man himself; most of Captain Naylor's submarine crew and a good many of the civilians who helped make up the strange band of survivors who had rescued him and his men from The Hole. He knew on an intellectual level that Pavel, the former Russian Spetsnaz, belonged with Skirjanek as much as any of them did. The end of the world was the only thing that had brought any of them together.

Pavel's story, delivered by Skirjanek himself, seemed even crazier. He and his fellow Russians were a very long way from home and had, for the time being, given up on an effort to get home. He understood the whole "Everyone is dead—what does it matter where you are?"

sentiment. During their two-man patrol following a state highway west towards the interstate, there'd been bodies, some scavenged down to skeletons; others were masses of rot and clothing covered in bugs. In the small town they'd just passed through, there'd been a reminder every few paces of the simple fact that the world had moved on from people. That said, he couldn't help but think if he were a Russian, or an Italian for that matter, he'd want to face the future at home, wherever that happened to be.

"I know the colonel seems like a good guy and all," he said as he watched a hawk or a small eagle dive on a rat the size of a house cat and then struggle for altitude. At least rats weren't the only thing making a comeback; they'd seen more birds of prey in the last two days than he imagined could exist in any single area. It was like watching nature's air show conducting bombing runs all around them. The rats were so numerous they were oblivious to the threat from above and wouldn't even register a response until one of their brethren was already airborne, squealing in the grip of a raptor. "I would have thought you and your countrymen would try to get home."

"I'm not a sailor." Pavel shrugged, watching the same bird struggle for altitude. "You did not see the survivors we encountered in Cuba or Miami. It is same everywhere. Moscow, Saint Petersburg, Rostov-na-Donu would be no different."

"Rostov . . .?"

"Na-Donu, it means next to the Don river. It is where I am from."

"It's a nice place?" Gunny Bruce had no idea what to say; he was just trying to be friendly, and if he was being honest with himself, it was a relief to talk to anyone who wasn't a member of his own unit. By this time, he knew details about his fellow Marines that he'd just as soon forget. There was no sane reason to explain why he should know that Elliot's family opened their presents on Christmas Eve, except for the nice one that was held back for the actual day. But he did know; that and a thousand other details about all of them.

"I have not been there for many years." Pavel stopped walking at the intersection they'd been working their way towards, pointed at the road signs, and then looked at him expectantly.

"I think this is why the colonel selected the two of us for this patrol."

"Sorry? You just lost me."

"Which way to go?" The Russian spread his arms, indicating the T intersection. "Who decides? You or me? We are both senior enlisted men. I think the colonel hoped we would come to an understanding while we are out here."

He'd been worrying about how to think of Pavel. Was he a comrade in arms? Part of Skirjanek's inner circle? Or just another survivor wondering where he fit in? The Russian, and apparently Colonel Skirjanek, were way ahead of him.

"I'm just a gunnery sergeant," he answered. "We were always told senior enlisted in the Russian Army were more like our officers."

"I believe this is true," Pavel answered, "because many of our men are still drafted and not good soldiers. The ones who stay for a career are the best soldiers. But we are not in Russian Army."

"What was your rank?"

"I was a *starshy praporchik*."

"*Starshy pra . . .?*"

"*Starshy praporchik*; Captain Naylor tells me this is like your chief warrant officer in rank."

"Then you have me beat by a mile." He indicated the intersection. "You decide."

"You would take orders from me?"

"We still talking about which road to take?"

"This is not what I meant."

He caught himself grinning and realized it was a relief to have a fellow NCO above him to screw with. "Look, I trust the colonel. He seems squared away, and he trusts you. That's good enough for me. You clearly outrank me, so unless you give some bullshit order that fucks with my Marines, I'll follow your orders."

Pavel accepted this with a nod and then looked at him strangely. "My English is still improving, so I may have made mistake in understanding the colonel." Pavel pointed to the two of them. "I believe this was his desired result."

"I'm sure it was," he agreed. It made sense to him as well.

"Why would the colonel not just order it so?"

"You heard his little speech to my guys, whatever he's putting together here; the Gypsies? He doesn't have the authority to order any of us to do anything—"

"But, that is no way to run a ship," Pavel interrupted.

"Exactly." He was about to continue when the Russians words caught him. "You're not a Navy guy, are you?"

"Stalin's balls! I am Army. Navy is perfect for getting you to a fight or maybe for rescue from a horrible death in a frozen wasteland, but a real soldier . . ."

"Right, OK, I'm glad we agree on that, because I was about to reassess our pecking order. But you get it, Skirjanek's right. He can't rely on authorities that don't exist, flags that no longer fly. There has to be something else holding us together. We trust the colonel's judgment. You and I have our professionalism, I guess you would call it."

"Professional respect?" Pavel offered.

"Exactly."

Pavel pointed at the road sign again. "So, which way? These signs make no sense to me."

"Left to the interstate."

They walked for nearly ten minutes under the trees that lined the road before Pavel turned to him. "Your Marines are subservient to your Navy, yes?"

He thought he could see the laughter in Pavel's cold blue eyes.

"Not anymore."

It was an hour later when the colonel radioed them.

"Wolf One? That's you." He smiled and handed the radio over to Pavel.

The conversation was short, and he listened in, raising his eyebrows at what the colonel reported he was seeing via the drone over Richmond. Skirjanek asked that they hold in place and wait for transport that would bring Farmer and Nathans to them as well as additional supplies.

"Rough count of between five and eight hundred militia on the offensive, circling city in an arc from northwest to southeast, driving southwest towards city and river on far side of city. They have assorted APC, and technical support, and at least one, I repeat, one Abrams tank. No sign of air support. Defensive force is holed up so far. We have no count, but resistance appears to be ineffective."

The surprise on Pavel's face mirrored his own.

"Please repeat, Eagle," Pavel asked. "Confirm number of troops on offensive."

"Offensive force appears between five and eight hundred, rough count."

"Understood, Eagle One. Holding position."

Pavel snapped the radio to his own belt as they just stared at each other.

"That is the largest concentration of survivors we have encountered," Pavel said.

"By how much?"

"We saw one group of perhaps one hundred people outside Miami. They were on the shore watching us as we sailed past. They were armed, and we did not make port."

"If this group has eight hundred shooters, how many people you think they'd have to have?"

Pavel just looked back at him for a moment before answering. "We can assume many more."

Skirjanek's Gypsies had access to equipment that could handle just about any contingency. The problem was they had a grand total of thirty-three personnel with military backgrounds and a roughly equal number of civvies, most of them glorified meteorologists with PhD after their names. They couldn't begin to use the gear they had access to. Now, it sounded like Poy's drone had found what Skirjanek had been looking for. It would be up to them to figure out if this was what the colonel had been hoping for or fearing.

Pavel just looked at him for a moment before moving farther off the road, taking a knee, and spreading out the map he had. "What do you know of this Richmond?"

"Not much, it's a small city about twenty miles west of here. A buddy of mine got married there a few years ago . . ." He noted the legs of another corpse lying out on the shoulder of the road ahead of them. Most of the torso had been reduced to the skeleton. "I'm guessing it's not the place I remember."

"No," Pavel agreed, following his eyes to the corpse.

*

"What the hell? This is more of a cattle drive than a battle." Lucas "Farmer" Hanson had the team's best pair of binoculars at the moment and had the best view of what was happening along the Richmond riverfront. Pavel had made the decision to set up on the south bank of the river, and it had proven to have been a fortuitous choice. Whatever was happening in the city had come to them. The city's defenders had been driven to a large riverfront plaza backed by two tall office towers.

"Tell that to the poor bastards who didn't run." Trey Nathans was lying prone with his sniper rifle. He had a much tighter, clearer view of what was happening through his scope than that provided by the binoculars. Gunny Bruce was having a hard time putting a label on what they were seeing, but he more than understood Nathans's anger. There were perhaps five hundred people down there. Civilians who had "escaped" the assault.

Driven through the city, they were now surrounded by the invading force that ringed the plaza with a weird combination of Bradleys, five-ton trucks, commercial "technicals" sporting what looked like M-60 machine guns, and one very conspicuous Abrams tank. Armed invaders worked through the crowd in small squads, disarming everyone.

The characteristic whine and rattle of other Bradleys operating out of sight within the city could still be heard from their vantage point on the south side of the river. At this point, the remaining gunfire was sporadic or seemed to be for show. It was a strange calm after every defensive position they'd been able to see had been overrun. In almost every case, for the defenders, to run was to survive. Those defenders who had stayed behind their guns had all been killed. The one exception had been a group that had managed to knock the tracks off a Bradley before plastering it with Molotov cocktails. The survivors from that group had been gunned down as they ran to their next position.

They'd only had direct eyes on that one firefight. If it had been indicative of other actions they could hear throughout the city, the defenders who had stood and fought had exacted their own price on the attackers, whoever they were.

"They are not very good soldiers," Pavel added, sounding a lot more clinical than most of the comments that had been put forth over the last few hours.

"They aren't soldiers," he replied. "I think they just got to the gear first."

"They are organized," Pavel replied. "They are staying with the units they arrived at the river with. They are following someone's orders."

He'd seen that too. It hadn't rained in the week since they'd emerged from The Hole. The river separating them from the city was spotted with hundreds of islands of exposed rock. There appeared to be some deep channels between the rocks, but they were deceptive. From their position, it almost looked like someone would be able to walk across.

"Same could be said for my old Boy Scout troop," Farmer replied.

"Your Boy Scouts do much in the way of mechanized assault?" Nathans fired back.

"Guys! Get your counts." He raised his voice an octave. "Get as much intel as you can." If he didn't stop them, especially Nathans, the arguing wouldn't end.

"All carrying your M4s," Pavel noted. "They are . . . what is the word? Homo . . . ?"

"Homosexual?" Nathans asked. He had to suppress a smile. Nathans wasn't being a smart-ass. He was confused."

"Homogeneous, Trey." Farmer didn't take his eyes away from his binoculars. "Means same as standardized."

He thought he could see Nathans shrug in response, but their marksman remained glued to his scope.

"Now that you mention it," Lucas added, "they all look to be carrying the same tac radios. These guys hit the surplus store hard."

"You are certain these are not military personnel?" Pavel asked them all, his own eyes glued to a smaller set of binoculars.

"I watched that tank struggle to stay between the buildings," he answered. "Whoever is driving it is a civilian. Those guys manning the M-60s in the backs of those technicals look as likely to shoot their own guys as they are the people they've been fighting." Bruce shook his head. "But I think you're right, Pavel. I think we've got a soldier running a clown show."

A clown show that had probably killed a hundred or more people over the course of the day. They'd know more if Poy had been able to refuel and get the drone back up. Once they returned, they could replay its camera footage over and over and compare it to what they'd been able to see firsthand for analysis.

"Another group being pushed down that main road," Nathans reported.

He picked the group up as soon as they cleared from behind a salmon-colored office building. It was a small squad of seven defenders who looked like they'd been through a meat grinder. They were disarmed, and most of them had been wounded. One woman in particular was being held up between another woman and a man, almost being dragged between them. A newish-looking Army JLTV rolled behind them, flanked by another dozen or so armed attackers on foot.

They watched, as did the gathered crowd of civilians, as the large truck pushed slowly into the crowded plaza. Whoever was riding shotgun in the JLTV hopped out, and climbed up on the hood of the truck as soon as it pulled to a stop. He was shouting at his men, who moved the seven prisoners to the river's edge atop the stone river walk. They could all see the man on the hood of the truck, shouting at the crowd with an occasional arm raised in the direction of the river. The man couldn't have known it, but he was also pointing at them hidden within the foliage of the opposite bank.

"We got ourselves a talker." Nathans shifted his position slightly. "Give the word, Gunny. Target acquired."

"Do not fire," Pavel answered.

Nathans ignored the Russian. "Gunny?"

"You heard the order. We're here to observe." When they got back to the base, he was going to have a sit down with the guys regarding his and Pavel's understanding. He wondered if pulling in the colonel for that would be a good idea. The lack of military discipline might be the right approach as far as the civilians were concerned, but within units like his, it was only going to lead to confusion. He had to assume Skirjanek knew that, and was waiting for at least some level of organic acceptance.

"Hell, as far as we know," Farmer added, "the attackers are the good guys here."

Nathans snorted from behind his scope. "I'll take whatever odds you're giving on that."

Whoever was atop the truck wasn't a happy camper. Nathans reported his view through the sniper scope. "Leader is early thirties. No visible rank or insignia."

The dismounted soldiers who had arrived with the last JLTV moved as a group in response to more yelling and took up a line in front of their prisoners.

"This doesn't look good," Farmer deadpanned.

It didn't, but there was piss-all they could do from across the river with four guns except to reveal their position. Gunny scanned the faces of the crowd in the plaza through his binoculars. They appeared to be somewhere between shock and horror at what was about to happen.

"VIP rolling in," Farmer announced. The honking of car horns reached them a second later as two black SUVs pulled up next to the JLTV. The rearmost SUV disgorged half a dozen men with guns who ran over and took up a position between the prisoners on the river walk and their erstwhile firing squad. The lead SUV took its time opening its doors. Four individuals hopped out and ringed the JLTV, signaling for the soldier on its hood to get down.

"Gray beard," Nathans reported, "exiting SUV. Full BDUs, he's wearing fucking stars."

"Get a picture if you can."

"Somebody's in trouble," Farmer sang. They all watched as the soldier who had been directing the erstwhile firing squad was led back to the general's vehicle.

Whoever he was, the officer on the scene directed the prisoners to rejoin their people held in the middle of the plaza. He was handed a bullhorn and began addressing the gathered crowd. Between the distance and the sound of the river rushing over nearby rocks, the words reaching them were indecipherable noise, but the tone was one of calm and reassurance.

"Looks like Mr. Pavel was right. The general is definitely in charge," Nathans added. "Army digicam BDUs, early to mid-fifties, maybe six foot, two hundred pounds."

John would have paid whatever went for money these days to hear what the general was saying to the crowd. From his limited vantage point, the penned-in people of Richmond looked deflated, but what had been abject terror a few minutes ago had passed. More than anything, they looked resigned to their fate. He even saw a few heads in the crowd nodding in agreement at whatever the general was saying to them.

School buses arrived ten minutes later. They had to have been waiting close by; hopefully, the drone was back up and recording all of it. The gathered survivors of Richmond, perhaps as many as five hundred people, were loaded onto the buses. Each group of four buses was escorted away by one military vehicle and its occupants. The process was organized enough that John was certain it wasn't the first time the attackers had done this.

Within an hour, the only vehicles left in the plaza were the two SUVs and the Abrams tank. The general stood off to the side of the others with a radio operator, talking to someone, when a tractor trailer pulling a lowboy trailer rolled into the plaza. They all had a good laugh, watching the multiple attempts it took the tank's driver to get the Abrams loaded on the trailer, but it was soon gone as well. The two SUVs were the last to leave.

"Up to Poy Boy's drone from here," he announced. "We can't follow."

"Wish we knew who was who." Farmer was on one knee, repacking his bag.

"This was theater," Pavel announced, looking at all of them.

"What do you mean?" he asked.

"Perhaps I use the wrong word; they planned to not shoot the small group of prisoners. The general's arrival . . . theater, for a psychological effect."

"You saying they faked it?" Nathans didn't look convinced.

He caught himself nodding. "That makes some sense. They terrify the shit out of them. Good cop, bad cop routine. General's the hero . . ."

"Son of bitch . . ." Farmer was shaking his head. "But why?"

*

General Marks climbed into the SUV, offered him a big smile, reached across the backseat divider, and clapped him on the leg. "Well done, O'Connell, you missed your true calling."

A degree in theater, three years as the lead actor for his community

Shakespeare company, and one lead in a local TV commercial said that he hadn't. The suck had just put an end to it.

"You had me a little worried, General. I was running out of shit to say." Sergeant Liam O'Connell wondered for a moment if he could have given the order to execute the prisoners. Which led to the question of whether his guys would have followed the order and pulled their triggers. On the latter question, he was sure they would have. He was just as certain that a part of him had wanted to give the order. That particular group of defenders had killed four of his team members. His performance atop the truck while addressing the crowd had been inspired, but he wasn't altogether sure he'd been acting.

Marks waved away his concern. "I was listening in on the open radio. We were close by. I wasn't going to have another Roanoke."

Roanoke . . . Liam hadn't been involved in that one beyond the role of carrying a gun. Whoever had addressed the battle's survivors at the end of the day had been just a little too keyed up and still angry over the effective defense that had been put up. As he'd heard the story from Marks himself, his predecessor had shot a pair of survivors at the front of the gathered crowd. The rest of the survivors, disarmed or not, had reacted in a very predictable manner and charged anyone holding a gun. By the time order had been restored, they'd lost another dozen soldiers and almost a hundred more of Roanoke's survivors.

In Marks's words, it had been a shit show. It was the real reason so many of those collected from Roanoke were still housed in the stadium. "It's all about trust," Marks had explained to him. "They can think whatever they want about the folks they've just been beaten by, but they have to come to believe that our leadership has their best interests and continued survival in mind. Don't fuck this up, or you'll join your predecessor under the fairway on the fourteenth hole."

As far as pep talks went, it had been effective. They all knew what the golf course's fourteenth hole was used for. Finding motivation for today's role hadn't been an issue.

Chapter 10

"Can we trust you not to run?"

Daniel and Reed were staring down at him. During his short time in Tysons, Ray had learned they pretty much ran the place. At least in terms of the day to day; he was pretty certain Daniel's girlfriend, Michelle, actually called the shots. She and some guy named Jason who hadn't been there during the nearly two weeks he had. It had taken two days for them to get the story of what had happened from Pro. They'd assured him the kid was going to be fine. He'd felt a little guilty that his first thought at the news that Pro was going to make it was all about the kid's story matching his own. It had. They'd released his cuffs and were standing over him now.

"You still good with setting my ass up for a trip out of here?"

"We are," Reed answered immediately. "Your story has to be that you've spent the last two days scouting with myself and Gabe. Neither one of us has been seen by Carla. We were scouting the area inside the beltway; in Gabe's case, it happens to be the truth. We'll get you out of here and once we are certain that Carla is around to notice, we'll roll you up with Gabe in one of the trucks. You have to figure out a time to sit down with her today."

"Why today?"

"'Cause we're going to arrest you and the whole group you arrived with." Daniel held out a hand to stop him. "Minus Sammy. He'll be with Michelle all day."

"We'll hold you together," Reed explained. "We're hoping she'll confide in you or say something that will help."

"This was her idea, wasn't it?" he asked.

"Whose?" Daniel asked.

He just looked at both of them and shook his head. He was tired of people thinking he was an idiot. "Michelle's."

"What difference does that make?" It was Reed's turn to play stupid.

"'Cause when the boss lady changes her mind about me, I'll already be under guard."

Daniel smiled at him. Reed rubbed at his face, concealing a smirk of his own.

"You may not believe this," Daniel started, "but from the beginning, you and Sammy were the only ones Michelle wanted to let in."

"Bullshit."

"Michelle doesn't trust anybody who says they're willing to give up their weapons. You were the one willing to walk away to keep your gun."

Reed held a hand up and grinned. "To be clear, she doesn't really like anybody except Daniel here."

"Fine," he relented. He didn't see that he had any options. Besides, if it helped nail that crazy bitch Carla, he'd give it a shot. "I'll do it."

*

Jason had taken almost a week to work his way back home. He'd gone west into the Shenandoah Valley and then north, moving only at night and checking out the towns during the day. They'd all been as stripped of people and supplies as he'd discovered Leesburg had been at the beginning of his trip. What was left was no different from the suburbs Sheriff Bauman's crew had hit. The towns had been professionally looted and left to small, scattered groups of survivors who had managed to escape the New Republic's personnel collection efforts. From Roanoke in the south, through Harrisonburg and Winchester in the north, the valley's towns had all been raided.

A small group just outside of Woodstock had told him the raiders had worked the valley all winter long, collecting people and looting everything they could carry. He'd intended to go west into the hills at Woodstock and try to make it to Wolf Gap where the Dagmans' small farm was located, but the same group that shared their information had also taken a little too much interest in him and his gear. They weren't a threat beyond the usual one of banditry, but he didn't want to take the time to deal with them. Wolf Gap could wait. He'd needed to get home.

He almost didn't make it. Raided or not, there were still people everywhere. The scattered survivors had learned the hard way that large groups were targets for larger groups. The survivors had dispersed. It was a lesson that he was desperate to deliver to Tysons. They'd been thinking their size offered protection, and to a certain extent it did. It also painted a target on their back. While he'd been traveling at night, by back roads paralleling state routes 9 and then 7, someone had shot out a rear tire of the beast. It had been pitch-black, and he'd heard the rifle report just as the right rear of the vehicle dug in hard and threatened to roll him.

It had been nothing but blind-ass luck, that allowed him to keep the rig on the road even at the sedate speed of maybe 35 mph. He hadn't stopped. Given a choice, stopping in the middle of an ambush was never a good idea. Accompanied by the sound of a flapping tire, and a rim that would send a rooster tail of sparks each time he steered to weave between abandoned cars, he'd continued for nearly two miles before pulling over in front of a line of abandoned cars that would offer some protection from whoever would be coming. He had no doubt they would be coming.

Somebody who had been able to shoot out a tire, of a moving vehicle, at night. He bailed out of the Land Cruiser and set up with his own rifle on the opposite side of the road, behind a Hyundai sedan that had the rotting remains of bodies sprawled across the front seat. There were times when he hated what the night vision goggles allowed him to see. Without them, his nose would have been perfectly capable of giving him the same information.

The sound of motorcycles reached him just as two bikes came around the last corner, moving slow. They rolled up, slowing even more when they spotted the beast. It looked like a man and a woman, judging by their builds. He confirmed it a moment later when the guy hopped off his bike and approached the rig with a hunting rifle held to his shoulder. The woman dropped her kickstand and followed. She didn't look to be armed, but that idea seemed ludicrous. He had to assume she was.

He waited until they were a safe distance from their bikes before letting loose a three-round burst at the gas tank of the man's bike. He was disappointed it didn't blow but then caught himself flinching when it caught fire and did. The woman threw herself to the ground, and the man came running around the back side of the Land Cruiser and let loose a round aimed at nothing in particular, in his general direction.

"Throw the rifle away!" he screamed. He could feel his anger building; he knew this petty bandit bullshit wasn't going to end any time soon. He so didn't want to deal with this right now and came very close to handling it in the most forthright manner he could think of. He told himself that they were probably just hungry, that he shouldn't kill them over that.

The man complied and hung his head. He stepped out from behind his cover, flipped up his night optical devices and crossed the road from where he could cover both of them. "Your weapons, all of them, toss them to the side of the road. I'll be checking you, and if I find one you forgot, I'll kill you. I don't have time for this shit right now."

"You a soldier?" the young man asked.

He hadn't thought of the light thrown out by the burning bike; they had a good look at him. "Used to be," he answered. "Lose your weapons, all of them. Now."

"You, too, miss." He prodded the woman's boot with his own. She was still lying on her stomach and hadn't moved.

"Don't do it, Will!" she spit. "He'll just kill us."

Jason stared at the young man and kept the barrel of his rifle aligned with his chest. Will couldn't have been any older than nineteen or twenty. The woman hadn't sounded any older than that either. "If I wanted to kill you, you'd both be dead. What I want is for you to change my tire while I keep an eye on you. You finish that, I'll let you go. You have my word."

"Your word?" the woman screeched from the ground.

He ignored her and focused on the guy. He could tell the young man had something holstered under his shirt. He tried to make his voice sound calm. "Your move." He was somehow reminded of his first encounter with Loki. Looking more closely at the young man, he wasn't convinced Loki wouldn't have been the smarter of the two.

"OK, OK." The man lifted his shirt and unsnapped his holster from his belt. He tossed it to the side of the road. He pulled another smaller gun from the back of his belt, plus a scabbarded bowie knife and a small folding knife from one of his boots. Maybe not so dumb after all, he thought.

"You know how to change a tire?"

"Yeah."

"Get to it. The jack is mounted inside the back door."

The woman started to get up, and he planted his boot on her lower back and pressed her back to the ground. "Not you. You didn't toss the knife I can see sticking out of your boot or the gun I'm guessing that you're lying on."

"Asshole . . ."

Yep . . . He'd rather be an asshole than take the easier and without doubt, safer route of killing them. She tossed her knife and the beat-up Glock she had been lying on. He let her get up and go sit on the remaining motorcycle, but only after zip-tying her wrist to the luggage mount behind the seat.

Will, if that was his real name, changed the tire quickly but took his time getting the lug nuts back on, delaying. Jason nudged him with the barrel. "I've changed a tire myself a time or two. Tighten them down. If you hurry up, I'll leave some supplies for you both."

"Seriously?"

"You two alone out here?"

"Yeah," the girl answered far too quickly from off to the side. She might as well have screamed "No!"

"Look, I don't know why I give a shit, but if you've got people depending on you, taking potshots at people is just stupid. When you get back to your group, you should come into Tysons. We've got food, shelter, and numbers enough to be safer than hiding out here in the hills." After what he'd seen in the last week, it sounded to him like a lie the second he spoke. But however long Tysons had, it had to be better than making a living off the road.

"Save your breath. We've heard about Tysons." The girl wasn't going to believe anything he said. If stories of Bauman's gang had reached them, he could hardly blame her.

"We ran those assholes out," he answered. "The place is under new management. If you ever do come in, ask for Michelle. She runs the place." He couldn't believe how good it felt to say that.

"That's it." The young man reseated the jack in its bracket on the door and stepped away from the back of the vehicle.

"You're down to one bike." He motioned with his chin in the woman's direction. "What do you want to carry? Water or food? I can spare either."

Will looked over at the woman before facing him again. "You wouldn't have any medicine, would you? Aspirin? Anything like that?"

"Will," the young lady almost growled at him.

He nodded. "I have some aspirin." He didn't have time to deal with whatever they had going on. He'd made the offer that would help them. It was up to them to take advantage of it or not.

"There's a first-aid kit under that packing blanket." He pointed into the back of his vehicle with the muzzle of the gun. "Take it, it's yours."

"You're really gonna let us go?" Will seemed incredulous enough that it left no doubt how this would have gone down had the situation been reversed.

"Take it," he repeated. "And start walking that way." He pointed with his chin back up the road from where he'd come. "You can come back for your weapons and the bike after I'm gone. You follow me again; I will kill you."

"What about me?" The girl had a set of shrill pipes on her that set him on edge.

"That's up to your friend here. You're going to sit right there until he gets back."

Will lifted the first-aid kit a few inches. "Thank you."

"Get going."

He waited until Will had passed the motorcycle and its occupant. "You two, and whoever you have in your group, should really come into Tysons. We have a doctor."

He saw the woman's head snap up at that news. "You're lying."

"We could help you, but I meant what I said. If I see either of you tonight, you're both dead."

He took his time getting situated and the NODs readjusted over his eyes. As he put the beast in gear, he glanced at the analog clock on the dashboard. He'd wasted more than an hour dicking around with the two bandits, who, if he was any judge of human nature, had a baby or a child out there somewhere.

The thought dredged up memories of how close he had come to being a father. Sam had been so excited, while he'd just been terrified. It had been all for naught. Sam's dreams had been stolen, and terror didn't begin to describe what had happened to the world. He glanced at the clock on the dash; it was nearly four a.m., and sunrise wasn't that far off. He'd already decided to push through. Pre-suck, this drive from Leesburg to Tysons would have taken him an hour with traffic and the never-ending construction along Route 7. Now it was just abandoned cars he had to dodge, and of course the occasional deer that would stand in the middle of the highway. Some things hadn't changed.

He wasn't headed to the mall; he wanted to talk to Rachel and apologize if she'd let him. He parked the beast in its customary spot behind the burned-out shell of a house at the edge of his neighborhood and walked the rest of the way. It felt good to stretch his legs, and he almost skipped up the driveway to the house, hoping Rachel would wake before Elsa. He wasn't worried about Pro; the kid never woke until someone did it for him.

The first indication that something was off was Loki. No Loki, to be more accurate. Everyone spent a lot of time in and around Tysons these days, so he didn't make much of it, and assumed Reed must have taken the dog with him. Given the early-morning hour of his arrival, he'd expected the house to be quiet, but it felt empty. There was a note on the kitchen island. He read it slowly, struggling to remain calm. He was moving out the back door before the note touched the floor.

He pulled up to the front of the hotel and hopped out just as Daniel and Michelle emerged from the lobby. He'd had to radio in before passing through the roadblock they'd set up. They'd known he was on his way in.

"He's going to be fine." Daniel jumped in front of him. "He's recovering."

While relieved, Jason was torn between wanting to learn more and the desire to move Daniel out of the way.

"He was shot once in the collarbone. Doc Adams says he'll make a full recovery."

"What happened?"

Michelle related what had happened, pausing at the end. "If you want to be mad at somebody, be mad at me. I sent him out there."

"Alone?"

Michelle just glared at him with her arms crossed in front of her chest. "I've been trying to get Rachel to quit blaming herself for not being there. Don't you dare pile on that, damn you. You're the one who left."

He didn't need Michelle to tell him it wouldn't have happened had he been here. "Where is he?"

"He's asleep in your old room." Michelle stuck a finger in his face. "Rachel is with him. Let them sleep."

"You look like you could do with some sleep yourself," Daniel said, trying to break off Michelle's attack dog routine that only managed to piss him off even more.

He *was* exhausted; he could feel it in his bones. "Tell me about this group, the one who had the radio."

This time, it was Daniel who filled him in. He started with an explanation that the guilty party was under guard in one of the top-floor suites. Good, he thought. There was a discussion he wanted to have with the man who'd shot Pro. Daniel went on, detailing his questioning of this Ray character. Between exhaustion and wondering what the hell he was going to say to Rachel, it probably wasn't the best time to be debriefed.

"Wait!" He grabbed Daniel's arm. "Say that again."

"Which part?"

"The dead guy, the veterinarian . . . What'd he say?"

"New Republic?" Daniel repeated the words that sent a chill through his bones. "This Ray character thinks it's related to whatever Carla and the dead vet were hiding."

"I'm sure it is."

"Wait a sec!" Michelle stuck her face in his. "You've heard it before, haven't you?"

It took every bit of control he could muster. He reached out, gripped Michelle tightly by each shoulder, and pushed her gently back half a step. Something in his face must have said what he managed to keep under wraps. She shut up and nodded to herself.

"What is it?" Daniel asked.

"A big-ass group," he almost whispered to himself. The images of the UVA campus and what he'd seen through the Shenandoah Valley drove him to one conclusion. The New Republic was sending out scouting parties, and Daniel had one of them locked up. "We aren't safe here."

"We aren't safe anywhere," Michelle agreed.

"I need to talk to this Ray character."

Michelle held both hands out slowly. "Jason, they aren't going anywhere. You need to get a few hours' sleep and then talk to Rachel." Michelle shook her head at him. "End it or don't, Jason. But, for that woman's sake, have the balls to put a label on it. She deserves to know one way or another." Michelle squeezed his shoulder gently and walked back into the hotel lobby, leaving him and Daniel staring after her.

Daniel let out a long breath. "So, there's that . . ."

"Good to see Michelle hasn't changed."

"Nope." Daniel gave his head a single shake. "She's still always right."

"I suppose she is," he admitted. "I'm going to catch a few winks until Pro and Rachel are awake. Can you pull the team together by this afternoon? We need to figure out what the hell we are going to do."

"Can I make a suggestion?"

"Don't start, Daniel. I have no idea what I'm going to say to her."

"I wouldn't presume." Daniel was smiling. "I was going to say, a shower and shave wouldn't hurt. You look like shit."

Chapter 11

Jason opened the hotel room door as quietly as he could and eased it shut once he was in the room. They were both still asleep. Pro in bed on his back with his right arm immobilized against his torso. Rachel had pushed two cushioned chairs together and was curled up within the small bowl they created. There was a pile of books on the table between them that made him smile. Putting Pro in what passed for their hospital was probably anyone's best bet to get the kid to study. He could picture Rachel torturing him with schoolwork during the day.

He crept around the edge of the bed to where he could look down at her. Kneeling at her side, he saw the peace that only sleep could bring. Rachel pulled at a part of him that he had begun to doubt he still had. He was past that now; he wanted nothing more than to get her out of here and take her someplace safe. As terrified as he was of letting himself care for someone that deeply ever again, or of letting Rachel do the same with regard to him, he knew they'd both passed that unspoken point. And he'd been too scared to admit it. She had every reason to be pissed.

He turned to look back at Pro. In his heart, he and Elsa were as much family as Rachel was. They weren't just his wards; they needed a parent's love as much as he needed them.

He turned his head back down to Rachel as he heard her stir under her blanket and ended up looking into the muzzle of the 1911 model .45 he'd given her.

"You came back," she whispered after her brown eyes swallowed him up. She let the gun drop to the side and offered the slightest of smiles.

"I came back." He nodded once, trying to make it sound like an apology.

Rachel strained to lift her head and look over towards Pro.

"He's asleep," he whispered, catching her face between his hands and kissing her much more deeply than he had intended. He laid her head back down as she just looked at him with what could have been suspicion.

"Rachel . . . I don't know how to—"

She stopped him with a finger across his lips. "I love you, Jason, and I'm pretty sure you feel the same way. But I'm not your charity case. I can't be. You have to understand that."

"I do." He nodded. "I love you too. I just don't want you to feel like you're stuck with me." He gave her his best smile. "The world has sort of curtailed your options, don't you think?"

"You're my world, Jason."

"And you're mine. That's what scares me."

She laid a hand alongside his face. "I think it's supposed to."

They kissed again; Rachel came out of the chair and fell halfway into his arms, and they just held each other tightly. He felt like his heart was going to explode.

Quiet laughter from the bed behind them broke the embrace.

"It's about time." Pro's ensuing laughter was all they needed until they both joined in. Jason realized he had a tear rolling his cheek. Rachel wiped away her own and looked over at their patient.

"How long have you been awake?" Rachel demanded.

Pro just smiled in embarrassment. "I knew you wouldn't shoot him."

*

Ray wasn't having to pretend house arrest was pure misery. When he'd agreed to do it, he'd assumed it would be Carla who would drive him nuts. Instead, it was Tina who wouldn't shut up about how these "animals" had done something to Tom. Carla, with the exception of the round of questioning she'd launched at him when he'd been pushed through the door by Reed two days ago, had been quiet. Too quiet. The woman was a natural busybody, always directing, always complaining, and her sullen silence was new enough that he was certain she was worried about something other than where Tom was.

Their large suite had two separate bedrooms and a large common area with a small kitchenette. The minders on guard out in the hall kept them fed and watered. They'd all been pulled out for questioning one at a time. His time was spent explaining to Daniel that Carla hadn't said anything useful. Charles, the old man, had explained that he'd been told his incarceration was just a precaution. Tina had been out of her mind that "they" kept asking about Tom, like he was a criminal or something and not a doctor. Carla hadn't said a thing about her questioning, but afterwards, Ray had caught her looking at him like she was trying to come to a decision.

He couldn't figure out what it could be. In terms of an escape, the were on the twelfth floor; windows weren't any more an option than the door and the guns on the other side of it. The dynamic in the room had changed an hour ago. The woman who in his opinion really ran Tysons, had delivered their breakfast in person. Michelle had stood there smiling at them before leaving.

"You folks had better be telling the truth . . . Jason's back. He's anxious to meet you all today."

"We don't even know why we're here!" Carla shouted, venting the frustration that he'd seen building in the woman over the last couple of days.

Michelle looked at all of them in turn and settled on Carla. "I'm betting you do."

"Where's Tom?" Tina cried. "Why won't you let us see him?"

"You tell us where he is," Michelle answered. "We'd be happy to let you see him."

He'd been staring at the door that Michelle let slam behind her. Carla was looking at him again, weighing something.

"This Jason sounds like a scary character." Charles didn't say much, ever. Ray thought the old man was just tired in a way well beyond his advanced years. Like someone who knew he'd lived his life and had been sentenced to a retirement that just wasn't fair—wasn't worth it.

"You don't believe those stories they tell, do you?" Carla spit back at him. "They make him out like some sort of demon who cleared out the goons who used to run this place, all by himself."

"Not a demon." Charles was shaking his head. "Just a tough son of a bitch."

Ray didn't doubt the stories. The people he'd met at Tysons seemed like good people, no different than most of the people he'd been held with in Kentucky. Good, solid folks who had fallen or been pushed into some horrific shit in the name of survival. Most of them, here or in Lexington, weren't the type to push back; that was a rare thing. There'd been a few hard individuals in Lexington who'd pushed back and tried to free the others. They'd all died; all except one. He'd live with the guilt from that for the rest of his life. He'd told himself more times than he could remember that he was done with the shit that came with other people—yet here he was again.

"These people have no idea what tough is," Carla responded and stormed out of the room. She slammed the door of the bedroom the girls had been using, and he was left in the living room with a tired old man and a juvenile girl who had somehow managed to hang on to the belief that the world, fallen as it was, still owed her something.

"What could have happened to him?" Tina mumbled mostly to herself and fell back into the couch. Her grandfather came up behind her and laid a comforting hand on her shoulder.

"I don't know, but she knows something she ain't saying."

Ray looked up at Charles, who was staring at Carla's shut door.

An hour later, as the four of them sat in the living room, trapped by their own thoughts and worries, the door to the suite opened without a knock. Reed and Gabe stood there, making a show of being armed. They flanked a man he hadn't seen before. The guy was of average height, very solid, with short-cropped hair and a week's worth of stubble on his face. So, this was Jason. He didn't need an introduction. He looked like a guy who could handle himself. The man's eyes were empty enough that he could almost imagine the things Jason had done to free these people.

Jason panned across the group slowly, twice, until the cold gaze fell on him. "You first."

Ray just let out a long breath and nodded. He'd shot the kid this guy thought of as his son. Playacting or not, this wasn't going to be fun.

He went flanked by Reed and Gabe, both of whom he'd spent some time with. They seemed like good guys, but he had no doubt either of them would put a bullet in his head if Jason told them to. Yet one look at Jason, and he was just as convinced the man wouldn't ask somebody else to do his dirty work.

Nobody said anything until the door to the suite shut. Then Jason just looked at him for a moment and held one finger up to his lips as he motioned towards the elevator at the end of the hall. He met the man's eyes; there was some depth there beyond the dead shark eyes that he'd seen a moment ago.

He was stunned when both Reed and Gabe stayed outside the room's door. Reed was about to protest when Jason waved him off and started walking to the elevator. He followed and waited for the elevator doors to shut before speaking.

"I take it you've talked to Pro?"

"He told me what happened. I don't blame you." Jason looked at him for a moment and then gave his head an angry shake. "It was my fault for being gone. You have any idea how much that pisses me off?"

"Yeah, I probably do."

"Ray? Is that your real name?"

"It is," he admitted. "Ray Hoover."

"Well then, Ray, you'll probably understand you'll want to be straight with me."

"I've been straight with Daniel; my story isn't going to change."

"No matter what?"

He caught himself shaking his head slowly. "I've been beat on before. Next to having the bends, it didn't even really register."

The elevator opened up on the second floor, and they stepped out into another hallway of rooms. The crazy stoner of a doctor was coming down the hall towards them.

"Where we going?"

"Pro wanted to see you."

And I want you to see him, Jason thought. Ray was different than what he'd expected. Jason watched Pro as he let Ray go in first.

The look of surprise on Pro's face was part of the answer he needed to be certain of. Pro wasn't at all fearful.

"How you feeling?" Ray asked as he moved to the foot of the bed and looked down at Pro. The teenager struggled to sit up a little higher.

"I'm OK." Pro grinned. "Not the first time I've been shot."

"Seriously?" Ray sounded shocked.

"Yeah." He moved up to the side of the bed between Ray and Pro. "He's not as smart as he looks, and this had better be the last time."

"It was my fault," Pro said.

"No, it was mine." Ray rubbed the top of his bald head as he spoke to Pro and then turned to face him. "It had been a while since I'd had to . . . I kind of freaked after I shot Tom."

"He deserved it," Pro announced. "The guy was up to something."

Jason watched Ray's reaction. He was pretty sure the man didn't think Tom deserved to die. It was the second part of the answer he was looking for. This guy wasn't a nut; he was just looking to check out, head to Georgia, and crawl into a hole. Jason understood that sentiment in a way that scared him. If it wasn't for those he'd come to love, he'd be in the same place.

"Maybe," Ray allowed after a moment. "I'm just glad you're going to be OK. Daniel told me you'll make a full recovery."

"I'll be good to go in a couple of weeks," Pro announced, turning to face him. "Doc Adams said so."

"Great." Jason flashed him a thumbs-up. He reached over, grabbed a book from the pile on the side table, and tossed it onto Pro's bed between his legs. "In the meantime, . . ."

"Come on!" Pro picked up the book and read the title. "*Nostromo?*"

"It's a good book," Ray said. "I used to have to sit around with nothing to do for days on end. Everything that guy wrote is good."

"It's like five hundred years old."

Jason was about to correct Pro's math, or maybe it had just been an assumption.

"Sure, it's old," Ray said. "People don't change, though. That's the point."

Pro looked between them for a moment, regarding both of them with nothing but suspicion. "Daniel sent you?" Pro's eyes narrowed. "Or was it Rachel?"

"No idea what you mean." He smiled, having no problem whatsoever with letting one of them take the blame for forcing Pro to make time for some semblance of an education.

Rachel came into the room a few minutes later, pausing at the door when she saw Ray. She took a deep breath and let it out slow.

Ray nodded a greeting in her direction. "I'm told you're one of the two I need to worry about. I *am* sorry this happened."

Rachel took a moment to digest the words and lifted her chin towards him and Pro. "If they can forgive you, so can I."

Jason spent longer than he probably should have just looking at her. Her hair was still wet from a shower, and she had an armful of clothes. She looked beautiful to him, and he was proud of her for giving Ray the benefit of the doubt.

Rachel offered a smile. "As for Michelle, I'd hire a food taster if I were you."

"She's fine," Pro assured Ray. "I talked to her."

Rachel flashed him a smile full of promise, and he found himself suddenly interested in getting this day over with as quickly as possible. Elsa had enough friends at the Ritz that she wouldn't mind spending the night here again.

"You two should go," Rachel said to him. "Pro isn't nearly as strong as he thinks he is."

"I'm right here . . ." Pro's protestations aside, he agreed. Business first.

Once they were back in the hallway, Ray turned and stopped walking. "Thank you for that. People kept telling me the kid didn't blame me, but . . ."

"I get it," he answered. "Besides, that was a lot easier on both of us than hooking you up to a car battery or removing fingernails. I trust Daniel's judgment; he's developed a highly attuned asshole detector. I just needed to see for myself."

Back in the elevator, Ray turned to him. "Maybe you should."

"What do you mean?"

"Tune me up," Ray said with a straight face. "That crazy bitch you guys have me locked up with doesn't know what to make of me. She needs a new friend."

"You're serious?"

Ray chuckled to himself. "Maybe we could skip the whole fingernail thing, but rough me up a little and throw me back in there. I'm sure there are plenty of people here who think you will anyway."

"Not my style," he answered, shaking his head. "Daniel made sure everyone here knows what we are doing with you. No one blames you."

Ray was silent for a long time. "That's more than I expected."

"These are good people," he answered. "Which is why I'll do anything to keep them safe. If I thought you were a threat to this place, I'd take you out. No fanfare, no torture, just—"

"Problem solved." Ray sounded to him like he was speaking from experience.

"Something like that, yeah."

They rode the rest of the way back up in silence until the elevator chimed on opening. "I meant what I said," Ray offered. "I was taking punches in Scottish pubs when you were still in high school."

"You worked there?"

"North Sea oil rigs; I was an undersea welder. My colleagues weren't exactly choirboys."

"You're sure?"

Ray let out a slow breath and pointed down the hallway. "Outside their door. Let her hear it."

"What about the others?"

Ray shook his head. "The old man is solid; he's just worn out. He thinks Carla's hiding something too. Tina?" Ray twirled a finger around his ear. "The girl's criminally naive or just broken. I'm not sure she even realizes the world has moved on. Whatever they had going on, it was just Carla and Tom. I'm sure of it."

They stopped a few doors away from the penthouse. He signaled Gabe and Reed to join them.

"Ray's just volunteered for a discussion. You guys stay out of it. When it's over, toss him back in the room . . ."

"What are you talking about?"

He just looked at Ray and cocked his head. "You're sure?"

"Stop talking ab—"

Jason's punch snapped Ray's head back into the wall. He followed up with a quick jab as his target's head rebounded. Ray, bleeding from a cut lip and nose, instinctively tried to move out of the way and then seemed to remember what was happening. Jason feinted high and drove a fist into the man's gut, doubling him over. He delivered an open-hand slap to the face that nearly spun Ray around and left Jason holding his hand in pain.

He nodded at Reed, who grabbed Ray by the collar and frog-walked him up against the penthouse suite's door. He held Ray's face between his hands and looked at the man, who smiled back at him with bloody teeth. "You hit . . . like a girl." The man drooled blood as he said it.

"Sorry," he whispered back. He stepped in and delivered an elbow to the side of Ray's face. His volunteer sagged against the door. Gabe had seen enough and pushed him away with one hand as he waved his keycard against the reader and flipped the door handle. Ray was barely on his feet, halfway to his ass, when his weight pushed the door open. He fell into the room, his legs still sticking out into the hallway. Reed gave him a confused look as he squeezed by and grabbed Ray by the armpits to pull him the rest of the way into the room.

Jason stood in the doorway for a moment, looking at the other three occupants, the bloody knuckles of his right hand gripping the door frame. The old man glared back in anger, while his granddaughter sat in numbed silence. He looked at Ray on the floor like he was a dead mouse some cat had left by the front door. Carla was looking right at him, wheels turning behind a look of surprise.

Jason followed Reed into the room and knelt over Ray. He slapped the man hard enough to bring him back around. He glanced up at the others in the room before refocusing his attention on Ray's bloodied face. "We'll try this again tomorrow, and keep at it until one of you steps up and comes clean."

"That was hard on you, wasn't it?" They were finally alone, and Rachel sat with him on one of the couches in Dagman's living room. She'd lifted the bag of ice off the top of his hand and frowned at the bruised and cut knuckles.

"It's not too bad." He tossed the bag of ice off and tried flexing his fingers. Nothing was broken, but he knew he'd gotten carried away with Ray. The frustration and blame for what had happened to Pro had come to the surface. If Gabe hadn't intervened, he wondered if he would have stopped.

"That's not what I meant."

He knew what she'd meant. What did she want him to say? That for a moment, Ray's face had become a stand-in for the fear that was gripping him? He wasn't going to go there. It was bad enough that he knew it for the truth.

"I know."

"Are you going to talk to me about it, or am I back in the land of people you don't let in?"

He tried to smile. Those brown eyes of hers saw right through him. "I'm not that bad."

Rachel reached out, grabbed his bruised right hand, and cupped both of hers around it. She gave it one shake before holding it in her lap. "I've never seen you like this. You seem . . ."

"Scared?" He caught himself nodding. "You're in, Rachel, believe me." He reached up and pulled her into a long kiss. He felt her flinch in surprise as his half-frozen hand gripped the back of her neck. She fell against him as he wrapped his arms around her, and he pulled his face back.

"I didn't think I'd ever feel this way again, and it scares the hell out of me. Not like you think, Rachel. I can't imagine losing you. What we are doing here? I can't keep you safe here; we're just a big juicy target. We need to get small, or at least disperse—"

Rachel reached up and put a finger tight against his lips. "Stop talking." She leaned back, pulled her shirt up and off in one quick motion, and dropped it to the floor. She leaned into him and kissed him again, this time longer.

"You're sure?" he managed between breaths.

"About everything," she answered with her face buried in his neck. "We have to do something about the ice-cold hand though."

Chapter 12

Northern Virginia

"I'm going to bed," Tina announced to the room. She was like that; didn't matter if the girl had to pee, was hungry, or had a headache—the young woman assumed the world had a desire to know. When they'd been on the road as a group, it had annoyed Ray to no end. A week or so without having to deal with her inane comments must have lowered his tolerance. He caught himself biting down on what he wanted to say. Her grandfather was already asleep in the other room.

"You do that," Carla fired back. Tina showed no sign that she'd even heard the comment. Once the bedroom's door shut, Carla looked up at him from the opposite couch with as much concern as he'd ever seen on her face.

"Can I get you another glass of water? More ice?" The suite's tiny freezer had one ice tray in it that he'd put to good use on his face.

"I'd kill for a real drink." His scabbed-over lips felt swollen and pulled tight with every word.

"You and me both." Carla tried to smile. It looked as unnatural as it did awkward. At the moment, she reminded him of one of the nuns from his childhood. There'd been a couple of them at St. Bart's Catholic school, who had apparently felt that smiling or speaking a kind word were akin to breaking their vows. He'd complained once about them to his mom, and she'd said they were a type—all they had was their faith, and it was so strong that anything else felt like a betrayal to them. "It's all they have," his mom had explained.

It was a strange thing to recall right now. He hadn't moved off the couch all day, and his fellow prisoners had left him alone. It was as if speaking to him would somehow throw them under suspicion. Carla, though, had cleaned up his face, and when dinner had been brought up to them, she'd told him to stay put and had brought his tray to him. It was so out of character for the woman that she'd seemed embarrassed by the simple act.

What is it that you believe in, lady? "I'm good, thanks. Not the first time I've had my face danced on."

"Was it Jason who did that to you?"

He gave a short nod in answer.

"What did he ask you?"

He shook his head slowly. "I think something might have happened to Tom; they can't find him. He figured I might have heard something from you all. They know I wasn't here when he went missing. I was with Gabe and Reed."

"He thinks we did something to him?"

He shrugged in response and let out a deep breath. "He didn't do a lot of talking."

Carla just looked at him for a moment. She reached for his water glass and walked away with it into the kitchenette. When she brought it back to him, she tried that forced smile again.

"We'll get out of here . . ." Carla nodded at him as if reaching a decision. "I'm going to need your help."

"We get out of here, I'm on my way to Georgia."

"I can beat Georgia."

"No offense, but I doubt that. I know I haven't been anything but an extra gun for you, since Sammy found me. Don't bullshit me, Carla. What is it you want?"

She nodded at him again. "When we get out of here."

"What makes you think we will?"

"Because I know we didn't do anything to Tom."

He tried to smile as he pointed at his face. "I get the feeling they already know that. It didn't stop the asshole from going to town on my face."

Carla leaned down and patted his knee like he was the new neighbor's dog. "Mark my words, when we're out of here, you and I are going to have a talk."

Wonderful. One more thing he didn't want to wait for before he could be on his way to Georgia. "If I get out of here," he repeated, "I'm gone the first chance I get. You'll have to do better than that." He'd been right; with Tom gone, the woman was desperate for a partner in whatever they'd had going. He closed his eyes, figuring he'd let Carla stew for a while. He wasn't going to show the least interest in whatever she was hinting at. Carla was so squirrely it would be the worst thing he could do.

"Right now, I just want to sleep."

"Oh, OK. Sure," Carla agreed, sounding almost surprised that he didn't want to talk to her. "If you need anything, just yell. I'll be up for a bit."

He didn't answer, just flashed her an upraised thumb.

The next thing he knew, he was being shaken awake by Carla.

"I need to talk to you . . ."

He rubbed his eyes against the harsh light of the lamp she'd turned on. "Can it wait till morning?"

"It really can't." Carla sounded almost desperate. She'd worked herself up with worry. "If they come for me tomorrow, I might not come back."

He didn't have to pretend he was clearing cobwebs out of his head as he rubbed his face, looking at her between his splayed fingers.

"You said you didn't know anything about Tom." He threw her own words back at her.

"I don't know what happened to him. I just know what he was doing." Carla stood up and paced in a circle at the end of his couch.

"What are you talking about?"

She stopped her pacing and turned to face him with her fists planted on her hips. "Tom and I are from a community in Charlottesville." She nodded to herself excitedly and held her arms apart. "A really big community."

Ray opened his hands on his lap. "So?"

Carla smiled again; it was the first time since he'd met her months ago that the light behind her eyes truly came on. And then she started talking.

By the time she was done, Ray was certain of three things. One, Carla was shit-house-rat crazy. This was not new information to him, but the woman had talked about Charlottesville like it was some sort of heaven on earth, led by the female version of George Washington. Carla could have been one of the nuns his mother had warned him of; *messianic* was the word that sprang to mind.

Two, this community of Tysons was on the New Republic's to-do list, and there was shit-all these people here could do to stop them. Three, any sliver of a chance he'd maintained, regarding sticking it out with these folks, evaporated. He was halfway to Georgia in his head as he told Carla he'd keep her secret.

*

East of Richmond, Virginia

"I saw the same drone footage as you did." Captain Naylor waved at the now blank screen at the head of the classroom, in the otherwise empty and quiet junior high school that they had made their temporary base. "I still don't know what to think. For all we know, what we saw . . . was a reprisal for something we didn't. Are we supposed to play judge and jury here?"

"We know what we saw," Gunny Bruce spoke up. "There is no way that group in Richmond was big enough to have started any shit with the group that rolled on them. I think it's clear who the aggressors were."

Drew nodded at both men's comments. They were both right. The gunny and Pavel's recon group had made it back to them in time to watch the drone catch the last of the vehicles in the line leaving Richmond turn off of I-64 at Charlottesville. The lowboy tractor trailer carrying the Abrams was far too heavy for the interchange overpass, and they'd watched it unload directly from the interstate and then follow the tank as it rolled the final three miles across terrain to the UVA campus. The tank had rolled into a field full of military vehicles; most of them were older Humvees and some JLTVs, but there had been a line of Bradleys sporting different configurations next to another Abrams.

By then, it was evident that a significant population was making the former college campus home. It was by far the single largest concentration of humanity they'd seen or heard of since arriving back in the continental US. To Skirjanek, it was a blessing, what he'd been hoping for; somebody else had preserved something, kept people together. Then the drone had observed and transmitted the images of the school buses unloading the former Richmond residents into the tent city set up within the football stadium at the edge of campus. They'd all seen the armed guards surrounding the stadium.

He turned to Pavel. "What do you think?"

"The gunnery sergeant is correct. The people within the city concentrated on defensive fortifications. They were not effective against those who attacked. They did not have capability for offensive operations."

"Sir, the stadium?" Gunny Bruce asked. "What's that all about? Nobody was given a choice between staying and getting on the fu—freaking bus, sir. They were POWs."

He could think of several ways to explain the stadium. Not all of them were as laden with negatives as the gunny was intimating; many were, but not all.

"Triage?" he suggested and gave a shrug of his shoulders. "Call it induction processing, separating out the troublemakers, or medical quarantine. From what we can tell from the drone, everyone walking freely around the campus appears armed. This looks like a community, not a prison."

"Thousands of them," Naylor interjected the most important point. "They can't be that bad."

He pointed at Naylor. "In answer to your earlier question, Jim, for the moment, we are judge and jury. Not for them, for us. It's not a question of who's right or wrong, but who can we attach ourselves to. We need to find a body of people who have the critical mass in terms of numbers from which to build something that can truly be secure." He stepped towards the map table they had set up and waved an open hand over Charlottesville.

"Secure enough, with enough numbers to expand and grow without having to resort to the kind of measures we saw today. This group is doing a lot right, and on the surface, based on our limited intel, a lot that turns my stomach." He paused, looking at the map of Charlottesville, noting the natural lines of defense the university grounds offered and the obvious weak points an attacker could exploit. He stopped himself and looked up at the other faces in the room. "If we are going to survive long-term, we may have to make some strange bedfellows."

"Sir?" Gunny Bruce was shaking his head. "Are you suggesting we help these people?"

"No," he answered immediately. "I'm saying we need more information. If it comes down to joining our strength to theirs, we need to know what behaviors we can reinforce and which to put an end to. I have no desire to become some sort of warlord, and even less to be used in the service of another. But . . ." He pointedly looked at Gunny Bruce for a moment. "The world has moved on. If we hold to all of the rules we used to play by, we could end up hurting more people than we help."

He paused and looked at every face in the room, holding up three fingers. "Three percent . . . that is the best official number we have as to the numbers that survived the virus. Throw in the riots that accompanied the die-off, the food insecurity, and the violence endemic to any failed state, and that three percent goes south rapidly from there. In the short term, stability may be just as important as our principles."

"But not more important, right, sir?"

It was clear Gunny Bruce was going to be his conscience. He couldn't have picked a better candidate himself, and he welcomed the challenging look in the Marine's eyes. Jim Naylor was a great organizer but would be harder to convince to fight at all. It went in keeping with driving a sub. In Captain Naylor's previous career, staying hidden and undetected was 95 percent of the fight. Pavel, he'd come to know, would be willing to take the fight to anyone. Period. He thought he could say the same for most of the other Marines and security contractors. The gunnery sergeant, and probably Corporal Hanson, the one they called Farmer, would need the same justification he sought himself.

"Gunny, we don't have the authority to enforce the laws of a nation that no longer exists. The same holds for the norms of a civilization that is gone. For myself, I believe our principles may be the only type of law and order we have any hope of enforcing. They are the only guidelines that I think this world can afford right now. I'll ask that you all keep that in mind, keep each other and me honest. Fair enough?"

Dr. Mandel, who had just listened so far, spoke up. "One man's principles are another's declaration of war. Given what has occurred to us as a species, survival of the greatest number of people must at least be given a consideration as an operating principle. Yes?"

He nodded in agreement. *To a point* . . . "That's why we need to learn who these people are, what they're about. I'd like to send a small group." He smiled. "I guess the right term would be diplomatic delegation."

"We're big enough to have a diplomatic delegation?" Hoyt Sweet asked in surprise.

"They absolutely don't need to know how few we are," he answered, pointing at Hoyt. "That's an important thing for you to remember. I'd like you to accompany Captain Naylor, who will lead the delegation. You'll both take your rank with you. Tell them where we hunkered down during the die-off." He nodded towards Gunny Bruce. "Pick three Marines, and I'll find a couple of the civilians who wouldn't mind a field trip."

"What do we tell them?" Naylor asked. "I mean, who do I say we are?"

"The truth," Dr. Mandel answered, "just not all of it. I suggest . . ." The discussion and planning went on for almost an hour before points already decided upon began to resurface. Drew ended the meeting at that point, and shared a sympathetic look with Captain Naylor as everyone started filing out of the classroom.

"Sorry to volunteer you for this, Jim."

"To be honest, I'm a little excited at the prospect."

He grinned a little. "That's why I want to send you. You'll give them a fair shake."

"You sound as if you wouldn't have . . .?"

He was about to answer when Gunny Bruce stuck his head back into the classroom.

"Excuse me, sirs. Could Pavel and myself have a moment of your time?"

"Of course, Gunny." He watched the Marine recon and Russian Spetsnaz operator shuffle in. He knew that look, and it seemed to hold true across cultures as Pavel's face shared the same formal mien.

"Why do I feel like a green lieutenant about to be counseled by his sergeants?"

Bruce smiled in response. "It's not that bad, sir. We just need some clarification."

"You two fighting over the Marines?" Captain Naylor joked.

"No, sir," Gunny Bruce answered. "But we could have. That's what we both wanted to talk to you about."

"Lack of a strict chain of command?" Drew guessed with a smile of his own. "Lack of military order and discipline?"

"Yes," Pavel answered. "Sergeant Bruce and I were able to come to an understanding. I'll be senior to him, as long as I don't . . ."

"Screw with my Marines, sir." Gunny Bruce nodded. "Pavel outranks me by a mile, and would be an officer in our Army. It works for us, but the men, sir . . . they need some structure, as I assume those we are training up will."

"You are absolutely correct." He nodded. "On all counts. I promise you, we'll get there with whatever force structure we end up with. We are one step closer to that, now that you two have come to an acceptable understanding." He gave a nod in Naylor's direction. "The captain and I will reinforce it after he pays me the dollar he owes me. I wasn't going to make a call regarding you two that you didn't both support. We don't have the numbers to be able to afford disgruntled leaders."

"You set this up, sir?"

"Did it work out for the best?"

"It did . . ." Pavel said slowly."

"In that case, *Captain* Pavel Eduardovich, and *Lieutenant* John Bruce, I have no idea what you are referring to."

"Congratulations!" Captain Naylor stepped forward and shook the hands of the two shocked men. "More work, longer hours, same great food."

"Pay's not what it used to be," Skirjanek added.

"Capitan?" Pavel said quietly before shaking his head. "I mean captain."

"Your surname, Pavel?"

"Volkov, Colonel."

"Well, you're officially Captain Volkov from this point." He turned to the Marine. "And you're Lieutenant Bruce. I hope we grow into needing two captains. If we don't, we'll have a whole different set of problems."

"Sir?" Lieutenant Bruce didn't miss much.

"Let's just say I have every hope that whoever is running things in

Charlottesville is someone we can work with." He left unsaid what could happen if they weren't. It was better that way, because at the moment, he didn't have a good answer.

Northern Virginia

They didn't come for Carla the next day. It was his turn again, just like he'd known it would be. The look of panic on her face as Reed and Gabe manhandled him out the door was one of abject panic. Ray had almost wanted to laugh. Her concern wasn't for his face or general health; it was the fact he now held her secret.

Jason listened to Ray's story, or rather Carla's, with a growing sense of dread. Daniel sat next to him, holding his head in his hands.

"This is the group you saw in Charlottesville?" Daniel asked him.

"Oh yeah, it's them. The New Republic."

"You knew about them?" Ray asked. "And you're still here?"

"Not like we knew they had ambitions this far north. They seem to have collected most of the survivors out of the Shenandoah I-81 corridor. They looked to have made it as far as Manassas and Leesburg. It seems they were gearing up for the DC metro area."

"If it makes you feel any better, the crazy bitch made it sound like they've got the whole country in their sights."

"It doesn't. They sent their advance team here. Here is all we can afford to worry about."

"What do we do with her?" Daniel asked.

"We see if she'll talk," Jason answered. "If she doesn't, I don't give a shit what we do to her."

"She won't talk," Ray announced.

"You sound certain about that," Daniel said.

"You didn't hear her. I don't think anything would make her happier than going out a martyr."

That works for me. "For now, I think we send you on your way to Georgia. We tell her you didn't make it through today's Q-and-A session and let the girl and her grandfather go."

"You're going to keep your word?" Ray almost sounded surprised.

"Of course," Daniel answered.

"I'm still going to try and talk you into staying." Jason surprised himself by how much he meant it.

Ray shook his head. "I've been to this dance before. I lost a lot of people I'd come to care about. I don't want to go through that again. If you're smart, you'll get out and let them have this place and your stockpile—everything you can't carry with you."

Jason found himself in total agreement. The only difference was the people he cared about were still with him. "It's not the place or the supplies we have, it's the people they want. They're playing the long game."

"All the more reason . . ."

*

Chapter 13

Charlottesville, VA

"*Boise* Actual, Raven Team . . ."

"Go, Raven." Jim Naylor thought it strange that his call sign was still tied to the now sunken USS *Boise*. It would be a very long time before navies were ever a thing again.

"Raven Team in place with eyes on. Alert level is low. One Bradley M2 with no, repeat, no AT missiles loaded. One 25 mike-mike gun. Bradley does not appear to be manned. Several civilian vehicles, total armed personnel on ground, fourteen—repeat, one four."

"Copy all, Raven, we are rolling. ETA five minutes."

Farmer as Raven lead set his radio down and stared through the break in the foliage, just east of the enemy roadblock he'd just described. "Enemy" was perhaps pushing it, regardless of how he felt. Lucas "Farmer" Hanson had been a Marine sergeant for less than a day, and Gunny Bruce—correction, Lieutenant Bruce had warned him that he'd be an officer himself, just as soon as Colonel Skirjanek thought they had enough troops to warrant it.

It was a little weird that even with the end of the world, his chosen career track hadn't changed one iota. He figured he was one of a very few people left who could say that. He'd signed up with the Marines as enlisted after graduating college, wanting the experience and the challenge. Six months in, he knew he'd found his calling and started angling towards Officer Candidate School. His acceptance letter for OCS had been in his pocket on the day they'd entered The Hole.

"What do you suppose they're barbecuing, Sergeant?" Salguero asked, his voice sounding muffled as his face was stuck inside the "Clue," the Command Launch Unit—CLU of a Javelin missile. Just one of the party favors they'd pulled out of The Hole.

"You have that Bradley locked?"

"Affirmative, Sergeant." Salguero was a smart-ass; he hadn't missed an opportunity to throw in "Sergeant" since they'd departed the Gypsies' camp. "No IR signature to target, they look to have just parked it. But I have it framed and locked, Sergeant."

Lucas thumbed his radio. "God, you there?"

Nathans came back almost immediately. "Hamburgers. They're grilling hamburgers with all the fixings." Nathans was glued to his sniper rifle, a hundred yards closer to the Charlottesville roadblock stretching across I-64. The roadblock of abandoned cars, set bumper to bumper in a line, lay just a quarter mile east of the Richmond Road interchange. The Bradley and a few working vehicles looked to be the movable gate. Right now, the guards appeared to be enjoying a midday barbecue, half of them sprawled in lawn chairs. The whole gathering was set half a mile east of where Highway 250 interchanged with the freeway.

"Great," he called back. "This goes smooth, maybe we can get one."

"With bacon," Salguero commented from beside him, "with cheese, fresh tomato, maybe some jalapeno slices, Sergeant."

"There they are." Newly minted Sergeant Kent Mason had retired from the Marine Corps three years earlier and had been serving as the director of the contractor security staff at McMurdo when the world had died. Here he was now, back at his old rank, escorting a former sub driver towards an armed encampment.

"That doesn't look too bad . . ." Captain Naylor's executive officer, Hoyt Sweet, said from the back seat of the Humvee. "One APC and bunch of civilians."

Mason shook his head. "That twenty-five on the Bradley could saw this vehicle in half in about three seconds, if they know what they are doing."

"What if they don't know what they are doing?" Hoyt asked.

"Then it might take twice as long; it's a serious gun."

"Oh . . ."

"Surely they aren't going to fire on vehicles rolling up with a white flag flying." Captain Naylor, in the front passenger seat, sounded as if he was trying to convince himself.

Kent could see the people at the roadblock scrambling as they were noticed, and he immediately let up off the gas and started braking. The large SUV following him had four of his "trainees" in it, two of them former *Boise* crewmen, two of them honest-to-God climatologists who had decided they needed a new profession in the fallen world. He reached down, grabbed the half length of broomstick, and stuck the attached white pillowcase out of his window as he rolled to a stop, a hundred yards away from the line of vehicles. There were enough rifles pointed at them over the hoods and trunks of abandoned cars that he figured the 25mm chain gun on the Bradley was a moot point.

The defenders didn't feel the same way. He heard the big 600-horsepower diesel cough to life on the Bradley, and a moment later, the turret of the 25mm main gun adjusted its aim by a few inches in their direction.

"OK, Captain. We are officially in their sights. You're on. Radio's on, ear shrouds in."

Naylor was carrying a smaller white flag that he waved out his own window before popping the door and stepping out in the middle of the interstate. "You two with me."

"Follow car, stay with your vehicle." Kent spoke into his open mic to everyone, including Raven Team, hidden in the surrounding woods after hiking in hours earlier.

"Bradley is hot, driver and gunner buttoned up." Hanson's voice intoned in their ears. "They all seem to be looking towards that group to the side of the Bradley for direction."

"I see them," Naylor replied.

Kent joined Hoyt and Naylor on the road in front of their vehicle. "Sirs—there's a culvert between the roadways. If this goes bad, it's as good as we are going to get for cover."

A thin man wearing a green baseball cap separated himself from the group they'd been watching and waved them forward. "Leave your guns on the ground!"

"Let's do it." Naylor unsnapped his holster from his belt and tossed it to the ground.

"Sir?" Hoyt didn't sound as if he liked the idea.

Kent laid his own M4 on the ground. "Do it, Mr. Sweet. We're covered six ways to Sunday."

Kent was keenly aware of what they looked like as they approached the barricade. Colonel Skirjanek had put them all in standard BDUs with flak jackets—the three of them looked like soldiers walking up to a citizen militia sporting various degrees of readiness. He saw a lot of M4s among the hunting rifles and shotguns covering them. The small man who was apparently running the roadblock couldn't have looked less like a soldier; he was wearing cargo shorts and flip-flops and had a tactical radio up to his ear, no doubt communicating with somebody back at the campus.

"Who are you? Where do you come from?" The man sounded bored, almost flippant, as if he were put off to have had his barbecue cut short.

"I'm Captain Jim Naylor, formerly of the USS *Boise*. I represent a group of former US Navy personnel that waited out the virus at McMurdo station in the Antarctic."

"The US Navy?" The little man's eyebrows flashed upward. "You're a little late in terms of defending us from threats foreign and domestic, aren't you?"

"We lost a lot of people as well." Kent thought Naylor did a good job in not looking or sounding like he wanted to throttle the dickhead.

"How?" the man asked. "You said you outlasted the virus?"

"Starvation mostly." Naylor delivered it in a matter-of-fact tone. "While our families were home dying like yours were. Who do I have the honor of addressing?"

"I'm a citizen of the New Republic." The man smiled. "My name is unimportant."

"I agree." Naylor got his own dig in. "Perhaps there is somebody more important we should be speaking to. I represent a sizable force, and your community is the largest group we've come across. We just want to talk."

"I'll bet we are," the man answered with a smile. "You thinking we're going to bow down to your GI Joe bullshit? You looking to recreate the United States? I don't know how long you've been back . . ." The rat-faced goateed beatnik waved his arms around him. "Take a good look around, Captain Jim. Your world is dead and gone."

Kent watched as Naylor held out both hands. "No argument there, friend. We aren't looking to enforce any authority we no longer have. We just—"

The New Republic man's radio blared to life with a mash-up of voices that talked over each other. The leader grinned and waved his radio at them. "You'll excuse me."

Jim Naylor didn't like how this was going. He hadn't expected a joyous "cavalry is here" mentality when they had rolled up, but the open hostility of the little dweeb was throwing him. In the world that they'd experienced since stepping ashore, the roadblock captain wasn't anything like the type of person he'd imagine in charge of anything. People like the jack ass in flip flops got authority through organization, laws, and bureaucracies—which, if the guy hadn't been a total prick, would have been a good sign. He watched the leader with the radio disappear behind the Bradley and took a moment to acknowledge the others standing around him.

"I don't think he likes me." Naylor did his best to smile. "How are the rest of you folks doing?"

A solid-looking guy with an M4 nodded at him. "He doesn't like anybody."

"I don't care who they say they are. We need to know more." General Marks's voice over the radio was full of excitement. "Invite them in. Talk to them."

Lisa wanted to agree, at least in part. A new player, a military one at that . . . in her mind, it came down to a choice between adding capability and the potential risk to her own leadership that came with it. In the end, the last thing she wanted was to infect this place with even more emotional detritus from the past. Having Steven handling her troops had been a necessity, but that benefit was starting to wear thin. She would have killed to have him in the room with her. She could have kept him off the radio, but he was out on campus with "his" boys, as he called them, running some training.

Thankfully, the leader at the eastern roadblock was one of her people. "Russel, bring them in. Send the rest of them packing."

"For God's sake, don't fire on them!" Marks shouted into the radio.

"Russel, take the three you have prisoner," she said calmly. "I think we need to send a message to the rest of them."

"Don't do this, Lisa," Steven pleaded on the radio.

She came to another decision. "I'll need you to talk to them, General. Why don't you join me back here?"

"Good news!" The rat face came smiling from back around the armored personnel carrier. He signaled to one of his people. "Drive these three to the university." He turned back to them. "You're going to be our guests for a short while."

"Guests?" Naylor asked. "That wasn't what we had in mind."

"I'm sure it wasn't." The young man bounced once on his flip-flops, pleased with his answer. "Like I mentioned earlier, you've got no authority here." He motioned with his fingers, and three men with M4s stepped forward, surrounded them, and herded them towards a pickup truck. They did as they were bid and crawled up into the bed of the truck over the tailgate. One of the men guarding them followed and sat against the tailgate, covering them as the other two hopped into the cab.

"You don't want to do this." Naylor was on his feet in the back of the truck, looking down at the roadblock's captain.

"You're right about that; I'd rather shoot you on sight—but the boss lady wants to question you."

The guard in the truck with him sat against the tailgate and motioned for him to sit with the barrel of his rifle. They pulled out onto the freeway behind the roadblock and sped off with him and Hoyt seated on the wheel hubs, staring at each other. Kent was sitting with his back against the cab. They'd just gone around a gradual curve in the interstate, losing sight of the back of the barricade, when the afternoon was split open by the ripping concussion of the 25mm chain gun opening up. It fired for what seemed like an eternity as their pickup slowed to a stop. The driver was in the process of stepping out to look back behind them. A stream of oily black smoke was clearly visible, rising over the horizon of trees.

"They just took out the Humvee and the follow car—no survivors." Lucas's voice in his ear sounded pissed off.

"You know what to do," Naylor said, as everyone was looking back behind them, all except the young man who was covering them.

"Who are you talking to?"

Lucas was seething as he looked out at the shredded remains of the empty Humvee and the burning wreckage of the Tahoe that had held four of their number. Including Katia, the cute Russian meteorologist he'd shared a cup of coffee with this morning. He was only dimly aware of Naylor's voice in his ear as he slapped Salguero on the shoulder. "Take it out!"

He looked further up the freeway. "Trey—weapons fr—"

Nathans's sniper rifle boomed before he'd finished speaking.

Mr. Rat Face, standing next to the Bradley, fairly exploded from hydrostatic pressure as Nathans's .50 caliber slug took him in the middle of the chest. Salguero launched the Javelin with the characteristic two-staged "boom—swoosh" sound. He followed the missile's short diagonal path across and down the freeway until it slammed into the Bradley. The shaped charge warhead was designed to punch holes of super-heated plasma through the armor of a main battle tank. The Bradley was a fine armored vehicle, but it didn't stand a chance of shrugging off the hit. It seemed to rock with the impact until the onboard ammunition, fuel, and oxygen within the vehicle ignited; then it exploded. It came apart with a massive secondary that took out a group of the nearby guards who had been manning the barricade.

Naylor couldn't see the anti-tank missile, but they'd all heard it hit. The lone guard in the back of the truck started to turn his head towards the driver, who had walked to the back bumper. "What the hell was that?"

Jim lunged at the guard in the bed of the truck, focusing on the barrel of the gun, slamming into him and pinning the man's rifle against his body and the tailgate. He was aware of the driver outside the truck shouting, and he looked up in time to see the man blown over. The report of a rifle rolled across the freeway a second later. Lucas, he thought for a second, but then remembered it was the smart-assed Marine Nathans who was the sniper.

He was face-to-face with his guard, aware that Kent and Hoyt behind were yelling something. The world around the pickup truck exploded in automatic rifle fire; the tailgate was hit, spalling something into his face. The man he was grappling with was hit in the head a second before he heard, more than felt, himself get hit twice. He sagged back, grabbing at the searing pain in his neck just as another rifle shot boomed out of the woods above the freeway.

Hoyt was suddenly on top of him, gripping him by the throat. His vision was fading, but he could see Hoyt screaming at him from above. Why was Hoyt mad at him? It was going to be all right.

"God dammit, NO!" Hoyt was screaming over Naylor's body as Kent jumped out of the truck and grabbed up the M4 from the dead driver. He made it around to the other side of the truck and confirmed the third guard, the one who'd sprayed the back of the truck with his M4, was dead. Most of the man's head was missing. The Marine sniper was good, but the shot had been just a little too late to save Captain Naylor.

"Hoyt! We gotta go now!" Kent scanned the freeway in the direction from which they'd just come. They'd have company soon.

"I'm not leaving the skipper!" Hoyt yelled back at him. Kent glanced over the bed of the truck, knowing what he was going to see; he'd seen the captain get hit in the back of the neck. "He could have left you all. He didn't." Hoyt was daring him to argue the point.

"Get out of there!" the detached voice in his earbud yelled at him. "You are about to have company!"

"Hoyt!"

The former Navy chief cum executive officer of the USS *Boise* lifted his head away from his captain long enough to just stare at him and shake his head. "I'm not leaving him."

Kent saw Corporal Nathans appear at the edge of the road, coming out from behind a line of thick foliage, before they'd made it halfway across the median of the interstate. The Marine was waving them on and screaming into his mic. "Move it!" Naylor's body between them was already getting heavy; the captain had been a big guy.

Nathans ran across the eastbound lanes to meet them and helped them drag Naylor off the road and into the thick woods lining the road. The Marine took one close look at their burden, grabbed Hoyt by the lapels, and stood him up against a tree.

"Chief! Your captain is dead! Don't waste what he did."

Hoyt made to shrug Nathans off, but the Marine was having none of it. He slammed Hoyt up against the tree. "The drone's got big numbers rolling in our direction. We need to move! We'll come back for the captain; I promise you."

Nathans turned to look down at him. "Make sure you get his radio; we are going now."

They moved deeper into the woods, uphill until they reached a rocky outcropping where Nathans had set up. The sniper took a moment to hand over his M4 to Hoyt, and slung his pack on and scooped up his sniper rifle.

"Farmer, Trey—we are three moving to you. Captain Naylor is KIA."

"Understood. Negative Trey, heavy traffic rolling down Richmond Road. Go to secondary."

"Copy all, meet at secondary—Nathans out."

"Colonel? Should I alert Gunny, I mean Lieutenant Bruce?"

Drew only half heard Private Park. They'd all been listening to the radio, transmitted back by the drone overhead the fiasco outside Charlottesville. It was his fault; he'd let himself get talked into this direct approach by Naylor. Now the man was dead.

"Alert them. Tell him to hold position until dark. Then move to retrieve our people at the secondary."

His failure? He'd failed to believe how far people had fallen; how hard they'd hold onto whatever power and authority they'd managed to grab since the die-off. It wasn't a mistake he'd make again. He'd overheard Naylor's conversation at the roadblock. These people felt power was the only authority? Fine; he'd give them a lesson that reinforced that.

"Captain Volkov?"

"Sir?" Pavel had been bent over the map with him, listening to the radio.

"Make preparations to move everyone and the two trucks of gear we have loaded to this location." His finger dropped on the map. "Zion

Crossroads, where Highway 15 and the freeway intersect. That will put us within about twelve miles of these people."

"Are we going hunting, Colonel?"

As much as he wanted to answer "yes" to that question, he knew they were too far outnumbered to contemplate offensive operations. What they could try to do was remove the permissive nature of the local area around Charlottesville; get them scared of their own shadow, test the leadership of whoever was holding the place together. Then they'd go hunting.

"Not yet, Pavel. But you, me, and the Marines now know what we are dealing with— people playing at soldier, and they just broke the oldest rule in the book. Maybe the most important rule we have in the apocalypse."

"I was not aware we had rules, Colonel."

"The Golden Rule, Pavel. Surely, you learned this as a child in Russia."

He watched a slow smile crack the Russian's face. "My grandmother tried teaching me that, but I ran with a rough crowd. We had our own version; do unto others before they can do to you."

Drew could only think of how excited Jim had been to make contact with another group. They'd put their best foot forward and lost it. He'd fucked up, and Jim had paid with his life. "Going forward, that may work."

*

Chapter 14

Northern Virginia

They had just entered the lobby of the hotel from the street side. Jason had been focusing on the duty guards. Daniel and Reed had them squared away and briefed up on what they were dealing with. Everybody was a little more on edge than they had been a day ago, which was all to the good as far as he was concerned. It just wasn't enough. Concentrated like they were here, in a semi-urban environment surrounded by high- rises, nothing was going to be enough. There were no exits from the area that didn't look like a street, and those could be blocked.

"Finally!" He and Rachel had been holding hands when Michelle spotted them.

Rachel seemed to take the attention in stride as he felt his face redden like he'd just been caught by his friends at a junior high dance. He felt Rachel's grip on his hand tighten. She wasn't going to let go.

"The tough guy has a heart?" Michelle looked far too happy for his taste as she finished beelining towards them across the lobby.

"He does," Rachel answered for him.

"Jason!"

He turned in time to half catch Elsa as the young girl slammed into him and wrapped him up in a bear hug around the waist.

"Hey there, kiddo!" He hugged her back and kissed the top of her head before he'd realized what he'd done. He caught himself; not for the act but for the heartfelt relief at seeing her again. Rachel and Michelle were smiling at him when he looked back up.

"Promise me you're not going to leave again?" Elsa pulled back and pointed at Rachel. "Rachel's been all grumpy bones the whole time."

"I wonder why . . ." Michelle whispered loudly enough that they all heard.

Jason felt something run into the back of his knee and looked down as Loki joined the reunion. He knelt and gave the dog a fierce rub, causing the Lab to do an immediate flop onto his back and expose his belly. He looked up at Elsa. "You've been taking care of him?"

"Yep! Reed takes him out during the day, but he stays with me. Can we go home now?"

Jason stood back up and wiped at something caught in his eyes. Rachel and Michelle had the grace not to say anything. He came to a decision.

"You bet. We've got some stuff to do here today. But if you'll get Pro and yourself ready, we'll all go back home tonight."

"He's ready," Elsa said. "He's been arguing with Dr. Adams and Nurse Sonia since yesterday."

"And anyone else who talks to him," Michelle added.

Jason looked at Michelle. "In the meantime, everyone ready?"

"Waiting on you two."

The meeting had gone down just about like he'd figured it would. Too many people wanted to stay and try to defend the refuge they'd built around the hotel and the supplies they'd foraged. In some cases, it was as simple as food security; others pointed out that they had power to run the lights and refrigerators; still others thought the numbers and the weapons they had were enough to defend against any threat.

Michelle in particular wanted to stay and fight. The amount of influence the woman had with most of the citizens of Tysons went a long way, and for good reason. She'd been a beacon of hope for many of these people when they'd lived under the sheriff, and they weren't going to gainsay her now. As she had put it, "The place was built with our sweat and blood. We aren't going to let anybody just have it."

"No, they'll take it," he'd said, getting heated. "They want the people, not your damned solar panels and canned vegetables. As far as I can tell, they'll treat the people who survive the attack fair enough as long as you toe the line and do their bidding—which amounts to rounding up more people who would just as soon be left alone. If you want that deal, stay."

"You've got your own fortress, power, water," Michelle had fired back at him. "You're asking the rest of us to pack up?"

"Pack up now," he agreed. "Do it in an organized fashion, plan it. Do it while you can. Take what you can. I'm not suggesting we disperse to the four corners; just find a couple of suburbs, where we can support each other. If you don't, those who survive will be limited to what they can carry while they're being hunted."

He watched Daniel's face as the room fairly exploded with people shouting over each other. He was sure Daniel agreed with him. He was just as certain Daniel would be staying with Michelle, whatever she decided.

He turned around and nodded at Reed and Gabe standing by the door. With a nod in return, they stepped out. It was time to play dirty. If he couldn't convince them, maybe somebody else could.

He slammed the tabletop with his palm and shouted for silence. It only took a second for the shouting to be reined in.

"I'm having Carla brought in." He looked directly at Michelle. "All I ask is that we all act like we are considering reaching out to Charlottesville. No threats, no yelling. Let's hear from their spy what her people are offering. If you still want to stay after that, I'll support it."

Daniel spoke up. "You expect us to believe anything that woman says?"

"All I'm asking is that you hear her out. Then make a decision about whether you believe her or not."

Michelle was glaring at him. The woman was a fighter, and there was no one he'd rather have on his team. But she was hanging on too hard to "a place." As stupid as it seemed, he understood it. They'd all lost everything. No one wanted to do it again.

Carla was put in a chair in front of the meeting room. Jason signaled for her handcuffs to be taken off. There were close to two dozen people in the room, all of them armed. Reed stood behind her with his handgun in hand. The woman looked like she hadn't slept in days, but it did nothing to dampen the hate that radiated off her as she took in the faces staring back at her. Her gaze settled on Ray, who leaned against the wall halfway down the table.

Jason saw some surprise flicker across the woman's face. "Let me save us all some time," he said. "Carla, you might be figuring out that Ray was onto you for some time. He volunteered for our interrogation session. He's told us everything you divulged to him."

Carla just glared at Ray for a moment and then turned to him. "So what? You going to torture an old woman now?"

Rachel reached for a bottle of water, stood up, and handed it to the woman. "Just hear us out, please."

Surprise and confusion battled on the woman's face for a moment, but after she drained half the bottle, her expression returned to steady suspicion.

"We don't want to fight with anyone," he said. "But, we will if we have to. We like the sound of some of what Ray told us. It doesn't seem like a bad idea to be part of something like you've built in Charlottesville . . . if it's true."

Carla looked back at him and took in the faces around the table as if really seeing them for the first time. "I don't know what he's told you."

"That you've got a large group, thousands strong. You've got crops in . . ."

Rachel jumped in on the conversation. "That you let everyone carry guns, especially the women?"

"That's all true," Carla said after a moment of staring at Rachel.

"Did the virus somehow miss Charlottesville?" Reed asked from where he stood behind Carla. "How is it that you have so many people?"

"They found us," Carla answered quickly. "The university pretty much sits next to I-64. Early on, people passed by, and we invited in everyone who wanted to stay. We don't have a Ritz hotel like you people, but the university and the hospital complex had been a FEMA and CDC site for a while. We had a bit of a head start."

"We've got I-95 less than half a mile from here," Michelle fired back. "We haven't seen that kind of traffic. In fact, anybody with half a brain knows to avoid the freeways."

"This was early on, I said." Carla seemed to nod in agreement. "Not now."

Michelle just stared back at the woman. "And now? How do you get your people?"

"We send out scouts." Carla sat up a little higher in her chair. "Like me, to make contact with people. Most folks are desperate for some sense of security."

"So, you can protect what you have? The place is secure?" Jason changed tactics.

"Very." Carla just smiled back at him. "But I'm not going to talk about that. I'm sure you understand why."

"Of course," he agreed. "I wouldn't either if our roles were reversed." He looked at the others around the room. Some were listening; a few weren't very good actors and were openly staring at the spy with disdain of their own. For her part, Michelle was a better actor than he would have given the woman credit for. Michelle had argued a day ago to march Carla outside and put a bullet in her head. He hadn't disagreed, and knew it might still fall to him to do just that.

"If we agree, we would just join up? How exactly does this work?"

Carla just shrugged. "I don't have the authority to answer that. I'm just a scout."

"Who does have the authority there?" he asked.

"Yeah, who's running the place, and what kind of place does he run?" Gabe stepped away from the wall next to Ray. "I've lived under a whack job; I'm not doing that again."

Carla almost smiled at Gabe. "Before you people locked me up, I heard the stories of what happened here. Trust me, we don't have anything like that going on. Our leader is a former professor at UVA, and she's a she. She doesn't have any patience for tough guys on power trips." Carla looked directly at him as she said the last.

Is that what you think I am? Jason just looked back at the spy, and then jerked a thumb at Michelle. "Don't look at me. She's in charge here."

"So, this lady professor?" Michelle leaned forward and put her elbows on the table. "She a one-man show? Her word law? Or does she rule by committee?"

"I'm not going to talk about any of that stuff either." Carla shook her head. "If you want me to take a message or escort a few of you down there, I can do that. But I'm not going to sit here and play twenty questions with you."

"You're a spy," Michelle fired back. "You're lucky we are asking anything."

"Like I said, I'm just a scout." Carla managed an awkward smile. "Call me a recruiter."

Jason turned to Gabe and motioned to the paper bag on the floor next to him. He accepted the bag, stood, and dumped the contents out into Carla's lap. It was one-half of the destroyed shortwave radio they'd found on the top of the roof.

"That's not what Tom said." He smiled as he sat back down.

"You're a scout alright, so was he. You were reporting on us."

"What are you talking about? Tom's . . ."

"Dead," he finished for the woman. "Told us all about the New Republic before he died too. How you're the advance team of what's coming for us. I've been to Charlottesville, you know. Took a nice stroll around campus. I saw the golf course planted with crops; I saw the field behind the admin building filled with military equipment. Tanks, Carla? What do you need tanks for? I saw the football stadium, too, the prisoners inside, living in tents. Listening to a recording spouting gibberish like some communist reeducation camp. I talked to survivors you missed when you rolled through Harrisonburg and Woodstock. I've heard firsthand how you collected your people."

He leaned back and crossed his arms across his chest as he swiveled his chair to face her fully. "Save us the I'm-just-a-recruiter bullshit. We know how you people operate."

Carla was staring at the piece of radio in her lap. "You killed Tom?"

"What would your people have done if they caught me sneaking around campus?"

She was quiet for a long time. When she looked up, she did a good job of putting on a brave face. "You do what you want with me. The only thing I'm going to regret is not being here when my people come through. Anybody who resists is going to join me. The rest of you will be taken and, in the end, you'll see it wasn't worth fighting in the first place. You'll be better off, safe and secure."

"Our survivors would just have to soldier for you at that point? Right? Forcing other survivors to join?" Michelle was shaking her head. "You should have stuck with scout; you're a shitty recruiter. I think we'll pass."

Carla smiled at the room. "Roanoke . . . Lynchburg . . . Blacksburg, Lexington, Harrisonburg . . ."

"Get her out of here," Michelle shouted at Reed.

"They all passed too! Every one of them. Staunton! Winchester! All of them." Carla kept yelling as Reed and Gabe cuffed her and dragged her out of the room. They were all silent a moment as they listened to her continue to scream down the hall. "You're all dead! You just don't know it yet."

Michelle was looking at him when he turned away from the door. "That was a dirty trick."

"Wasn't sure she'd say anything, but I'm glad she did. You have to realize what you are facing."

"I don't have all the answers," Michelle said, shaking her head, and then leveled a finger in his direction. "Neither do you. I think we have to fight, but you're right—there's no need to make it easier for them. I'll support dispersing, getting away from the hotel and the mall, as long as we make every effort to keep our people together and take as much as we can with us. Will you help us with that?"

He glanced at Rachel; her eyes were pleading with him. They hadn't spent much time sleeping the night before. They'd even spent some time talking about the future and different scenarios. In every one of them, his main concern had been to get Rachel, Pro, and Elsa away from Tysons. If Michelle could agree to move the people out, he'd help them.

"I will," he said. "Let the hotel and the mall be their target. We can defend it a lot more effectively if we aren't actually living here and don't plan on ever coming back."

"You lost me," Daniel said.

"You mean to turn this place into a booby trap?" Michelle was frowning.

"I was thinking more along the lines of a death trap," he admitted. "But yeah, you've got the general concept. All of it hinges on them thinking we are here. It also means our perimeter is going to have to be extended; scouts out as far as Leesburg to the west, and south watching 15 and 29."

"We can do that easy enough," Reed responded.

"And our rules of engagement need to change. We're operating under the assumption they've lost contact with their eyes and ears here. We have to assume they'll look to send more before moving on us. We need to be prepared to vet or engage anybody coming towards us."

"Definitely," Ray added. "Carla flat out told me they'd sent teams to different cities. She mentioned Richmond, Norfolk, and here. She even said they'd sent a team into Pennsylvania and another to Knoxville. It sounded like they're pretty ambitious."

"Well, Richmond isn't very far from Charlottesville," Daniel countered. "Maybe they'll head in that direction first."

"Maybe," Jason agreed. Everything they could plan for was based on a series of maybes. "We can't count on anything. We need to start now, and you are the last people in the world I need to tell how much stuff there is to move—you built the mountain."

"Where to?" Rachel asked.

He nodded and flashed a smile in Michelle's direction. "I've been thinking a lot about that . . ."

"You're going to make me beg, aren't you?" Jason had to try, but he could see the determination on Ray's face. The guy was anxious to be gone.

Ray straddled a BMW touring bike, wearing a shit-eating grin and holding a pair of night vision goggles. He waved the goggles at him and ignored the question. "Thanks for these, by the way."

"If I were you, I'd travel only by night. Stay off the interstates," Jason said. "All the former FEMA sites have been within a mile or so of an interstate, and good or bad, they all seem to have collected people."

"The one thing I don't want." Ray grinned. "Will do."

Reed handed him a radio. "I imagine you'll be out of range shortly, but we're always listening on this frequency."

Jason watched as Ray pocketed the radio. "I'll radio in if I see anything for you to worry about. I've spent a lot of time with the map book." Ray patted his chest.

"You want to give us your route in case you need us to come get you?"

"Would you?" Ray was smiling.

"If I thought you'd come back with us." Jason smiled in return. "You bet your ass I would."

"I'll take 15 south all the way to Durham, then work my way west through North Carolina. I'll go south at some point; my folks had a farm in northwest Georgia. A little community called Trion. It's on the map."

Reed laughed. "Not sure I'd tell Jason where you're headed."

"No worries." Ray waved away the concern. "It's Georgia hill country; somebody doesn't want to be found, they won't be."

Jason held out his hand. "Good luck to you, Ray. You're wasting moonlight."

Ray shook hands with both of them. "You as well."

They watched the motorcycle disappear behind a building and listened to it grow more distant.

"Wish that was you?" Reed asked him as they turned to walk back to the hotel.

Jason kicked at a loose nugget of asphalt and watched it until it rolled to a stop. He could see Rachel and Elsa standing at the doors of the beast; he thought he could see Pro already seated in the back. Michelle was right; they were going to have to fight.

"Not anymore."

*

Chapter 15

"Frog? You hear that?"

Former or possibly current Marine; he wasn't exactly sure what he was at the moment. Ogoro Uwasi stared at Elliot, wondering what had ever possessed him to divulge the fact that his given name meant "frog" in his native tongue. It wasn't like he could pull rank on the fool; all the Marines were now corporals except for Sergeant Farmer and Lieutenant Bruce. According to Bruce, the colonel had plans to make them all sergeants at some point.

Beating some sense into his fellow Marine wasn't an option. They'd tried that when they'd been stuck in The Hole, and it hadn't worked. Besides, the colonel didn't seem to be in the mood for horseplay at the moment. Skirjanek had been all business when he'd ordered the two of them three miles north of their new base. If anything went down at their makeshift roadblock, he'd need Elliot.

"I don't hear anything," Uwasi answered.

They both stared at each other for a moment from where they leaned up against the side of the Humvee that anchored the serpentine track of abandoned cars along the straightaway of Highway 15.

"Me neither." Elliot shrugged. "It's gone."

"What was . . .?" Uwasi stopped. He'd heard it. Now, they both did. It was a motorcycle, its high-pitched whine growing louder. The back end of their roadblock sat two-thirds of the way up a rise in the road, and they had a good view of Highway 15 stretching north into Virginia farm country, or at least they'd had one before the sun went down.

He ignored whatever Elliot was about to say, climbed up into the back of the Humvee, and stood up in the cupola, sporting a .30 caliber M-60 machine gun. He flipped an NVD monocle down over his left eye.

"I see him. He must have night vision too!"

Uwasi knew they weren't outlined on the ridge. They were below that, but something had caused the motorcycle to start slowing. They hadn't built a barrier with the abandoned cars; it was more a serpentine course designed to force anybody not driving a tank to slow down.

"I got him," Elliot whispered from the ground. He bent over, sighting down the length of his rifle over the hood of a car.

"Captain Volkov said we need intel," he answered as he brought the machine gun around to the target.

"We really going to take orders from a Russian?"

"I certainly am." Uwasi had been with Pavel before he'd become Captain Volkov in Newport News. They'd been on patrol and walked into an ambush set up by some scavengers. The three men and a woman had been dead, courtesy of Pavel, before he'd picked himself off the ground after catching a round with his vest. "Besides, the colonel made him captain. Gunny . . . I mean Lieutenant Bruce agreed."

"But he's Russian, Uwasi."

"So what? We have a dozen Russians with us. I'm Nigerian, Cruz is Puerto Rican, Poy Boy is Samoan or some shit, and all those folks from the sub—they're Navy."

"You got a point there," Elliot admitted.

And you, Elliot, you're an idiot. "What's he doing?"

"Just looking around . . . no! Here he comes, moving slow." Elliot was breathing hard, starting to get wound up.

"Relax, Elliot, it's one guy on a motorcycle. We got this." His Humvee was halfway hidden behind a small building holding a massive irrigation pump of some sort that would never run again. Elliot's cover was in the middle of the road; the bike would have to go around his colleague. "I got an idea," he said when the bike was within a hundred yards of their position.

He let go of the M-60 and maneuvered his M4 up through the cupola. "I'm going to shoot out his front tire when he's in front of your car. You knock his ass off the bike when he tries to get by you."

"What!"

"Just do it, Elliot."

"Wait! He's stopping again."

Ray rolled to a stop again. He'd been dodging abandoned cars for the last two hours. He'd even had to leave the road once when the traffic snarl had involved two tractor trailers, but this was different. These cars looked like . . .

He spotted the rear half of a Humvee ahead, sticking out from behind a concrete pump house. He sat frozen with fear, his eyes crept upward, taking in the outlines of the top of the vehicle. A bright flash bloomed in the middle of his vision, and he felt the impact of the bullet through his hands on the motorcycle's handles. The whole bike dropped a couple of inches at the front end. He half jumped, half flew off the bike in reflex. He'd had it in gear; when his hand let off the clutch, the motorcycle lurched forward with a sputter and died, tipping over in front of him just as he reoriented himself on the asphalt.

Scrambling forward on his hands and knees, he passed the BMW that he'd thought would see him home, and reached the back end of an abandoned Toyota SUV. He ripped off the NVDs to try to see what was around him. The sky was overcast, but there was a full moon somewhere behind the clouds, and it wasn't nearly dark enough to sneak back the way he'd come. Besides, whoever these assholes were, they'd been able to shoot out his front tire, so it was a good indicator that they probably had night vision too.

"You're surrounded! Toss the rifle!" The deep bass of the voice had a strange accent.

The world had it in for him. It had killed everyone he knew. He'd been trying to get to Georgia when he'd been shanghaied by the assholes in Kentucky. He'd fought his way out of that shit show only to fall in with Carla and her group before finding Tysons. Giving him a rare glimmer of hope, they'd set him up and sent him on his way. And now this . . . all of a sudden, the world still seemed to have too many people in it for his taste.

"Not going to happen!" he shouted back. "Looks like I'll be needing it shortly."

"You assholes picked the wrong people to fuck with. The Marines are here now!" It was a different voice shouting, sounding like it was coming from the middle of the road. Maybe he *was* surrounded . . .

"Drop the weapon, and approach with your hands on your head."

The Marines? How stupid did these people think he was? He glanced at his motorcycle; he'd ridden right into their roadblock—maybe it wasn't the right question to be asking himself. Then again, they could have shot him just as easily . . .

"Look, I'm not looking for any trouble. I'm just trying to get south to Georgia."

"Why?" the second voice shouted. "Nothing going to be there. Where you coming from?"

"I started in Cincinnati," he yelled back. "I'm from Georgia."

"You don't sound like you're from Georgia."

He shook his head in confusion; what in the hell was this guy's issue?

He peeked around the bumper of the SUV. "Well, I am! I'm just trying to get home."

"You're not from Charlottesville?"

He did a double take. "You trying to tell me you're not?" This guy didn't sound like the sharpest tool in the shed.

"We are not." The deep voice came from directly behind him and was punctuated with a rifle barrel against the back of his head. "Place your weapon on the deck, now, sir."

He looked up and saw the dark-skinned Marine, in full battle rattle. He'd worked on building and repairing pipelines in Iraq during the reconstruction effort. It was all familiar to him; the gear, the polite phrasing, the smile, and the absolute willingness to do violence were all evident.

His hands went up off his weapon. "I swear, I'm not with those folks. I'm just trying to get—"

"I don't care." The Marine above him shook his head and nudged him with his rifle. "Toss your weapon, now."

He sat against the pump house, his wrists and ankles zip-tied together. The Marine who snuck up on him had the name "Uwasi" on his BDU top. They had been polite enough with him, even when they'd told him in no uncertain terms that they'd kill him if he tried to escape.

The other Marine, Elliot, had been the one who zip-tied him, and he hadn't stopped talking since. He'd almost had trouble overhearing Uwasi's radio call telling someone that they had a prisoner.

"You really from Georgia?" Elliot looked young to him, as only a redhead could. The kid could have been twenty or thirty.

"Yeah . . . you guys really Marines?"

"Bet your ass we're Marines—the last Marines."

"Elliot!" Uwasi had yelled. "Leave the detainee alone and get back on your scope."

He watched the Marine wander off into the darkness, mumbling to himself as he went.

Detainee? He could just barely see the outline of Uwasi in the cupola of the Humvee above him. "You guys really not with the group in Charlottesville?"

"Save your breath, sir."

"Who's coming to get me?"

There wasn't a response, and there was nothing but silence for nearly a quarter of an hour until he heard another vehicle roll up, coming from the south. He was fully expecting a replay of Lexington;

142

a mishmash of survivors carrying military surplus and looking like they'd just raided Bass Pro's hunting gear department. Instead, it was three more Marines.

One of the new arrivals, close to his own age, maybe a few years younger, knelt at his feet, drew his knife, and cut the ties around his ankles. "I'm Lieutenant Bruce. If you'll come with us, we have a few questions."

"Aren't you a little old for a lieutenant?"

"It's a long story, sir. If you'll come with us, maybe some of your questions will be answered."

"Do I have a choice?"

"Not at all, sir. I'm just trying to be polite."

The man he'd been speaking to, Drew Skirjanek, the one they called the "colonel," grabbed three glasses off the shelf behind him. They'd been sitting at a table in the back-office lounge of a large landscaping company for the past two hours. He'd been watching as they drove in; they were in a building just off Highway 15, a quarter mile south of I-64. He'd told them his story, twice. The false dawn was starting to glow out the window behind the third man at the table, who had yet to say a word.

The colonel filled the three glasses and pushed one across the table to him. "That is quite a story, Mr. Hoover."

He handled the glass and looked at the amber liquid. He could smell the peaty scotch. If it was going to be his last drink, he couldn't fault the choice. He lifted the glass. "Is this supposed to make me feel better?"

"Relax," the colonel said after taking a sip of his own drink. "I believe you, and I apologize for being the one to interrupt your trip home, yet again."

"So . . . not a last drink?"

Skirjanek was rubbing his face; clearly, his thoughts had taken him elsewhere. He glanced up. "Not at all, we'll see you on your way. But first, I wonder if you'd do us a favor, possibly help out your friends in Northern Virginia as well."

"I'm not telling you where they are, or anything more about them." He'd been very careful to hide any details about Jason and his group.

"You'd have to be either a world-class asshole or insane to tell me anything like that. Your reticence speaks volumes to your character." The colonel swirled the liquid in his own glass. "I'm asking that you contact your former group on our behalf, arrange a meeting. Whenever, wherever they'd feel comfortable. I'm willing to be the one at risk."

"Colonel? I advise against this course of action." The statue of the third man at the table finally spoke. Ray did his best and failed in hiding his surprise at the thick Russian accent.

Ray held up his glass in a mock toast. "Here's to someone farther away from home than I am." He drained his glass; it looked like it might be his last drink after all. He was shaking his head as he slammed the glass down. "I'm not going to do anything until I hear your story, and probably not even then. Near as I can tell, these people at UVA have lied to the people of every city they've attacked."

The colonel nodded to himself. "I'll tell you our story, but I've got something that may help you believe me when I do."

He watched as the colonel got up and went to dig through a backpack next to a fold-up cot on the other side of the room. The man moved slowly, like he was tired from more than being up all night. He came back with a ruggedized laptop.

"I was stationed at McMurdo Station in the Antarctic." The man waved a hand around the room as he waited for the laptop to start up. "We all were, everyone except for the Marines you've met. Our Russian contingent was at their primary base there . . ."

"Vostok Station," the Russian said simply as he appeared to be reading the back label on the bottle of scotch.

"Riiiight, I've heard this story. The one where you paddled an ice floe before it melted."

The colonel's face twitched a little at his statement before he turned the laptop around so he could see the screen. It was a recording of a split-scene video conference. He recognized the colonel on one side of the screen straight away. It took his brain a moment to process the man visible in the other half of the screen.

"Is . . . is that? Son of a bitch, is that the president?"

"President Eugene Huffman." The colonel reached forward and hit play. "The last president, giving me my last orders."

He watched the conversation, noting the date/time stamp on the bottom of the screen. As far as he could tell, he'd already been at the training seminar in Cincinnati for a day when the video call had been recorded. The same day, he'd started out of town as people had begun dropping dead all around him.

". . . if they're free of infection. Make every effort to get them a ride home as well." The president was talking about the Russians in Antarctica. When he looked up at the Russian next to him, the Russian was staring back at him. He pointed at the screen and then at the man. "You?"

"And others you have not been allowed to see."

Ray listened until the president asked the colonel about his family. He reached out and pulled the lid of the laptop shut. Nobody needed to relive one of those conversations. He shook his head, coming to grips with what he'd just heard. Holy shit! These people had survived the virus in Antarctica.

The colonel was holding out a hand for him to shake. "I'm Andrew Skirjanek, formerly a colonel in the US Army. It's a pleasure to meet you, Ray."

He gripped the man's hand; he'd already decided he was going to trust these people. Nobody would have made up or could have faked what he'd just seen. "So . . . the Navy came for you?"

"A single Los Angeles attack submarine, down to a skeleton crew, came for us and brought us home. A week ago, the captain of the USS *Boise*, a man we all owe our lives to, a man who had become a friend, was killed by the people running Charlottesville. We didn't know who they were; we approached them under a white flag." Skirjanek held out his glass to the Russian, who still held the bottle of single malt. "My fault."

"Is not your fault." The Russian poured two fingers into the colonel's glass and then waved the bottle at him.

He was exhausted, he needed sleep, but the drink sounded very good at the moment.

"I am Captain Pavel Volkov." The man nodded at him. "Will you help us?"

He glanced at Skirjanek, who was appraising him over the rim of his glass. He nodded to himself and slammed the drink back. "I can't promise anything, but I'll try on one condition."

"Which is?"

"When this is over, if you can, you get my ass to Georgia—stick me in one of those tank things I saw in the garage and escort my ass home. I don't seem to be able to make it on my own."

"Not tank." Pavel was shaking his head. "Is Bradley infantry fighting vehicle."

Skirjanek gave a short laugh to himself. "It's a deal, Mr. Hoover."

"It's just Ray, Colonel." He looked back to the Russian. "And Bradley infantry . . . whatever will do nicely."

*

Chapter 16

University of Virginia

Josh Keynes was suddenly a popular guy. He figured it had everything to do with the shredded and burned-out hunk of metal that had been the Bradley anchoring Charlottesville's eastern roadblock. General Marks and Miss Cooper had finally run into a group that had real teeth. Josh had almost succeeded in convincing himself that they had, in Miss Cooper's words, "grown the fastest and farthest," so no one would be in a position to challenge them. He'd heard those words a lot early on, and they'd been an important part of the effort to grow their community as fast as they could.

He'd been part of the twenty-five-person-strong group of locals that had figured the UVA campus offered a lot of advantages after the virus, especially after the FEMA center it hosted was overrun and then abandoned by looters. That had happened before the dying was truly over and the looters had the run of everything.

They hadn't quite made it to the campus and by the time he and his group had emerged from the church basement where they'd been hiding for two weeks, they were scared and hungry. It was technically his group at that point; not out of any wonderful leadership on his part, but more of a process of elimination. People had continued to die during those two weeks, and when they emerged, it had been him they'd all looked to for guidance. He could still remember the sheer terror he had felt when it hit him that these people were depending on him to keep them alive.

Before the virus, he'd been a townie, from a long line of townies. He'd grown up and worked in a small city dominated by a university where many of the region's best and brightest got their start. He had been serving them beer for a decade, behind the bar of a place he owned. He might have been a pillar of the local chamber of commerce, a deacon in his church, a scout master to his nephew's Boy Scout troop, but every night, he'd been surrounded by young people who never even saw him, not really. The respect he saw in those faces looking to him for answers had been something new, and something he'd worked hard to maintain in the year since.

When his group had reached the campus, Lisa Cooper was already there and in charge. She'd recognized his worth right away; a leader who had the trust of his people. He'd been her right hand for a short while. Eventually, he was replaced. People were found who could keep the power on. Doctors were found who could keep people alive. General Marks had shown up and was put in charge of the militia. Lisa Cooper could have forgotten him. He wouldn't have even faulted her for it. He figured the list of things more important than his ego was a long one.

But she hadn't forgotten. She always took the time to speak to him, ask how he was doing. She'd gotten him assigned to Lewis Hall; he and a couple of others from his group had the run of one of the prettiest buildings on campus. With the arrival of General Marks, she'd made sure he was given command of one of the militia companies. It was a job he'd carried out with enthusiasm. To his own surprise, he'd been good at it, even if he had some issues with the way they did things. General Marks had come to rely on him more and more. Which, he supposed, was why he was here with the man now.

They were surveying the eastern barricade across I-64, the old one that had been abandoned after the attack. There was a new one being built fifty yards further east. It would be three cars deep, and would have what the general was calling a tank trap dug across the interstate. He could see the bucket arm of the backhoe already working just beyond the thick wall of abandoned cars.

Marks had been studying the remains of the Bradley that had anchored the former roadblock. When he turned around to face him, the look of worry on the general's face seemed to have grown. "Show me the device your guys found."

"We've left it where they fired their missile from, hoping they'd come back for it. It's right across the freeway and up into that hill," he explained, pointing at where he knew the site was, about five hundred yards away.

"Your people are set up on the site?"

He nodded. "At a distance, yes, sir. But they have eyes on it. Do you feel like a stroll?"

"Hell, yes." Marks started walking and waved over his shoulder for him to join. "Anything that gets me off that damn campus is welcome."

As they crossed the median between the freeway lanes and proceeded towards the new barricade, Josh pointed at the backhoe. "Will that really stop a tank?"

"Stop?" Marks shook his head ruefully. "Maybe, if someone is dumb enough to drive into it, but it will direct a tank or any other vehicle around the barricade, where we'll set up a choke point and some nasty surprises." He was about to ask what the odds were that these military folks had a tank or other heavy gear, when the general turned to face him.

"We've scoured every military base in the region, and tried to disable whatever we couldn't grab. I think the odds of them attacking with gear we can't handle is remote. Besides . . ." Marks pointed at the two hundred militia soldiers manning the new barricade. "I don't think there can be very many of them, and most are likely to be former sailors—that little shit of an art history professor did manage to convey that they'd arrived on the USS *Boise*; that's a submarine. How many people from Antarctica could it have brought with it?"

Josh had no idea how many people a submarine held, but he liked Marks's reasoning. He'd served two years in the Virginia National Guard right out of high school, and his military experience had been limited to responding to hurricane relief efforts. For his part, he'd never liked Russel either. He didn't know the guy had been an art professor, but that kind of made sense with all the solidarity bullshit the guy had always spouted. He'd just assumed the dead militia leader who had been in command here had been just another trust fund baby who had taught at the university before the suck had killed all of his students.

"How many?"

"Christ, I don't know. If you had to, I suppose you' could put three or four dozen folks in one of the things on top of its crew, but it would be standing room only. They certainly couldn't have anything remotely approaching what we have in numbers."

He reminded himself that Marks wasn't a real general. Josh was part of a very small number of people who knew that. The man had retired from the Army as a major and spent the previous three years running the ROTC program at Virginia Tech in a reserve billet. He was by far the most experienced military person they had, and the rank Cooper had bestowed on him had made sense. But for Josh, there was still the fact that Marks might just be as far out of his depth as the rest of them.

"Could they have more than one ship?"

"It's possible." Marks grunted. "I was privy to a lot of the command traffic during the die-off. All of us reservists had been called back up—everything I heard or saw regarding naval assets was pretty pessimistic."

They walked in silence past the new barricade for about a hundred yards until the general turned to him. "Josh, I'll be honest with you. Lisa . . . I mean Miss Cooper wants me to take you under my wing. You've done well, and with your guard experience, you at least understand what I'm trying to do in terms of training up the militia."

"I hear a 'but' in there, sir."

Marks grinned at him. "Not a 'but,' more of a concern that you'll answer to me and not her." Marks held out a hand as if to stop an expected argument. "Strictly in terms of the militia, you understand. What she's managed to do here is nothing short of miraculous. She's held us together and built a solid foundation from which to grow. But she'll be the first to admit that she doesn't know a damned thing about leading people in battle." Marks jerked a thumb over his shoulder as he walked. "Yesterday's shit show back there highlights that.

"Josh, I need you to understand that we have no idea who we just started a fight with and how very fucked up that is. I've tried to make her understand that we won't be the only ones who managed to hold people together and raid the local armories. Do you understand what I'm saying? She needs us, but we need her to understand that we have to be able to direct our military affairs. I know you've been with her longer than almost anyone—it's why I'm being straight with you."

"I understand, General. I see what you're saying, and for what it's worth, I think you're right."

Marks looked at him as if he was expecting something more by way of a response. The general wasn't going to get anything more. Marks had already said enough to him to sign his own execution if Miss Cooper felt it was warranted. It would be up to her, and she'd asked him to make a full report of this meeting. Josh could still feel where she had kissed him on the cheek when she'd asked him to become her eyes and ears with the general. He knew he was infatuated with the woman, had been since he'd first met her. If he could gain the trust of the militia, he might be able to replace the general in more ways than one.

"Right here, sir." He took a game trail uphill, off the road, until they came to a small depression where the foliage was squashed flat. The area still held a funky chemical smell that was similar to the cordite of firearms. He pointed at the launcher that had been discarded.

"Shit . . ." Marks was rubbing his face. "That's a clue, C-L-U, Command Launch Unit for a Javelin missile."

"How bad is that?"

"Well . . . it's not standard issue on a submarine, that's for damn certain. I can't imagine any use for one at our base in Antarctica. Whoever these folks are, they must have done some foraging on their way home."

"Could we have missed a base here? I mean locally?"

Marks was shaking his head. "We hit them all, I'm sure of that. South Carolina, Georgia, and Florida, though . . . there's a lot of hardware down there that they could have grabbed on their way north."

Josh took a knee and hoisted the launcher unit onto his thigh. "Well, maybe they left it here because they only had one missile."

General Marks was looking down at him and shaking his head. "If you're going to work with me, you have to get out of the habit of wishful thinking—we have enough of that shit going around already."

"Yes, sir." Josh filed away the words for playback later, but as he held the missile launcher that had destroyed the Bradley, he found himself thinking Marks, pretend general or not, might have a valid point.

"We might as well bring it with us. It'll make a hell of a thermal sight for the roadblock, and I'm pretty sure we even have some extra batteries that will work with it."

As they worked their way back downhill to the freeway, the general pointed back behind them. "Talk to your teams, Josh. No sense having our scouts within shouting distance of the barricade. Push them out further east, another couple of miles. Whoever these people are, I can't imagine they'll come at us directly."

That made sense to him. He took in the new automobile barricade when they reached the freeway. Sandbags were being placed between the cars, firing steps were being built behind the wall, and there were now three Bradley M2s anchoring the roadblock. There were similar improvements being made at two other roadblocks; one eight miles to the west on I-64 where Highway 29 crossed the freeway, and the third on 29, north of the city. He wouldn't want to attack something like that.

*

Trey Nathans had watched through his rifle's scope as the two Charlottesville assholes walked out to where Salguero had fired the Javelin. He could generally find something to hate in any orders, but his current ones really rubbed him wrong; he could have serviced both of the targets with ease. The colonel wanted these assclowns to think they'd been scared off. He'd managed to get a decent photo of the guy wearing stars on the lapels of his BDUs. It wasn't anybody he recognized, but Skirjanek was an Army full bird; maybe it would be somebody he knew.

*

Chapter 17

For Jason, the last week had been a blur. They'd started moving people and supplies out to the Lansdowne resort and the surrounding subdivisions. The whole area was about fifteen miles northwest of Tysons towards Leesburg, set back off of Route 7 in the direction of the Potomac. There were large cleared green spaces, parks and two golf courses they could farm, with close access to the river for irrigation. All of it was surrounded by a sea of housing anchored by a resort hotel and an upscale retirement home. There was more housing than he thought they'd ever need, but it was spread out and had, compared to the Tysons area, wide-open spaces from which to see an enemy coming.

It was going to be a process. The dead were the problem; their remains "remained," as Pro had pointed out with a snicker during the first day of the effort. They could only move people as fast as the cleanup crews could "reclaim" the respective housing. Wells were being dug, but the old man, Charles, was really the one who knew what he was doing, and they were running the old coot ragged. For his part, he'd spent the last two days with a large team, patrolling the routes between Tysons and their new home and beyond.

Most of the survivors they'd come across had wanted nothing to do with them and taken off at the first sign their space was being invaded. A couple of the team members had expressed some concern or guilt over the fact that they might be scaring away good people. He didn't agree. They weren't forcing anybody out; they were forcing people to focus on his patrols and NOT the growing caravans of trucks moving back and forth on Route 7. Caravans that could have been followed. They wouldn't be able to keep the new location secret forever, but he wanted to push that envelope as far as he could. Every day they had to work on the defenses and infrastructure was a gift.

A few of the people they'd come across had stuck around long enough to hear them out, and signed on. He'd enjoyed being out of the fishbowl that he considered Tysons to be, and spending time with Rachel was a bonus.

At the edge of consciousness, he was aware of her sleeping form next to him. They'd been so exhausted from working a sixteen-hour day that they both had figured they'd pass out after their showers; they'd been wrong. Probably to be expected since they'd shared the shower. He was still worried about how Elsa was going to deal with the fact that he and Rachel had taken over the master bedroom, but Rachel had laughed it off and told him to quit worrying.

None of that helped when the bedroom door opened after a couple of very quick knocks. "Jason, Jason!" He was just awake enough to realize it was Elsa. In a panic, he sat up in the bed just as Loki slammed into him. Loki jumped back to the floor and ran in a circle, barking once.

Awake but still in a fog, he did his best to focus on Elsa. "What's wrong? You OK?"

"Yeah, Daniel is on the radio. Says you have to come meet him right away." Elsa glanced over at the lump in the bed that was Rachel. "Sorry, he said it was really important."

"It's OK, you did good." He gave his head a shake. "I'll be right down. Do me a favor and take him with you." Loki knew when he was the subject of the conversation and got excited all over again. He made a couple of tight circles and let out another bark in expectation before Elsa could get him out of the room and shut the door behind him. He stared at the closed door, thinking that maybe Rachel had been right. If Elsa was wigged out at the thought of him and Rachel sharing a bed, she'd hid it very well.

"I hate that dog . . ." Rachel mumbled without moving.

"Liar." He glanced at the clock; it wasn't even eight a.m. yet. The schedule had them starting at noon today. "Sleep, I'll be on the radio if it's anything important."

The top of the mall's parking deck looked like the carnival had just arrived. Pallets and piles of supplies were strewn all over in a rough line fronting the entire edifice. Lines of trucks were being loaded to be sent out to the new site later in the day. He was almost amazed at the industry of the place. They were well over six hundred people now, and everyone was working. What didn't get moved in the next few weeks probably wouldn't be. Gas was starting to go bad. Tanks of the stuff had been located, but it all had a shelf life; same with the tons of food they were moving.

Crops they'd planted at the nearby sports fields would be tended. They had to be; it was too late in the year to plant all over at the new location. That said, on Charles's advice, they had already starting plowing and turning over the parkland along the Potomac River in preparation for next spring.

He was staring at a team manhandling a cast iron stove into the back of a panel truck. He could see a half dozen of the things already loaded. More shit he wouldn't have thought of, he realized. A lot of their people would be in single-family homes whose gas furnaces were never going to run again.

Daniel clapped a hand on his shoulder as he walked up from behind. "When Bauman had us collect those, I didn't imagine we'd live long enough to need them."

Jason shook his head. "What's happened?"

Daniel gave his head a jerk and walked off a few paces. "Ray came up on the radio this morning. He wants to meet with you."

"He came back?"

"Not exactly." Daniel shook his head. "He says he ran into another group, led by an ex-Army colonel. They asked him to arrange a meeting."

Ex-military? How was that possible? People in the service had died along with everyone else. They had been the first group to be hit really hard; they generally lived on top of each other in ships or barracks. They hadn't stood a chance against the virus.

"*Asked* him?"

"That's what he said," Daniel confirmed. "Ray sounded fine, a little pissed off that he wasn't on the way to Georgia, but he didn't seem squirrely."

"Where?" There was no way he was going to take people to a meeting with someone he didn't know.

"That's the part that sounded legit. Ray said the colonel insisted on leaving that to you. He and two others are waiting with Ray at the 66 and Route 28 interchange. Ray said he wasn't going to bring them any closer."

"Huh."

"What? That's a good thing, right?"

"Yeah. It also means whoever has Ray isn't stupid. Either a good thing, or a very bad thing."

"What do you want to do?"

He thought for just a moment. "I'll need Reed's team. Gather them up quietly, stay off the radios. Have them meet me at the Reston Town Center, at the fountain in an hour. I'll call in Rachel." Part of him didn't want to involve her, but there wasn't anyone he'd rather have watching his back through a rifle scope.

"I'm on it." Daniel made to move away.

"Daniel?"

"Yeah?"

"Have you told Michelle?"

"She was the one on the radio with Ray. Something about how this was your rice bowl."

He shared Daniel's grin. "Good." The last thing he needed was another pissing contest with Michelle.

"He looks to be alone." Rachel's voice in his ear was welcome. He found himself wishing they were on a private channel, but Reed and his twenty-person fire team were all listening in back at the Reston Town Center, a mile and a half away. He'd set up to meet Ray, alone, at the toll road's interchange with the Fairfax county parkway. Rachel, with Pro acting as her spotter, was set up on the roof of an adjacent office building, and they had a line of sight back down the parkway.

He heard Ray's motorcycle before he saw it appear at the bottom of the overpass. Jason knew he was exposed in the worst way, but he was putting his faith in Ray. The guy could have screwed them over a number of times by now, starting with the whole Carla thing. He'd told Ray to come alone, and it looked like he had.

That said, as Ray came to a stop in front of him and pulled off his helmet, he very much wanted to raise his rifle. He settled on the crosshairs that he knew Rachel had painted on the man's back.

"Didn't expect to hear from me, did you?" Ray grinned.

"Can't say that I did. I'd be a lot more welcoming under different circumstances."

"Yeah . . . I get that," Ray said slowly.

"How far did you get?"

"Ran into their roadblock on 15, about four miles north of I-64. They thought I was with Charlottesville. A couple of Marines almost punched my ticket."

"Marines?"

Ray looked at him and shook his head, smiling to himself. "You aren't going to believe this, but . . ."

Ray's story was beyond incredible, but he figured if anybody had outlasted the virus, they would have had to have been somewhere like Antarctica or sealed deep underground in a bunker. He'd listened to everything Ray knew about this Colonel Skirjanek, but it was at the point where Ray had handed over his gun and radio to him, saying it had been the colonel's suggestion, that he started to hope he wasn't being played.

Ray had followed him back to the Reston Town Center on his bike.

Jason waited for Rachel to report that the toll road and parkway remained clear of traffic and then ordered her to keep a watch as he picked up Ray's radio.

"Colonel, do you copy?"

He was about to repeat the question when the radio sparked to life.

"Copy, this is Andrew Skirjanek, formerly an Army colonel."

Jason held the radio to his chest, thinking, and looked at Ray.

"I think you can trust him," Ray said.

"Colonel, you and your two men are clear to proceed to the Reston Town Center. Are you familiar?"

"Affirmative, I'm familiar with the area. I did a tour at the Pentagon. Lived in Arlington for a time."

"Copy," Jason said back. "I'll meet you at the main fountain."

"Do you have a preferred route for us?"

"If you are not playing straight, Colonel—your route is unimportant."

"Understood. Proceeding toll road. Myself, two passengers. Twenty mikes."

"Copy, twenty mikes."

He sat Ray's radio down on the lip of the fountain and relayed the arrangements to the rest of his team on his own radio.

"We are going to play it straight. If they roll in here with just three people, fingers off triggers unless something happens. We'll have them surrounded, and they know it. Let's give them a chance to say their piece."

He turned to Ray. "What are they driving?"

"Ford truck, one of those Raptors—all black, shiny wheels. The Russian's evidently a huge fan."

He did a double take. "Russian?"

"They brought a bunch of Russian scientists with them from Antarctica. Sorry, I should have mentioned that."

"You think?"

"He's a soldier like you. The colonel guy seemed to trust him. He was a Spits nast, or something like that."

"Spetsnaz?"

"Yeah, that sounds right."

Jason rubbed at the bridge of his nose, thinking that he really could have used another hour or two of sleep this morning.

Shit . . . "People, be advised. They are driving a black Ford pickup." There were so many ways this could all go wrong.

Pavel brought the pickup to a stop on Reston Parkway in front of the Town Center. They could see into the large courtyard surrounded by high office buildings. Ray was in plain sight, standing next to his motorcycle and beside another man with an M4 harnessed to his front, two hundred meters down the far-too-narrow bricked roadway.

"Colonel? You are certain you want me to drive in there?"

There wasn't anything to like about the tactical situation. The courtyard was a killing ground surrounded by bunkers. Drew had figured on something like this. Whoever this Jason was, he was playing this smart.

"This is their show, Pavel. And we will play it very cool, gentlemen."

Lieutenant Bruce spoke up from the back seat. "Not like we have a choice, sir."

He didn't have a choice. They had to find an ally, someone they could trust, or he might as well give up on what he was trying to do and live out his days in The Hole as the world's most heavily armed shut-in.

"Go ahead, Captain Volkov."

Pavel patted the steering wheel once. "Is pity to destroy such a wonderful machine."

"Oorah, sir." Lieutenant Bruce at least pretended to be a little more enthusiastic.

"What are they waiting for?" Ray and he were looking at Skirjanek's truck, sitting in the median of Reston Parkway, pointed at the entrance to the Town Center.

"He's taking a big risk," Jason answered. "Tactically speaking, this place *is* the barrel you shoot fish in—and your friend knows it." He had every intention of hearing the guy out and playing it straight, but he hadn't asked for this meeting; the other guy could take the first step.

"Not my friend," Ray countered. "Just the guy who abducted me and plied me with some good scotch."

He was about to make a joke about how he hadn't figured Ray for a cheap date.

"Doesn't look like the driver's too excited about this." Reed's voice in his ear was comforting. He knew Reed was watching with binoculars from the fourth story of the office building directly behind him.

I wouldn't be either. "Copy. Remember, we play it straight."

"Here they come," Ray said.

Jason made a show of rotating his M4 around to his back, where it was far less accessible. "I sure hope you're right about these guys."

The truck came to a stop twenty feet away. Ray let out a breath that sounded like he'd been holding it. "Me, too . . . that's the colonel riding shotgun. The Russian is behind the wheel, and the guy in the back seat is one of the Marines."

Here goes nothing. Hyperaware of his sidearm in its holster, he took a step forward and beckoned them with a wave. He let out his own held breath when the doors opened slowly and the three men landed in the roadway with empty hands, except for the laptop held by the guy Ray had said was the colonel.

His worst fear had been one of the many versions of asshole full birds he'd come across while in the service. The type of officer who'd memorize a new power word for each morning's briefing and then use it repeatedly during what followed. Or the guy whose grandfather had gotten men killed in WWII, before fathering a son who had been fragged by his own troops in Vietnam—but not before siring the asshole who thought he was the second coming of Napoleon, fighting insurgents in the Ghaki pass in Afghanistan while holding to a belief that they could "win these people over." He'd dealt with all types, and even a few he'd have followed into hell on a word.

Skirjanek didn't look like a colonel—period. Holding the laptop, with a pair of reading glasses lassoed around his neck, if it hadn't been for the boots and BDUs, he'd have guessed he was some ultra-fit college professor. Just shy of average height, with a slim wiry build and a hawkish-looking face that was all sharp angles, the guy looked like a triathlete.

The two bodyguards *were* soldiers. There was no mistaking that. He already knew the Russian was a soldier from Ray. The man was taller than Skirjanek by an inch or two but built like a fullback. At the moment, the Russian was ignoring both of them and scanning the surrounding buildings with what looked to be a practiced eye.

The soldier who had been in the back seat was as tall as he was and about the same age. A Marine, he guessed, and a lifer by the looks of it. One didn't get the fused-vertebrae look in the Army, and the look on the Marine's face was screaming that he thought his CO was insane.

"You're Jason?" The colonel sounded friendly enough, almost conversational.

"I am, Jason Larsen."

"Shit." Ray gave his head a shake. "I suppose I should have handled introductions."

"No worries, Mr. Hoover." The colonel waved away the concern as he walked up to him, holding out his hand. "Jason, I'm Andrew Skirjanek. Drew to my friends."

"It's good to meet you," he said. "Is it Colonel Skirjanek?"

The man's eyes were laughing as he took in the surrounding courtyard. He lingered on the burned-out shell of a minivan in the middle of what used to be the ice rink. "Certainly not in any official capacity. Everything I swore an oath to is well and gone." Skirjanek nodded in greeting at Ray and then turned back to him. "I understand from Mr. Hoover, you're the leader of your group."

"Not exactly," he answered. "I didn't want the job. I guess you could say I'm the head watchdog for our civilian authority, and by civilian, I mean a former soccer mom with anger issues."

"Fair enough." Skirjanek nodded to himself. "We've all got that in common, I suppose." Turning to his subordinates, he said, "I'd like to introduce my colleagues. This is Captain Pavel Volkov, formerly Russian Army Spetsnaz. He and his people were in Antarctica as well, and hitched a ride off the ice with us."

He offered what he thought was a friendly nod of respect in the Russian's direction.

"How many guns are looking at us?" the Russian asked, as he continued to scan the surrounding buildings.

"Enough," he answered with a smile, before turning back to the colonel. "No disrespect intended, just playing it safe."

"More than understandable." Skirjanek waved away the concern and turned to his other bodyguard. "This is Lieutenant John Bruce, former Marine gunnery sergeant, Marine recon."

"It's a pleasure, sir," the Marine answered, sounding a lot more like the Marine sergeant he had been than a postapocalypse field-promoted lieutenant.

"It's just Jason," he responded. "Good to meet you, all of you." Jason made a point of turning back to the Russian, whose focus was taken up with the upper stories of the office building behind him and Ray.

"Captain, my people have been told to stand ready. They aren't going to start anything. You're all safe, as long as we remain friendly."

"Am only worried about truck, limited edition."

"Mr. Larsen," Skirjanek cut in and motioned with his laptop when the shared laughter died down. "I learned a lesson when I spoke to Mr. Hoover. Perhaps I can answer your question of how full of shit I am, right off the bat."

He smiled and nodded. "Not sure I'd put it that way, but Ray did mention a video I had to see."

As the video of the conference between Skirjanek and President Huffman played, Jason was struck by a sense of the surreal; watching the classified meeting from a laptop, sitting on the hood of a pickup, in the middle of the Town Center's courtyard. The collapse of civilization that the president referred to had happened. They were all part of the "lucky, or possibly unlucky, few" who were mentioned.

When the video ended, Skirjanek stepped away and looked again at the metal carcass of the minivan on the ice-skating rink. Jason had watched the entire video, and caught the last part where Skirjanek had basically told the president that his family had been in touch, and was dying. He closed the laptop and regarded Skirjanek's back for a moment.

The colonel turned back towards him and jerked a thumb towards the ice-skating rink. "Last time I was here, my wife and I came with my daughter." Skirjanek tried to smile and failed. "She wanted to ice-skate. My wife drove our minivan."

Jason wanted to tell Skirjanek that thinking back on the past was a short road to anger and madness that didn't fade easily. "Colonel . . ."

Skirjanek held out a hand and waved off the concern in his voice. "I was just wondering how long it will be, if ever, before we build a place to go ice-skating. The idea is like the recording you just watched. It's an artifact of a dead world."

"And your last orders?" he asked. "Another artifact?"

"Without a doubt," Skirjanek agreed and walked closer. "But, if there's a better way to help the people who managed to survive, I haven't thought of it. Do the most good, for the most people." Skirjanek indicated his two men and himself. "In terms of a grand strategy—that's it in a nutshell."

Jason glanced at Ray, who had retreated a few steps to where he was leaning against his motorcycle. The man's face was, as usual, unreadable.

"I'm still here," Ray announced and then gave a nod in the colonel's direction.

"So the Navy rescued you?"

Skirjanek described the trip north for his group and the Russians in a single submarine. He was far more detailed regarding their interaction with Charlottesville, and the loss of Captain Naylor and four others. Jason had already decided he'd share all he knew about the Charlottesville group when the colonel's description of the skirmish mentioned they'd fired a Javelin.

"Wait." He shook his head. "A Javelin? Where'd you manage to loot a Javelin?"

Skirjanek smiled and pointed to Lieutenant Bruce. During the discussion, the Marine had continued to loosen up and was sitting next to the Russian on the curb.

"That brings us to our Marine contingent. Lieutenant Bruce's squad spent nine months sealed underground, in Virginia, in a classified continuity of a government site that was meant to be an arms cache, supporting the same mission I had in Antarctica. Which was basically to ensure the survival of a coherent command authority with which to restart and rebuild in the event of nuclear war."

"Underground? For nine months?" He glanced over at the Marine, wondering how the guy was still sane.

Bruce nodded slowly. "And eleven days."

The colonel looked twenty years younger than his late forties when he smiled. "When I showed up with the proper authentication codes to let them out, there was a moment when I wondered if I would ever see them again. To answer your question, the Javelin, as well as a great deal of other gear we have availed ourselves to, came out of that facility—The Hole."

Every time he'd listened to someone's tale of the die-off and their personal aftermath, he usually came away thinking that he'd been relatively lucky. He'd been with Sam when he lost her. What had followed had been a result of his choices. These guys? Trapped and starving in Antarctica or locked underground for nine months was a new level of suckage.

"Humor me for a moment." Skirjanek moved to the laptop and brought up a new screen. "What was your SSN?"

"Seriously?"

"You worried about identity theft?" Ray barked out with a laugh from behind him.

He provided the numbers that Skirjanek typed in and was shocked when his Army personnel jacket, with a photo, appeared on the screen.

He overcame his surprise quickly. "If you're going to try and reenlist me, you should have brought more people."

"Nothing like that." Skirjanek nodded at the screen. "Just an example of what I have access to in The Hole, and forgive me, I wanted to know who I was talking with as well."

Jason nodded at the laptop. "You've convinced me . . . and you've got anti-tank missiles. Why did you request this . . . meeting? It doesn't sound like you need our help."

Skirjanek turned himself around and leaned his ass against the front bumper. "When I accused Ray of being from Charlottesville, he mentioned that you've already had a run-in with them."

"Far as we can tell, most of the state outside of the DC metro area has already been steamrolled by them." Jason couldn't see how it would hurt anything to share what he knew. Trust didn't come easy, but the concept of "the enemy of my enemy" still applied. "I spent a night sneaking around their campus. I've seen their . . . I guess you'd call it a reeducation camp up close. They've got a lot of people."

"The stadium? We wondered what was going on in there."

He found himself nodding. "PowerPoint and audio playing twenty-four seven. Whoever's running the place is not a fan of the way things were." Jason added his own air quotes. "Who are we going to help? Everyone. Who's going to stop us? No one."

"To hell with that." Lieutenant Bruce was shaking his head. "We've seen how they go about collecting people, at least in Richmond. We'll stop them."

"That we will," Skirjanek added softly.

He wasn't about to stand aside and let others fight his battle. "Well, we know our group is on their to-do list. They've already scouted us.

If I can help, I will. A few others might agree to as well."

Skirjanek seemed relieved, but was shaking his head as if he wasn't sure about something. "Would you feel the same way, if I told you I'm trying to save as many lives in Charlottesville as I can?"

"They've attacked you, attacked everyone they could . . . killed your friend. You're going to try and save them?"

"Do the most good . . . for the most people. It's the only kind of math that makes any sense to me. I could destroy the entire campus, right now with one MLRS strike."

"Wait! You mean to tell me you've got an MLRS battery?" The Multiple Launch Rocket System had been at times known as the "grid square removal system" or "the finger of God" for its ability to destroy everything in a single map square.

"Mr. Larsen, I've got the equipment, gear, and fuel to outfit and operate a Mechanized Infantry Division, including the armor, and aviation brigades and the artillery battalion. Not to mention a lot of civilian equipment that, given the time and security to put it to use, could be utilized to jump-start a civilization worthy of the name. What I don't have is the stomach for killing four or five thousand people of the so very few we have left."

Skirjanek came off the bumper and walked in a tight circle before facing him again. "I'm not interested in adding to the butcher's bill out of revenge. I don't want to take over, any more than I'm willing to be someone else's attack dog. As for Charlottesville? And the New People's Republic? I very much think a change in leadership, not to mention a name change, is in order. I think we might have something in common there, you and I."

What Skirjanek wasn't saying clicked in place for him. "How few are you, Colonel?"

The man shared a look with Lieutenant Bruce, who just shrugged and then smiled back at him. "Pretty smart for Army."

"We have a total of sixty-four people, half of whom I'm beginning to have some confidence won't shoot me or someone else by accident.

Including my seven Marines, Captain Volkov, and some former military contractors, we have twenty-one people who have at least deployed in the past with a weapon in hand. Out of the remaining crew of the *Boise*, we have another dozen or so who are coming along."

Skirjanek put a hand atop his head and smiled. "What I do have, our secret weapon for the long term . . . is what I'm guessing is the single best-educated group of survivors on the planet. Outside of strictly military personnel, I'm overflowing with scientists and researchers. There's a bunch of graduate students who would have been PhDs if it weren't for their doctorate review boards dying. That includes the Russian contingent that basically staffed a mirror of McMurdo at their Vostok base. Giving those people a place, the time, and the security to work their magic is my job one. Charlottesville is just in the way."

"You really think you can build something . . . lasting?"

"If I didn't, I'd take one of our MRAPs and just drive off into the sunset. I'd be lying if I said the idea hasn't sounded pretty good some days."

Jason understood that on a fundamental level. He'd almost done it himself. Ray was in the process of doing it. "I can understand that."

Skirjanek held out both hands, like he was pleading. "Whether I can talk you and some of your people into helping us or not, I'd like to suggest . . . hell, I'm flat-out asking that you take in my noncombatants. I assure you, they'll more than pull their weight."

"I see . . ."

"The rest of my group, we call ourselves the Gypsies; we *are* looking for a little payback. If we can buy a larger group like yours the time and security they need—it's as good a chance as we are going to get to start over."

Jason was aware of his head shaking. "One thing I've learned in the last year, those people aren't going to sit back and let you challenge their leadership to a duel. They will fight. Their scout we captured is a certified true believer."

"I'm sure they will," Skirjanek agreed. "The best we can tell, they have between four and five thousand people."

"Civilians . . ." Pavel's tone couldn't have been more derisive.

"Yes, civilians—who have been forced to fight." Skirjanek was getting excited. "You can't tell me that among that number, there one or two folks competent to lead that would make for a better neighborhood."

"Restart the HOA?" Jason knew he sounded incredulous. The memory of what Bauman had created in Tysons, what Ray had been through in Kentucky, what Charlottesville had done to its neighbors. "We're barbecuing the carcass of civilization atop a dumpster fire."

Skirjanek barked a short laugh before pointing at the laptop. "I saw you have a degree in history; so do I. We aren't the only population center trying to stand up. We won't be the only one that manages to get their hands on military gear. The satellite feeds I had access to at McMurdo and the more limited feeds I have access to at The Hole show that clearly."

The colonel ran a hand through his short hair, shaking his head. "I think for the next century, if not longer, we'll be lucky to progress to the city-state level of civilization. We'll have all the wonderful rivalry and hate-filled baggage that went along with it. The whole concept of 'us versus them' pretty much got codified and perfected during that stage of our development. Throw in a civilizational collapse, mass psychological trauma, and some charismatic leadership, and your dumpster fire is going to grow into something far more dangerous that we, and I mean the human race, might not recover from."

As much as he tried to find fault with Skirjanek's logic, he knew he couldn't. The man wasn't saying anything he disagreed with. He'd been wrong—this colonel wasn't a PowerPoint warrior. He might be somebody he could respect enough to follow. Every time he formed an argument in his head, an image of Elsa or Pro or Rachel would manifest itself. They'd said much the same to him months ago. This world was all they had; they had to fight for it.

"I push too hard . . .?" The disappointment on Skirjanek's face was clear.

"No, Colonel. I was just remembering something that was said to me a few months back, by some kids who have come to mean a great deal to me. Different words, but same message. I'll help."

"We'll help," Ray added. "Just so long as you keep your promise when this is over."

"What promise?" Jason did a double take.

"Mr. Hoover extorted an armed escort to Georgia out of me, in exchange for arranging this meeting with you."

"Not bad." He felt himself smile as he shook his head.

"We drink now?" Pavel suggested. "Make official."

"Oorah!" Lieutenant Bruce piped in.

Chapter 18

"North Team, this is Gypsy One. We are on the beltway, five minutes out."

Jason thumbed his radio. "Copy, Gypsy One."

"Gypsy One?" Michelle and Daniel spoke with one voice. The rarity of that happening gave him pause.

"Made sense." He shrugged. "They call themselves the Gypsies." Both Michelle and Daniel were standing next to him, outside, on the top of the mall's parking deck. The day was hot, and the humidity was getting bad, which had everyone's temper on a short fuse. It wasn't just the heat. The stench of rot from the dead was back, worse than it had ever been the year before. They were now all paying for whatever reprieve the cool fall and hard winter had provided last year.

Fear of disease had forced them to work hard clearing the remains from the immediate area, both during Bauman's reign and after. The smell now was in the wind, coming from everywhere. They'd taken to opening the doors and windows of houses to give nature's scavengers access to what they sought, but it was a slow process and one more reason to abandon Tysons for something more suburban.

"Making themselves right at home, aren't they?" In the week since his meeting with Colonel Skirjanek, Michelle had vacillated back and forth between ecstatic to take on newcomers, and resentful of the extra work it entailed.

"We did agree to this," Daniel pointed out with a smile; he was thrilled to be getting some technical help. The move westward to the new site, a series of compounds each able to support the others, had continued unabated. Every day, there were new problems; distributing the power from the solar farm taken from the roof of the mall, wiring up the pumps that still needed to be installed in the wells they had yet to finish digging, and the seemingly endless list of builds and repairs that were needed to make the new site livable and secure. They had the need for technical expertise that very few of them even understood well enough to explain. Skirjanek's promise of equipment and expertise was enough to quell, for the most part, even Michelle's concern that they were going to be taken over by the military.

"Who are you going to leave with us?" Michelle had turned on him and almost barked the question. He knew she was overworked, put-upon, and exhausted; that said, it was all he could do to keep from firing back.

"I'm taking Reed's security team, Pro and his scout team, Rachel, and a couple of the folks she's been training up on the long guns." He stopped Michelle's comeback with an upraised hand. "That will leave you with both Daniel's and Gabe's security teams, and everyone Reed and Mitch have been training up. We'll be keeping Charlottesville busy in their own backyard, so you should be all right from that direction. You'll have the river at your back, and the only direction a real threat can come from is the Maryland-DC direction or out west. Either way, they'll have to use Route 7 to get to you, and we're only two hours away."

Michelle was nodding to herself. "And if they beat you, or whatever you call it, down there? What the hell are we supposed to do then?"

"Michelle, you wanted to fight. Remember? Would you rather fight here, or on their turf?"

The heavy growl of vehicles and the sound of a tractor trailer downshifting stopped whatever she was about to say in response. He was getting pissed off himself; the last thing Skirjanek needed was to get ambushed by "bad" Michelle, and it was starting to look like that kind of day. A big, four-wheeled JLTV, the light tactical vehicle that was replacing the Humvee in the Army, turned onto International and rolled to a stop. It had what looked like an M-60 machine gun mounted on its top. An eighteen-wheeler pulling a flatbed trailer, carrying an M2 Bradley, pulled up behind it.

"Oh shit." Daniel let out a breath. "A tank."

"Not a tank," he said, letting out a breath of relief of his own as a familiar black Ford Raptor pulled around the stopped vehicles and came towards them. "And I think it's a present for us."

"How do you know?" Michelle asked.

"They dragged it up here, and it wouldn't be tied down with chains if they were looking to use it."

"You're sure?" Daniel sounded worried.

"If I'm wrong, it won't matter for long."

The Raptor turned onto the parking deck and drove slowly towards them. He again credited Skirjanek's common sense. The guy had to know what was going through the minds of the people watching. Jason turned to look behind him. Most of the mall's roof was lined with people watching, probably terrified by what they could see stacked up behind the eighteen-wheeler out on Dolly Madison.

"I thought he'd be taller" was the first thing Michelle said when Skirjanek hopped out of the passenger side of the pickup. The driver seemed to fill the driver's side of the truck and looked Samoan; had to be one of the Marines, he guessed.

"Jason." Skirjanek waved in greeting and walked right up to Michelle. He'd warned the man.

"Ma'am, I'm Andrew Skirjanek. I guess you're my civilian authority at the moment. Where do you want us? We've brought a lot of stuff that Jason mentioned you could use."

Skirjanek might as well have hit Michelle in the forehead with a hammer. She was stunned. "Uhh, I'm sorry?"

"You are Michelle? The leader of this group?"

"Don't look at me." He shook his head at her when she turned to question him. "You wanted the job."

"Well, I suppose you could just park the stuff right here for now. We've cleared it out for you."

Skirjanek looked around at the expanse of the parking lot, and Jason thought he saw the guy wink at him. "Yes, ma'am. Might I suggest we keep the Bradleys out on the roadway? I'm not certain this parking structure would hold them."

Michelle again turned to him. "Those would be your tanks." He smiled. "Sounds good, Colonel."

Skirjanek nodded once at Michelle and backed off a step. "Let's do introductions after. I'll get these people moving."

Skirjanek was on the radio on his way back to the jeep. "Bradleys and tanker, up along the road fronting the mall. The rest of you, park on the deck here."

Michelle turned back to him and almost smiled. "Is he serious?"

"About?"

"Civilian authority?"

Skirjanek had enough firepower to level Charlottesville without a fight. The guy preferred to risk a fight in order to try and save lives; and if he'd wanted to, he could have rolled over them here with one of the Bradleys. "Yes, I think he is."

Nothing he'd seen in a long time gave him as much pleasure as the look of surprise and panic on Michelle's face. He shared a look with Daniel, who wore a shit-eating grin on his face.

It had been a very long day; the supplies were unloaded, and his civilians were mixing with and making new friends among the fellow survivors of what had been labeled the Potomac settlement. They were barbecuing dinner in the welcome shade, just behind the Landsdowne conference center. Drew felt a pull he couldn't have imagined. Part of him wanted to stay.

"This is much more defensible than where you were," he pointed out to Michelle. "The Potomac behind you, Goose Creek on your north. You just need to build up a line of defense covering your west and south."

"It's going to be a lot of work," Michelle said, "but I'm starting to see it."

He pointed at Hoyt. "Mr. Sweet here is a former master chief in the Navy. That's a long way to say that he can get things done. You don't need to do everything; delegate. Let him help you manage the work."

"Gee, thank you, sir."

He traded smiles with Hoyt. "Face it, you were getting bored." He turned to look at Michelle again and smiled at Daniel and Jason. "Never let Navy people get bored."

"I'll have a week of work just getting all the solar panels tied in with the extra capacity we brought up. Then we can start supplementing with some windmills. I can't promise AC this summer, but you'll have ice for our drinks."

Andrew rattled the ice cubes around in his glass of whiskey and smiled. He was used to living out of a tent, but even he wasn't immune to the allure of some creature comforts.

"AC? Seriously?" Michelle almost gasped. Jason's description of the woman had been spot-on, and he could already tell he'd scored some points with her. He'd dealt with far worse during his Pentagon tour, where he'd had to schmooze with politicians for budget dollars. He had no interest in running a society; he needed Michelle to feel secure enough to leave him alone to do what needed to be done. He knew it was the same arrangement she'd managed with Jason, but if everything went as he hoped, this community was only going to grow, and with it, whatever authority and legitimacy she had. Whatever "arrangement" they came up with would likely have some staying power. He was thanking his stars that, her temperament aside, Michelle seemed more than up to the task.

"If Dr. Mandel says he can build a power plant, he can do it, yes, ma'am." Hoyt was pointing toward the barbecue, at a large group of people who were in line for food.

Michelle held out her drink. "First off, people need to stop calling me ma'am. I'm not the damn school principal."

"The hell you aren't." Jason spoke up and put an arm up ward off the incoming backhand.

"Dr. Mandel?" Michelle looked back at him. "He's the older Russian gentleman?"

"That's right, he's the one with three doctoral degrees. Anything technical, he's your brain. Let Hoyt be your clipboard."

"Again, sir, thank you." Hoyt was shaking his head, but he looked happy.

Michelle stood slowly and raised her glass. "When Jason ran this plan by me, I have to admit I thought it sounded too good to be true . . ." Michelle paused and looked around at the gathered people, new and old. "A part of me can't stop thinking how fragile this all is, but sometimes I can almost see a future again. Thank you—all of you."

He shared the toast and then stood up himself. "That's a future we can all believe in, but I don't think anybody here thinks it's going to be handed to us." He looked at the young man seated next to Jason and Rachel. "A week ago, Jason told me that a kid told him that the world as it is was the only world he had. Wise words that we all need to keep in mind. Charlottesville is the current challenge; they aren't going to be last. As we deal with that threat, it is we, the Gypsies, who should be thanking you.

"Any future we build isn't going to be built through armed conflict. It's going to be built here with crops; it's going to be the protection and passing down of the knowledge the old world left us. Maybe that includes AC, maybe not, but it will have people sleeping securely. We *are* going to have to fight, but the war for the future will be won or lost here, and in places just like this."

He paused, and looked around at the group of people that he had seen work so hard during the day. They were survivors. "For that, we thank you."

If he ever got to thinking Skirjanek was some sort of superhuman, he'd think back on this moment. Skirjanek was in the front passenger seat of the Ford Raptor, slumped over and snoring up a storm. Jason was in the back seat along with Rachel, who was curled up against him and sound asleep. One of the Marines, Corporal Park, who was called Poy by everyone except Skirjanek, was driving. There was no doubt as to where the handle had come from. The guy had to be close to three hundred pounds and had mentioned at the barbecue that he was on a diet when he was told to go back for more.

"What was The Hole like, Mr. Park?"

"It's Cameron, sir—or just Cam." The Marine waved a hand, not taking his eyes off the road. They were driving south on James Madison Highway, Route 15, and just passed through what had been Orange, Virginia. He didn't know if the destruction he saw around him was recent or had occurred during the riots, but the small city center appeared to have burned to the ground. He and Sam had taken a day trip down this way a couple of years back and toured James Madison's home. He hadn't been able to stop thinking about that trip; a different world and a lifetime ago. They and the vehicles that followed were driving without headlights, and the ghostly glow through the NVDs seemed to accentuate how empty the land was.

"You can call me Poy. Everyone else does, except the colonel."

Skirjanek stopped snoring at the mention of his name. He could see Park shaking his head in admonishment. The corporal didn't speak until Skirjanek started cutting logs again.

"The Hole's a lot better than you are probably thinking," Park whispered. "It's really, really big. It was just the idea that we were trapped, and that everybody we knew was dead—it messed with us pretty bad. Guys started 'suck starting' their sidearms, sir. It got bad. Corporal Kearney almost did for all of us; he went nuts and rigged one of the ammo bunkers with C-4. Lieutenant Benoit handled the issue."

"Lieutenant Benoit? I haven't met him yet."

"You won't, sir. He went crazy two months later, though if you ask me, it was taking care of Kearney that did it for him. He was a good man, solid. A lot like Gunny Bruce."

"Now Lieutenant Bruce?"

"That's him; he could have gone to OCS years ago. But he's a Marine's Marine, sir."

"I'm not a sir, Cam." He felt himself smile. "Haven't been one for a long while. It's just Jason."

"Not true." Skirjanek shifted in his seat and then gave his head a shake. He wondered if the colonel ever truly slept. It was common knowledge in the military that the ability to function on the bare minimum of sleep was almost a mandatory superpower for officers. "You'll have command of the people who are coming down with you, which will be our largest contingent. I'd say captain, at least."

"Congratulations, sir!" Poy slapped the steering wheel in excitement. From where he was sitting, it seemed as if the corporal was laughing at him.

Charlottesville

"Miss Cooper . . . respectfully, you can't be serious." Dr. Naomi Vance was having a hard time processing what she'd just heard. For the briefest of moments, she'd considered just agreeing with Lisa Cooper and trying to figure a way out of it later. The former chief of obstetrics at Roanoke Memorial Hospital had been a guest of Charlottesville since early December, and she'd had to treat a lot of people who had disagreed with this woman in one way or another. Most recovered and were returned to the community; a few had been pulled from the university hospital that she ran, and had never been seen again.

At the end of the day, she was a physician. Her oath was all she had to hold onto in the fallen world; that, and moments like she'd had yesterday, when she'd helped bring a baby girl into the world. She had been very careful to keep her misgivings regarding Cooper private. Whatever the woman's issues, Charlottesville worked. It was safe. That baby girl would grow up in a world different from what any of them had known in their childhoods, but she would grow up. The greater good . . .

"Dr. Vance . . ." Cooper got up from her chair, slowly walked around to the side of her desk, and pointed out the window. "These men are coming to destroy what we've built. If what they've said about being in Antarctica is true, correct me if I'm wrong, but they shouldn't have our immunity to the virus." The world's coldest blue eyes stared back her, above a smile that looked nothing but inquisitive. "Would it somehow be more ethical or moral to shoot them?" Cooper sounded incredulous.

Yes, by a long shot. "Even if I could do it, and I'm not saying I could, I'm not a virologist. I do know it would risk a mutation that *we* might not be immune from."

"We live with that risk every day, don't we?"

She shook her head and looked directly back at the woman who controlled her life, controlled everyone within the radius of her bullyboys. One of whom had arrived with Cooper and had stood at the door of her office without saying a word.

"Yes, we live with some small chance of that happening. It would be increased by orders of magnitude if we were somehow able to find live cultures and rerelease it into the environment."

"Find? What do you mean?" Cooper's tone was back to conversational. "The world is carpeted in the bodies of people who died from it."

"If the virus were active after all this time, within or upon the remains of the dead—the people you're worried about would have already succumbed. Viruses are living organisms; this particular one needs a living host to propagate. The world simply ran out of those . . ." She could tell her tone wasn't doing her any favors. She'd almost gone the psychiatry route after med school. She didn't need any of that formal education to know Lisa Cooper scared her. It did give her insight enough to know the woman looking down at her was a high-functioning sociopath.

In the old world, it had served her well; if Lisa Cooper had chosen business rather than academia, given her intelligence and charisma, she would have risen just as fast and just as far in any corporate boardroom. Throw in seven billion dead and the end of civilization, and the constraints of normal society were gone. Those societal norms were normally what acted in place of a conscience in people like Cooper. All that was gone; what was left was a highly intelligent, hyper-motivated individual, wrapped in the kind of body and face that usually had the opposite sex eating out of her hand. In sum, she knew Lisa Cooper saw only the ends—the means to get there were nothing more than events to mark the passage of time.

"Where could we find some live virus?"

She wondered if Cooper had even heard her. "Research facilities that were working the problem," she answered. "They would have super chilled the live virus down for preservation, to maintain a stock for study. But they've all lost power. With the temperature rise, the clock starts ticking." *Thankfully.*

"This was a research hospital, and it was crawling with CDC folks during the last days. The power here only went down for a short time during our fight, and then we got the generators back up."

The woman was too smart to lie to, too dangerous. "It's possible," she admitted. "I can certainly check. Although, if they knew they were dying, I'm certain they would have destroyed any samples they'd collected." If there was any live virus down there in the virology vault, she knew what she had to do. *"First, do no harm . . ."*

Cooper regarded her with a cool smile for a moment and then nodded to the man standing at the door. "I think we'll make sure you don't have to do that alone."

*

Chapter 19

A feeling of relief washed over him as a sand-colored JLTV came into view around the gentle curve of I-64. They'd had a heads-up they were inbound. Poy's drone had spotted the convoy thirty minutes ago. Within moments, a line of flatbeds loaded with gear, M2 and M3 Bradleys, and if his eyes weren't playing tricks on him, one Abrams tank, followed. Rachel and Pro were somewhere in that convoy, and the relief he felt wasn't due solely to their return.

The Gypsies were stretched thin. There was no getting around it. More so over the last week, as Lieutenant Bruce and three of his Marines had been absent with the fifty people from Reed's security team that he'd brought south with him. They'd all been sent east, back to The Hole for equipment and a week of intensive training. Reed's team was the most capable group of "soldiers" he had, followed by Daniel's team that had remained up north. Within Reed's group, there were exactly three individuals who had ever served in the military, including Reed. After almost a year of fighting for their survival, they weren't exactly civilians, but he wished that some of Skirjanek's people would quit referring to them as soldiers.

While they'd been gone, learning to operate the small M72 rocket launchers, heavier Javelin missiles, and the assorted weapons sported by the Bradleys, he'd been inserted into the rotation of patrols and observation posts that Skirjanek had emplaced around Charlottesville. He'd understood what Skirjanek was doing; plugging him in with as many different team members as he could, giving both him and them a chance to get to know each other. What it now meant was that he'd been "on" for ten days straight, and life was about to get more interesting.

As much as he wanted to go check on Rachel and Pro as the line of vehicles pulled off to both sides of the I-64 interchange, it was Lieutenant Bruce who caught his attention in the front vehicle, waving at him. There wasn't a whole lot of time to waste. The overhead feeds from Poy Boy's drone had revealed that Charlottesville was prepping for something.

"How'd they do?" he asked as Captain Bruce and a Marine he hadn't met yet walked up to him.

"Mixed bag." Bruce shook his hand. "A lot better than I expected, better than our own civilians we've been training up."

"Most of them have had a lot of experience they'd just as soon forget, but I suppose it counts."

"It showed." Bruce didn't look as if he'd slept a lot either. He turned to his fellow Marine. "I want you to meet our newly minted lieutenant, Lucas Hanson, aka Farmer. He's my right hand, and before the shit show, he'd been accepted into OCS."

He regarded the young man, who looked like he belonged on a Marine recruiting poster or in Hollywood. "Farmer?" He smiled. "I'd have guessed 'Terminator.'"

"Grew up on a farm, sir. The name kind of stuck during basic."

"Just Jason, Lucas. It's good to meet you."

Bruce patted Lucas on the back and grinned at his fellow Marine. "You two have a lot to talk about. I need to go find the colonel."

Bruce was gone in a flash and yelling at people to start unloading before he'd gone three steps. Once a sergeant, always a sergeant.

"What's that all about? Everything alright?"

"All good, sir . . . I mean Jason. I just wanted to check on you regarding Pro."

He could feel himself start to grin. He figured he knew where this was headed. "How'd he do?"

"That's the problem." Lucas nodded to himself. "The kid's a natural, and even with a bum shoulder, he's better than anybody in that group outside of Reed. He insists on being at the pointy end."

"Welcome to my world."

"In the old world, IF he was eighteen, and IF he was a Marine, he'd be sidelined for another two weeks with that shoulder. But you were a soldier; you understand he just fits in. Salguero, one of my squad, pretty much adopted him as a little brother. I warned him we probably wouldn't let him in on this next fight, but he made me promise I'd check with you."

"If he's at a hundred percent, I'd have no problem adding him to one of the scout teams." He recognized how strange it felt to say that, but Pro *was* that good. "The kid can just up and disappear; he actually headed up our scouts. But I'm in complete agreement about waiting until he's healed up."

"He going to accept that, if it comes from you?" Lucas sounded dubious.

"No." He smiled and shook his head. "Short of tying him up and having him watched, he'll figure out a way to insert himself. Kid's a bit of a barracks-room attorney when it comes to the subject of him being a legal adult by way of the world ending."

Lucas laughed at that. "'Bout what I figured. So . . . I kind of had him cross-trained."

*

He was driving a tank! Pro had the driver's hatch open and the seat in its elevated position so he could see out. Tommy was sitting on the hull outside, next to his head.

"This will be easier than when you loaded it. You just drive straight off—sloooow and straight."

"What happens if I screw up?"

"To you and the tank? Nada. But we might need to use this transporter again."

Transporter? It was a flatbed. Pro wanted to say something, but held off. Why did everything in the military have to have a different name just because of its paint job?

"Remember the rules about driving this thing?"

"There are no rules, only things that go squish."

"Right. So . . . slow and straight, pull ahead."

His seat and his whole body vibrated with the 1500-horsepower turbine engine, but he was amazed at how quiet it was. The tank almost seemed to whine more than rumble. He was already in gear; he popped the emergency brake and then let up on the brakes controlled by the left-hand yoke on the T-shaped steering bar. He applied some power and almost panicked—he couldn't see what was in front of him. Then he remembered the training; you go where and when the commander says to go. Salguero was the tank commander, so he went.

The trailer moaned as the sixty-nine-ton beast shifted and eased itself down onto the trailer ramps.

"*Bueno, ese.*" Salguero flashed him a thumbs-up. "Till I say stop."

Pro breathed a sigh of relief. The tank was sitting on flat ground.

"Bring it around, big circle to the right. Park it next to the tanker— not too close though."

Riiiiiight . . . Not too close to the tanker truck full of fuel. Jeez, did they think he was stupid? Still, he was driving a tank! They could harp on him all they wanted.

"OK, stop." Salguero made a cutting motion across his throat. The vehicle seemed to float, rocking back and forth smoothly as he came to a stop. "Emergency brake?"

He reached down with his right hand and pulled the handle up. "Engaged."

"OK, kill it."

He did as he was told and sat there for a moment, listening to the turbine wind down. Holy shit! They might actually let him drive the tank.

Jason watched Pro crawl up out of the driver's hatch and waved. He couldn't believe he was considering letting Pro drive the thing. There probably wasn't a safer place for Pro to be in the kind of fight they were planning, but his mind was busy playing catch- up.

"He's actually got about eight hours of terrain work under his belt," Luca explained. "It was all we had time for. Took longer than we thought it would to prep the tank."

"I'm sold," he said. Pro's shit-eating grin as he slid down the forward glacis of the tank was priceless. He watched as Pro bumped knuckles with the people he'd been training with and had to smile. Pro's mascot status had transferred over to the Gypsies.

"There's something else I wanted to say, sir."

"It's just Jason, Lucas . . ."

"Right." Hanson's radio went off. It was Skirjanek, wanting him to report immediately.

"It'll wait, sir." Hanson looked almost relieved as he turned away and moved off at a jog.

It took him a couple of minutes walking down the line of flatbeds until he found Rachel off the back ramp of an M2 Bradley. She saw him, dropped her pack and her gun on top of it, and came running.

She slammed into him and kissed him hard. "Miss me?"

"You know I did. How was it?"

"It was more fun than I thought it would be, but long days."

"You teach them how to shoot?"

Rachel's face glowed as she pushed herself away. "There's some guy here, Nathan? They want to put me up against him on a range."

He nodded. "Trey Nathans, and he's been warned. You do know he's a Marine sniper?"

"That doesn't mean anything against St. Mary's British School's best."

"That's the spirit." He pulled her into another hug. "I still wish you weren't here."

"I know," she said into his shoulder and gave him another squeeze. "But you're going to manage, right?"

"Hey!" Pro came around the side of the Bradley. "Did you tell him the Marines were hitting on you?"

Rachel shook her head, annoyed at Pro, and looked up at him. "Just one." She smiled. "And he could not have been more polite. I think I scared him to death when I told him I was spoken for. Pro's the one who can't seem to let it go."

"Let me guess, Lieutenant Hanson?"

The look of surprise on Rachel's face was priceless. "How . . .?"

"I think he was about to tell me about it."

"Why? It was harmless."

"Man code." He smiled and turned to Pro. "And you need to mind your own damn business."

Pro's excitement wasn't going to be sidetracked. "OK, OK . . . are you going to let me drive the tank for Sergeant Salguero? He was a tanker for a year before he went recon, he said——"

He held up a hand and stopped Pro. "I need to talk to the colonel first, see how he wants to use it."

"The tank?"

"Yes, the tank. Now, if you don't mind, I'd like to talk to Rachel for a moment . . ."

"Right." Pro flashed him a two-fingered thing that might have started out as a salute. "Tell him, Rachel, you saw me drive that thing back at The Hole."

"Go!"

"OK, OK . . ."

They both watched the irrepressible teenager skip off.

"As much as I don't want to admit it, he really did a good job. Even followed the Marine's orders. I think he wants to enlist."

"Yeah, Bruce and Hanson told me."

"So, you did talk to them?"

"Yes, I spoke to the movie-star handsome Marine lieutenant."

Rachel gave his hand a squeeze. "You know, if Clark Kent had blond hair . . ."

He smiled at her. "I missed you."

"Me too. Any chance we'll get any time for ourselves down here?"

"I do have my own tent."

She slapped his arm. "Not what I meant, not entirely at any rate."

"I think things are going to get busy over the next couple of days."

"That's it, that's the plan." Skirjanek motioned towards the map on the table. "I'll take the infantry, as a diversion only, right up I-64 and hold their attention. We'll avoid a pitched battle at all costs, and what actions we do take will be focused on the enemy's vehicles. Captain Larsen will take his team and hit the outpost that they have established on Highway 29 at the Rivanna River crossing, and destroy the two bridges there if possible.

"Major Volkov will swing north of their roadblock on 64 and attempt to destroy the Long Street Bridge over the Rivanna that leads into town; it doesn't look to be guarded, so after blowing the bridge he should be available to hit their roadblock on 64 from behind, in the event, and only if they move out up the freeway against our diversion. Captain Bruce will swing south and take out the I-64 bridge west of the eastern roadblock and then move back along 64 to hit them from behind on the south side if needed, again only in the event they come out looking for a fight . . . Questions? Concerns?"

Skirjanek looked around the room at them. "Remember, this isn't do or die. We are just trying to dick with them by creating a siege mentality. I want to deny them any way of moving their heavy equipment east or north by transporter; taking out the bridges will do that. They'll still be able to cross that stream in a dozen places with their vehicles, and anywhere on foot, but they won't be loading up Bradleys or M1 Abrams for any field trips unless they want to go the long way around into the Shenandoah. Meanwhile, they'll be burning more fuel we don't think they can easily replace."

Bruce spoke up. "What is our ROE?"

"If you engage, whether initiated by you in pursuit of your mission or in self-defense, you will utilize all means to protect the lives of your people—that is priority one. This is more of a probe with some distinct goals. Avoid stand-up fights if you can. We are not at war with these people, not yet—just their leadership. Killing large numbers of them, which we could do at any point, would be counterproductive to our long-term goals."

Jason could appreciate Skirjanek's sentiment, and as he glanced around the break room of the large landscaping business that was acting as Skirjanek's HQ, he thought most present would agree. Major Volkov was a glaring exception; the former Spetsnaz thought it better to soundly defeat Charlottesville and then treat with the survivors. Jason wasn't certain he didn't agree with Pavel, and they'd both said as much to Skirjanek in private. The colonel freely admitted it might come to that, but he'd asked for their support, and they'd given it.

That had been an easy conversation to have back at Zion Crossroads. Now, looking at his assigned bridges and the manned guard posts on the north side of the river through his NVDs, he was leaning in support of Volkov's argument.

"Rachel, do you have angles on both bridges?" She was set up on the north side of the river, far to the right of him, between the two bridges, the main Highway 29 bridge and the smaller, newer-construction bridge four hundred yards to the west.

"I have them, except for easternmost group on the main bridge. The ones on our side of the river."

Somebody had known what they were doing when they'd set up what they were labeling guard posts. Both bridges had sandbag emplacements at either end. The small Rivanna River, which at this time of year wasn't much more than a big creek, ran sixty feet below the bridge. The ravine created by the river was more of a geographic feature than the waterway itself. Across the river, on the south bank, two more emplacements had been set up between the bridges, both able to fire on either bridge.

"How about positions across the river?"

"I have them both. I am almost directly across from middle guard post. They look to have knocked off."

"Say again."

"Position directly across river from me, they are asleep."

"Copy." He supposed it would be too much to ask that the ones on their side of the river would catch a few z's; they seemed very alert; their attention focused on Highway 29 stretching north out of town.

Ray and Sergeant Uwasi were somewhere down in the riverbed, making their way slowly west until they were under the bridges. He'd known Ray had been a deep-sea welder, but he'd been pleasantly surprised when it turned out he had a lot of experience with demolition charges. "Usually set them to go off under four hundred feet of water, blowing damaged wellheads or pipe," Ray had explained as if it were something everyone could do. "How hard can it be to rig up something where I can see clearly and breathe the air?"

It wasn't setting the charges that he was worried about. Uwasi had some real-world experience in that box as well. It was getting to the underside of the bridge unseen, and then back out, that would be the issue. If Ray and Uwasi were discovered, it would be up to him and the rest of his small team to keep the enemy on the bridges engaged.

He glanced at Sergeant Elliot next to him. The Marine was focused on his binoculars, which were pointed across the river, towards the glow of light from the campus that stood out on the horizon like a beacon.

"Anything?"

"Lots of activity, sir. Vehicle headlights moving around. Can't see where they're headed."

Chances were, the colonel's diversion had been spotted. It was too big a threat for Charlottesville to ignore. Jason wasn't sure what to make of Elliot. He knew Elliot was the target of a good bit of ribbing. The kid was so gung-ho, so "Marine," that at times, it didn't seem like the fact that the old world had died had set in with Elliot. So far, though, in the field, he hadn't seen anything to give him pause. All the

Marines were now sergeants, except Farmer, who was their lieutenant, and Bruce, who had vaulted to captain alongside him.

"Keep an eye out there. They'll be rolling soon."

"Will do, sir."

He activated his mic. "Ray? Status?"

He had to wait for the one-click response; so far, so good. It was just taking too long. His team had traveled farther than any other to get to their target, and on top of that, they had two bridges to wire. The plan was to hold off detonating anything until Skirjanek's diversion got a response, but at that point, it was going to be "fire in the hole" for anyone who was ready.

*

The thrill of driving the seventy-ton tank had worn off in about ten minutes. Salguero wouldn't let him go any faster than three or four miles an hour, which was harder to do than he'd thought it would be. This thing wanted to run. The last time the tank's commander had yelled into his head phone to slow down, it had been followed by a "last warning!" It had taken him an hour to get up the courage to ask why they were moving so damned slow.

"Because we're going to be the surprise. We can't do that if we're first in line." Salguero's tone was calm, much calmer than it had been when he'd been yelling at him to slow down. "There's two Bradleys out ahead of us, as well as two Javelin teams on foot. We don't want to outrun our support. Remember, we want them to shoot at us."

It all made sense, except that last part.

"Stop! Skew left sixty!" Salguero's voice screeched in his headset a few minutes later.

He was already turning as he engaged the brake. He watched his rotating compass heading continue to spin until the tank was aligned roughly 60 degrees to the left of their previous direction of travel.

"Good! Much better." Salguero's voice came through clearer without the track's road noise. "Why do we do that, Pro?"

"To put us at an angle to a threat you have spotted." He repeated the answer he'd given the last two times Salguero had ordered a stop. "It increases the depth of our armor relative to the threat." He couldn't see any threat.

"That is correct. Cruz! Were you standing where the recoil wouldn't have broken you in half?"

"You bet your sweet ass!"

"Good deal. Remember, I might not have time or might forget to give a warning for that first shot. It's already loaded, so you don't have the muscle memory of loading, stepping back, and enabling the shot— we are in battery. Most injuries in these things look a lot like a mashed loader who was standing behind the breech during a recoil. More often than not, it happens on the first shot."

"How are you doing, Mr. Mason?"

"All good, looking for something to shoot."

Mason was their gunner. As Pro understood it, Mason had operated the cannon on a Bradley in the past, when he'd been a real Marine. Not that it mattered at all, but Pro realized that Mason was the only one in the tank who wasn't Hispanic.

"OK, we're going to camp on this spot. Scouts are picking up headlights and movement a few miles ahead. Pro, up and out. I want you to take a quick look at the surrounding area and tell me where you want to park this thing."

"We could come up right behind that abandoned truck," Pro suggested. "It won't hide us, but it might break our . . . uh, profile."

"Points for the suggestion. But no, where else do you see?"

He didn't see anything that looked like one of the firing positions they'd shown him in the training manuals. In desperation, he pointed at the concrete Jersey barrier at the inner edge of the road. "Hide behind one of those? We could push it around."

"You could, but what's it going to protect? It'll just be something you have to crunch if we need to move out."

Salguero grabbed him by the shoulders and forcibly turned him to the side of the road and the barrow pit. "Remember, the only things that have to sit up high enough to operate are our gun and the sensors in the turret, so we can see. Two ways to do that—dig a firing position or . . .?"

"Find a hole." Pro nodded. It made sense.

"Outstanding, we'll make a tanker out of you yet."

He'd already decided he wanted his own rifle back and the freedom to move on his own. There was enough moonlight that it must have shown on his face.

"Why do you think I went recon?" Salguero patted him on the shoulder. "Recon oh-rah. OK, quick, do a walk-around. Decide where you are going to park, get a picture of what's around us in your head, remember it, and get us moved."

Chapter 20

Pavel and Nathans saw the approaching headlights at the same time. Pavel was almost insulted; the enemy was either stupid or so confident from rolling through unprotected towns that they didn't even think to douse their headlights when moving in their city. The column was headed right towards them down Route 250, out towards the enemies' roadblock on the freeway.

"Looks like they've spotted our diversion. I know we're supposed to wait . . ." Nathans let the obvious question hang there. He and Nathans had finished wiring the small, two-lane Long Street Bridge an hour earlier. Once they'd made it past the roadblock, it had been no issue avoiding the single patrol they'd seen. They'd been able to sneak to the bridge and wire its two concrete support pillars with cutting charges. In this case, two shaped charges of C-4, emplaced opposite each other, and wired with matching lengths of detonation cord. A pair for each of the two columns of reinforced concrete.

Pavel wasn't certain it would bring the bridge down, but no one of sound mind would be driving infantry fighting vehicles or heavy trucks across it when they were done. They were *supposed* to wait until the diversion was engaged out on the highway. But he took Nathans's suggestion for what it had been.

"Be prepared to blow the bridge." He could wait until they had a better idea of what was coming towards them.

"Been ready."

He knew Nathans very well. Pavel was sure the type existed in every army. The young Marine was the soldier who was always right, and for whom orders were almost always wrong. The attitude wasn't one he shared, but that didn't make Nathans wrong . . .

"Cremova, can you see them?"

"*Shkol'nye avtobusy, a zatem tanki.*"

"What the hell she say?"

"School buses, with tanks following," he translated.

"Tanks? As in more than one?"

He was getting a clearer picture as the column approached. A block from the far side of the bridge, the buses were visible. The headlight from the second bus in line backlit the profile of the full bus in front. And those were more Bradleys following behind, not tanks. He couldn't fault Nadia Cremova, her specialty had been related to ice core samples not very long ago.

"*Soldati* in the buses—infantry," he finished before Nathans could complain. "Infantry fighting vehicles following."

"So now?"

"No, we wait." He clicked his radio. "Cremova, move your team back to our rally point." He turned to Nathans. "We will let school buses cross, then explode the bridge."

"Blow the bridge, we say 'blow' the bridge."

"Call it whatever you will. Do not do it before I give the word."

"Those school buses will be headed towards our people on the highway."

He was becoming tired of the whining. "It is nothing the colonel cannot handle. The more of the enemy that witness their defeat, the more progress towards the colonel's goal."

"Yeah, but . . ."

"Corporal Nathans, you are making me angry." He pulled his binoculars away and turned to glare at the Marine. "Is not a good thing."

Nathans was about to say something else but thought better of it and turned away to look down the barrel of his rifle.

The first school bus was across the bridge and rolling past their position on the roof of a restaurant. Pavel crept along the rooftop and waited until the last bus was across.

"Now!"

Nathans didn't hesitate. The dark gully beneath the bridge flashed, as if a massive camera had just snapped a picture, followed immediately by the sharp crack of the charges. They watched as the bridge tilted for a moment before the roadbed seemed to steady itself. The Bradley in the middle of the bridge gunned its engine, and the momentum transferred from its tracks did the trick. The near side of the bridge pulled away from the embankment as the middle of the roadway rotated to the sound of shearing reinforced concrete. It completed its turn, dumping the lead Bradley into the ravine forty feet below.

In what Pavel took as an engineering miracle, the far side of the bridge remained, and the Bradley there began backing up, trying to get its weight off the bridge. It almost made it before the bridge seemed to sag against the far hill. The Bradley was deposited with the front of its tracks on the sloping bridgeway and the rearmost of its track trying to grip the hillside.

"It won't be getting out of there." Nathans sounded pleased.

Pavel was more concerned with the three Bradleys in a row behind. Their autocannon began to slew around, looking for a target.

"We go! Now!"

He was pleased Nathans had no issue with that order.

*

John Bruce's whole body spun in place at the sharp crack of the explosion to the northeast of his position. It had been Pavel's target bridge. So much for plans. He glanced over at his own team, who were all looking back at him, waiting. They'd seen no patrols and had worked quickly to wire both lanes of I-64 over the Rivanna. It was only going to take out one short section of the roadway, but it would be enough to stop truck traffic from moving east out of town on the freeway. The colonel had ordered radio silence, not because they worried about Charlottesville breaking the encrypted signals of the radios, but because the traffic itself could be heard as static and was a good indicator that something was in the offing. That was now a moot point.

"Major Volkov, report." Skirjanek's voice sounded calm.

It was nearly a minute before Volkov's voice came back, sounding out of breath. "Target destroyed; strong enemy force was halted. Infantry continuing towards roadblock."

"Copy, stick with your plan. Captain Larsen, report."

"One target prepped, still working on second. Heavy guard presence."

"Copy, beware of reinforcements."

"Copy."

"Captain Bruce, execute as soon as ready and then proceed with as planned."

He turned to Antwan; the naval petty officer had been assigned on active duty to McMurdo and was a long way from where he started. The rest of Antwan's trainees stood around him, burdened with their gear. "You get the honors, Mr. Sikes."

"Fire in the hole!" Antwan didn't have to shout, but he did anyway. Everyone plugged their ears before the sharp cracks; four distinct flashes from beneath the freeway's bridge lit up the night around them. From two hundred yards off, they could hear the crashing of the roadway into the shallow ravine below.

It took nearly two minutes before the dust had cleared enough that his NVDs were able to process a clear image. The freeway was only missing about twenty feet of pavement, but the gap stretched across all four lanes. "Well done, Mr. Sikes! You missed your true calling."

"Yes, sir. Been preparing for the apocalypse all my life. Just figured there'd be angels and the sounds of trumpets."

Not so much. "OK, people. We move back along the freeway, east. Stay on south side of the hill as we move up to assist the colonel.

Antwan, you and I in front. Beware of people from their roadblock trying to get to high ground. Weapons on safe while we move." He had half a dozen trainees with him; everybody needed experience, but he didn't need to catch a round in the ass from somebody who had been monitoring weather balloons not very long ago.

The echoes from Bruce's bridge reached them as a dull rumble. Pavel's bridge going up had already woken the guard force. Now they were hyperalert, and Jason could see several talking on the radio. It was only a matter of time before somebody down there did some critical thinking.

"Headlights coming this way," Elliot whispered. "Two vehicles, coming fast."

Shit... He tapped his microphone. "Ray, status? They've got reinforcements coming. Talk if you can."

Ray's response was one click.

Shit. He was going to have to buy Ray and Uwasi some more time so they could finish wiring the second bridge. "Rachel, mark whoever looks to be in charge when the backup arrives. Be ready. Wait for my fire before engaging."

Rachel came back with a single click of her own. The headlights were less than a mile south of the river and coming at them in a hurry.

"Elliot," he whispered and pointed down at the main bridge to his left. "Get an angle on the guard post, this side of the river with the LAW. Take it out, but wait for my fire." He had the radio control for the detonators with him and could take out the first bridge right now, IF Ray and Uwasi had used the correct detonator. They'd carried two, set to receive two different frequencies; in the dark, working on foot, up the edges of the river, they could have used the wrong one. If they had, nothing good was going to happen.

"It's not stopping." Rachel's voice brought his head up from where he'd watched Elliot squirm his way out of sight down the hill.

One of the suburban-looking vehicles stopped on the far side and disgorged half a dozen guns. The lead vehicle crossed over and disappeared from his line of sight, behind the small hill that hid his perch from the guard posts on his side of the river. He thought it sounded like the tires squealed to a stop well past the terminus of the bridge beneath his location.

"Elliot, the vehicle that crossed. Take it out as soon as you have a sure shot!"

The LAW was nothing more than a modern version of a bazooka, except that there wasn't anything modern about it, and the punch it packed wouldn't have done more than scratch the paint against a tank. Against an SUV, it punched through the driver's-side window of the open middle door and kept going until it met the back seat.

Jason had a moment's panic as the back blast from the small rocket lit up Elliot's unseen firing position, but the explosion from the suburban dismissed it out of mind. If he lived through this, he was going to make sure the other Marines cut Elliot some slack. Rachel's big gun barked twice in quick succession as he maneuvered around the back of his hill.

"Rachel, move!" he screamed into the radio. "Shoot and move!"

The enemy on the far bank was spraying automatic rifle fire into the dark from across the river; he could hear rounds impacting the trees above him and whistling past overhead. More fire erupted below him. He wasn't certain if it was Elliot shooting or if it was enemy fire aimed at the Marine. He moved fast, half sliding on his ass, half running. Twenty feet and three tree trunks later, he discovered it was both. Elliot was pinned down behind a fallen tree. There were at least two or three guns firing from below at the Marine.

He had a line of sight on Elliot and could see where one guard was hunched down behind some rocks at the edge of the road. "Elliot, toss a grenade down there."

"Copy." He watched as the Marine pulled a grenade from his webbing. "Grenade out." Elliot's voice was full of adrenaline. He tensed as he watched Elliot toss the grenade down the hill. It wasn't going to get near close enough to cause any damage, but he just needed a distraction.

When the grenade exploded harmlessly on the near side of the burning suburban, he was already moving. He curled around the hill, away from Elliot, towards the now empty guard post at the end of the bridge, moving farther downhill as he went. He pulled up with a tree trunk between him and the guards as they opened up on Elliot's position again.

Peeking around the tree, he could see three of them. He dropped one with a head shot before they knew he was there. He might have hit another as they reacted quickly and turned their fire in his direction.

"Elliot, move!" he yelled as he kissed the dirt. A heavy, wet-sounding THUNK impacted the tree just above his head, followed by the echo of heavy-caliber rifle.

"Rachel, they have a rifle across the river with night vision. Do you have him?"

"Was moving," Rachel came back a few second later. "I don't have him. Can you get him to fire again?"

That's the challenge, isn't it? "Wait one." He slid deeper into the shallow depression he'd found in his panic, rolled onto his back, and dug out the packed rain poncho from his fanny pack. It took him longer to find a stick in the forest than it should have, but he stuck it through the hood.

"Going to give him a target, Rachel."

"Copy, I'm watching."

He paused for a moment as Elliot fired a couple of bursts; the Marine had moved to where he could threaten the nearer threat from the remaining guards on this side of the bridge.

He thrust the poncho up slowly and then moved it incrementally to the side, trying to mimic the profile of a man looking around the edge of a tree. The incoming round missed his elbow by a couple of inches and his head by not much more. The poncho hadn't fooled whoever was behind that gun, and the shooter clearly had some very good night vision. He pulled his arms in, out of reflex, as the booming echo reverberated back and forth across the shallow ravine.

It was followed by another shot; this one he knew had come from Rachel, given its source.

"Shooter is down," Rachel breathed into his ear. She fired again and then a third time a few seconds later. "Doesn't look like anybody wants to pick up the man's nice rifle."

He popped his head up and looked across the portion of the bridge he could see, which was only about halfway across. It wasn't good. There were three more of the enemy crossing on foot.

"Tangos on the bridge," he called out before lining up a shot and dropping one of the reinforcements.

"I don't have a shot," Rachel came back.

"Blow the first bridge." Ray's voice cut in.

"Ray, say again, confirm."

"Blow it!"

He dug for the detonator, flipped back the safety shield, and made certain it was set to channel A, which would trigger the detonator that Ray and Uwasi were supposed to have used for the first bridge. "Fire in the hole—cover."

The road surface of the bridge blocked the blast itself, but the flash of the cutting charges and the sharp series of cracks lit up the entire area for the briefest of seconds. He'd had his eyes mashed shut, but for a brief second, it seemed like daylight behind his lids. A creaking rumble of falling concrete started, followed by an earthshaking collision as the roadway of Highway 29 fell forty feet into the ravine below.

Jason was up on his feet and moving as the dust and smoke was still billowing up. The cloud had reached the road by the time he did. He moved quickly, tossed a flash-bang grenade behind the rocks where the guards had been hiding, and moved again. There were two unmoving forms and one who was on his knees, screaming with his hands over his ears. He serviced all three of them and then looked for cover for himself. There were still a lot of enemy guns across the ravine, and it wasn't the type of river canyon that would prevent anybody from walking down, across, and back up this side.

"On your six." Elliot's voice in his earbuds helped clear some of the deep tonal ringing leftover from the flash-bang.

"Rachel, what can you see across the river?"

"They are taking up positions on the roof of that motel. A few are behind vehicles in the parking lot. No movement across the second bridge."

"Ray—status."

"Second target wired; we are moving to safe distance. Three minutes."

He breathed a sigh of relief. "Signal when safe. Keep moving back to our vehicles. Rachel, you, too, move now. Elliot and I will bring up the rear."

Four minutes later, he pushed the button on the second bridge. They were in the woods, a quarter of a mile from the river, and moving quickly. The bright, momentary flash behind them almost had the feeling of flashing a middle finger at the enemy as they moved away.

*

"OK, the idiots are coming on." Salguero sounded excited. "Our infantry has dismounted and gone to ground above us on either side of the freeway. Does everybody see our two friendly blue force Bradleys?"

"Affirmative," Mason said, "I have them marked blue."

"Got them." Pro nodded to himself, with his eyes glued to his own thermal view screen. The M3s were maybe two hundred yards ahead of them. One in the median strip, the other in the borrow pit across the eastbound lanes.

"Where are you standing, Mr. Cruz?"

"My ass is kissing the wall of this thing."

"Outstanding, Cruz. What happens in the tank, stays in the tank . . ."

Pro hated having his world reduced down to a three-by-six-inch screen. But it beat sitting back at the base, "healing up," which had been his only other option.

"Remember, we have two Javelin teams out in front of us as well. Nobody shoots the good guys."

They sat silent, waiting. Pro could barely take it anymore. "Time for a question?"

"The judge's only option was the Marines or the Army," Salguero fired back instantly.

"You chose poorly," Cruz responded in kind.

"I had a choice; Army has to take what's left."

When the laughter died down, Pro inserted himself. "We're a tank. How come we're so far back?"

Mason spoke up. "If we were fighting the Russians, we wouldn't be. The Bradley's TOW missile range is twice or more what our gun has. They'd usually be scouting the edges or behind us. But these assclowns are bringing two Bradleys and a bunch of technicals against us. I think the colonel wants to make the point that we're here, and not even needed, but I'm guessing."

"Sounds right," Salguero agreed. "Hold on—" The tank's commander abruptly cut off, and once again, Pro was alone in his hole, reclining within the front armored glacis of the tank.

"OK, Javelin teams have them in sight, Bradleys leading the way, infantry riding school buses and trucks. A couple of JLTVs, Humvees, and technicals as well; we should see them soon. Javelin teams have the ball. Be ready . . ." Salguero's tone had lost all humor.

This sucked . . . Pro's view screen showed dick-all, besides the two friendly Bradleys ahead. *"Here, and not even needed";* Pro hated that more than anything. Reed was on one of those Javelin teams. He should be as well.

"I have the lead Bradley, sir, and what looks like a JLTV close behind at four thousand meters—still coming on." Lucas Hanson was seated next to him, buttoned up within the M3 Bradley, and manning the suite of sensors and targeting that controlled the TOW missile launcher mounted on the outside of the turret.

Hanson had been the one Marine Lieutenant Bruce had singled out to him as borderline indispensable; as such, the young Marine had either been out on patrol or off training Jason's folks for the last three weeks. It was the first chance he'd had to spend any real time with the Marine.

"Very good, let me know when they stop or get within twenty-five hundred meters."

"Stop or twenty-five hundred meters, aye, sir."

"What're we you going to do after OCS?"

John had told him that Farmer had been selected for Marine OCS just before the squad had begun their rotation in The Hole. He knew Lucas had joined the Marines as a grunt *after* college, which, in the days prior to the suck, made Farmer a unicorn of sorts.

"You'll laugh, sir."

He was about to give orders to kill fellow Americans, or fellow survivors who'd been countrymen. He could use a laugh. "Try me."

"I was thinking intel, sir. Maybe try to pick up a foreign language."

"I would have guessed flight school."

"The idea of being trapped in a cockpit? No, sir. Not my thing."

"Claustrophobic?"

"No, sir . . . Range to lead elements thirty-four hundred meters, still coming on."

"Copy—thirty-four hundred meters."

"It was the idea of being chased by an air-to-air missile and not being able to do a damned thing about it. Sort of wigged me out."

He could understand the sentiment, though it wasn't likely to be a concern for anyone, not for a very long time. Not unless there was a group of survivors somewhere in the world staffed with enough technical people to keep planes in the air, which was something he couldn't imagine.

"Javelin teams—Gypsy One. Target your nearest enemy Bradley. Wait for my word." The two hunter-killer teams were well off the highway to either side, closer to the target than he was, and would be targeting different enemy vehicles by virtue of their own locations. He was more concerned with getting these people some experience than he was with either Javelin team actually hitting their target.

"Our new people are more motivated than I'd feared."

"They are that, sir," Hanson agreed after a moment. "I heard some of their stories while we had them back at The Hole; most have had a real tough time. Slaves to whoever was running the place before Jason showed up."

"So I've gathered; I think they understand better than we do what Charlottesville is or could become."

"Sir, can I ask what our long-term plans are?"

"Salguero, Gypsy One—advise me when you have enemy heavy vehicles in effective range." He switched channels and called the Abrams, hull down behind them.

"Copy, Gypsy One. Will advise when they are in our box."

"Jason asked me the same thing, Lieutenant. Best I could do is some sort of federation of city-states, independent, but hopefully willing to come to each other's defense."

"That's why you haven't bracketed Charlottesville with artillery. You think we'll need that?"

He turned his face towards the young man, who was still glued to the padded viewfinder. "I hope not," he said. "But I've learned not to put too much faith in hoping. What's their range?"

"Just passing twenty-three hundred meters," Hanson replied. "More JLTVs and technicals visible behind the infantry transports. I can't believe they haven't seen us yet."

"Your first target is the Bradley in the westbound lane," he said after another glance at his own monitor. If the Javelins missed, that one would be closest.

"Target framed and locked."

"Gypsy One—Salguero; we are in range."

"Copy. Salguero—target enemy Bradley in eastbound lane. You are weapons free, heavy vehicles only, after Javelin strike."

"Copy all—Salguero out."

"You ready?"

"Ready, sir." Hanson was as calm as could be.

"Javelin teams, fire when ready."

Reed heard the colonel's voice over the radio. He didn't need the slap on the back from Sam Hirai, letting him know he was clear to fire. He'd fired three practice rounds at The Hole. The Javelin was a fire-and-forget weapon, and they'd be running the second the missile left the launch tube on his shoulder. None of the practice targets had been moving; this one was. It was also, he had to assume, full of people. He could see Sam in his peripheral vision. One thing that had been made very clear to them; you needed to make sure there wasn't anyone standing behind the launch tube.

The enemy Bradley, just short of a mile away, stood out clear as day in the infrared viewfinder. He locked the targeting reticle and fired. After a short delay, he was momentarily stunned by the explosive booster charge that pushed the missile from the tube. He opened his eyes too soon and was half-blinded when the missile's propellant ignited thirty feet in front of them. He watched as he followed the track of the missile. He was going to miss. It was far too high.

"Shit!"

"Come on!" Sam was pulling at his flak jacket.

"Wait." He pushed Sam off as he saw the missile arch over and begin its terminal dive. It slammed into the Bradley with a massive bloom of orange fire.

"Dude! Come on!" Sam pulled at him again. It was time to run. The Marines had called this technique "shoot and scoot," and when they'd trained for it, they had another missile waiting for them at their next position. They'd only packed the one missile in—it was time to just run.

Skirjanek watched the Bradley being taken out and had time to swivel his camera on the turret to the second Bradley. That missile missed its target, but plowed right through a pickup truck that had been following close behind.

"Switching targets," Hanson reported without being told.

"Engage when ready."

He watched as Lucas depressed the firing stud. There was a delay of a few seconds as the gyroscopes within the TOW missile spun up. Insulated as they were inside the Bradley, the actual launch sounded like a large gun going off outside the armor.

"Tracking . . . Tracking . . . That's a hit!"

He switched to the internal circuit of the Bradley. "Julie!" He kicked the internal metal wall that separated them from their driver. "Back us out of here, pull back." The Bradley's twenty-seven-ton frame jerked him in his seat even as heavy machine gun rounds could be heard slapping the hull.

"That's got to be fifty cal."

He activated the servos on the Bushmaster 25mm chain gun and selected low rate auto fire. He fired three quick bursts well above the muzzle flashes he could see in his viewfinder. He was just trying to keep their heads down as his driver backed them even farther out of range.

He spotted two JLTVs racing forward of the enemy column, the rest of which had stopped cold.

"Salguero, two JLTVs headed our way. Take them."

"I don't have a shot!" Mason yelled.

"Pro, forward! Drive it like a rental. Just keep an eye peeled for our Bradleys pulling back. Don't rear-end the colonel."

He'd never driven a rental; he didn't know what that meant. But given Salguero's tone, he gunned the engine and released the brake. The Abrams went nose up as it climbed back onto the roadway surface. He made the turn out and straightened their path. Even he could see the two vehicles coming down the freeway at them, one in each lane.

"Full stop!" Salguero yelled.

He slammed on the brakes and could tell from how the tank slid to a stop that he'd just chewed up a section of the freeway with the tank treads.

"Gun ready!"

"Fire!"

Pro's whole world recoiled. He could feel the shock of the cannon firing in his bones. The 120mm cannon fired a narrow bolt of depleted uranium enwrapped in a sleeve of some sort that Salguero had called a sabot. The sabot was supposed to keep the arrow straight inside the barrel and flew away after leaving the muzzle. At over five thousand feet a second, the tank round was converted into superheated plasma as it met the target's armor. The cannon and the penetrator it fired had been designed to kill other tanks.

In this case, it passed clean through the engine block and firewall of the lightly armored truck, killing everyone inside in a spray of expanding shrapnel. Most of the penetrator was still intact as it shot out the back of the JLTV and plowed into a hillside, three hundred yards behind the burning fireball that had been the JLTV.

"Holy shit . . ." Pro mumbled to himself. He couldn't believe how fast that had happened.

"Load!" Salguero yelled.

"Target second JLTV!"

"I got him!" Mason yelled.

"Gun ready!" Cruz yelled a few seconds later.

"Fire!"

This round was a little high; it went in through the windshield and must have hit something solid inside, as the fireball shot out the back of the vehicle.

"Pro! Straight at them, no hurry, they're running!"

He put the tank in motion. He could see the mass of vehicles and buses down the freeway turning around and heading back the way the way they'd come. One of the buses had a large group of people running after it, trying to catch up.

Skirjanek's command Bradley rolled forward until it reached its original firing position. He popped his hatch, and took a deep breath of cooler air, even if the night was humid, and watched the enemy move back as fast as their legs or vehicles would carry them.

"Not used to somebody else being the hammer," Lucas shouted up at him from inside. He crawled the rest of the way out, and dropped his headset back down into the vehicle.

"Tell Julie to pop her hatch. You two get some fresh air."

"Yes, sir."

He pulled the radio from his webbing as he watched the fleeing enemy, if indeed that's what they were.

"John, Pavel—Gypsy Actual. They are headed back your way in a hurry. Deploy psyops material at the roadblock. Avoid all contact."

Chapter 21

"How the hell did this happen?" Lisa's head was in her hands. She sat on the other side of the room from him. The physical distance separating them was another message that he would have had to have been an idiot to miss. Whatever personal relationship they'd had, it was over.

Marks was done trying to sugarcoat events for her, especially after last night's activity that could be laid directly at her feet. "We attacked their people without cause, under a white flag—we've been expecting a response. Given their apparent resources, I'm surprised they waited this long."

Her hands dropped away from her face as she took on a confused look. "Under a white flag? Are you fucking kidding me? This isn't the sixteenth century, and we aren't playing by the Marquis de Queensberry rules."

He kept his calm. Lisa could get angry, and often did, but it would pass and she'd come out of it as if the ensuing conversation never happened. The few people who he'd witnessed get angry with her were notably absent. They hadn't been demoted; they didn't fall out of favor - they were quietly fertilizing the 14th hole's fairway. "That is now for certain," he answered. "But we could have been, and we may come to wish we were."

"You want me to say it?" she screeched. "Fine, I made a mistake. I fucked up. I thought with the size of our army, you could have handled them. I got that wrong as well."

One way or another, their fates were tied; he was still of that mind, even if he was beginning to wonder if Lisa still felt the same way. "You weren't wrong." He managed to give her that concession. "Other than in making the same mistake I did in assuming that they were no different than everyone else we've come across."

She stood up, smoothed her dress down, and walked slowly to the window. "Tell me, then, how are they different? I mean besides the fact that they have fucking missiles."

"They are well led." There was no point denying that either in his own mind or to her. "And their initial reaching out to us was probably genuine. Part of me hopes that may still be on the table."

"How can you say that?" She spun back to her desk and held up one of the flyers that had been strewn all over the eastern roadblock and discovered by the militia as they were retreating. "They're calling for our heads. Mine and yours!"

"Lisa, if they'd wanted to, they could have killed hundreds last night out on the freeway. They didn't pursue; they didn't fire on the infantry. I think there's a message in that, as well as the one you're holding."

Her militia jackboots had collected every flyer they'd found and rounded up anyone who talked about them. Even he had to admit, her militia had been damned effective in their efforts. The flyer's message had been simple and straightforward; "We are not at war with Charlottesville, only your leadership." As part of that leadership, he was thankful for the militia's efforts, but the rumors and whispers would be impossible to stamp out completely.

"You're not suggesting we turn ourselves in to them? They have no authority here. I . . . we built this."

"Hell no." He shook his head. "My takeaway is that they don't have the numbers to take us on. Some very effective ordinance, yes, but not the numbers to defeat us. Otherwise, they wouldn't be trying this psyops bullshit."

"What *do* you suggest, then?"

"Let them think it worked." He nodded. "We've come to our senses. Ask for a meeting."

"You think they'd be foolish enough to buy that?"

"Not a chance, but we play for the time needed to locate them, and then we throw everything at them. Their anti–tank weapons aren't going to stop three thousand infantry. It'll be ugly, and you need to know that going in. We will lose . . . a lot of people. But I'm convinced it's people they don't have."

"I've got another option," she said smugly. "But you need to find them."

"The virus?"

She hid her surprise well. "You knew?"

"No, not until this second," he admitted. "Your boy Josh and some of his team have been spending a lot of time at the hospital. I put two and two together."

"You're OK with the concept?"

The idea sickened him, but whatever principles he had left had been permanently and justifiably bent by the apocalypse. "I don't like it; any more than I imagine you do. I do think it's cleaner than losing half of our people trying to fight them." Besides, he, Lisa, and all their people had been winnowed by the virus. They had lost everyone close to them, lived through the hell of the die-off. Why should a group of people that had managed to avoid all that be allowed to dictate anything on moral grounds to them?

Lisa nodded at him agreement. "Josh is not my. . . anything, Steven. But I do trust him. You said you did too."

*

"You really don't want to be in here with me."

"Dr. Vance . . . Naomi," Josh corrected himself before she could do it for him. "You know I have to be."

"I get it." She zipped up her orange biohazard lab suit as far as she could and then spun slowly in place to allow him to finish the process. "Not like I don't mind the company." Her voice was suddenly modulated by the flexible bag helmet and its oversize rigid face screen.

"But I can't imagine this as anybody's idea of a third date."

He had to laugh at that. He'd initially taken Dr. Vance as the typical stuck-up, overly privileged type he'd learned to despise having grown up in a college town. Two days of working together had disabused him of that. He'd discovered that they'd almost known each other in the old world. They'd gone to the same junior high and high school here in Charlottesville. Naomi had been a senior when he was a freshman at Charlottesville High, and they hadn't known each other, and even if they'd been the same age; she had been in the chess and science clubs while he'd played baseball.

He had actually known her father; Mr. Vance had been the head maintenance guy/janitor at the junior high they'd both attended. Which had blown his silver-spoon preconception of her out of the water. Two days of navigating the previously sealed and abandoned virology lab in the basement of UVA's medical center, in these claustrophobic moon suits, engendered a certain level of trust in who you were working with. Given the fact he didn't have a clue what he was doing, he had no option but to trust the woman. As he finished zipping up her suit and checking the seals, he realized that she was trusting him as well.

"I have to admit, Doc. For an orange balloon with a face mask, you look good."

"Are you flirting with me before we begin to look for live cultures of a virus that killed everyone we knew?"

"But we're safe? Right?"

She turned to look at him. The plexiglass face shield distorted her face a little bit at the curves, but he was again struck by her girl-next-door attractiveness. "We're immune from the CBR-2a, which mutated from the 1d variety; at least that's the best I can come up with from the notes we've found. I'm a baby doctor, Josh. Remember? I'm relying on what I recall from a virology class I took nine years ago."

He gave a nod. She'd been nothing but honest about how this wasn't close to her field of expertise or study. "I also remember you telling Cooper that it could mutate again."

He could see her nodding inside her helmet as he zipped up his own suit as far as he could.

"That's right. Viruses use RNA to reproduce, not DNA. If I remember correctly, it's hardier than DNA and capable of mutating more readily. Viruses have been around a lot longer than we have."

He turned away from Naomi and pulled on his helmet, allowing her to zip him up the rest of the way. "Kind of makes you wonder whether this is something we should be screwing with at all, don't it?" He couldn't see the reaction on her face as she continued the seal check on the back of his neck without comment. After what he had heard went down on the freeway two nights earlier, he'd given a lot of thought to what these military guys had said on the flyers they'd left behind.

She gave his shoulder a squeeze. "You're good."

He let his unanswered question go as he turned back around. She was smiling at him. "You ready?"

The cold room was inside what Naomi had told him was called the "hot lab." The lab was accessed via an anteroom or air lock through a simple heavy steel door with rubber gaskets. He'd been through the process twice now and knew what to expect. They waited for the red light above the heavier inner door to turn green, signifying that the air pressure in the anteroom was significantly higher than in the lab.

At the green light, he pushed the door open with a hard shove, breaking the seal. Even in the moon suit, he could feel the air flow behind almost pushing them into the lab. He waited for Naomi to step across the threshold and then shut and sealed the door behind them. The first day, when they'd come just to access files and laptops, he'd asked why they were wearing moon suits if they were immune. The answer had frightened him to the core. The virus they were after was far from the only one in cold storage within. Even if the suck hadn't mutated, if the cold storage had remained cool enough, there was other nasty shit in there that he'd just as soon avoid.

On the first day, Naomi's research had found a catalog of the viruses warehoused within the cold storage. None of the strange-sounding names made him feel better, and the ones he did recognize—SARS, bird flu, West Nile—were just icing on the cake. He could remember thinking that shit like that shouldn't ever be stored, anywhere, anytime, but who was he to say what the eggheads had needed to try to find a cure?

Yesterday, Naomi's efforts had confirmed the presence of CBR-2a in cold storage. Today, they'd be going into the actual cold vault to check the temperature logs, and see how warm the place had gotten during the short period of time the hospital's power had been down.

"There it is. Hope you remembered to wear your long johns." The doctor was pointing and moving towards another heavy, polished stainless-steel door at the back of the room. The bright yellow biological hazard stickers on the door shouldn't have given him pause at this point, but they did.

"Everything's sealed up? Right?"

She turned to face him, and thumbed the sleeve of her moon suit. "Won't know until we get in there, but I would think so. The suits will protect us." She paused a moment, and waved toward the door. "You really don't have to go in there with me . . ."

But he did. "Don't let that halo-wearing doctor out of your sight." Those had been his orders directly from Lisa Cooper. "Watch her like a hawk and ask questions so you know what she is doing at every step."

He shook his head, comically aware that the head of his oversize helmet didn't move at all. "Yeah . . . I do."

The door didn't want to open at first, but with a heavy push, it popped open, and they stepped in to the sound of rushing air following behind them. Once the door was shut and he found the light switch, Dr. Vance looked around slowly at the wire-framed shelving running down both sides of the freezer.

"Shit . . ." he heard her whisper.

He almost jumped in panic. "What?"

"There's a box of dry ice here, still solid."

"And that means . . .?" Christ, dry ice was stuff he used to see in kids' drinks at the fairgrounds.

"Means it stayed really cold in here. It would have evaporated otherwise."

"But that's a good thing, right?"

She was moving slowly down the wall, looking at the stainless-steel thermos-like containers and their labels. Once again, she ignored his question until she came to a stop and pulled a container off the shelf. She held it out in front of her.

"This virus in this container killed seven billion people, Josh. It's not a good thing."

"Not what I meant, Doc."

"Josh, I know what you meant. I'd been hoping for a room full of spoiled samples."

"Yeah . . . I guess I was too." He was surprised at his own admission.

"Where's that leave us?"

"What do you mean?"

"You know exactly what I mean." She squared her shoulders up a little and just stared at him.

He knew Dr. Vance was good people. Her heart was in the right place. As for lying to Cooper, there was no way the woman would believe anything but success. She knew the power had only been off for a short period of time, and he'd already reported that the files indicated the presence of the virus.

"There's no excuse you can think up, that Cooper will believe," he said. He flopped his arms out to his sides. "I've kept her informed of the records we found."

"I know you have. You're going to have to do what you think is right. But if she thinks I'm going to build her a biological weapon, the bitch is crazier than I thought she was, and that's saying something." Naomi held the bottle out in front of her.

"It's not that simple, Doc."

"It's exactly that simple."

He took a step towards Naomi.

"Whatever you're going to do to me, Josh, just be careful. You definitely don't want to rip your suit in here."

He almost laughed. It was a snapshot of the young Virginia girl he'd imagined her as. She thought he was going to hurt her, and she was concerned about his moon suit.

"Don't think I'm not serious . . . Cooper knows there's virus to work with."

"I understand," she said.

"Well?" Lisa got up, came around her desk, and sat back against the front edge. Josh was hyperaware of how close she was to him. The woman oozed sex appeal when she wanted to. A promise of things unspoken; he'd seen it before, in the early days of Charlottesville. He'd watched General Marks fall prey to it. He couldn't fault the guy; there was no way he would have turned her down if the casual flirting had gone further. For a short moment, he wondered how far he could push it. He stopped himself; if it was going to happen, it already would have. He needed to be the guy she could trust.

"It's a process," he answered. "I think Dr. Vance is relearning a lot of stuff along the way."

"Like what?"

"I mean, she's fond of pointing out that she's a baby doctor and had never been involved in this kind of stuff. But as far as I can tell, she's working the problem. She said she'll know more in ten days to two weeks."

"Why so long?"

"That part I actually understand, sort of. We used to do a lot of craft beers in my place; it's not just an issue of the right ingredients. In the case of beer, yeast only works so fast. She has to cultivate enough of the virus to be able to test it, and then attenuate it—and I have no idea what that means yet, but I'm learning." He used the words Naomi had provided for him. He'd even practiced them in the shower.

"She had some real concerns about the virus mutating again . . ."

"Oh, she still does," he admitted with a strong nod. "Listening to her, the more I learn, at this point—so do I. I've reinforced the issue of how many of our lives this is going to save. Believe me, it's the only reason she's doing it."

"It's the best argument for it," Lisa agreed. "If there were another way, rest assured we'd be doing it."

"Well, we're the guinea pigs and going into lockdown tomorrow. So, I'll have to report by radio from here on out."

"What!"

"The only way to be sure we aren't producing a virus that has mutated into something that will kill us, is to work with the live virus. She's the only one who can do that. At this point, I'm the only one who understands what she's doing well enough to mind her."

"Christ, she's the only doctor we have! Can't she use somebody from the stadium as a guinea pig?"

Thank you for your heartfelt concern for my sorry ass! "We can't live in the moon suits for the next two weeks. Dr. Vance says the chance for a mutation isn't negligible, but the odds of any variation happening in a direction that would be harmful to us is remote."

"She'd better be right." Lisa shook her head and then looked back down at him, seeming to see him once again. "My God, for your sake too."

Nice recovery. Naomi was right; the woman was a sociopath. Like most guys, he'd been taken in by the package and spent too much time staring at her tits to notice.

Cooper moved back around her desk quickly, as if she'd suddenly realized that he might already be carrying something. "You be sure to stay in constant contact, and if there is anything you need, just ask. We don't have a higher priority right now."

He stood up to leave and before turning back; "on that note, we have to keep the hospital's backup generator running. I heard that one of the diesel tanks was destroyed the night of their attack. We good on that score? There's zero chance of this working without some of that equipment."

He could tell Cooper didn't like the question. "The highway to the west is still open. We're bringing in some tankers from a depot off I-81. Stay on the radio, and keep me updated."

*

Chapter 22

Farmer put down the radio. "That was Poy. He's got the convoy turning onto 64 at Staunton and headed this way. Twelve miles, figure fifteen minutes or less."

Jason looked at the team he'd brought with him. All the Marines, minus Jon Bruce. Pavel was dragging the last of the Jersey barriers into place with one of the JLTVs and a heavy chain. Reed and half a dozen of his team rounded out the fourteen people he had with him. The barrier only had to be enough to stop the fuel convoy, or at a minimum slow it down to the point they could safely target it. He didn't like the idea of shooting at tanker trucks full of diesel any more than he imagined those riding in the enemy convoy were going to like it. Skirjanek had left I-64, west of the town, available to the enemy in the hopes they'd try to use it, and they had.

It had taken Charlottesville four days since the fight on the freeway to risk a fuel run. Skirjanek's scouts had watched the convoy pull out and head west the day before. The drone had tracked them to a fuel depot south of Staunton off I-81. The colonel had marked the location of the depot for later use, and Jason and his team had spent the previous night navigating back roads south of I-64 to bypass Charlottesville and set up this ambush for the convoy's return trip. The highway here was raised over the rural interchange and surface roads; the trucks wouldn't be able to go off-road.

"Where do you want us?" Rachel asked. Pro was standing next to her, balancing her rifle off his good shoulder. He pointed east at the overpass where the Blue Ridge Parkway crossed the interstate.

"Up there, but over the westbound lanes, not this one. There's some cover there."

Rachel nodded at them both and jerked her chin at Pro. "You heard him, let's go."

Pro had begged to be allowed to accompany the ambush team, but he was still unhappy that his role was going to be limited to spotting for Rachel.

"Might as well be a mule," Pro complained as he turned and started walking. Rachel rolled her eyes. "A mule would complain less," she whispered.

"I can hear you," Pro shouted back over his shoulder.

Rachel looked at him and shook her head. "Be careful?"

"Always."

He watched her walk away, glad that the two of them would be far enough from the makeshift roadblock to be safe should the bad guys do something stupid. If they were stupid, Rachel would be doing more than watching.

"The kid's a handful." Farmer laughed to himself.

Jason shook his head. Pro wasn't sixteen years old yet, and the teenager had already been shot twice, concussed, kidnapped, made a slave, and hunted. He worried that Pro was enjoying his own legend a little too much, to the point the kid felt he needed to feed it. "You have no idea."

"You going to let him join the Marines?"

Jason smiled back at Farmer. Skirjanek and Bruce were already well into the planning stages of a volunteer force among their own people and any of the Tysons crowd who wanted to join what they hoped would be a real fighting force, beyond the rough collection of civilians they had now. The colonel had already fleshed out the plans for setting up a very basic boot camp where the volunteers could learn how to be proper soldiers or Marines as the training cadre was almost entirely

Marine. It was a good plan, and one that was going to have to wait until they had some breathing room, but they had already filled the first class of forty. Pro's name had been the first one on the list.

"He informed me that I didn't have a choice." Jason laughed to himself. "He had a whole prepared speech about how he should be considered a legal adult and I didn't actually have any authority to stop him. I think I confused him when I told him I thought it was a wonderful idea."

"We'll see what he thinks after a week under Gunny, I mean Captain Bruce."

He glanced back up the road to watch what family he had remaining, walk away.

"I assume Rachel told you I asked her if she'd join me for a drink when we were at The Hole? I had no idea you two . . ."

"Farmer."

"I mean, if I had, I wouldn't have."

"Relax." He swatted the Marine on the shoulder. "She told me; and if she'd been offended, which she wasn't, you'd have known it right then and there."

"I don't doubt it." Farmer smiled to himself. "I just didn't want there to be anything hanging out there between us."

"Lucas." He pulled his eyes back in from looking down the highway in the direction the convoy would approach from. "There isn't, forget about it."

Farmer held up both hands in surrender. "Done."

"OK, get on the radio and confirm with Poy that it's still just the two tankers and two escort vehicles. Who knows how many people they already had out and about before we shut them down?"

He watched Lucas out of the corner of his eye; the young Marine was solid. Lucas fit anyone's definition of a "good guy," and he was only a year or two older than Rachel. He liked Lucas enough to almost feel guilty. He was nearly the old man he felt like some mornings, and he still talked to ghosts in his dreams. He'd said as much to Rachel a couple of nights past, leaving out the ghosts. He'd been shocked at her anger. It shouldn't have come as a surprise; the apocalypse hadn't improved his understanding of women one iota.

"Same two Humvees, lead and follow," Farmer relayed back to him.

Both of the escort Humvees had M240 machine guns on roof mounts. If the assclowns crewing the guns got cocky, this could get messy. That was his big worry. It would be easier to hit the convoy hard, but they had all bought into Skirjanek's long game of trying to win hearts and minds, and that meant trying to kill as few of these people as they could. They all assumed the tankers were transporting diesel for the generators supplementing the massive solar farm that Charlottesville had constructed; if they were wrong, and the tankers were carrying gasoline, the degree of difficulty went way up.

"Alright, get everyone in position." He picked up his own radio. "Reed, your team ready?"

"Reed here, we're ready."

"Copy, remember, don't let them see you until we've stopped them."

"Copy."

It was almost ten minutes later when Reed radioed back. "They just passed our position, two tankers, one Hummer leading, the other following. Pulling out in two minutes."

The freeway between Reed's initial position and their roadblock crawled up the western slope of the Blue Ridge Mountains, though from his perspective, having grown up out west, these were just hills. Beautiful, heavily forested, and standing out above the plains on either side, but hills just the same. Given the steady grade the trucks would be pulling against, he didn't figure they'd be moving that fast.

They heard the tractor trailers downshifting before the first Humvee appeared, coming around the curve. Whoever was driving the lead vehicle acted quicker than he would have liked. Having seen the Jersey barriers, someone in that lead vehicle had to have been on the radio immediately. The air was split by the sound of air brakes and squealing tires as the second tanker truck appeared already slowing. The follow vehicle came around the corner a second later and didn't slow, as it swung around the two trucks and joined the lead vehicle. Its own brakes locked up, and it came to a skidding stop next to its twin. Both machine guns on the roof mount were manned and swiveling, looking for a target.

"Not my idea of an ambush," he complained as he reached for the battery-powered bullhorn at his feet. It would have been a lot safer to just fire them up. He faced Farmer; "tell Reed's vehicle to move up close enough that they can get a lock on one of the Humvees." He pointed at Uwasi and Elliot, who were each holding a LAW rocket. "You guys target them as well."

He thumbed his radio. "Pro, have Rachel mark the shooters, hold fire unless they shoot."

"Copy, Pro out."

They were hidden in the trees south of the interstate, about a hundred yards from where the convoy had stopped. Uwasi and Elliot were already moving out, trying to get closer to get a better shot with the short-legged LAW.

He put the bullhorn up and aimed it down the freeway. "You are surrounded! All vehicles have been targeted by stand-off weapons. We don't want to hurt anyone. If you stand down, you will be released and can return to Charlottesville. The tankers are going to stay right where they are."

He looked at Farmer. "Reed?"

"He's moving up, not there yet."

"Flash your headlights if you have heard me, otherwise I will open fire."

The driver of the nearest tanker truck flashed its headlights. He could only assume whoever was leading the convoy in the Humvees had heard him as well; they were even closer. He waited another ten seconds and repeated the warning.

Farmer was slapping his leg. "Reed's got a lock on the lead vehicle, the one in the fast lane."

"Thirty seconds until we fire. Un-ass your vehicles and walk forward! Leave your weapons. You will not be harmed."

Nothing happened, but he could see the two figures in the cab of the closest of the lead vehicles, and they appeared to be arguing.

Come on, guys, don't make me do this. "Twenty seconds!"

Farmer slapped his leg again. "Reed says the two truck drivers are out of their vehicles and moving forward."

He couldn't see anyone on foot yet, but someone in one of the escort vehicles had seen the truck drivers approaching. The passenger door opened, and whoever stepped out began yelling at the unseen truck drivers to get back to their trucks.

"Ten seconds!" he yelled. "You have ten seconds to get out and lay your weapons down, or Javelin missiles are going to light up each and every one of you. If they don't kill you, the fireball from the tankers will. Get out! Five seconds."

He should have opened with the threat of burning to death. The doors to the two Humvees popped open. One machine gunner dropped down inside to exit that way; the other crawled farther up and out and hopped down off the back of the vehicle. The man who had been screaming at the truck drivers lifted the barrel of his weapon and pointed it at his colleagues, yelling at them to pick up their dropped weapons.

The man fired once at the road. Jason cringed, half expecting either Rachel or one of the Marines to open up.

He hefted the bullhorn. "You have three seconds to drop your weapon."

The man panicked and spun in the direction of his voice and loosed a salvo of automatic fire that smacked and whined off the roadway, fifteen yards from his position.

Shit . . . "Rachel, take him."

The report from Rachel's .338 Lapua overrode and put a bookend on the bouncing echoes from the M4. He risked a look up and over the rock he hid behind. The rest of the enemy had their hands over their heads and were looking down at the body of their former leader.

He pushed his radio. "Reed, move up slowly. Everyone else, break cover and move in. Hold fire unless fired on. Sniper team hold."

"You're really going to let us go?" Whoever Rachel had killed had been the leader of the convoy, that much was clear. One of the truck drivers was speaking for the rest of them.

He just nodded in reply and looked to where Farmer was patching up one of the men from the escort vehicles who had been hit by the ricochet from the dead guy's warning shot. The bullet had popped off the road and clipped the guy in the ass. The man hadn't even realized he'd been hit until the shock wore off. By the time his guys had closed in, he'd been on the ground and screaming.

"He going to be alright?"

Farmer nodded back at him. "Creased him, he'll be fine."

He turned back to the gathered crowd of prisoners and addressed the truck driver who had spoken. "We're going to let you go, just like I said. Your vehicles are staying here though."

"You're going to make us walk?" One of the younger men didn't sound too happy at that prospect.

The convoy's new leader looked like he wanted to take a swing at the man who had spoken up. "Thompson—shut it."

"We'll transport you as far as Yancey Mills, and drop you off. That'll leave you with about twelve miles to walk. I'd do more if I could," he explained. "Under the circumstances, you'll understand that we don't want to get any closer to Charlottesville, unless it's for our own reasons."

"I get it." The truck driver nodded. "It's much appreciated."

"We aren't at war with you people, just your leadership."

"And anybody who sides with them," Reed added. "Charlottesville isn't going to control anything but Charlottesville. If people want to leave and return from wherever you were taken from, they'll be allowed to do so."

The truck driver just looked back and forth between him and Reed. "What's that mean?"

"In short, turn over your leaders to us, and Charlottesville gets new leadership decided by you all." Jason flashed Reed a smile. "As my friend said, we aren't looking to be warlords, but we aren't going to allow anyone else to be either."

The one the driver had called Thompson spoke up. "Who are you guys? If you think Miss Cooper is going to lie down for you people, you're crazy."

The truck driver stared down Thompson but then looked back at him. "He ain't wrong, they'll fight."

Lucas walked over, stuffing his first-aid kit back into his bag. "Fine by us; it gets really boring running roadblocks like this. But how many of you people are we going to have to kill just so this Miss Cooper can be in charge?"

Jason took a step towards Thompson and stared at him until the man nervously looked away. "That's really the only issue here." He tried to make eye contact with each and every one of their erstwhile enemy before stepping back and pointing at one of their Humvees. Salguero was just finishing up dismounting the M240 machine gun.

"It'll be a tight squeeze, but you'll all fit." He pointed at the truck driver. "You're driving. Stay in between our vehicles, or we'll turn you into Swiss cheese. OK?"

"Yeah. . . I can do that."

Northern Virginia

Carla had come to a decision. She wasn't going to sit here as a prisoner waiting for these fools to find the courage to kill her; not without trying to strike a blow. On that score, she figured it was only a matter of time. She was a threat to them. Not anything like what her people would do to them, but a threat nonetheless. It was past time for her to start acting like it.

In the excitement and activity of moving their settlement, things had gotten hectic outside the doors of her hotel room prison cell in Tysons. She'd had a view of the parking lot below the mall and had watched for nearly two weeks as these people loaded up all they had collected and moved. It was an endless cycle of material being piled up outside on the parking deck, until it was loaded up in anything with wheels and disappeared out of her line of sight. She'd timed how long it took some of the pickup trucks, which she assumed could be unloaded at their destination quickly, to return for another load. Wherever their new home was, it wasn't far.

She couldn't help but be impressed with the volume of gear they had collected, nor could she deny the pride she felt in knowing she was, in large part, the reason they were running away. Her own people might have lost the advantage of surprise with this settlement, but in the end, it wouldn't matter. The people she watched out the window, her grips who kept her fed, had every right to be scared. These people's wariness and a new address wouldn't save them. That was enough for her to hold onto, enough to keep her going.

She'd been a little concerned when some of their looters returned with a convoy that included some military equipment. But the armored trucks and two APCs had moved out within a few days of arriving as the crowd around Tysons first thinned, and then disappeared. Her minders thinned out too. What had been someone bringing in a tray of food, watched over by an armed guard while another stood in the doorway, became just a guard in the hallway.

The day they'd actually transferred her, the double guard had been back, but the woman who'd been sent in to collect her tray from the night before was new and hadn't noted the missing butter knife. The knife, hidden in her sock, and the small duffle bag of clothes she'd been allowed had made it with her to her new cell. Wherever "here" was; they'd put a hood over her head during the transfer and driven around for a lot longer than necessary to try and confuse her.

The new cell was a serious downgrade from a room in the Ritz.

Whatever type of building she was in; the room had a concrete floor and a heavy-gauge steel door. It looked like a storage room of some sort that had been cleaned out to make room for the fold-up cot and a single chair to sit on. Bathroom trips were guarded affairs down an austere hallway, with no view of the outside world. It was a miserable existence, or would have been had she any intention of remaining a prisoner.

Within a week, the cheap butter knife was ground down and honed to the sharpest double-edged stiletto she and the concrete floor were capable of. By the end of the second week, she knew the schedule of her guards as well as they did. The minders bringing her food and water varied widely, but were almost always women. A few were roughly her build. The armed guards, of whom she had so far counted four different individuals, always remained outside the door. There seemed to be three men and one woman in that rotation.

She had a plan, but she needed the female guard to be on duty to have any chance of overpowering her—and she needed that to happen when the heavy-boned, short- statured woman, who was a mirror for her own build, brought her meal. The right combination had happened once already, but the guard in the hall had been talking to another unseen individual at the time. Bad luck; but she knew the schedule and only had to be patient.

Michelle walked into the town house that she and Daniel had claimed for themselves. It was just down the road from the resort and retirement home that many of their people had chosen to live in. Others had opted for a new subdivision of single-family homes on the far side of the resort. The town houses were nice and had filled up quick. Daniel had put a hold claim down on the end unit for Rachel and Jason. Michelle was smiling to herself in the entry hallway.

"Must have been a good day," Daniel teased her. "You haven't yelled yet."

She smiled back at him, and held an accusatory finger out in his direction. "I just had to listen to Marli and that worthless layabout she's shacked up with complain that their unit's refrigerator hasn't been wired up to the grid yet."

"And yet you're smiling . . . You didn't hurt them, did you?"

"No, as a matter of fact, Hoyt stepped in. He explained his people are wiring the houses as fast as they can, but priority is being given to those who have been working, and not, as he put it, sitting at home reading back issues of *Home and Garden* and working on their tan."

Daniel could only laugh. Most of their people took pride in how hard they were all working to make a new home. A very small minority were close to getting an attitude adjustment. "Well, all right . . . See? All you have to do is delegate."

Michelle walked towards him with her arms out, asking for a hug.

"Daniel, this might actually work," she mumbled against his shoulder as he wrapped his arms around her.

"Things are coming together," he agreed. They just needed the time, as Colonel Skirjanek had pointed out, "to dig in and sink some roots."

"Did you ever think we could really make a go of it?" Michelle pulled her head back and looked at him.

"We still talking about our little community here? Or . . .?"

"No, I mean yes." Michelle smiled and patted his chest. "You, I take for granted. For the bigger picture, I think I've just been waiting for the other shoe to drop."

"I know you have," he said. "You know I've been there. I thought I was going to lose you to it. You have to believe in what we're trying to do, Michelle. It's the only way I managed to pull myself back. Without hope, we aren't really living. If we give in, and just accept our lot without pushing back? I'm not sure what that makes us, but I know I didn't like the way it made me feel."

"It's all so fragile," she whispered.

Daniel tightened his hug. "I think it always has been, the old world just lulled us into believing that we were somehow invincible. We're awake now."

Michelle squeezed him tight. "Yes, we are."

"You hungry?" He pulled back. "One of the Russian ladies next door made some *pelmeni* and invited us over."

"I saw the crowd coming in. What's *pelmeni?*"

He shrugged. "Something that didn't start in a can."

They were coming down the front steps and waving at the dinner crowd who were across the narrow street with red solo cups in hand, when both their radios exploded in a jumble of excited voices talking over each other and washing each other out. Michelle stopped and pulled hers off her belt. She'd heard one word that sent a chill down her neck—Carla.

She looked up at Daniel as she pushed the talk button, confused by the strange expression on his face. His hand shot out, punching her in the shoulder before stepping in and knocking her aside. The blast of a gun split the air as she was falling. She slammed into the bricked sidewalk on her side, and caught a glimpse of Daniel struggling with someone on the ground as she rolled.

She'd made it to one knee and was moving to help when another shot went off. She froze in horror as a fountain of blood erupted out of the middle of Daniel's back, and the reality of what she was seeing hit home. Daniel's flailing stopped, and she could only watch as Carla's face appeared from under his shoulder as the woman fought to lever his weight off.

She saw the gun Carla struggled to pull free from where Daniel had trapped it against her body. The woman's face was a mask of rage, and she was screaming something that she couldn't hear. Michelle was staring at those empty eyes when several gunshots rang out. She didn't even flinch when Carla's gun fired; she watched, detached, as a round sparked off the pavement next to Carla's shoulder, followed by two more shots that turned the woman's head inside out. She could only stare until she was aware of hands pulling her away. Daniel's dead face and the pool of blood spreading out beneath him was all she could see as a waterfall of white noise drowned out everything. Her lags failed and strong hands caught her.

*

"Tell me what you need, it's yours." Skirjanek looked back at him with an empty mess-kit cup held against his chest. Jason's still had half a finger of whiskey in his. Gene and several others from Gabe's security team had shown up a couple of hours ago, having driven down from Northern Virginia with the news that Daniel had been killed and Michelle seriously wounded by Carla.

Gene, whom Jason still thought of as "Miami," had reported that Carla had somehow killed the woman who had brought her evening meal and then overpowered her guard. Wearing the clothes of her first victim, the crazy bitch had the run of the place for an hour before her escape had been discovered. The only thing that made sense to them was that Carla must have spotted Michelle and followed her back to the home she shared with Daniel.

"I know he was a friend."

Jason just nodded and slammed back the whiskey. "Drew . . . thank you. I think right now, I have to get Rachel and Pro back up there to say goodbye. Especially Pro; Daniel was the first decent person the kid came across after the suck."

Skirjanek flashed him a look of confusion. "I thought I'd heard you'd come across Pro first."

Jason remembered that night when he'd "met" Pro, when he'd gotten the kid captured. "I had."

Drew poured him another finger of whiskey. "You can't blame yourself for not being there."

"I don't. I blame myself for not putting a bullet behind the woman's ear the moment we knew who she was. She was that poisonous."

"We're going to see more of that shortly."

"We will," he agreed. He swirled the whiskey in his cup and looked back at the man he'd decided to follow. "Please tell me you aren't going to give this Cooper character a soapbox, put her on trial, detain her . . . what have you."

Drew shook his head with a sad smile. "Not in the cards. If I could, she'd be dead already. With luck, we'll get her own people to do that for us."

That wasn't going to happen any more than the sheep had risen up against Sheriff Bauman. People were just too damned scared. They were fed, housed, and had a modicum of safety in a world so ugly the air still tasted dead.

"You and I have a very different relationship with luck."

"Go say your goodbyes, Jason. Take one of the JLTVs, and be careful. Your man who brought the news down reported taking fire just outside of Gainesville. When we settle our present issue, I think these nuisance-level road gangs either need to be brought into the fold or pushed elsewhere."

Jason stood slowly. "The to-do list never gets any smaller, does it?" It would be dawn soon. He could afford to let Rachel and Pro sleep before he'd share the sad news.

Skirjanek stood and held out his hand. "I have to believe, at some point, it will."

Chapter 23

The graveside service was delayed for three days, waiting for Michelle to heal up enough that she could attend. Carla's last act had been to get one round off at the woman she'd been trying to kill. She'd almost succeeded. Hit in the leg, Michelle's femoral artery had been nicked. If it hadn't been for the gathered crowd of Navy personnel as well as a quick-thinking Russian physician's assistant on the scene, they'd be burying two people.

Jason knew Michelle, in a wheelchair with her right leg extended straight out in front of her in an inflatable cast, felt anything but lucky. The Navy personnel and a few of the Russians had assumed the security duties out at the newly constructed observation posts ringing the Potomac settlement, so that everyone from the Tysons contingent could attend. By now, all of them knew the role Daniel had played in freeing them from the hell that had been Tysons under Sheriff Bauman.

Jason was listening to Reed's words. The former Navy Seabee probably would have been studying to become a Navy chaplain by now if the world hadn't died. He was the closest thing they had to a man of the cloth. Surprised to learn that Daniel was Jewish, Reed had panicked. He knew nothing about what was supposed to be done. Two of the Russian scientists, in addition to Dr. Mandel himself, stepped in and put the man at ease. They'd washed Daniel's body and wrapped him in a shroud, and explained that those close to him should take part in helping to bury the body.

As Reed was finishing up, Jason glanced at the shovel stuck in the pile of dirt and knew they'd run out of dirt before they'd run out of people who felt they'd been close to Daniel. In a lot of ways, he'd been the glue that had held this group together. Michelle was their spirit animal, but Daniel had been the steady, calming figure who had refused to stop believing that things could and would get better. Rachel stood behind Michelle's wheelchair with one hand on her shoulder; the other grasped Elsa's hand. Next to them, Pro looked more like a young man than a teenager. There were none of the tears that had been present a short time ago when he'd helped Pro bury his mother's and sister's remains. The kid just stood in rigid silence; his hands balled into fists.

Jason couldn't help but think that despite their cleanup efforts, there were hundreds of thousands of bodies, within miles, that would never be buried; millions further out and billions across the planet. Daniel's burial was different; it was separate and distinct from those who had lived and died before. In contrast to the billions who had died from the virus, even his wife's death, when the scope, suddenness, and mass trauma of the die-off had been so overwhelming—blame or reasons had become meaningless. Daniel was a loss suffered in the new world, after they'd started over. His death was accountable. Blame could be assessed; justice could be sought.

Outside of Charlottesville

"Gypsy One, Tag One—we are in place." John Bruce was breathing hard. They'd been set up where they thought the convoy of empty trucks was headed. They'd guessed wrong, and had to bust ass along back roads to reposition their ambush. After the frenzied drive, they'd left their vehicles behind a highway repair depot's pile of road salt, and ran the last quarter of a mile carrying far more gear and weight than the human body was meant to do. He was gassed, and it had been all he could do to get the words out without sucking in another lungful of air.

Charlottesville was trying to sneak another supply run past them. They'd stopped three forays in as many days, and Skirjanek's description of today's quarry made it sound as if the enemy was changing things up. The drone had been grounded and sitting ready when the line of three panel trucks and three pickup trucks loaded with militia had rolled past where Uwasi and Elliot had set up an observation post on the edge of the city.

The scouts had radioed in and reported the movement, and Poy had launched his bird. Captain Bruce; he was still coming to terms with that title, and his team had already been prepositioned five miles south of the city. Another team led by Pavel was northwest of the city, waiting to pounce as well.

Pavel's team had seen the action yesterday. They'd stopped a convoy of trucks, shot up the vehicles, and sent the survivors packing on foot back to the campus. Today, it looked like it was his team's turn, and there were a lot more of the enemy escorting this convoy. Poy's best guestimate had been thirty-plus enemy combatants, and that was only if the panel trucks were truly empty.

"They are two miles east of you." Skirjanek's voice was calm. "Stop the vehicles and fall back, John. You don't have enough people to get in a stand-up fight with them."

John knew the colonel would be looking over Poy's shoulder, staring at the drone's camera feed right now. He glanced back at "his" team. He had ten people, four of them actual Marines. The rest he considered on-the-job trainees. He wished that kind of internal math wasn't relevant, but he knew that wouldn't be the case for some time. The volunteers from Northern Virginia were motivated and getting better with every patrol; there was no denying that. They were a long way from the cold-eyed warrior staring back at him.

"Lucas, I'm going to ask you to fire two Javelins. Target the first two vehicles in line. The rest of us will keep their heads down while you reposition and reload between shots."

"As long as I don't have to carry this thing much further."

The Javelin's CLU weighed thirty-five pounds and was not exactly ergonomically designed to be carried by hand, let alone sprinted with. If Farmer was complaining, the run they had just made from their vehicles would have killed a normal person. In addition to the CLU, the Marine was weighed down with his rifle, ammo, and normal pack that weighed in close to seventy pounds.

"Take your two mules and go set up."

The two new guys behind Farmer each carried a hard-case-enclosed Javelin missile. One of them, Sam Hirai, had a lot of potential but was giving him the stink eye at the moment.

He smiled back. "It's a technical term. Remember, your job is to stay hidden until you fire, and for the second guy, stay hidden until Farmer gets to you, and needs your reload. We clear?"

"Clear." Hirai nodded. "Where do you want us?"

The lead vehicle, a Ford F-350 with a bed full of armed-up militia, was driving a lot slower than it needed to be. Skirjanek thought it could be out of caution, or it could be what he feared; these guys were looking for a fight. John didn't have enough firepower out there to confront them directly—not without destroying the convoy and targeting everyone in it. It was the same problem he had with Charlottesville in general, just on a smaller scale. His gut was telling him that his counterpart in Charlottesville was calling his bluff. *You want to stop our movement—you're going to have to pay a butcher's bill to do it.*

It was a wager that he didn't have enough chips to match. "How much do you want to bet those panel trucks are full of more infantry?"

"Not going to take that bet, sir." Poy didn't look up from his laptop controlling the drone.

He was walking a fine line; trying to drive a wedge between the Charlottesville militia and their leadership, knowing full well his actions had the potential to strengthen Lisa Cooper's position. They'd learned a lot from the people they'd captured so far and then released; Cooper and this General Stevens were the enemy. His data holdings at The

Hole hadn't told him anything about Stevens, other than the fact there wasn't a general grade officer with the last name Stevens, and hadn't been since the 1980s—and that one had been in the Air Force.

He grabbed up his radio. "Tag One—Gypsy One—hold fire, I repeat, hold fire. Stand down. Do not engage."

"Gypsy One, that's a copy. Do not engage."

Bruce switched channels, and shook his head. Farmer was going to be pissed. He and his team would have to carry their weapons back.

*

Twenty miles north of Bruce's position, on a rural two-lane back road confusingly labeled both Highway 665 AND Millington Road on his map, Pavel was about through with the American system of road nomenclature. A proper road should have a number, period. An important road might be allowed a name, but it should not confuse the issue by having a number as well. And the names! Stalin's balls, these Americans could even make that confusing—most of the roads had several names. Richmond Road became Long Street close to Charlottesville, and then became Ivy Road west of the city. In some places, it was just Route 250, and in others, it was Route 250 and Route 29 simultaneously.

He'd given up and requested that Skirjanek direct him using map coordinates. It helped somewhat, but only until one of the other Americans hopelessly confused the issue.

"Major, one tanker truck, one escort coming up the hill. Three minutes out."

This was information that made sense. His team was set up near the intersection of the north-south-running 810 road and the east-west-running 614. The enemy was trying to get yet another truck out of town via the back roads that networked the area. He had Trey Nathans and the sniper's .50 caliber rifle on his team, and the Marine had an excellent position to see down the hill and observe the approach of the enemy.

"Mr. Nathans, target both vehicles, their engines. Disregard enemy combatants."

"Affirmative."

He nodded to himself. Nathans's skill as a sniper was a credit to the American Marines, and he had told the man just that before he had delivered, with John Bruce's enthusiastic permission, some attitude adjustment. He'd waited until he had Nathans alone. He knew the type; Nathans would suffer private admonishment far easier than he would a public shaming. He hadn't even had to get physical. A cold description of how he wanted to handle the matter of Nathans's attitude in the standard Russian Army tradition had been enough. The Marine was learning to keep his opinions and random thoughts to himself, at least within range of his hearing.

"Targets in sight, and in range," the sniper reported a minute later. "Where do you want them stopped?"

A moment later, he spotted the lead pickup truck himself, closely followed by what he assumed was an empty tanker truck. "Right there is acceptable, Mr. Nathans."

The drivers and four soldiers who had been acting as escort guards stood in front of the steaming radiator of the pickup truck with hands atop their heads. One round from the .50 caliber had penetrated the engine block and brought the vehicle to a standstill twenty yards in front of where the tanker had been stopped.

"Again?" The truck driver did not look happy.

"We stopped you yesterday, didn't we?" Petty Officer Cruz was doing the talking. Skirjanek didn't want to reveal that they had Russians with them, and provide a potential rallying point for Cooper to use. Pavel had no issue with the reasoning. Had they been in Russia, "the Americans are invading" would have provoked a similar reaction. He sat quietly on the tailgate of one of their own trucks and watched Cruz work.

"Yeah, but that was a lot closer to town. You can't expect us to walk from here. It's close to twenty miles!"

"It's just over twelve," Cruz pointed out and then waved a hand around him. "Hey, nobody says you gotta go back, but wherever you go, your weapons and vehicles stay here."

"We're just trying to go for some fuel for the generators," the driver countered. He was a tall man of thin build, perhaps fifty years old. "Fuel that runs refrigerators and lights for a lot of women and children."

Cruz nodded in understanding. "And assault vehicles, and tanks, not to mention your trucks. How many more of those do you have, by the way?"

"Enough!"

"Fine," Cruz added. "Get going; maybe we'll see you all again tomorrow. You can fill your water bladders or canteens from our supply." Crus grinned, as he glanced up at the sky and wiped a sheen of sweat off his own face. "It's going to be a scorcher."

The driver looked around at the rest of his team for a moment and then nodded in acceptance. "Would you let us get our tennis shoes out of the vehicles?"

"Your what?" Salguero spoke up from the ring of guns around their prisoners.

The truck driver shook his head in frustration. "I just hiked eight miles yesterday in these boots. Packing tennis shoes seemed like a smart move this morning."

Cruz smiled. "What's your name?"

"What the hell does that matter?"

"I'm just being neighborly," Cruz laughed. "Chances are, we'll be seeing each other again."

"Lawton, Ed Lawton."

"Well, Mr. Lawton, you can grab your sneakers from your truck. That was good thinking."

Pavel cleared his throat, reached into his thigh pocket, and retrieved an MRE pouch while Cruz was watching.

Cruz smiled back at him and turned to the prisoners. "Look, we don't have anything against you all. If you're hungry, we've got plenty. Like you said, it's a long walk."

"We ain't gonna eat with you," one of the guards almost shouted.

The driver just regarded Cruz for a moment and then nodded. "The rest of us will, thank you. Bates, you should eat too. I don't want to listen to you whine for the next twelve miles."

*

"Well done, both of you." Drew had just finished listening to the reports from Pavel and John. "It appears our efforts are having an effect. Poy was able to track that convoy I called you off of. It circled back to town and unloaded. Those panel trucks had fifteen or twenty soldiers apiece in them."

"So, it *was* a patrol in strength." Pavel nodded.

"Perhaps; I think it just as easily could have been a sacrificial lamb. Hoping we'd attack it and kill a bunch of folks. An event Cooper could have used to strengthen the will of her militia."

"We are certain they have a militia separate from what they call their guard force?" Pavel asked.

"Near as we can tell, it looks that way. The guard force is what they've managed to train up into standing units under this General Stevens. The militia seems to be just that, and if we believe the snippets we've collected, it appears the latter answers more to Cooper than General Stevens. Although the drone has spotted a lot of joint training activity involving both, so any real division between the two forces could very well be wishful thinking on our part."

John ran a hand through his close-cropped hair and gave his head a shake. "It's just a matter of time before they move against us in force. It sounds like they know where we are."

Pavel nodded in agreement. "The men we captured today were quite clear that they knew we were camped at Zion Crossroads."

"What are they waiting for?" John sounded tired. They were all tired. Maintaining the constant patrols and roadblocks with their limited numbers was far more taxing than preparing for the stand-up fight that he knew both his subordinates were anxious for. He was, too, if he was being honest with himself.

Drew shook his head as he stared down at the map spread out in front of him. "I wish I knew." He was sure of one thing; they would see them coming. They'd prepared and practiced moving out on short notice. Let them come. They would move, set up at the fallback location, and continue harassing them. He wasn't going to stand and fight over a meaningless freeway exit. What were they waiting for?

Chapter 24

"Lisa, there's no coming back from this, whether it works or not. You need to be clear on that."

She turned to him after glancing around to make certain she wasn't going to be overheard. "You said you agreed as well."

They were standing outside their vehicle in the parking lot fronting the football stadium. Their guards—her guards, Stevens corrected himself, had established a cordon around them, thirty feet away.

"I do." And God help him, at this juncture, he did. She'd left him no choice. Her actions had created an enemy when there didn't have to be one. "The risks are real. Dead men have nothing to lose."

"Relax, Dr. Nance says the risks to us didn't present themselves. It didn't mutate."

"I meant them." He shook his head, doing a good job of controlling his anger. "If they figure out we've attacked them with a biological agent . . . I can only imagine how I would react if I knew I had a week or so before I died."

"It's not like we are going to tell them." Lisa waved away his concern, and then her face melted into a malicious grin. "At least not until it's too late."

Why tell them at all? He'd known she was crazy for a long time. Not just in the sack, which he was in no position to complain about, but she truly didn't seem to be able to see anything that didn't conform to her image as to how things were.

Four pickup trucks loaded down with supplies came around the edge of the stadium and stopped anything he was about to say. He could see Josh driving the lead pickup and Dr. Vance sitting across the cab from him. Part of him had been surprised that the doctor had agreed to formulate the virus into something that had been sprayed onto every piece of equipment in the beds of the trucks. In addition to being sprayed on the clothing, tents, and backpacks that they'd soon be handing out, Josh had even reported they'd added it to the water they'd be handing out.

He could only assume Dr. Vance was in the same boat as he was and had read her situation correctly. Her "assigned" minder was very much Lisa's animal. Josh had been an unspoken threat, far more than a volunteer lab assistant.

"This will work," Lisa said to him as Josh pulled up. "It was a good idea when you proposed it; it's still a good idea. It's going to save lives."

When he'd proposed it! Christ, all he'd mentioned was "it was their dumb luck that the virus had burned itself out." The rest had been her idea. He knew correcting the record was pointless. More than that of any person he'd ever met, Lisa Cooper's view of the past was as flexible, as it was justified.

"Dr. Vance." Lisa waved with a smile when the doors popped open. "Welcome back to the light."

"Thank you." The doctor shrugged, flashing a look towards Josh that was somewhere between hostility and fear. "I'm just glad it's done."

Lisa pointed at the cargo in the trucks. "All of it is . . ."

"Thoroughly infected," Josh added confidently. "And correct me if I'm wrong, Doctor, but it will be for a couple of weeks even without susceptible hosts."

"That's correct, for at least two weeks, longer for items that don't get exposed to direct sunlight."

Lisa clapped her hands together once and beamed at Josh. "Listen to you. You sound like you know what you're talking about."

"I've learned a lot," Josh admitted with a shrug.

"Is that true?" Lisa was magnanimous in her victory. Having forced Vance to do her bidding, she'd gotten what she wanted. Now it was all smiles and sunshine.

"I couldn't have done it without him," the doctor admitted, sounding as if she'd wanted to say "wouldn't have."

"So how do we do this?" he interjected. "As safely as possible."

Dr. Vance pointed at the trucks. "Have the personnel come out and collect the gear themselves. No need to test fate and have any of our people handle it."

"But it's safe to us?" Lisa looked like she wanted to take a step back.

"It is," the doctor replied. "We've both been exposed to it for ten days; we continue to test positive for the antibodies we had before we started the process, with no change. That said, there's no reason to have anybody handle the infected gear who doesn't have to."

"OK then," he said. "I'll go let our Trojan horses know they are going to be released."

"No, I want to do it," Lisa said. "If this doesn't work, we may have to bring some of them back into the fold at some point. You'll just scare them."

Dr. Vance turned to look back at the campus. "If it's alright, I'd like to go and get back to my office, and maybe take a long shower."

"Of course, Doctor," Lisa allowed with an understanding smile. "I know how difficult this was for you, for all of us. Our volunteers know you from their medical check; they shouldn't see you here at any rate."

"I'll drive you back," Josh offered.

"No!" Vance turned on her minder. "Sorry, I think I'd just like to walk."

The three of them watched Dr. Vance go until she passed through the cordon of armed guards on her way back to the main campus.

"Not a happy camper." Josh shook his head.

"That can't be helped." Lisa nodded in agreement. "You're certain she did this right?"

"As much as I can be, yes." Josh shrugged. "I'm not a scientist or a doctor, but I know people. She feels guilty as hell. I'm pretty sure she was disappointed that the virus hadn't mutated and we weren't going to get sick. Me . . .? Not so much."

"I'm not going to forget what you did for us, Josh." Lisa's praise was so natural, so genuine, Stevens recognized it for the true superpower it was. He'd been the recipient himself many times before. Witnessing it deployed against someone else was almost disconcerting. He recovered and held a hand out to Josh.

"Nor will I, Josh. They used to give medals for this sort of thing. You risked everything, son."

"Saving lives, right?" Josh asked. "That's why I did this; the doc too. If it's not a problem, I'd just as soon nobody know it was us who did this. For the doctor's sake as much as mine."

*

Michael Anthony wasn't going to believe anything that came out of Lisa Cooper's mouth, not after spending three weeks as a prisoner, sleeping in a tent on the thirty-yard line inside Scott Stadium. Listening to the unending loop of her recorded message of solidarity and a new beginning had been heaping insult on injury. But their release and outfitting with food and supplies had been real enough. He wasn't going to stand around waiting for the assholes to change their minds.

They'd been walking east for two hours, he and a group of thirty-two others that included two young children being pushed in strollers. The majority of those released from the stadium were from Roanoke and had gone west when they'd hit I-64 as a group. He was headed to Williamsburg, along with a few others who had been taken with him in Richmond. Their ragtag group looked like the stream of refugees it was, and it was a much smaller group than it should have been. Most of those scooped up in Richmond had lasted a week or so in the stadium, before they'd given in and sworn the oath of loyalty that their jailors had wanted from them.

He'd almost caved himself, and had started to wonder why he was holding out. Beyond the confinement and the mental wear and tear of having to listen to the same recorded message twelve times a day, they hadn't been mistreated. Frequent visits by former prisoners reinforced the story that people were being treated well upon release.

This morning, Lisa Cooper herself had come into the stadium and made an announcement that everyone was free to go. "We'd like you to stay and see what we have to offer. If you still want to leave, we'll set you up with supplies and send you on your way. Please know that you are always welcome to return. We will never turn away anyone." It had been a nice speech to put the cap on a mass abduction and internment, but he'd been moving towards the gate before she was done speaking.

Kim Dawes, walking next to him, turned around and walked backwards towards the interchange over Black Cat Road for several steps before resuming forward.

"Nobody seems to be following us?" She didn't add the "yet." Kim had checked behind them every few minutes since they'd made it past the manned roadblock east of Charlottesville.

"I figure if they wanted to off us, they wouldn't have gone through all this trouble." He patted the hunting rifle on his shoulder. At the roadblock, they'd given him a single box of twenty rounds and a 30.06 rifle. Half a dozen others had been given hunting rifles or shotguns. They weren't going to be able to put up anything but a pretense at defense if they needed to, but it was something.

"Whatever," Kim almost spit. Kim had been one of the defenders of Richmond who had been lined up next to him, in front of a firing squad on the riverfront. "It just feels weird is all I'm saying."

*

"This is new . . ." Poy was watching the refugee group tramp down the middle of the eastbound lane on his laptop. A few minutes ago, he'd thought the drone had been spotted, and he'd taken it up another thousand feet. From the current altitude and with the angle of the sun's shadows cast on the smooth roadway, the group looked like a strange herd of colored cows.

"It's certainly unexpected." The colonel never seemed to get excited. "Why release their prisoners, why now?"

Poy had learned to take his cues from Skirjanek, and one thing he'd discovered early on was that Skirjanek liked to talk to himself and bounce around ideas. He also liked to teach. The man had gone on for an hour a week ago, about siege warfare during medieval times, and how there were countless conflicts in the distant past that could inform their present situation.

"Maybe they just don't want the mouths to feed, sir. We going to let them off-load refugees on us?"

The colonel nodded once and smiled at him. "So, you were listening?"

"Yes, sir. I've always liked history, never thought we'd be reliving it, but I always thought the olden days were kind of cool. You know, except for the whole no-penicillin-or-Internet thing."

"I can think of a lot of scenarios where your thinking would be correct, but the mass grave they have behind the golf course argues against a humanitarian approach. So yes, I'd say they are looking to weigh us down or gather intel. Probably both."

"What are we going to do?"

The colonel was silent for a long moment, watching the group grow closer with each step. "I think we'll take the bait."

"Sir?"

"We'll learn something as well, Mr. Park. Besides, these people were prisoners this morning; we might even get a few recruits out of this. If not, we'll see them on their way. Least we can do is feed them when they pass through."

Poy wiped the sweat from his brow. The skies were clear, and it was going to be a hot day. "Sir, before I climbed the drone, I was pretty sure I saw some kids and even a couple of baby strollers. It's gotta be pretty shitty on top of that road. I mean . . ."

Skirjanek dropped a fist on his shoulder. "That's good thinking, Mr. Park. You're right, we'll go to them, offer some transport."

"You're fighting them?" Kim asked the guy calling himself Colonel and then looked at him in expectation. "Where do we sign up?"

Kim's enthusiasm aside, Michael didn't know what to think. They'd been trudging along, the threat they were leaving growing more distant with every step, when they'd crested a rise in the freeway and come face-to-face with a bunch of well-armed soldiers, blocking the road and holding a white flag. He did the only thing he had a mind to and stood there, wondering if they'd escaped the frying pan and jumped into the fire. Some of the group had taken off running, either back the way they'd come or into the woods off the freeway. Most had stopped after about a hundred yards and were just watching to see what was going to happen.

"One thing at a time." The Skirjanek guy held up a hand and then pointed skyward. "We saw you get released this morning with our drone and have been tracking you. They aren't pursuing you. We're trying to figure out what Cooper's angle is and thought in the meantime we could get you off the road in this heat and see what you know. That is, if you're willing to share."

"We don't know what's going on either." Michael shrugged. "It was like they just gave up on converting us and let us go. There's a much bigger group of us that headed west. Cooper was all smiles, acting like it was no harm, no foul; said we be welcomed back if we changed our minds."

"Fat chance," Kim said. She'd stood with him in the middle of the freeway when the others had run. If she wanted to sign up with these people, IF they were taking volunteers, he'd probably do the same. Kim had been the only thing in his life worth hanging on to for the last six months. He could see others starting to filter back out of the woods. "They attacked us, took us prisoner, and the bitch has the stones to tell us they'd welcome us back? As if!"

The colonel nodded in understanding at Kim's outburst and then turned back to face him. "That's all for you people to decide. For now, if you can corral your people up, we'll get you down the road a bit. We might be able to provide some transport for you and your people, help get you to where you were headed, within reason."

"Why are you doing this?" He'd asked the question before he'd realized he was speaking.

"No reason, beyond the fact you people have had a rough time and could use a break. That, and I still want to know why they released you. It's far outside what we've come to expect of them."

"For us too," he answered. "If I knew anything, I'd tell you."

Skirjanek believed Michael, and the half dozen others he'd had a chance to talk to since getting them all back to Zion Crossroads. Which wasn't as helpful as it should have been; none of them could add anything of use. Trapped inside a football stadium for almost a month since they'd been rounded up in Richmond, they were completely in the dark as to what had been happening around them. They'd taken the explosions they'd heard two weeks past as nothing more than training exercises.

The enthusiasm that some of them had shown for signing up wasn't anywhere close to universal. Most of these people just wanted to be left alone and were ready to continue their journey eastward, with or without any help. As much as he wanted to take the half dozen gung-ho members of the group at their word, he knew he couldn't. A quick discussion with Pavel and John reinforced his thinking.

"We've discussed your situation," he began as he walked up to where the group had been given an opportunity to take a load off their feet. Most were sprawled out on the ground after eating the meal they had provided; some were resting in lawn chairs. Those who were armed were alert, almost as if they could sense the hidden rifles he had covering them. "And we're going to get you to wherever you want to go, or at least give you gas for the trip. Vehicles we have plenty of."

"You don't want our help?" The woman, Kim, wanted payback, or at least that was the way she was playing it.

"Want . . . and can use," he began, "are two different things. I hope you can understand that. If you're willing, you can tell us where you're headed, and we'll reach out to you after we've settled this. If not, that's fine too. Either way, we'll set you up with some real weapons. What you've got may feed you, but you'll need more, and we'll provide it."

"Sounds more than fair," their leader, Michael, agreed after a moment. "And you're right, it makes sense. Before they attacked Richmond, they managed to get their people inside our groups. Road people." Michael looked at Kim and gave one shoulder a shrug. "People like us."

"But we're not . . ." the woman began and then stopped herself, deflating. "You're right."

"I wish the situation were different," he said. "I really do. Thank you for understanding."

The next morning, they had gassed up a dozen civilian vehicles from a car dealership a mile up the road. The refugees were in good spirits; the unexpected assistance and their rediscovered freedom had most of them hugging their benefactors. Kim gave him a big hug and planted a kiss on his cheek. "Thank you!"

Michael's car was the last to depart, and the man shook his hand. "Most of us are going to Williamsburg, the colonial town. We figure all the reenactment stuff might come in handy if it hasn't been looted. Sooner or later, we're all going to need to get back to basics."

"That's good thinking. We'll try to buy you a little security." He handed over a radio and two spare batteries. "Today's a Tuesday, in case you were wondering, July thirteenth. Monitor this thing every Sunday at noon for an hour to conserve your batteries. If we resolve this situation here, we'll give you a call. We're in contact with another, larger group up north that just wants to be left alone as well. Like-minded people need to stay in touch. I seriously doubt if Charlottesville is the last group we'll see with delusions of grandeur."

Michael hefted the radio in thanks and got in behind the wheel of the pickup. "July thirteenth?"

"Yes."

"Did you all do anything special for the Fourth?"

"We tried; we were more than a little busy. We raised a few drinks in remembrance. Maybe next year, we'll have time for something more."

"Colonel, I don't know what to make of this." Michael waved a folded-up slip of paper at him. "I found this in the bottom of my sleeping bag last night. I wasn't the only one. There was a bunch of them inside our bags, inside the MRE cartons. I had half a dozen people handing me the damn things this morning. Somehow, I don't think it was meant for us."

He read the message and could feel his eyebrows furrow in confusion.

"Doesn't make sense to you either?"

He read the message again.

Do not believe what you are told. I take my oath seriously.
— Dr. Naomi Vance

"Can't say that it does. Do you know this Dr. Vance?"

Michael shook his head. "Maybe, there *was* a doctor. A real one. We weren't given her name."

He waved the paper. "Thank you for this. I think."

Michael nodded. "Please keep us in mind, and good luck to you."

"Will do." He shook the man's hand again through the open window.

Watching them drive off, he felt better than he had since his trip to Northern Virginia, where he'd seen people trying to build a future. Given half a chance, most people were basically good. Without that chance, he knew better than most how ugly they could be.

Chapter 25

"Colonel! Sir." Elliot slid to a stop in the gravel of the landscaping company's parking lot. "Poy's drone is watching them fuel their Black Hawk. They've got a big crowd gathered watching. He thinks they are getting ready to fly."

That answered one question, he thought; they had a pilot. "Thank you, Mr. Elliot. Your radio, please."

"Gypsy One for all units, retrans for all units—enemy is going airborne. Get everything and everyone undercover like we've planned. Patrol teams, report any sighting of enemy air, but do not engage." Between the car dealership, a fire station, the Dept. of Transportation equipment sheds, and the Walmart supercenter, they had all their vehicles under a roof, and the personnel all knew where to hide so that they'd be in a position to protect their critical gear.

He listened to the callbacks, satisfied that the message was getting out to everyone. He handed Elliot his radio back. "Sergeant Salguero is out with Major Volkov, correct?"

"Yes, sir. They are set up on the north side of town again."

"No worries, Mr. Elliot. I assume you are familiar with the firing of a Stinger anti-aircraft missile?"

"Uhh . . . yes, sir. I've seen one demonstrated, sir."

"You'll do fine, Corporal." He pointed at the D.O.T. maintenance garage across the highway from them. "Go grab a Stinger case from the armory and meet at the firehouse."

"Yes, sir! Right away, sir!"

*

"This is insane," Tim Calhoun muttered to himself, or so he thought.

"What's your problem?" Scott Mackey had been one of General Marks's ROTC students at Virginia Tech, one of only two who had survived the virus. As such, the little punk thought his shit didn't stink. Calhoun was fairly certain the general agreed. "You're a pilot. This is a helicopter."

And you're an asshole . . . "It's not that simple. I've never flown anything like this." Calhoun repeated what he'd been saying for the last week to anyone who would listen.

He'd learned to fly helicopters thirty years ago at a civilian crop-duster school outside of Richmond. It was a career that had lasted him all of three years. The local farmers had stopped growing tobacco, and he'd quit to go to work for an aerial surveying company. His actual flying time with that company had been infrequent at first and then disappeared altogether as commercial satellite imagery really took off. He hadn't flown a helicopter in over twenty years and was regretting ever having mentioned that he could.

"You've been studying up on the manuals, right?"

"Sure," he admitted, before pointing at a bank of switches in front of his right knee. "See those? I've no fucking idea what they do; they weren't in the manual." He could see the nervousness light in the younger man's eyes, and he reveled in it. "Still want to come along? Because I'm guessing the maintenance crew have been reading the same manuals that I have. We're relying on guys who used to service your dad's car." Which wasn't exactly true; Calhoun had more confidence in the ground crew, which included a genuine mechanical engineer, than he did in his own ability to actually fly the damn thing. They brought it here on a flatbed and then put the word out for a pilot as they worked on it all winter long.

He'd been just stupid enough to mention that he had some flying experience. The role had promised a bigger room, one without roommates, and a more robust meal ticket. He'd have done for the room alone; at his age, he was way past wanting to share a dorm room. Especially with somebody who had to have been threatened with violence to avail themselves of the showers they had running in the gym complex.

Mackey held up a hand while he donned his flight helmet and plugged it into the cockpit's intercom system. "Do you want to go tell General Marks that you are unable to perform this mission?"

"Mission? I thought we were just going to overfly the freeway to the east?"

"Depends what we find." Mackey was yelling unnecessarily into his mic over the sound of the turbine spinning up. "We may have you drop us off out there."

"Who's us?" he asked, just prior to four of General Marks's soldiers piling in through the starboard door. One look at their gear, and he realized they were all members of Marks's assault squad. Some of them, he'd heard, had been actual soldiers at one time or another; others were civilians who just really enjoyed playing at it. Who was he to complain? It wasn't like he was a real pilot either.

He did a quick scan of his temps and pressures and didn't see anything that struck him as out of the ordinary. There were too many damned screens and buttons that he didn't recognize to worry about it. He knew the fancy displays and a lot of the inputs were related to navigation, autopilot, communications, damage control, and a rash of other shit he had no business monkeying around with or had the time to learn. He carefully engaged power to the rotor. He caught sight of General Marks standing outside, at a safe distance, next to Lisa Cooper, as he looked out the cockpit to confirm the blades had started turning. Marks was flashing him a big thumbs-up with a shit-eating grin on his face. He responded in kind, knowing something dramatic was expected. *Asshole . . .*

Ten minutes later, they had completed the second slow circuit of the campus, and he was starting to believe he might survive the flight. He'd had a moment back there when he'd learned just how heavy this bird was; he hadn't had enough collective lift engaged as he banked the helicopter, and they'd lost a hundred feet of altitude in the blink of an eye. He'd corrected quickly; the interaction of the collective and cyclic worked via the same laws of physics as the old Bell he'd flown, spraying tobacco fields.

"We good?" Mackey looked a little less sure than he had a moment ago.

"All good," he lied. "Just getting a feel for it." He proceeded south to the freeway and started bending their flight path east when it came into view.

Even from their location on the top floor of the practice tower of the fire station, they heard the Black Hawk well before they spotted it. They'd had a heads-up; the UH-60 had overflown one of his scout teams alongside the freeway to the west, a few minutes before.

"Tell me when, sir."

Skirjanek knew Elliot was referring to initiating the battery on the launcher. The Stinger was a great weapon, but its battery and infrared targeting acquisition required a coolant that ran on compressed argon gas. The system would be operable for less than a minute after it was initiated. There were two spare battery coolant units in the open case at their feet, but he knew from personal experience that having to switch the BCU out when you were in the middle of setting up a shot was never good.

"Not yet, Mr. Elliot. Don't energize the seeker until I say."

"Affirmative, sir. I will remind you that the FIM-92 J variant requires time to cool the targeting unit, necessitating a lag time of approximately ten seconds. High ambient temperature may increase that interval by as much as an additional five seconds, sir."

He glanced over at the young man. "I thought you said you hadn't fired one before."

"I have not, sir. I read the manual once, sir."

And memorized it, apparently . . . No one quite knew what to make of Sergeant Elliot. The kid was more than a little off. He'd asked then Sergeant Bruce about it early on, wondering if the time in The Hole had affected him adversely. Bruce had said the kid came out of advanced infantry training like that, and had test scores that were off the charts. Anybody who interacted with him socially just came away thinking the guy was a little off and maybe a lot slow.

"Do you have an eidetic memory, Mr. Elliot? I have a hunch you know what the word means."

"I don't know, sir. I do remember things I read, sir. If they interest me."

"Such as the operation of a Stinger missile system?"

"Anything associated with the Marine Corps, sir."

"Outstanding, Mr. Elliot." He could see the Black Hawk now, moving slowly towards them over the freeway. "I have eyes on our target, but are we going to continue this discussion?"

"Yes, sir. I have eyes on as well, sir."

Drew pushed his lapel mic. "All units, remain under cover. Enemy air overhead." *Nothing to see here, nothing at all* . . .

*

"I don't see shit!" Mackey shouted into his headset. "They must have bugged out?"

Calhoun had arced the helicopter south at the freeway interchange and followed Highway 15 for two miles before doing a wide, slow, 180-degree turn and starting back north. Mackey's confidence aside, he wasn't so sure. This was a good place to hide; the area had a lot of businesses with big buildings or garages to store vehicles out of sight. That included the DOT vehicle repair lot and its half dozen barnlike structures they'd just overflown. In addition to the subdivisions of housing, there was even a newish-looking hotel next to the freeway where the bad guys could be bunking.

"You didn't expect them to be on the streets waving flags at us, did you?" There was something strange about the stretch of highway that he couldn't put a name on.

"Looks empty to me," Mackey replied.

That was it! No cars stalled out or left on the road. They'd cleared the area. "Somebody sure as shit has been here, no cars on the road. And take a look at that parking lot next to the hotel." The asphalt surrounding the parking lot was chewed to shit, like what the tanks and APCs did to the roads around campus if the drivers weren't careful.

"Sure enough!" Mackey agreed and then flashed something with his hand to his asshole buddies in the back. "They look to be gone now though. Set us down in that clear space in front of the hotel. We'll check that out."

"You nuts?" he yelled. "What if they're just hiding?"

"Just do it," Mackey yelled back. "The mission is to try and get a head count on them. We will recon the area—might be able to see how many rooms in that hotel look lived in."

He wanted to argue in the worst way. Not just because the nineteen-year-old ROTC student wannabe was so fucking stupid, but also because his last name was Calhoun and he came from a long line of assholes who called bullshit when they saw it. "You're putting the helo at risk. You have no idea what's down there."

It almost worked; he could see the indecision on the kid's face. It was followed by a firm shake of his helmeted head. "I'm in command of this mission. Put us down."

The rotor wash kicked up a year's worth of debris and trash that had blown into the area. Part of it was his fault; he hovered just off the ground for far too long, but hell, it wasn't like he was a real pilot or anything.

"Just wait for us here. We'll be right back."

He wanted to bite the idiot's head off, but he knew the kid had only completed a single year of college before the virus had hit. Mackey was as out of his depth as he was, sitting in the cockpit of a Black Hawk helicopter, wondering if he could remember how to safely shut the turbine down. *Fuck me . . .*

Drew dropped his binoculars against his chest and gave his head a shake after watching the five occupants of the helicopter enter the hotel. "Bring the jeep around, Corporal. Leave the Stinger."

"Yes, sir."

He watched the Marine pound down the metal stairs of the fire station tower and pressed his mic. "Gypsy One for Corporal Uwasi and Mr. Reed—roll your teams to the hotel. Stay on 15, do not turn in. Weapons hold unless fired on."

*

He had the flight manual open on his lap, trying to make sense of the controls and readouts in front of him. The helicopter creaked and groaned with contracting metal sounds as it cooled down. He could only hope those noises were 'normal'. Mackey and his "team" had been gone for just a few minutes, and he took the lack of gunfire as a good sign. Maybe he'd just been paranoid.

The sound of boots landing in the metal compartment and the barrel of the gun inches from his head when he turned around argued otherwise.

*

"Shit! Where the hell is he?" Scott Mackey asked the universe. They'd already looked around the helo. He'd sent one of his guys back into the hotel in the hopes that Calhoun had gone in after them. No such luck.

Wells spoke up. "Dude! That cranky old coot either took off, or he was taken. If he was taken, we need to get the hell out of here, now!"

David Wells was the oldest of his team and might have been pushing forty. He at least had some military experience; he was a former campus policeman and had done a stint as a military contractor, some kind of gate guard in Afghanistan, a decade ago.

"What about the chopper?"

His team just looked back at him in expectation that he should be able to answer his own question. He didn't know what to do. General Marks was going to go ballistic, and Miss Cooper . . . he didn't even want to think about her reaction. He wondered if running away might be *his* best move at this point.

Wells took a step forward and waved at the rest of them to follow. "We sure as shit aren't going to carry it. Let's go!"

*

Their "prisoner" let out an angry cackle at the sight of his former passengers cutting through the narrow strip of trees separating the hotel's lot from the freeway. "Serves the stupid little bastard right!"

It was not a reaction Drew had been expecting. He was seated in a booth inside the IHOP that shared a parking lot with the Best Western. He'd been holding a gun on the pilot while he watched the enemy soldiers argue with one another. Reed and a dozen of his team were quietly doing the same thing, across the interior perimeter of the restaurant that still smelled like old coffee and maple syrup.

"Gypsy One—Poy, do you have eyes on?"

"Affirmative, Gypsy One—they are on foot—westbound on the on-ramp, sir."

"Holy shit!" The pilot, who appeared to be in his early sixties, slapped the table with an open hand. "You're real soldiers, aren't you?" He looked around at the members of Reed's team and shook his head. "I told him you all were probably hiding. But he was feeling his oats." The pilot snorted in derision. "In charge and all that. Little shit had no idea what he was doing."

Drew holstered his gun and just looked across the table for a moment before extending his hand with a smile. "I'm Colonel Drew Skirjanek, former US Army. You are not a prisoner. You can do what you like; we'll even help you do it. But there's a place for you here if you want it."

The old man just nodded once to himself and then gripped his hand firmly. "Name's Tim, Tim Calhoun, and Colonel . . ." The old man gave his hand another pump. "Before you ask—I am NOT a pilot. Nearly shit myself twice just getting here."

Drew smiled to himself and started laughing along with his first pilot. Another piece fell into place.

Chapter 26

You don't have to talk to me, if you don't feel like it," Jason said, glancing at Pro across the cab of the JLTV. "But trust me, I've been there. You need to talk. Building walls around yourself isn't the answer." He wondered if he sounded as much like a hypocrite as he felt. He and Rachel had given Pro his space for the week since Daniel's burial; until a moment ago, he had been content to leave the teenager alone. For his part, Pro had been content to provide one- or two-word answers and then shut down.

"I'm OK . . ."

Riiiight . . . He let it go and concentrated on his surroundings. They hadn't seen any of the road bandits Gabe had reported spotting a week ago, but as they passed through Culpepper, headed south on Highway 15 back to the Gypsies' camp, his head was on a swivel at every crossroad.

"Nothing we say is going to bring Daniel back." Pro sounded like he wanted to argue, but it was more words strung together than there had been in some time.

"No, it won't. Neither will shutting out everyone else."

"You did."

And there it was; it wasn't something he could even try to deny. "And I almost paid for it with my life, yours, Rachel's and a whole lot of innocents. I wasn't myself for a long time after my wife died, Pro. It wasn't losing her and all that happened afterward that drove me to shut everyone else out—I was just flat-out scared. I caught myself starting to care again, after I promised myself I wouldn't. Pro, look at me . . ."

Pro finally turned to face him after wiping at his eyes. "I care about you as much as anyone I have left in this world, but I am not a role model. That was Daniel's gift; he believed in the future. Don't waste it."

"Nothing's ever going to be fair again, will it?"

"Fair?"

"He was just trying to build something." Pro was almost shouting. "The future he was always talking about—it's not right . . . why was he the one killed?"

It wasn't fair; life never had been fair. He doubted if it ever would be. "Daniel's not the first person I've been close to who I've lost—and I don't mean my wife or what the virus did to all of us. Years ago . . ." He stopped himself, wondering if telling this story would only make it worse. But Pro was looking back at him in expectation, engaged, present for the first time in a week.

"Tell me."

"It was in Afghanistan . . . my squad made it out of a two-day running battle. It was bad; there were fourteen of us, and we had almost that many gunshot wounds between us. We were shot to hell, low on ammo, water, and time. If air support and reinforcements hadn't gotten to us when they did, I doubt if any of us would have made it out of that mountain pass.

"One of my sergeants, Roger Lewis Smith—we called him 'Smithy'—came through it all without a scratch. He was as good a soldier, a man, and a friend as they come. He got a Bronze Star for what he did over those three days; the guy was amazing, always joking. Kept me and everyone else loose and able to think, which is to say he helped keep us alive.

"We were back at our forward operating base a day later; he was one of about four or five guys who were actually on their feet. He got hit by a single mortar round lobbed out of the surrounding hills by a kid about your age. Smithy had just left the phone shack, where he'd been able to talk to his wife on a sat-phone. She'd just told him that he was going to be a dad.

"It's never been fair, Pro. Not ever." It had been a long time since he'd thought of Smithy. "Maybe that was the reason I pushed so hard just to get you, Rachel, and Elsa out of this, go find a place where we could hide. But we decided we weren't going to run. Daniel and what he thought we could build was a big part of that decision. I'm more convinced now than I was before we lost Daniel. It is the right decision. But it's not a game."

"I didn't—"

He stopped whatever Pro was about to say with a wave of his hand. "The bad guys get to vote too. So does Murphy."

"I know."

He watched as Pro wiped at his eyes. Part of him felt sorry for the kid, given the world he had left to grow up in, even knowing it wasn't pity that Pro wanted or needed. He knew what Pro needed, and it was scary how much he wanted to give it to him.

"Daniel didn't want you to have to fight at all; but I think even he got his head around the fact that it's what you have left—that it's part of who you are. It took me a while to get there myself. He wouldn't want you to forget the people you're fighting for or to push them away."

Pro sat up a little higher. "You're right. I know."

"You good?"

Pro didn't answer for a long moment. He shook his head and let out a deep breath that he'd been holding. "I think so, thanks."

"Thanks? For what?"

"For not treating me like a kid."

He had to lean across the width of the cab to punch Pro in the shoulder. "We'll get through this."

"Who's Murphy?" It was the first time he'd seen Pro smile in a week. "Is it one of those sayings that only old people know about?"

Jason laughed out loud. "You know Mr. Murphy as well as anyone. I suppose your generation would just say 'shit happens.'"

*

"Welcome back, Jason, Pro." Skirjanek was waiting outside to greet them when they pulled in. The colonel had a huge grin on his face and pointed up Highway 15, which they'd just come down. "You see Charlottesville's most recent donation to our war effort?"

It had been impossible to miss the Black Hawk helicopter, sitting in front of the hotel at the freeway interchange. "Theirs? I assumed you pulled it out of The Hole."

"They paid us a visit, three days ago. The pilot decided to stay with us. Things have gotten weird while you've been gone."

"Good weird? Or other?"

"Not certain yet." Skirjanek waved them inside. "Come on, I'll get you caught up."

"Before I forget, Colonel." Jason pulled out a slip of paper and handed it over. "Hoyt finished his radio tower at the Potomac settlement. These are the frequency schedules and security protocols of the communications plan he pulled together."

Skirjanek waved the paper. "Good deal, that's going to save us some gas. How are things up north?"

"Getting back to normal. Michelle is going to be in a wheelchair for another couple of weeks, then crutches and a cast, but she'll make a full recovery. Your people were able to save her. The other work has made huge bounds; I hardly recognized the place."

"That's good to hear, but it wasn't my people who saved her, Jason." Skirjanek glanced at Pro for a moment and then back at him. "There's just us."

Skirjanek turned to Pro and held out a hand. "I didn't get a chance to express my condolences to you, young man. I understand you and Daniel were close."

Jason watched Pro shake the man's hand. "Thank you, sir."

"I'd understand if you wanted to take some time . . ."

"No, sir." Pro shook his head. "If I have a say, sir, I'm fine. It's been explained to me that the enemy gets to vote too."

Skirjanek glanced between them, and Jason gave a slight nod. Skirjanek's smile looked sad. "That they do. Come on, I'll get you back to current." The colonel paused in mid-thought. "Rachel didn't come back with you?"

"Michelle needs her up there more than we need another sniper," Jason answered with what felt like the truth. There'd been something else going on with Rachel, though, and damned if he knew what it was. The day before, Rachel had walked out of Michelle's room and run into his arms, hugging him so hard it almost hurt. "I love you, Jason. But I can't go back with you. Not now. I'll wait for you, here." He was more than OK with keeping Rachel away from this fight, but he didn't think anything could have stopped her from wanting to be a part of it.

"I understand." Skirjanek grinned. "She'll be missed. I *was* hoping to have her help putting a certain Marine sniper in his place."

*

"Say again?" John Bruce wasn't certain he hadn't misheard the driver of the eighteen-wheeler that straddled two lanes of the rural road behind them. Steam was still hissing out of its radiator.

"This is the fifth time you assholes have stopped me. It doesn't hurt my feelings to say I haven't gotten through yet—but I am done walking back to town only to have to do it again tomorrow. Where do I sign up? One group of assholes is the same as another."

"What's your name?"

"Ed Lawton."

John looked down to see the brand-new pair of running shoes on the truck driver's feet and resisted the urge to laugh.

"Alright, Mr. Lawton, we'll take you on board." He wasn't sure what the colonel would do with volunteers, but that wasn't his problem.

One of the guards from the escort vehicle spoke up. "Don't do this,

Ed. We don't know anything about these folks."

"Like hell I don't." Lawton turned on his own group. "I know they ain't the murderers we've been told they are—so do you. Shit, Pauley! That guy gave you a pair of shoes for the walk back to town a couple days back. They could have just killed us every time they've stopped us."

"Yeah, but—"

"But nothing, you do whatever you want. I'm done pretending Cooper and Marks know what the fuck they're doing."

In the end, Lawton and one of the guards, a younger man named Greg whom Lawton just called "G," elected to stay behind and watch as their former colleagues started a seventeen-mile hike back to where they'd started.

"What now?"

It took John a moment to realize their new volunteer was speaking to him. "I have no idea, Mr. Lawton. We weren't expecting guests."

"In short, you're free to do whatever you want, go wherever you want." Skirjanek was addressing the half dozen defectors that they'd pulled in. John had figured he'd have some explaining to do regarding his two, but Pavel and Farmer had returned with four of their own.

"You'll have to understand," the colonel continued. "I'm not going to arm you and put you in the middle of my own people. It's nothing against any of you, but that kind of trust has to be earned. We will see you armed, and driven back down the road to Richmond with some supplies. When this is over, if you're still there, we'll make contact. In the meantime, you can go your own way. After, if you still want, you can sign on with us, or rejoin the others in Charlottesville."

"Not happening." Ed Lawton, the loud, angry, and talkative truck driver he'd brought in, took the opportunity to launch a pseudo mumble, loud enough that everyone heard him.

"Or not." Skirjanek grinned and held up both hands. "I'm just saying we have no intention of laying waste to the place; you could go back if you want. Rest assured, it will be under new management. In the meantime, go where you want. I will warn you to stay away from this area and Charlottesville. To my people, from a distance or through a rifle scope, you aren't going to look any different than the people we *are* worried about."

John knew what Skirjanek was doing. This group of volunteers were turncoats, in some sense of the word. They weren't the released prisoners from last week. They were all former "citizens" of the enemy, and as much as he believed their defection was legit, there was no way to be certain they weren't here to learn what they could and report back. If that was the case, the colonel was just reinforcing the message that their problem was with Charlottesville's leadership and not its people.

"Sounds good enough to me," Lawton announced, taking in the faces of the other group of men who had elected to jump ship. "Then again, so did what I heard from Charlottesville six months ago. I guess we'll just see."

*

UVA Campus

From the top-floor office overlooking the UVA campus, the view was as it should be; ordered, calm, and most critically, hers. From her vantage point, Lisa Cooper had a good view. There was the ever-present crowd of people in what had become the market commons, stretching out from the front of the Madison building beyond the Rotunda. She could remember students sitting out there with their book bags, waiting for class or playing Frisbee, oblivious to how fragile their existence was. Now, it was a makeshift sea of folding tables, tents, and spread-out blankets heaped with the detritus of a fallen civilization. A swap fair at the end of the world.

She was struck by the crowd. A quarter of a mile away through her window, and she could sense the restlessness. There weren't as many goods to trade lately. They couldn't get anyone out of town to forage, and she'd already cut back the generators supplying power to the dorms; what diesel they had left on-site was relegated to keeping Steven's toys running. To make matters worse, those making yesterday's supply runs had returned on foot, again, and missing half a dozen people who had elected not to return.

The militia had stopped another group from trying to sneak out the night before. Warnings hadn't been enough, and they'd had to be shot when they refused to return to campus. The same militia was even now among the crowd in the commons, spreading the story that the "enemy" had attacked the campus last night and been repulsed. Something had been needed to explain the gunfire that had awoken her as well.

She needed to reestablish a firm hold on her people, and fast. They needed to be as invested in their own survival as she was in her own; that wasn't going to happen while she sat here and allowed her people's morale to be sapped by what Steven had labeled a siege. She'd let her "general" convince her that attacking the enemy would lead to a slaughter of their people, and maybe he was right. These Army assholes had certainly been able to run rings around anything that Marks had come up with.

But beyond blowing up the main bridges out of town, they hadn't attacked yet either. Maybe Steven was right and there just weren't that many of them. It was starting to be the only thing that made sense to her. If she'd been in their place, and had the numbers to do, she'd have attacked long ago.

She took a sip of her freshly ground coffee, and realized forcing the enemy to attack would solve many of her issues. They could afford the losses. It would unite and focus her people, revitalize her authority; and it would have the added benefit of winnowing out the enemy's limited numbers. Besides, they should be starting to get sick and die by now. Hell, she caught herself smiling . . . Steven might even get himself killed in the fighting. All of *his* people, most of them men who enjoyed playing soldier, would have a dead hero to revere. Promoting one of them to take his place would just further tie them to her.

There was only one sure way she could think of to force them to attack. Steven had warned her against it, but it wasn't the enemy blocking the roads outside of town that she worried about. It was her own people; the crowd milling in the distance, full of insecurity and worry. Steven was incapable of understanding that. When push came to shove, he was stuck in his old-world patriarchal construct where the military was the protector of the people. He would never grasp the simple fact that the people's insecurity and dependence were the ultimate tools for creating a path to and maintaining power.

"Karen!" she shouted at the closed door to her office. Her aide opened the door just a few seconds later.

"Ma'am?"

"Get a message to General Marks; I need to see him as soon as possible."

"Ma'am, he left a message that he was accompanying one of the patrols this morning."

Even better. "Do you know if Josh Keynes went with him?"

"No, ma'am." Karen shook her head and then waved a hand in front of her face. "I mean to say, he is not with the general. I saw him coming in this morning. He looked to be arranging another training session with one of the militia companies."

She knew Karen's interest in Josh was more than professional. She didn't have the heart to tell the woman that she believed Josh had fallen for Dr. Vance. She wasn't sure of it, and she was uncertain about what she thought of it herself. She was going to need Josh going forward.

"See if you can find him. I do need to speak to him."

*

Chapter 27

Pro knew what Jason was going to think. But the "what would Jason do?" question hadn't gone through his head once. There was only what he knew he had to do. He'd known since Daniel's funeral. The colonel hadn't said a thing about his presence when he had filled Jason in on everything that happened while they'd been gone. He'd kept his mouth shut and just listened, while trying not to be too obvious as he took in the big map of the UVA campus stapled to the wall.

They'd learned a lot from the drone, and even more from the people Skirjanek had labeled defectors. Many of the buildings on the campus map now had labels. A lot of them just said "Dorm"; the library had its name scratched out and replaced with "Armory." One building in particular, labeled "HQS," and surrounded by a large parking lot labeled "Heavy Equipment," dominated the northeast quadrant of the campus. While Jason and the colonel talked, he focused on the map, the surrounding neighborhoods, and the roads stretching out to the edge of town.

He could go where they couldn't. In his head, it was that simple. He was the best sneak he knew. Even Farmer and Salguero had heaped praise on him for his ability to move without being spotted. Nathans had wanted to get him on a sniper's slow-crawl course, whatever that was. If he was spotted, he could just be the kid everyone expected him to be. He could use that. He'd use anything he could to get close enough to kill the crazy bitch he knew was responsible for Daniel's death. He had to do something, and Skirjanek was still treating him like the walking wounded. He was fine.

Jason, the colonel, Pavel, and John had been planning something all day, and they'd said that he wasn't yet back to full strength and would have to wait "a while longer before taking an active role." Screw that! He managed to keep a straight face to hide his disappointment. That had become impossible when Jason had given him some bullshit message to run over to Reed while the rest of them filed into the office of the landscaping company that Skirjanek called his war room. When the door had shut in his face, he'd wanted to scream and kick the damn thing down. Tell them how wrong they were; but he'd delivered the message to Reed, wiping away tears of anger during the long walk.

His "escape" from the main Gypsy camp at Zion Crossroads almost ended before it started. He'd collected what he needed during the previous day, slowly, never carrying more than a few items at a time. He spent enough time bullshitting with Poy that the big guy had ended up helping him fix up the mountain bike that he was going to use. All the while saying that Pro should just use one of the "cruiser" bikes that Poy liked to use to pedal around the camp because they were somehow cooler.

Jason had left on a patrol with Farmer and Pavel an hour after dinner. He was left in his tent alone. He was surrounded by friends and people he trusted with his life, but as he snuck out of the tent, through the yard, and around the back of the landscaping office, carrying his pack like a duffel bag, he thought back on the night he'd spent shuttling canned goods out of Pete's old house. It had been the night he'd first met Jason . . .

"Dammit, Pro!" Ray's voice snapped him back to reality. He'd been checking behind him and had almost stepped on Ray and one of the Russian ladies; he thought it was Valeria or Valentina or something like that. It was dark enough that he couldn't be sure. He did his best not to look as the woman started laughing and tried to cover herself with Ray's shirt.

"Kid, you have got to quit surprising me!"

"Uhhh . . . Sorry."

"Where you headed this time of night?"

He was glad it was dark; he could feel his face flush. "Jason said I could go with one of the patrols in the morning. I'm just getting ready; I couldn't sleep."

"Us either." The woman laughed again.

"Oh . . . Jeez, really, I'm sorry."

"Pro." Ray waved him off. "'S OK . . . I'll see you in the morning."

"Right!" He felt himself nod in agreement as he remained frozen in place with embarrassment. "OK, then, you all have a good night."

"Pro." Ray was smiling as he jerked his head in the direction of the parked vehicles. "Go . . ."

"Sorry, really," he half mumbled as he set off around the equipment shed, thinking that this was what Jason must have meant about "Murphy."

"This is why I wanted to stay in my tent!" he heard the woman complain before he passed out of earshot.

His bike was where he'd left it, and he only had to get his rifle from where he'd stashed it earlier in one of the JLTVs. He had a long way to go in order to avoid the scouts that the colonel had scattered around the eastern edge of the city. He was going to ride north on 15 until he found Louisa Road and then bend west until he ran out of rural roads to follow, and he knew he would. Hammock's Gap was like a giant swath of green on the map, stretching out from the eastern edge of the city. The only thing he could see that crossed it before he'd have to swing too far north was one of those massive power lines and a railroad.

He was aiming for the power lines; he could follow them all the way to where they crossed over Highway 20. From there, it was a straight shot into the city, coming from a direction where he didn't think he'd be spotted. He wasn't worried about the pretend soldiers of Charlottesville; it was Jason, Skirjanek, and his Marines that he had to avoid. He checked his water bottle and made sure his CamelBac wasn't leaking. For the two weeks before Daniel's death, and since he'd come back, he'd been one of Skirjanek's gophers. He knew where everyone was scattered around Zion Crossroads, on either side of the freeway.

He pedaled slowly, past the settling ponds behind the McDonald's, then around the back side of the massive Walmart supply depot before swinging back to Route 15. From that point, he took off to the north like a rocket. There was enough moonlight that he didn't need to use his night vision, which was a good thing; he hadn't been able to scrounge an extra set of batteries the day before. He had roughly fourteen miles of easy pedaling before he'd have to leave the road. By then, the Gypsy camp would start waking up, and his clock would start ticking.

*

Charlottesville

Eric was giving him the "you've got to be kidding" look. They'd known each other since the meltdown. Together, he and the big guy had kept control of the situation in the basement of the church where they'd hidden with a bunch of other strangers. Since emerging and falling in with Lisa Cooper, Eric had been pretty much engaged in keeping the juice flowing through the part of the campus they had occupied. He'd been a lineman for the power company before the virus, and not somebody Cooper would have spent a minute of effort on getting to know.

"Look, they haven't fired on any of our people who didn't start shit with them," Josh explained. "Cooper told me to get somebody I trust to keep their mouth shut to deliver her message." Which was only partially true. He needed somebody he trusted to deliver *his* message. If Cooper found out that he'd put at risk the guy who kept the lights on . . . he might as well pack his bags and go deliver the message himself. A big part of him wanted to do just that, but that would only put him under suspicion.

"Just drive up, white flag flying? Fuck . . . you."

"They're twelve miles up the road at the Zion Crossroads overpass. You can be up and back in less than half an hour."

Eric just grinned at him and shook his head. "It's so safe, you do it."

"I would, but Cooper doesn't want me talking to them. Trust me."

"She that paranoid?"

"What do you mean?"

"Look." Eric waved away the question. "I do trust you; you know that. We had each other's backs when no one else did. You want me to deliver the message, I will. But only if you drive." Eric pointed at the open-topped jeep sitting behind the roadblock on the freeway. He'd already mounted a white flag from the whip antenna.

He immediately warmed to the idea. No one would be excited to drive up to the enemy that had them encircled, and he'd say as much to Cooper if asked. "Deal!" He smiled. "But remember, I'm just your driver."

Eric made to hand back the sealed envelope, and he refused it with two upraised palms. "You're the messenger." He jerked a thumb at his own chest. "Driver."

The people manning the roadblock all looked at them like they were crazy as they sat in the jeep and waited for the Bradley, acting as the gate, to be started up and rolled away. Eric smiled at him and indicated the surprise on the faces of the guards watching them. "You think they know something we don't?"

"It's the militia," he whispered. "She'll have told somebody here exactly what we are doing."

He put the jeep into gear, and rolled slowly through the gate opening. Cars were welded together four high and reinforced with Jersey barriers and rough, unfinished concrete. Behind them, the wall itself was six cars high and stretched across the entire freeway to anchor itself in the hills lining the interstate.

"What *are* we doing?"

"Cooper thinks she's delivering a message that all the soldiers surrounding us are going to start dying of the virus."

Eric shook his head as if to clear it and then turned on him. "And you asked me to deliver *that* message? What the fuck!"

He smiled at his friend. "That's not the only message in the envelope; I added a message of my own."

Eric sat quietly for a moment as the jeep picked up speed on the freeway. The hot, humid air felt like a blast furnace until they picked up enough speed to get some degree of cooling. "If this is a long story, you'd better slow the fuck down. I mean it, Josh."

*

"Get out slowly! Move away from the vehicle." Uwasi didn't yell. He didn't have to; Kent Mason, Reed, and six of Reed's combat team had met the jeep at the end of the exit lane off the freeway. In terms of uniforms, gear, and of late, deportment, there was little difference, if any, between one of the volunteers from Northern Virginia and one of the Marines. In a real fight, Drew knew the difference would be huge, and would stay that way for some time, maybe forever. But, as he observed the two men stepping lightly out of the jeep, he was pleased with what he saw.

"Jen! Marcum! Pat them down." Reed was starting to sound like an officer. Two of his people slung their weapons onto their backs, and moved forward under the barrels of their colleagues.

"What is that?" Reed pointed at the manila envelope that Marcum had swatted to the ground.

"It's a message for your colonel, from Ms. Cooper." The big guy, dressed in what looked like work overalls, pointed at his feet. "We're just the messengers here, flag of truce and all that."

"Were you at your roadblock when we showed up, under a white flag?" Kent Mason sounded pissed. Drew couldn't fault the man. He'd been wondering the same thing.

"I was working on campus when that went down."

"How 'bout you, slick?" Mason adjusted his rifle and focused on the other man, who was dressed like some throwback to a contract group in Iraq; 5.11 pants, boots, and a wisely empty thigh holster. He may have driven the vehicle, but he looked like he was leading this circus.

"I wasn't," the man said. "I was with General Marks, miles away. He did try to stop what happened."

"He tried?" Drew knew Mason and Naylor had become good friends. The man was justified in his anger. If Chief Sweet had been here, the messengers would probably have already been shot.

"What's the message?" Drew interjected, as he walked forward to step out in line with his people, between Reed and Mason. "I'm Colonel Skirjanek."

The contractor-looking guy turned his gaze to his larger companion in expectation. The big guy shook his head and took a slow step backwards. "Sorry, bud. I'm out of this."

"May I?" The contractor pointed at the envelope.

"Go ahead," Drew answered, as he stepped closer himself.

"The message from Cooper was sealed, but I can guess what it says. The other message in there . . . was from me."

Drew thumbed the envelope and regarded the two men.

"I wasn't supposed to be here," the driver explained. "I was supposed to find somebody I trusted to deliver it. I ended up agreeing to drive."

"I see." Drew tore open the envelope. There was another, smaller envelope inside. A fancy, monogrammed thing with gold filigreed letters on it. Cooper must have been "someone" before the fall, he figured, though for the life of him, he couldn't imagine the type of person who would have hung on to something as useless as personalized stationery during the apocalypse.

He dumped the envelope on the ground and began reading. It was a short note, full of justifying bullshit and identification as a victim of military oppression before it simply announced that they'd all been infected by the virus - "and if you're not already sick as you read this, you soon will be." It went on to explain how the released prisoners they'd taken in had all been infected, as well as their gear. He wasn't able to prevent the chill that crept up his back as he read the message, but his mind had already gone back to the message the refugees had found hidden in their gear. Whatever was on his face when he looked up, it caused the man in front of him to take a step back.

"And your message?" He held up the piece of folded paper.

"Cooper thinks we recreated the virus from the CDC lab at the university medical center," the man got out in a rush. "We didn't. We destroyed it."

"Who's 'we'?"

"Me and our doctor. She's a doctor, and I was . . . trusted enough to help her."

"Dr. Vance?" He enjoyed the look of surprise on the messenger's face.

"How . . . how could you know that?"

Drew read the note the man had inserted into the envelope. It was a more verbose version of what Dr. Vance had planted in the refugees' gear. The note was signed "Josh" at the bottom. "You're Josh?"

"Yeah, Josh Keynes."

"Cooper truly believes she's had us infected?"

"She does." Josh nodded. "She's trying to egg you on to attack us. She waited until she thought you'd all be sick."

"How many people were party to this plan?" Drew felt his throat constrict, as if he were trying to talk through an iron pipe. "How many people were OK with bringing back a bug that killed seven and a half billion people?" He dropped the papers to the ground and took a step towards the man.

"Far as I know, just Cooper, General Marks, and the doc and I."

"I sure as shit didn't know about it," the big guy drawled. "That's fucked up."

Drew regarded both of them. "Tell her you just saw a few of us, and that we looked sick. You go back and tell her we'll be coming."

"But—"

"But nothing, Mr. Keynes. I have to believe you and Dr. Vance. No one here is sick. It's something we've been on the lookout for since making landfall. Cooper is correct though—this isn't something we are going to ignore."

He turned to look at the faces behind him. Reed and his people, who would have been immune to the biological attack, looked every bit as pissed off as Mason and Uwasi did.

He faced the messengers. "We will attack, and we will destroy Cooper, Marks, and anybody who stands with them." He looked at both of them, forcing himself to admit he owed a debt to the man standing in front of him. He and the doctor who took her oath seriously. "If you want to save your own people, then you've got your own message to start spreading."

He regarded both of them. "I know there are people who will stand by her, just as I know there are a lot of people who aren't there by choice, especially at this point. You'd best get going. You've got until tomorrow night to get your people out of the way—or take care of the issue yourself. We've been very judicious as to our use of force up until this point; I'm starting not to care. Tomorrow night. Tell here we're coming for her."

Chapter 28

Jason unfolded the map and checked where he, Pavel, and Farmer were in relation to Pro. The kid was probably going to be pissed off, but he'd had a drone tracking him since he'd ridden out of camp. Poy was taking care not to lose sight of him, and the infrared camera had worked well during the night. If Pro stayed on his present course, he'd be coming to them. It was a different world than it had been when they'd pulled up for the night. Skirjanek's message to them this morning, following his visitors, made that crystal clear. They were done waiting.

John was bringing the rest of the Marines and a squad of Reed's people to them; "rolling heavy," as Skirjanek had put it. With luck, they could intercept Pro before the kid wandered into a battle. He had figured Pro was going to do something stupid, and he'd taken precautions. Ray and Skirjanek had been watching him like a hawk yesterday evening, and Pro's "escape" hadn't been nearly as clean or as unobserved as they'd led him to believe. He'd planned on letting him go and intercepting him before he'd enter the city, but Cooper's messengers this morning had changed all that.

Pavel took a knee next to him and looked at the map. "You are still thinking to take the rail tracks into the city?"

The rail bridge would support any vehicle John and his team would be bringing, and they'd kept a close eye on the railway for the last week. Beyond an occasional foot patrol, the enemy didn't seem to be interested in using it themselves.

"I am," he confirmed. "I think we should break a small team, possibly two, off on foot. Get some eyes on to direct the main strike."

"And the boy?"

"He comes with us." Jason had spent sleepless hours the night before, trying to come to terms with bringing Pro along. The alternative, short of handcuffing him inside one of the Bradleys, would be to just see him go lone wolf again.

"I can appreciate his skills." Pavel nodded to himself. "You are certain?"

No, he wasn't certain. "He's the best scout we have."

"I'm uncertain about that." Pavel's finger dropped on the middle of the campus. "Though he may be able to walk among them without raising suspicion."

"Until he shoots someone." He did his best to smile.

An hour later, Farmer's voice came over the radio. "I spotted him. He's coming down the north edge of Highway 20. I'll let him pass my position before I fall in behind. He's on foot."

Fifteen minutes later, Farmer radioed back. "Following."

Jason picked up his own radio and switched channels. Pro was going to be pissed off, but he took more than a little enjoyment in what he was about to do.

"Jason for Pro, over."

Jason looked up at Pavel who was looking at him strangely. "I hid a radio in the bottom of his pack; volume is cranked up."

Pavel gave a short grunt of laughter. "Hopefully, he has an extra pair of pants with him."

Pro lay still, frozen in surprise at the bottom of a dry ditch overgrown with weeds. Jason's voice had nearly caused his heart to stop before he realized it was coming from his bag.

"Jason for Pro, over. I know you can hear me."

"You hid a radio on me?"

"Sorry, you aren't as sneaky as you think you are."

"Doesn't change anything," Pro came back.

"We are attacking tonight." Jason was worried Pro would just toss the radio; he wanted to get the message across quick. "I want you with me for that, and be advised, you are approaching our position."

There was a long pause during which Jason pictured Pro having already thrown the radio away and running. "Who's behind me?"

Jason looked up at Pavel, who was nodding in appreciation. "That would be Farmer," he answered, smiling to himself.

"You'll let me go with you?"

"Yes."

"No tricks? Because you old guys aren't as fast as I am."

Jason just shook his head, smiling. "No tricks. We are at the next crossroad, or you can wait for Farmer and come in together."

Farmer had been following the clear path of broken weeds, stepping on grass and the occasional boot print, until he wasn't. He had stepped around a tight pair of oak trees growing out from the bank of the ditch when Pro's trail disappeared. He froze for a moment and then looked back behind him.

"Pro, I know you're here."

"I've had you for the last couple of minutes." The voice came from directly above him. He looked up to see Pro lying along a thick limb of the nearest tree. He'd just walked underneath the kid.

"Done resting?"

"How'd you guys know where I was?"

"Ray radioed Jason last night. We've had Poy following you with the drone."

"That's cheating."

"There's no such thing, Pro." He hid his embarrassment at letting the teenager get the drop on him. "You coming or not?"

Pro's legs swung off the branch, and he dropped to the ground after hanging by his hands for a moment.

"Yeah, I'm coming. Jason hid a radio in my pack. He told me about tonight. Why'd he put you out to creep on me?"

Probably because he didn't know if you'd be smart enough to listen. "I'm wondering that myself."

Charlottesville

"Did you believe him?" General Marks's face was a full of concern. The general's voice sounded like it wanted to crack in excitement, or maybe it was fear; Josh wasn't sure. The look on Cooper's face couldn't have been more different; she'd been looking at him with unbridled suspicion since he'd walked in.

"Yeah, I believed him," he answered. Josh glanced at Cooper. "Maybe he was playing it up for his own guys, but he believes it—they are going to attack."

"But he looked sick?" Marks leaned forward across the table, desperate for the answer.

He nodded in reply. "More than looked; he was sick. One of his guards could barely stand, eyes were bloodshot." His mind drifted back to the die-off; it was easy to remember the symptoms. He rubbed at his own face, not having to fake the visceral reaction. "The one guard who was wobbly, you could see where he'd started bleeding under the skin, at his neck. He'll probably be dead by tonight. We only saw nine or ten of them in total, including this colonel."

"Why did you go yourself?" Lisa didn't seem to be concerned with Marks's line of questioning.

"Wasn't the plan." He shrugged. "I found somebody I trusted, but he wasn't going to go by himself. After what we did to their messengers, no one thought driving up to them was a good idea. Erik delivered the message; I just drove." He couldn't tell if Lisa believed him or not. Maybe he was the one being paranoid now. He'd tended bar for his entire adult life; he knew people. If Lisa had been a guy with a few drinks in him, she would have looked like she was about to start swinging.

"Skirjanek . . . I recognize the name." General Marks seemed oblivious to the tension radiating from Cooper's side of the table. "He was one of those shadow think-tank colonels in the Pentagon. One of those guys who would have gotten his first star a long time ago if he'd had a political bone in his body. Wrote a bunch of strategy papers and policy critiques that made a lot of people angry."

"Is that important?" Lisa finally stopped looking at him and focused on Marks. "I mean really! Right now?"

Marks slammed a palm down on the conference table. "Yes! For God's sake, it is. We have to know what we are dealing with! Who we are dealing with . . ." Marks put a hand on top of his head and let out a deep breath. "I've said that from the beginning. That man, well equipped as he seems to be, with two or three companies of trained soldiers, could roll over our people with ease."

Josh could see the finality of the decision in Lisa's eyes, even if Marks couldn't. He'd walked the fence between these two for too long. He had no doubt as to which side offered the best chance of survival over the next forty-eight hours. Not just his survival, but Naomi's too. He had to get out to the hospital and warn her that their secret had a distinct shelf life. As soon as they were attacked, Cooper would know she'd been lied to. He knew the woman well enough to know Lisa would waste no time in hunting them both down.

"General, I didn't see any evidence of those kinds of numbers. Those I did see were sick. This Skirjanek, whoever he was in the old world, seemed desperate. 'Pissed off' doesn't begin to describe his reaction when he read the message. He came very close to having us shot." He turned and faced Lisa. "And we would have been, but he wanted you to know, in his own words—he was coming. We can beat them."

"And we will." Lisa laid both of her hands on the table and offered him a smile as she stood up. It felt like a temporary reprieve. She didn't even look at Marks. "You two, go and get our people ready. I'll do the same. I'll address everyone this evening at dinner. Just because he said tomorrow night, why would he wait?"

*

"The colonel's going to dance around them tonight, knock on their door with the tank, overfly the campus for a message drop and maybe even let them get a look at the drone, all starting with the drone in a couple of hours." John Bruce's briefing was short on details. The mission wasn't at all complicated; locate the Charlottesville leadership and eliminate it.

"All diversionary, but in force," Bruce continued. "Give your team some noise to hide in as you make your way to the campus."

His team . . . Jason had already decided on splitting it up. Pavel and Pro would be one team. If they were questioned, it was an easier sell for a teenager and a guy who spoke broken English with a Russian accent to say they were new additions to the community. Farmer, and he would be their backup, there to eliminate anybody who didn't buy their story.

"We'll keep the pressure up during the day tomorrow. Hopefully, by nightfall, you'll have had some success. The colonel will roll for real, either through or past their block, starting at 2000 hours, and he'll use the ford we located just north of the freeway to cross the Rivanna. From there, he'll proceed northwest towards the campus. With luck, he's hoping they'll try to stop him. My team will roll down the rail bed." Bruce paused and jerked a thumb at the four Bradleys he and his people had brought up. "My unit has my Marines minus Poy, and Salguero filled out with Mr. Reed's best people. Twenty-four infantry; we'll be on call to assist you as needed or otherwise react. The train tracks roll right to the southern edge and northern edge of campus, but we can get off anywhere along the line."

"Poy staying home to fly the drone?" Farmer asked.

"Yes," Bruce answered. "But he's also got two M triple seven howitzers laid in. He's convinced the colonel he's tied it into the GPS network. He's been training up some of Mr. Reed's people, but targeting time or rate of fire isn't going to be anything like we are used to. Skirjanek expressly ordered me to make certain that no 'danger close' -fire missions are requested. It's stand off and stay away only."

"Poy playing video games with 155mm, what could go wrong?" Nathans piped in from the edge of the gathered crowd stacked between two Bradleys.

"We need arty; I for one will be glad it's him at the other end." Bruce shot Nathans a withering look.

"Oorah, Captain Bruce."

"Questions?"

"Simple enough." Jason nodded to himself and looked over at Pavel, who was regarding Nathans with an evil smile. "I think Major Volkov and I just had the same idea. I'd like to take Nathans with us, get him and his gun in a good position before the balloon goes up."

"Works." Bruce nodded. "With luck, we spot her and cut the head off this snake, and it dies quick."

Bruce turned and looked at everyone gathered around him. "The colonel has taken pains to limit any casualties, and that will continue. We are going to hit them hard, especially any military hardware we see. Where they stand and fight, we'll hit them hard, but it's all to get them moving. Which we are going to let them do. These are civilians who have been playing bully. Most of them haven't had a choice in that. That said, this will be a fight. Do not hesitate. The decision process is all on their side." John had turned and was speaking directly to Reed and his team who would be the infantry inside the Bradleys.

"We are here to fight—do not take any risks in trying to determine their intentions. Until you see a white flag or their asses running away, they are the enemy. They will have a chance to choose wisely." John's face broke out into a wide smile. "We'll be starting leaflet drops with clear instructions for them, starting in about an hour."

*

Drew shook his head at the sight of Poy trying to "fix" the copy machine. The tight spaces of the big machine weren't designed for a forearm the size of most thighs. He took in the extension cord that snaked across the floor, out the window, to a portable generator, and could almost laugh at the thought that the initial step of their first battle was delayed by, in Poy's descriptive parlance, the "freakin' mother of all paper jams."

"This mean I don't have to fly? If he can't fix it?" Tim Calhoun, his reluctant helo pilot, was almost smiling at the single sheet of paper the machine had produced before it had starting making a grinding noise that sounded like it was eating itself.

"We'll handwrite the damn things if we have to."

He watched his "pilot" walk back outside, mumbling to himself. Poy and a couple of Jason's people who had shown some interest had been buried in technical maintenance manuals for the Black Hawk for a week. Spare parts he had plenty of; they just had to pull them from The Hole. The hard part, according to Poy, was identifying the right part, then locating it in the massive underground warehouse. The upside was that the helo was in better shape now than when it had arrived.

Poy's current difficulties aside, the technical whiz had been a godsend. Cameron "Poy" Park was going to be promoted very soon. As much as he could use another trained Marine, the guy was invaluable in keeping what technology and gear they had working.

"Drop your crayons, Colonel," Poy announced. "I think I found the problem."

Poy started dropping shredded paper and what looked like grass over his shoulder. "Mice, sir. An old nest."

He rubbed the bridge of his nose and did his best to roll with the punches. *Mice* . . . "What do you need, Mr. Poy? How can I help?"

"Sir, I usually have Elliot playing gopher for me, but I could use a vacuum cleaner. One of those hand jobbies—like for cleaning the inside of your car. A can of compressed air if we can find some. It's a mess in here, sir."

"Keep working the problem, Poy. I'm on it."

Shakespeare sprang to mind immediately—something about "my kingdom for a horse." West Point, the Special Forces, a graduate year at Harvard Business School, CENTCOM Chief of Operations), and more command staff positions at the Pentagon than he cared to remember, interspersed with three combat tours; the apocalypse had changed everything. Right now, he needed to find a vacuum.

"Just like you're spraying fields!" the colonel yelled into his helmet mic. Calhoun almost cringed; why the hell did everyone think they had to yell into the thing? "Stay low and fast. We'll be out of there before they have time to react."

They were coming in from the south and had just crossed over the freeway. The colonel had told him to pass to the east of the football stadium, past the hospital, and then straight down the main lawn, using Jefferson's famous Rotunda as his aim point. He could do that; as much as it killed him to admit it, flying sixty feet off the ground at over 130 miles an hour was fun. Or would be until someone started shooting at them. He hoped the colonel had an appreciation for how many things could break or wear out on a helicopter. The damn things basically tried to shake themselves apart between maintenance checks.

For the hundredth time in the last twenty minutes, he wondered why the colonel had insisted on coming along. His people in the back, with the cardboard boxes of flyers, had guns. It wasn't like he had anywhere else to go in the event he just decided to fly off.

"I've been studying this place for almost a month by map. I want to get eyes on." The colonel seemed to answer him, and for a moment, he feared he might have spoken out loud. It wouldn't have been the first time his mouth outran his brain.

"Get your boys ready to dump your cargo, Colonel."

"If you see a large group of people, aim for them. We want to spread the message as wide as we can."

"They'll have guns, Colonel. They all have guns."

"Far as they know, you are bringing their helicopter back. I doubt they told anyone they lost their pilot—not that type of leadership."

Calhoun stifled his laughter. "Lost! Is that what you are calling it? Shanghaied, more like."

"Semantics, Mr. Calhoun."

"OK, lots of people stay in these neighborhoods between the hospital and the stadium. Get ready to dump." He made certain the colonel signaled his team in the back of the bird as he checked his airspeed and eased up on the collective a little bit. He wasn't too worried about being shot out of the sky. The colonel was right; as low as they were, they'd be through and gone before most people even saw them. He even thought he'd have time to swing west at the top of the campus so the colonel could paper the dining hall and dorm areas past the baseball field.

"OK, now! Bombs away!"

Josh had heard the beating blades of the helicopter fading in and out of earshot for a few minutes before it suddenly grew in volume and shot past where he stood, near the entrance to the hospital. Its appearance caught him by surprise; by the time he started pulling his rifle around from his back, he could see the masses of paper fluttering out in the downwash. The paper looked like big feathers shedding off an even bigger bird.

Smart, he thought, as he let out a held breath in relief. He'd been trying to warn as many people as he could without falling under the suspicion of Cooper or one of her hard-core minions. Colonel Skirjanek had just done that for him. He was at the hospital to warn Naomi and get her somewhere safe before Lisa figured out her invaders weren't dying, or even sick. When that happened, he and Naomi had to have a plan to avoid Cooper. Their survival depended on it.

He watched as the helicopter quickly dropped past the horizon of trees at the edge of the parking lot, before focusing on the dumped debris floating down. Some of it was going to land in the parking lot.

Most had hit the ground before he had made it out there, and he had no problem picking up several.

Citizens of Charlottesville—Your leadership has just advised us by messenger that they purposely infected our group with the virus. I won't go into the morals or ethics of such an action; that is for each of you to decide. What concerns we have had with your leadership have now passed into the realm of vendetta. We may be dying, but our last actions are going to be taking Lisa Cooper and Steven Marks with us. Any and all occupants of Charlottesville who support what they have done, or attempt to defend them from our wrath, are warmly invited to join them. For those of you who wish to see a newly elected leadership from your own ranks, you have two options. Lay down your arms and signal your surrender when we attack—OR—take matters into your own hands before we do. Save yourselves from a fight you cannot win.

Colonel Andrew Skirjanek, Former US Army

"They just dropped these all over campus." He handed the flyer to Naomi. "You need to hide . . . now."

"I've got a place picked out in—"

"I don't want to know, and don't tell anyone. Don't let anyone see you go."

She looked at him with concern. "I thought you'd want to come with me."

"I do." He was surprised at how much he wanted to do just that, right this instant. He also wanted to keep her safe. Not Dr. Vance, but Naomi. She'd risked everything to save lives, lives of people she didn't even know. With her looking at him the way she was right now, he couldn't do any less.

"If I disappear now, Cooper will know we lied to her. She'd burn this place down looking for us, and Marks might actually get better prepared to face them; right now, he thinks they're all half-dead. I'll get somewhere safe, but it can't be until the fight starts. Cooper will need me then. Right now, I'm just another potential threat." He pointed at the flyer in her hands. "Especially after this."

"You promise?"

"I promise." He leaned in to give her a hug, but she threw her arms around his neck and kissed him, hard enough that he immediately questioned his judgment.

"I'm going to hold you to that."

Josh's radio was going berserk before he made it back to his vehicle. Calls were coming in from all over campus. He switched to the command channel, and before he could check in, Marks's voice was screaming for him to report back to the admin building.

"On my way." He paused and brought the radio back up to his face. "General, did you catch the tail number on the helicopter?"

"Affirmative, get back here, Josh."

The drive back across campus was a study in mood swings. He could sense the unease in the faces he saw, looks that left no doubt as to whether the paper drop had been successful. Some of those people knew him and how close he was to Cooper and Marks. They looked scared.

Driving up to the admin building, he was stopped at the gate by a group of militia.

"What the hell?" he almost shouted. "I got orders to report."

"We know." Brian Casper was one of the students who had been with Cooper from the very beginning. He had almost a dozen of Cooper's diehards standing behind him, blocking his pickup from entering the fenced parking lot. "We heard the radio call."

"So are you going to get out of my way?"

"We were told to disarm anyone and everyone before they go in the building." Brian tried to give him a smile. "Miss Cooper's orders."

"Because of the flyers?" He tried not to shout. "It's what they are trying to do, drive us apart. This is stupid."

Brian looked like he might agree with him, but he knew it wasn't going to matter. "Sorry, orders."

He handed over his sidearm, and jerked his head back at the assault rifle resting in his gun rack. "It'll stay in the truck; one of you can babysit it. I figure on needing it soon."

Brian held up the sidearm. "That'll work."

"You said they were on their last legs!" Lisa started yelling the minute he entered her office. Marks was there as well, and he tried not to let his surprise show that the general was still armed. Lisa had a couple of her civilian advisors in the room with her, as well as a trio of bodyguards that Marks had always referred to as Cooper's Praetorian Guard. "How they'd manage to fly a helicopter?"

"I don't think they did," he said. "I think it was Calhoun flying; I know it was the same helicopter."

"You think they are forcing him to help?" Marks asked.

"Maybe he volunteered," he offered. "Doesn't really matter, does it?"

"Makes sense," Marks commented, filling the surprised silence. "If they'd had a helicopter before he went missing, they'd have used it."

Marjorie Elster spoke up. "I'm in agreement with Josh." The woman was another academic of some sort, "rescued" from James Madison University in Harrisonburg. She had been attached to Lisa's hip ever since. "It doesn't matter; what matters is the content of the flyers. It's affecting morale."

"So is replacing my guards with those militia bullyboys outside." Marks was getting worked up. Josh wondered how long this meeting had been running before he'd arrived. The flyers had been dropped less than an hour ago. He got the immediate impression that Marks was severely outnumbered in the room.

"That was a political decision, General," Karen, Cooper's personal assistant, answered.

Marks's face went red in anger as he spun in place to face the woman.

"It was a stupid decision! One that undermines the morale of the very people you all are going to be relying on for your survival."

"It was my decision, General." Lisa's voice was calm. Crazy or not, Josh thought it was an effective counterpoint to Marks's panic.

Marks looked at Lisa for a moment, a myriad of emotions flashing across his reddened face. Josh could see the resignation in it. "Are we supposed to pretend that makes it a viable decision?" Marks shook his head in disgust. "You're all nuts. You aren't leading a revolution here; you're sitting on a group of traumatized survivors."

Where had *this* general been for the last year? Josh noted the guards all had their hands clasped behind them. He was betting they had guns already in hand. He figured Cooper had already made her decision regarding Marks. He'd been ordered to report to see where his loyalties lay.

"Steven." Lisa shook her head as if disappointed in an answer given by a student. "No one appreciates the role you have played here more than I. But I think the time has come for you step down."

Marks barked in laughter. "Is that what you are going to call it?"

"It's preferable to other things I could call it." Lisa nodded at the guards. "Please relieve the general of his weapon and place him under arrest. He'll hold until this current crisis is over."

Marks reached for his sidearm. Josh had been waiting for it and grabbed the general's arm, pinning it to his body. For a moment, his back was to the rest of the room, and his face was inches from Marks's. The man stared back at him in wounded shock. He offered him a quick wink. The way he figured it; he'd just saved Marks's life. It might not matter. The man was firmly on Skirjanek's list as well.

He was left holding the general's sidearm as he watched two of the guards frog- marched him out of the room. He held the handgun out, grip first, to the remaining guard, who had his own gun leveled at his head.

"Ronnie, that won't be necessary." Lisa came around the conference table to him. "Why don't you keep the general's gun? We don't have any reason not to trust you at this point."

Oh, yes, you do . . . but I'm too chickenshit to pull this trigger and trade my life for yours. "For the record, I think you could have trusted the general too," he said.

"You might be right." Lisa tilted her head to the side as if she was considering his opinion. "But I couldn't be sure he was as committed to the survival of Charlottesville as he was to his own skin. You . . . I don't worry about."

*

Chapter 29

Jason watched Pro and Pavel as they crossed the street, and the corner lawn of a frat house that appeared to have been converted into permanent housing for some of the citizens of Charlottesville. Neither of them bothered to hide their weapons; they were wearing street clothes like the rest of the citizen militia they seemed to be following down the road, west, deeper into the campus. Everyone they saw was armed.

Skirjanek had attacked the roadblock about an hour ago. The 120mm main gun on the Abrams had a distinct sound. There had been half a dozen of the shots, and the light from a couple of secondary explosions had reflected off the low-hanging clouds and been easily seen from the edge of the city that they crept through. By the time they reached the eastern edge of the campus, their small group spotted the groups of citizens, all walking in towards the center of campus. Pavel and Pro had scrambled out of their flak jackets as fast as they could to join Charlottesville's call-up.

Jason had pulled Pro in close. "Remember, we're trusting you with the mission. There's no room for the personal here. You follow Pavel's orders, whatever he says."

"I will." Pro had seemed genuine. But watching the two of them disappear into the darkness was hard.

"I got a dollar that says he gets some before we do."

He turned and looked behind him at Trey Nathans.

"Trey, you're messed up. You know that, right?" Farmer beat him to the punch, which was probably a good thing.

Nathans looked at both of them in surprise. "Relax . . . I meant the Russian; dude's stone-cold nuts."

Jason couldn't imagine Pro in safer hands. Now the three of them had to get to the other side of the medical complex so they could get Nathans to a perch on one of the rooftops. With their heavy packs and Nathans's sniper rifle, they weren't going to blend in as easily as Pro and Pavel. They'd seen two roving security teams in campus security golf carts in the last five minutes. They seemed to be acting like sheepdogs, directing everyone to the middle of campus. He desperately wanted to get eyes and ears onto whatever was happening there.

"You probably don't want to talk too much," Pro whispered to Pavel, "like at all." They had a group of half a dozen men and women a block ahead of them, and another, smaller group behind them. At the last crossroad, they'd been able to see yet another group walking in the same direction, backlit by a couple of vehicles.

"You will speak for me," Pavel whispered.

"OK . . ." Pro regarded the Russian for a moment. The man looked keyed up, not in a nervous way, but like he was ready to break the neck of anybody who got close to them. "Remember, there's people from everywhere here. We'll just blend in."

"I am blending."

"You know, you look like that guy from that old *Terminator* movie, the one who was made of liquid metal."

Pavel looked down at him for a moment and shook his head in confusion as they walked underneath a trellis of some sort at the end of the road. They were entering what appeared to be a garden, with a statue that looked like a lump of rock in the middle of it. "Not Arnold . . .?"

"No, the other guy, the bad terminator."

"Ahh, yes. Was good movie." Pavel turned to check behind him and then gripped Pro by the back of the neck and guided him firmly off the stone path and into the bushes. "We will wait here for everyone to pass, and then follow."

"But . . ."

Pavel's finger mashed against his lips. There wasn't enough light that he could see the Russian, but he could almost imagine red, glowing eyes. Voices reached them a moment later as the group that had been following them entered the garden.

"What the hell do they expect us to do?" A woman's voice was heavy with worry.

"I suppose they'll tell us, won't they?"

"You believe them, from the flyers they dropped?"

"How the hell am I supposed to know? If they're for real, I'm going . . ." The group passed out of earshot.

"We should follow them," Pro whispered.

"Yes, from a distance," Pavel answered. "We do not want to be in the middle of a crowd. We will wait."

Pro wanted to argue on principle, wanted to be doing something, but realized it made sense. They waited a couple of minutes before another, larger group of over twenty people streamed past. The group broke in half to go both ways around the statue within the garden alcove. There were so many voices, they drowned each other out, but it was easy to tell that no one seemed excited about this muster.

Two more smaller groups passed; the last group was walking slow enough that Pro thought they were looking for them. He could feel Pavel tense up next to him. A whirring sound startled the four laggards as they were lit up a by a handheld spotlight.

"We going to have a problem here?" one of the men yelled from the open-sided electric cart that swung into the garden alcove from the neighborhood side.

"No, we're good," one of the men from the group shouted back, holding his arm up to block the spotlight shining in his face.

"Hurry the fuck up, then! Or we'll collect names."

The group picked up their pace and disappeared down the trellised walkway. The cart stayed where it was, its spotlight centered on the laggards until the pathway bent out of sight.

"Should be the last of them," the passenger said as he clicked off his spotlight and put his legs up on the dash of the security cart. "Let's wait here for a few minutes, and then we'll make another loop to see if we have any stragglers."

"Sounds good." The driver hopped out and walked over to the edge of the path. He fumbled with his belt for a moment before turning back to the cart. "You think Marks is going to have them roll out or just reinforce all the gates?"

"Dude, I heard Marks ain't going to be deciding shit. Mendoza told me Cooper had him arrested."

"Yeah, right! He get that off one of those bullshit flyers?"

"I'm serious. He's pretty tight with some of those militia dudes; he'd know."

"Who the hell are we supposed to be taking orders from, then?"

"Keynes for now, I suppose."

The driver finished taking his leak. "This is messed up; we got no business fighting the fucking Army."

"They ain't the Army, Benny. Just a bunch of—"

The radio on the cart stopped whatever the man in the passenger's seat was going to say. "Security three, when you finish your rounds, can you swing up to the north campus? We got a bunch folks with a lot of questions."

The passenger fumbled with his radio for a moment. "You're not there to answer shit; just get them moving to the lawn. We got stragglers at the frat houses. We'll come up when we can." The passenger threw his radio back onto the seat.

"That was Gorelic?" The driver paused with one hand on the roof, looking in at his seated partner.

"Yeah, I don't see why we have to do our job and his."

"I hear that."

Pro was startled by Pavel's movement. The man was there next to him one moment; the next, he was walking out of the bushes towards the cart.

"Who the hell are . . . ?"

Pro saw Pavel raise his handgun with a suppressor. Two muted shots split the night air just as he was starting to stand up.

The driver had collapsed in a heap outside the cart, and the passenger slumped down and slid out the far side. Pavel had already reached down and grabbed the driver. Pro reached him a second later and knelt to help him. Pavel stopped him, picked up the driver's baseball cap, and seated it gently on Pro's head.

"Now we will go. You will drive."

Two quick minutes later, the two bodies were in the bushes, and they were both wearing the borrowed navy windbreakers over their gear and matching UVA baseball hats. Pro was sweating up a storm underneath the extra layer of clothing, but he wasn't about to complain.

"What now?"

Pavel gave him a quick grin. "You can drive this . . .?"

"Golf cart." Pro jumped behind the wheel. "Yes."

Pavel cracked two infrared glow sticks and taped them to the roof of the cart, then fell in next to him, fumbling with his radio. "All units, Raven One and Two are mobile. We are in possession of security vehicle . . . it is golf cart, marked with infrared."

Pro wanted to laugh as he followed Pavel's pointed finger and began turning the cart around.

"Affirmative, Raven One." Jason's voice came back. "Any chance you can deliver Mr. Nathans for us?"

*

Drew listened to his own radio and set it down. Jason and Pavel were on campus. John and his strike team of Bradleys had rolled across the railroad bridge over the Rivanna and were pulled off the tracks a mile from campus. They'd accomplished everything he'd wanted to this evening. It had taken half a dozen shots from Salguero's Abrams, directed against the wall of stacked cars stretching across the freeway, before the people manning the roadblock had started waving T-shirts at them and filing out of their makeshift positions.

They'd stopped the approach at the maximum range of the M1's cannon and fired directly into the wall of stacked cars. It had been for psychological effect only, and Salguero had taken pains to shoot the wall of metal. It had worked; Poy had reported ten minutes ago that the former defenders were still moving back up Route 250 towards the ruined bridge, running into town.

"All units, Skirjanek—we are moving forward to occupy freeway roadblock at Route 250. We will hold there and let them stew for the night." He waited for the confirmations to come back and then pointed down the dark stretch of freeway; patches of small fires amid the still-burning cars were all he could see with his naked eye. He was heads-up in the commander's seat of his Bradley and could see Salguero ten feet away, similarly perched out the top of the Abrams's turret.

"Lead the way, Tommy. Button up, and take out the two Bradleys down there as soon as you are close enough to be certain of hitting them." He hoped whoever was manning them had retreated as well.

"All vehicles will follow in two lines." He looked behind him at the three other Bradleys besides his and the half dozen JLTVs as he transmitted. "Maintain one- hundred-yard separation, just like the approach."

"They are coming." Roberto Giron wasn't a happy camper. He looked over at Mohamed as he crawled through the Bradley's rear hatch and pulled the heavy door shut behind him. If he had a friend inside this metal coffin, it was Mohamed. He'd seen the enemy formation up the freeway with one of the night vision scopes that had been dropped and left behind by the fleeing guard force. Supposedly there to defend the roadblock, they'd turned and run, waving white T-shirts over their heads as they went. The fact that so many of them seemed to have had white T-shirts ready and at hand said more to him than the fact that they'd used them. He'd been careful to keep the pillowcase he had crammed into his thigh pocket out of sight, but it was past time to use it as far as he was concerned.

"No shit, they're coming," Jack spit back at him. "You think they'd have lit us up if they were just going to sit out there?"

Roberto spun towards Jack; he was sitting in the commander's chair where he could control and fire the Bradley's main gun. "We're the only ones left here for them to shoot at! This thing isn't going to scratch the paint on that tank."

The three of them were buttoned up inside the Bradley that acted as the rolling gate for the roadblock. He and Mohamed weren't even supposed to be here. They'd been pulled off the wall to "help" Jack inside the Bradley when his other crew hadn't shown up, earlier in the evening. There was a lot of that going on; everyone had read or heard about the message on the enemy's flyers. Their bad luck; otherwise, he and Mohamed would be headed back to town as fast as their feet would carry them, along with the rest of their unit.

"They've got other vehicles we can hurt." Jack sounded scared, which he could more than understand.

"They have those rockets," Mohamed blurted out. "They will fire before we can."

Jack's hand dropped to his sidearm as he turned towards them in his seat. "We're staying."

"Everyone else is gone," he tried again. "Why?"

"You think these assholes are going to show us any mercy, after what we've done?"

"Who gives a shit? I'm not waiting around to find out; I'm headed west. So are a lot of other people," Roberto said as he looked over at Mohamed, who had slid one seat closer to the front while Jack took another look through his scope.

"What about our other tank? Why aren't they answering?" Jack almost sounded confused, like his brain wasn't working.

"They're gone, too, and this isn't a tank! We're dead men sitting in here."

Jack drew his revolver from his belt and pointed it at him. "We stay and fight."

Roberto's hands went up over his head in reflex. "Easy there. I'm not saying we run, just that this thing is no match for that tank they have. We need to get out of this coffin." Once outside the armored vehicle, Jack could stay and fight if he wanted to; he had no intention of doing anything of the sort.

"We stay." Jack sounded like he was trying to convince himself.

"Why?" Roberto could sense the enemy tank rolling closer. He didn't want to burn to death in a steel box. God had spared him from the virus; he was certain it hadn't been for this. He was already moving as Jack started turning towards him in his seat, the gun coming up slowly. He slammed into the Bradley's commander, the tight spaces doing as much to protect him as having Jack's gun arm pinned against him.

He felt Mohamed next to him, reaching past for Jack's legs. The gun clattered to the deck as the two of them tore Jack out of his station and dumped him on the floor. Mohamed's heavy boot slammed into Jack's face to stop whatever he was going to say. Roberto scooped up the revolver and waved it at the back door, hitting the ramp release control. "Let's go!"

The back ramp came down slow on its hydraulic hinge. Too slow . . . Their Bradley, acting as the barricade's gate, was oriented at a right angle to the freeway. It was presented in an almost perfect profile to the tank bearing down on them. The same tank that had already fired.

The depleted uranium penetrator rod struck the Bradley slightly forward of the midpoint of the upper half of the armored box. There was no explosion of a warhead. The uranium rod and the armor it bore through were converted into a superheated plasma by the kinetic force of the impact. The plasma jet sprayed through the interior, killing them before they knew they'd been hit. Roberto Giron's last thought had been a good one; he'd cheated death again.

*

"They lied to me . . ." Lisa barely heard her own voice. Her office was a madhouse of activity with her people running in and out, shouting orders and requests at their colleagues. Orders that no one was answering. This team she had handpicked and trained to help her administer what she had built was staying by her side. She was enough of a realist to know they weren't the team that could protect her. She'd arrested the man who could have. Marks was being held in the basement of this very building and wouldn't be inclined to help her. Not now.

"Ma'am." Jerry Moser came to a stop in front of her desk. "The scouts we sent to the freeway say that the enemy has complete control of the roadblock. They seem to have stopped. They spotted over forty individuals and say there were probably more within the vehicles they have, which includes a tank."

"Over forty?" She looked up at her newest commander of their supposed defense force, the third one of what had turned out to be a very long day and night. "Did any of them look sick?"

There was an instant of confusion that flickered across Moser's broad, pale face. She realized her mistake right away. Up until a few seconds ago, Jerry had believed her explanation; that the enemy's accusation that she had purposely infected them was bullshit; that the claim printed on the flyers was meant to sow confusion.

"They didn't say." Jerry checked behind him at the others in the room before turning back to her. "Should I have asked?"

"I should have told you; I'm sorry. We had some earlier intelligence that the virus had caught up to them." She held a palm out in front of her face. "Not that we had anything to do with it. If their story about being in Antarctica is true, they wouldn't be immune, would they? They're just blaming us for something that we couldn't possibly control."

"I see," Moser deadpanned. It was clear he didn't believe her. She was past tired of this worthless moral posturing. The world didn't have room for that shit, not anymore. Why couldn't the rest of them see that?

"I'll send more scouts," he said after a moment. "Get you an answer."

"If there are only forty people, why don't we just attack them?"

Jerry shook his head. "Ms. Cooper, it would be suicide. They have a tank, four of those Bradleys like ours, and a half dozen other lighter military vehicles. They've got those missiles that we know they can use. The units General Marks had on the barricade? They've all retreated, and have gone to ground somewhere within the city; most didn't return to the campus. The teams we had guarding Route 29 in the north and the western approaches aren't reporting in. There are reports of groups fleeing the campus to the west."

She already knew all that, and waved her hand at him to make him stop. "Any word on Josh Keynes?"

"Nothing. He hasn't been seen in hours."

Josh had gone out to check on the barricade. He might have been caught in that fighting, or, more likely was off hiding somewhere after having lied to her.

"Who do we have left? That will actually fight to defend this place?"

"Most of the militia, ma'am, but right now, they are on campus, trying to corral our people and stop them from running, and it's getting ugly . . ."

"Go on. You seem to be the first person to be honest with me all day."

"Ma'am, I used to be the head of marketing at a vineyard in the valley. I don't know anything about this . . . sort of thing. It just seems that if we put up a credible defense, they'll want to negotiate, or at least give us a chance to explain. Your militia is what we have left to do that with. It might save some lives."

She'd been counting on the militia to keep her and her people safe while Marks and then Josh and their supposed military people fought. It wasn't supposed to have come down to this. "How many of them will fight?"

"If they show half the enthusiasm for defending us as they have for shooting our own people, I'd say most of them."

She let the criticism go. Moser probably didn't know those orders had come from her. The last thing she needed right now was yet another worker bee who suddenly had a crisis of conscience.

"Give the order. I'll follow it up with one of my own. They are to fall back to this facility and make a stand here."

*

Jason listened in on Poy's intelligence report. He didn't bother to wake Farmer. The young Marine was out cold, stretched out on the floor underneath the classroom's windows. Having spent the previous day and night first corralling Pro, and then inserting into the campus, they were tired. Spread out on the carpet of a ground-floor room in the school of architecture, they'd alternated to catch maybe a couple of hours of sleep apiece.

Pavel and Pro had abandoned their golf cart a few hours earlier, when the campus had descended into chaos. They'd gone to ground in a building a few hundred yards away from their own position, but not before managing to deliver Nathans to Cabell Hall. The sniper was now lying low on the roof of that building and had an unobstructed view of most of the central campus and the main lawn. The four of them, he and Farmer and then Pavel and Pro, were less than half a mile away from the president's office, where the militia had all pulled back to. Just behind the building was the sunken, fenced-in field where Charlottesville had parked all their heavy military gear.

Jason was only half listening to Poy's report over the radio; most of the information had come from him and his people on campus. He turned the volume down, hoping to let Farmer sleep a little while longer.

"I've spotted seven distinct groups making their way off campus to the west, towards the lake at the edge of the golf course." Jason smiled to himself at Poy's practiced diction; he sounded like he was reading a prepared report, at odds with the broken pidgin he spoke when he was relaxed.

"Several hundred have already reached the lake," Poy continued. "They look to be waiting this out." Jason couldn't fault them. Where were they going to go on foot that they couldn't be caught, regardless of which side won out on campus? As far as he could tell, it was a good sign that they seemed to be sticking together. Some of those groups, he knew, had fought with the militia just to get clear of the campus. That fighting was the reason they'd gone to ground; it had been impossible to tell who was who. Pavel and Pro's security golf cart had come under fire before they'd managed to ditch it and hide themselves.

"As of the last few hours, I've gotten a clear view of their militia having pulled back around the administration building and the adjacent equipment park. They have sortied their two Abrams' and assorted APCs in a rough perimeter around the site and dug a narrow trench for personnel. No visual on AT missile loadouts on their Bradleys—I repeat, no visual—but not confirmed. Estimate between three and four, repeat, three and four hundred enemy personnel visible on the perimeter with crew served weapons. No sign of principal targets." Poy's transmission broke for a moment. "Uh, I think that's it. Over to you, Gypsy One."

"All units—Gypsy One. Thank you, Mr. Park." Skirjanek's voice cut in. "Hold positions for now; we are in process of returning recon bird for fuel and turn around. They are consolidating their forces at the moment, and we do not want to interrupt them. Schedule will be moved up as soon as recon is back on station. Be ready to step off, starting at 1300 hours. Captain Bruce—your strike team will start rolling before general attack as will Gypsy One. Be prepared to roll at 1200 hours.

"Captain Larsen, you are still up on their radios, correct?"

"Affirmative," he answered, eyeing the three radios they'd collected during the night. "At least two distinct channels, no radio discipline—but we catch most of it. No mention of principle targets or this Josh character." It was far worse than that. At one point during the night, it had sounded like a troop of Boy Scouts arguing over their walkie-talkies during a weekend camping trip.

"Copy—I'll have you deliver a final plea to their common sense before we begin."

"Copy all," he replied.

Chapter 30

It was a typical late July day in Virginia. If there had still been weather reporters on TV, or any TV for that matter, the forecast would have been hot, hazy, and humid, with a high chance of thunderstorms in the late afternoon. Same as the day before, same as tomorrow. The classroom on the fourth floor of their building that they had climbed to had a wall of southern-facing windows. Jason figured it was close to 120 degrees in the room, and it was a sauna. But it was where they needed to be in order to broadcast.

"To any and all people who can hear this transmission. My name is Captain Jason Larsen. I'm in command of our forces that are already on campus and watching you at this moment." He let up on the transmit and smiled at Farmer. Lucas was holding another radio on a different channel up to his face.

"All five of us?" Farmer grinned back at him and shook his head.

Jason nodded at the radio and pushed his own button again. "To those of you with the good sense to have laid down your arms and vacated the campus during the last twenty-four hours, stay where you are. We will render aid and assistance as soon as we are able. To those of you who have taken up position on the perimeter of the admin building, the ones who call themselves 'militia' . . . be advised we observed you openly attacking your own people during the night.

"You've given up the right to live among them. Instead of protecting your people, you are defending the ego of Lisa Cooper. Is that enough to die for?" He let up on the button and waited until Farmer did the same.

"Tough to tell if they are getting in any of this."

"They are." Farmer nodded. "They were chatting up a storm a few minutes ago. Probably in shock we have some of their radios. Idiots."

He waggled the radio to signal he was going to start again. "You have fifteen minutes to throw down your weapons, exit your military vehicles, and empty the administration building. Proceed to the central lawn and remain there. You will not be harmed as long as you comply with these instructions. What happens to you will be up to the people of Charlottesville and whatever leadership they elect. This will be our last communication. You have fifteen minutes, starting now."

He and Farmer set the captured radios down and just looked at each other.

"You think they'll cave?" Farmer asked, risking a look out the window.

"I hope so."

"Fuck you! Fascist pigs!" blasted out of one of the captured radios. "You have no authority here."

Jason grinned back at Farmer. "I'm going to go out on a limb here and say no."

"As much as I want to stand here and watch Poy's artillery strike, Nathans has a much better view, and he's probably at a safe distance."

"Probably?" Jason had to smile at that. Nathans was on a rooftop, eight hundred yards farther from the admin building than they were at the moment.

Farmer grinned. "Poy is an oh three-eleven, rifleman. He's had some secondary training in comms, and as technical as he is, it probably should have been his MOS. Right now, he's ten miles away, aiming two 155mm howitzers in our general direction."

"So, basement?" Jason asked.

Farmer shook his head after a moment. "We'd lose comms."

They settled on a classroom in the west wing, on the ground floor.

It was as far from the target area as they could get without leaving the building. The windows were facing away from the target area, and they weren't going to see anything. They'd have to be satisfied listening to Nathans adjust the fire.

"Nine minutes," Farmer breathed and wiped the sweat off his face as he took a knee under the windowsill.

*

"Movement, Gunny!" Elliot yelled from the Bradley behind him. John Bruce heard it in the clear and over his headset. He was so jacked up that he didn't even think of reminding Elliot that he was now a captain. A direction to look would have been nice though; *that* he would remind him of. They'd rolled along the train tracks all the way through town and hadn't left the rail cut until they reached the southern edge of the university hospital center.

His four Bradleys were parked in a lot just two hundred meters south of Cabell Hall. Somewhere on the roofline of that massive edifice, Trey Nathans was set up and had the best seat in town.

"Movement left, civilians!" Elliot yelled again. John spun his turret around and immediately saw a group of twelve or fifteen men and women and a couple of kids emerging from the tree line fronting what looked like a residential area, dotted with houses. Most of the adults were holding a white T-shirt or pillowcase over their heads. Several of the adults were armed, he saw straightaway, but the weapons were slung. He moved the turret, and the 25mm Bushmaster canon it held, away from the group.

"Uwasi! How much time do we have?" he yelled. Regardless of the answer, he didn't have time for this right now.

"Six minutes!"

"You people are in no danger from us, but you need to find some shelter, and I mean right now!" He shouted across the distance.

A woman turned and said something to the rest of the group, then kept walking towards him while the others stopped.

She stopped ten feet away from the Bradley. "Ma'am, you don't understand. It's not going to be safe out here in the open in a very short moment."

"We've been hiding since you dropped those notes. They turned the water off to the campus. Please." The woman clasped her hands together under her chin. "Can you spare some water, the kids . . .?"

Water? He did a double take. They'd brought plenty, and the colonel's force had even more.

"Hell yes, send a couple of your people over." He pulled back in his hole and yelled down into the interior of the Bradley. "Uwasi, pop the ramp, off-load our watercoolers."

When he looked back up, the woman was crying. "You're really going to leave us be?"

"Yes, ma'am, as soon as we've done what we said we would do."

"They tried to kill us!"

"I know, ma'am," he answered, keeping a close eye on the two approaching men as he heard the back-ramp smash down on the asphalt. Two of Reed's combat team off-loaded two large watercoolers as Uwasi watched over them, with his assault rifle held ready at his chest.

"It's all going to be over soon," he added as the two men started waddling away with the ten-gallon coolers.

"Were you the one we heard on the radio?"

"Uwasi! Time?"

"Four minutes, twenty, sir."

"No, ma'am," he answered, and pointed at the nearest house he could see through the break in the trees at the edge of the lot. "Get your people inside that house, the basement if it has one. Right now, ma'am!"

He felt bad about the way the woman jumped at his voice. But that would be the least of their worries in a few minutes.

He'd yelled loud enough that the larger group was starting to move back, helping with the heavy coolers.

"What's your name?"

"John Bruce, ma'am. Please, you need to go, right now."

"Thank you, John." The woman nodded, turned, and started back to her people at a jog.

"Mount up, Uwasi!"

"Sir!"

He watched the group disappear into the house he'd directed them to, as he listened to the hydraulic whine and ratcheting click of the ramp coming up and sealing the rear of the vehicle.

"Time?"

"Three minutes, sir!"

He turned around to face the rest of his vehicles and waved his arm over his head in a looping motion. Satisfied they all had running engines, he clicked his command link. "Button up!" He confirmed all the hatches coming down before he slid down into his chair, dropped it to the interior position, and sealed up his own vehicle.

That had been a first; a local saying "thank you" before he blew the shit out of their home. It had never been an expectation in Iraq or Afghanistan, even if there had been a few after-action offers of gratitude from populations that had been held hostage by the local muj or Sunni warlord. He'd been a Marine his entire adult life; he'd never been anything else, but he'd never imagined he'd be fighting Americans on US soil.

They weren't Americans, he corrected himself; not the people trying to protect the crazy bitch running this place, not anymore. They were the enemy, and they were about to reap what they had sown.

*

Drew checked his watch; just over two minutes to go. He hadn't thought Cooper's militia would surrender, but he had hoped Jason's transmission would cause some more infighting. He had just brought his column's approach to a stop on Main Street, after crossing over the rail tracks that Captain Bruce's units had utilized less than an hour ago.

They were twelve hundred meters from the target area and could get there in a hurry; the road they were on was crossed by another rail line that looped through town. It passed within fifty meters of the northern edge of the Madison Bowl, where the enemy had dug in.

The whine from the turbine of Salguero's Abrams caught his attention. The German Army in the 1980s, during training maneuvers, had nicknamed the Abrams "whispering death" for the relative quiet and distinctive sound of its turbine engine. The name made sense; something that big and heavy should just make more noise. Salguero was "up" in his turret behind the small glacis that mounted a machine gun as it pulled to a stop next to his Bradley.

"Two minutes, Mr. Salguero."

"Yes, sir." The Marine saluted him. "I've been wondering if the colonel wouldn't be more comfortable in here, sir. We can squeeze you in."

"You've been wondering?"

"Captain Bruce was very convincing, sir."

"I'll be fine, Sergeant. Better button up."

"Sir, with all due respect, I can read a map. We are in the flight path of Poy's artillery; if he's short, anything but a direct hit isn't going scratch me. You are a lot more . . . squishier, sir."

"Have some faith, Tommy. I'm a lot more worried about Jefferson's Rotunda; it's an historic landmark."

Salguero jerked his head back in shock. "It's a building . . . sir."

He shook his head and grinned. "Button up, and roll up fifty yards, Sergeant." He pointed forward.

"Yes, sir." Salguero shook his head in disgust and saluted.

He checked his watch, and then the sky above. "Please, Lord, help that kid shoot straight."

Everyone had checked in and was in position. He watched the sweep of the second hand on his watch, a Rolex; it had been a gift from his parents when he'd graduated from West Point. He realized this was the first time he'd worn it in combat. It had always seemed stupid to him that some of his colleagues went into the field with their prize watches. It was a damned strange thing to think of at the moment, and he knew he was deflecting his attention from the issue at hand. He fundamentally wished he didn't have to do this, but was just as sure that he didn't have an option. He reached down to the microphone inside the tank, the one attached to the Bradley's radio and the twenty-foot whip antenna above him.

"Fire when ready, Mr. Park."

He waited for a few seconds. "One gun, fire when ready. Out." Poy's reply was calm enough. He knew the Marine directing the M777 artillery piece was a bundle of nerves, but he was confident that Poy had tied in the fire-control targeting computers to the still-functioning GPS system.

"You reading this, Sergeant Nathans?"

"Affirmative, one round, out. I will direct." He didn't envy Nathans's being on the rooftop on a day like this; the sniper was probably cooking on the metal sheeting of Cabell Hall's roof.

Poy spoke again. "One round, out. I say again, one round, out."

Any artillerymen of the last hundred years would be screaming at the call for fire direction, but Poy was wearing so many hats at the moment, the only thing he cared about was that the Marine had the basics down.

He thought he heard the howitzer fire in the distance, but he couldn't be sure until he heard the incoming round ripping through the air. He ducked back down inside and pulled his hatch shut behind him. "Please, God, not the Rotunda."

*

Trey Nathans couldn't bring himself to give a shit what Skirjanek thought of Poy's technical acumen. As far as he was concerned, Poy was still the lazy, fat piece of shit who had almost eaten himself to death in The Hole. Which was why he covered his head with his hands the moment he heard the incoming round. He knew Poy didn't like him;

the fat bastard would probably get away with an errant shot that went wide.

The pitch of the ripping sound in the heavens above altered; snipers were often cross-trained to act as Fire Support Men in the Corps. It made sense; they were often well concealed and a lot closer to the target than most of the units they supported. He'd never directed arty fire before, and only called in one air strike, but he'd had enough arty rounds go over his head to realize he wasn't going to get hit.

He raised his head to look down the length of the lawn, past the Rotunda to the admin building beyond and the large field behind it. The map of the campus he carried with him labeled the field the "Madison Bowl." It was where most of their foraged gear had been held until they'd moved it to create the perimeter of men and machines around the building.

The ranging shot blossomed fifty yards to the east of the field. The fireball consumed a house and blew the adjacent structures into kindling as the sound of the explosion reached him. He glanced at his map of the campus as he fumbled with his radio.

"Fire base—Nathans, adjust fire. You are close. You just took out a bunch of frat houses. Adjust fire, up 50, left 50."

"Adjust fire, up 50, left 50, out," Poy came back immediately.

"Affirmative," he replied.

"Adjusting fire, two shots out."

"Two shots out, copy." He put his radio down. "Come on, Poy, just walk those rounds across the street and you're money, Marine."

This time, he had the confidence to keep his head up during the incoming flight of the shells. The first one impacted near the middle of the field and threw up a massive funnel of dirt amid the fireball. The second round hit the western edge of the admin building a second later. Bits of construction—he hoped they were bricks, not pieces of occupants—sprayed the area.

"Fire control—Nathans, you are on target—west end of target building hit. Fire for effect."

"On target—copy," Poy came back. "Fire for effect, out."

"Fire base, Gypsy One. Five rounds, each gun." Skirjanek was back on the air. "Then cease fire."

"Fire for effect, out. Five rounds, each gun, and then terminate fire mission, out."

Nathans brought up the butt of his rifle and tried to use his scope to see through the smoke and dirt hanging in the air. The Rotunda and its wings blocked his line of sight to the nearest of the makeshift trenches that had been dug around the admin building. The portions that he *could* see stretched along the sides of the Madison Bowl and across the back of the field. Poy's first ranging shot must have landed a lot closer to the adjacent road than he'd first thought; there were several unmoving bodies across the road from the destroyed and burning frat houses.

The front of the admin building was seven hundred yards from his position, the farthest edge of the bowl almost nine hundred. He had a great view of the anthill that Poy's shells had kicked over. The defenders were starting to stick their heads back up; others appeared to be in shock as they stood around staring at the missing chunk of the building they had been all set to defend. Someone waving a piece of white cloth stuck over the end of a rifle caught his attention along the far edge of the grassy bowl. One of his trench mates shot him a second later.

He was thinking that a normal artillery battery would have already fired, but they would have had extra guns with shells already loaded and would have just needed minute adjustments. Both of Poy's guns, all of them in other words, would need to be reloaded, and he didn't exactly have a trained crew to work with. He was still watching the enemy when he thought he heard the distant, deep boom of the howitzers. It was a second and a half later before his ears picked up the incoming rounds. He could see several of the defenders yelling at their colleagues to get back down. Like that was going to help.

His scope picture was jarred as the two shells landed almost simultaneously. When he pulled back from the scope, he saw that one had overshot the bowl and plowed into the courtyard of a modern-looking building across the street. The other had landed just behind the admin building, and what was left of a pickup truck was in the process of spinning out of the sky. Nathans smiled to himself; two down, eight to go. This was so much better than having to shoot people; but his head went back down to the scope to find targets. Somebody would be trying to hold them together. There was always somebody.

He spotted just that someone screaming into a radio. The target stood up; he cursed to himself, as *she* walked along her section of the trench line. He imagined he could hear her words of encouragement, or given what they knew about these people, maybe they were threats. Training took over; he sighted in between her shoulder blades and waited for Poy to fire again. No sense in advertising himself, not yet.

*

She'd brought just three others with her. Karen had come, of course. If there was one person absolutely devoted to her, it was Karen. Two of her personal guard had led the way down the stairway into the basement; Ben Pierson, the oldest member of her security detail, and Terry, whom she realized in embarrassment she had never really spoken to. She didn't even know his last name, and that wasn't like her.

They'd just reached the musty-smelling basement that was far older than the renovated brick mansion above, when the ground pulsed under their feet.

"What the hell was that?" Karen cried out as dirt and dust filtered down from above and was knocked into the air from the floor.

"Artillery, I think," Ben said.

"You think!" Karen could be a bitch sometimes, but that's why they had worked so well together.

"We've got to go." Ben ignored Karen. "Now, ma'am."

"We need Marks," she said, hating the words as she said them. "He knows the way."

Ben was already moving down the hall covered in linoleum tiles that appeared to be fifty years old. He stopped at a metal door, slid back a bolt, and jerked it open. She walked through the doorway of the storage room where they'd jailed Steven. He was sitting on his cot, with his back against the brick wall. One arm was handcuffed to a pipe coming out of the wall.

"You waited longer to run away than I thought you would." He didn't even sound smug or frightened to her.

"You can lay on the 'I told you sos' all you like," she pleaded. "Right now, I want you with me. I always have; I think you know that."

He just smiled back at her and shook his head. "God, you're good."

"Steven!"

"They have artillery," his eye brows arched in what might have been surprise. "That tremor you felt was a ranging shot. I'm surprised they haven't fired yet."

"I need you!"

"No . . . you need me to lead you through the tunnels, get you to the rig you've got fueled and waiting for your escape." He looked behind her towards the others. "She ever mention that to any of you? She's had a getaway planned since before the people shooting at us even showed up."

"That's not—"

There was a shrill, earsplitting whistle just before the doorjamb she was standing in was propelled at her. A pain exploded in the middle of her face, and she heard something snap in her head. It all happened in slow motion, but the lights went out with a suddenness that her stunned brain noted even before she hit the floor.

She lay there, stunned, for what seemed like hours. She thought she could feel the earth moving, pulsing repeatedly at slow intervals like there was a massive heart beating somewhere deep beneath them. She cried out and opened her eyes, blinking at the thick air-dirt mixture that coated her wet eyes and covered the inside of her mouth and throat as she sucked in a breath. Someone was screaming in the darkness. She thought it was her for the briefest moment, until a rib-racking cough exploded out of her bruised chest. There wasn't any air! In a panic, she sucked in another lungful of the earthen cloud that was hanging around her.

Someone was shaking her. There was a dim light dancing around above her head.

"Ma'am, can you move?"

She thought she recognized Ben's voice. He almost sounded like he was underwater. No, it was water she could hear and feel pooling around her.

"I can't see!"

"Your face, ma'am . . . hold still."

"What's wrong with my face?" Her panic rose as she felt another tremor through the floor and heard another explosion. She felt more dirt trickle out of the ceiling.

"Hold still, there's a broken water pipe here. I'm going to lift your head up."

The cold water felt better than anything she could remember. And she could see again, sort of, at least out of one eye. Ben pulled her slowly to her feet and held onto her for a moment to make sure she wasn't going to fall as he swung his flashlight around.

She caught skewed snapshots as she tried to follow the beam. The doorway had partially collapsed. There was a pair of legs sticking out from under a pile of bricks that had almost blocked the hallway, and she could see a pale arm waving at them from the far side of the blockage.

She grabbed Ben's arm and directed the beam further into the storage room. Steven's very still body was held up by the handcuffs; the side of his head and most of his shirt were covered in blood.

"Shit!"

"Ma'am?"

"He knew the way . . . the tunnels run underneath the whole campus."

"Where's the vehicle parked?"

"I . . . near the stadium, I'm not sure. He took care of it."

"Do the tunnels reach that far?"

"I don't know!" she yelled, and wanted to say more but was racked with another round of hacking.

"Breathe through your shirt." Ben pointed the flashlight up at his own face; he was holding the collar of his shirt up over his nose. He turned away and was looking for something on the ground.

"Don't leave me here! Please!"

He didn't answer her, but when he turned back around, he put a flashlight in her hands. It was wet and sticky. Ben coughed and then shook his head and moved her flashlight out of his face. She felt bad; she needed him and didn't want to anger him. Nothing terrified her more than the thought of being alone.

"Come on, I know where the tunnel starts in this building, and the stadium is south of here."

"Which way is south?" She didn't like the way her voice sounded. She couldn't breathe through her nose, and even holding the collar of her blouse up over her face sent sharp waves of pain through her head. Ben didn't answer her, just turned and started climbing across the pile of bricks that had buried the top half of Terry in the doorway.

She almost rolled down the far side of the pile. She would have if her slide hadn't been stopped by Karen, whose shallow hiss of pain almost made her jump out of her skin. Her flashlight beam swam over Karen's face. The woman looked untouched except for a trickle of blood coming out of the corner of her mouth.

"Lisa! Help me . . . I can't . . . feel my legs."

The beam of her flashlight revealed Karen's lower half, buried in the pile of bricks. She could see blood soaking through the dirt near her waist.

Lisa felt her head nod once in a decision that had been near instant. "We'll get you some help. Just hang in there." She reached out and gave the woman's hand a squeeze, and then moved to the edge of the pile of bricks until she could stand in the hallway beyond. She could feel

Karen's eyes burning a hole into her back. For the briefest of moments, she was grateful for the darkness.

"Don't leave me here!"

She ignored the cry and set one foot in front of the other, towards Ben's flashlight hanging in the darkness.

*

Chapter 31

"Gypsy Two—Gypsy Actual—kickoff is go."

It was about time, John Bruce thought. As far as he was concerned, Poy had produced the slowest ten-round artillery salvo in the history of modern warfare. He had to smile though; he knew the defenders had just endured the longest six minutes of their lives.

"B troop roll," he called out. Mason's two Bradleys were rolling past him as he popped the lid of his own and raised himself back up. "Remember, don't get in a pissing match with them. Use your TOWS—spot, shoot, and scoot their Bradleys. Dismount your people as soon as you can; light up the heavies with Javelins if you get a shot. We'll let Tommy deal with the tanks and help as we can. Target all enemy vehicles and hardpoints." The order was for his own nerves; he had to stay focused. They'd gone over and over the tactical plan a dozen times. Mason knew what he had to do.

B troop had a little farther to go than his two Bradleys in the pincer movement they were pulling off. They'd both roll north to either side of the lawn; Mason's team on McCormick until they passed the Rotunda and bent east toward the enemy. He'd parallel them on Hospital Drive until cutting across the manicured lawns and hitting them from the opposite direction. He counted to thirty in his head.

"A troop, roll, get us to the anthropology building!" He grinned to himself. The building was perfectly situated to give him some cover, and if it still stood, an elevated position to put out his own hunter-killer team. Uwasi was one of the best Javelin operators he'd ever worked with, and without a doubt, the best the Gypsies could muster.

He lowered his seat as the Bradley jerked into motion; he wanted to stay "outside" for as long as possible. He had his protective glacis to hide behind, but he doubted Nathans was the only guy out there with a long rifle and a scope.

He switched to his internal-only channel. "Come on, Tasker, kick it in the ass!"

He nodded in appreciation as the Bradley's engine gunned and they wound up to thirty-plus miles an hour as the buildings swam past on either side. Tasker was from somewhere up around DC and had worked remodeling kitchens less than a year ago. The story would have been similar for the majority of those fighting today, but the people who had come south with Jason were a step above where they had been six weeks ago. He just hoped it was a big step.

His Bradley, and the one following him, commanded by Henry "Naks" Nako, jumped the curb and plowed through a bike rack as they left the road and hugged a line of what looked like dorms. He thought he saw more than one face looking back at him through the windows. All he could hope was that they were civilians, in hiding like the ones who had approached them. He didn't want to imagine what this day was going to turn into if they had everyone shooting at them.

Trey was aware at the periphery of his senses of Bruce's Bradleys rolling past on his right; he'd heard Mason's team roll behind him a moment before. "Gypsies—Nathans, be advised, two Abrams active. One in the middle of bowl, the other anchoring southeast corner of defensive perimeter. One Bradley destroyed, another damaged or abandoned. Others at corners of perimeter. One rolling north inside the bowl. Gypsy One, your approach has been spotted."

Yep, he was sure of it. Skirjanek's column, led by Tommy in his tank, was rolling up the train tracks through town; they'd be near the top of the far edge of the bowled area within a minute. He watched as one of the friendly Bradleys stopped and disgorged two Javelin teams. He lost sight of the four soldiers as they disappeared into the backyards of frat houses that still stood in the artillery savaged block of houses across from the eastern edge of the bowl. He tracked his scope back to the northernmost enemy tank, sitting in the middle of the grassy depression; he could only see it because it was in line with the half of the admin building that had collapsed.

There was a target standing behind the tank, talking with the crew inside on the "grunt" phone. He noted his breathing, ignored the puddle of sweat that his position had become, and ranged the target at 645 yards. He missed having a spotter, but they only had so many Marines to go around. The other half of his sniper team had died five months ago in The Hole, accidently, while cleaning his handgun.

The shot felt good, and he had time to refocus his sight lock just as the target was spun around. He'd just winged the guy, but he'd been hit in the arm with a .50 caliber bullet. He could see his target lying in the torn-up field, his free hand trying to stop the bleeding at the remaining stump of an arm below the shoulder. The tank's grunt phone was left hanging, unused. The crew inside the enemy tank would have to rely on their own eyes for the moment.

He swung his sight picture up to the northern edge of the bowl, and could see Tommy's Abrams "track" left out of the rail bed and start to roll between two wooden-framed frat houses. The enemy infantry in the opposing line could see them coming. One soldier in particular looked to be a leader; at least the man was screaming orders. 710 yards; he took up the trigger, focused, and fired. The man fell back, and he went looking for another target just as a bloom of fire erupted from the front of the enemy tank. The sound of the shot rolling across the campus reached him a moment later.

Drew winced as the frat house directly to his forward left erupted in a blossom of fire. Tommy was directly ahead of him in his Abrams and had departed the rail bed. Salguero's tank had been squeezing between the Delta Upsilon frat house ahead and another he couldn't yet identify when the Delta U house came apart riding a wave front of wood shrapnel. He was "down" in his command hole, but he'd had the turret open. He triggered his hatch and got it closed by the time the frat house had stopped pelting his Bradley.

He cursed his stupidity; there was no doubt the enemy Abrams had fired an older <u>HE</u> round, High-Explosive rather than the anti-tank (AT) penetrator rounds that Tommy was loaded with. It wasn't the ammunition of choice if you were trying to kill a tank, particularly another Abrams, but it would have put a serious hurt on them in the much more lightly armed Bradley. Particularly so, if said Bradley's commander had been more worried about situational awareness than his own crew's survivability and had the hatch open. It didn't make any sense to him, but he had no idea what kind of tank ammunition Charlottesville had managed to scrounge.

"Elliot, weapons free. Fire the TOWS the second you can lock that tank or an APC. Don't wait for an order."

"Affirmative, sir."

"Javelin teams, Gypsy One," he called out to the two, two-man Javelin teams he'd dismounted during the approach. "Hammer that tank as soon as you are able. Direct fire mode!" The enemy Abrams was too close for them to utilize the far more effective "top-down" attack mode wherein the missile would climb for altitude before plunging down on the top of the turret, or onto the engine deck where tank armor was thinner and more vulnerable.

A Javelin was capable of disabling an Abrams in direct mode, if it got lucky, and if the target in question wasn't cheating with active-reactive armor packs. Poy's video shots of the enemy tanks hadn't captured any indication of the extra defensive measures. Two missiles might mean they could get lucky with an engine kill, or maybe they could de-track the beast. He doubted if the Javelins would "kill" the tank unless they got very lucky; for that, the best tool was another Abrams.

"Copy all, prepping to fire."

Salguero grinned to himself at the radio exchange. The HE blast had impacted the frat house five feet in front of his tank. If Irina hadn't paused and brought them to a jarring halt as she turned off the tracks, the round would have hit them. As it was, the exploding HE round had given the Abrams a slight jolt, and had probably scorched a layer of paint. The noise of the explosion had been much worse.

"Irina, punch it! Go, go, go! Right at him, don't show him anything but your nose. Gun check?"

"Gun's up!"

The first part of the enemy tank he spotted was its canon barrel, pointing right at them.

"Stop!" he screamed into his mic as the rest of the opposing Abrams came into view. He glanced at his own targeting screen, slaved to Cruz's gun sight. The reticle was holding at the junction between the turret and the front glacis of the enemy tank.

"Fire!"

An explosion powerful enough to rock the seventy-ton behemoth beneath him went off two feet away from where he was sitting. Contained within the breech of the canon, he still felt the concussion in his bones and teeth. He'd always loved this part of being a tanker. Nothing could beat letting loose with the big 120mm canon. He didn't wait to see what the effect of the hit had been. With fewer than sixty yards separating them from the enemy tank, he knew it was a hit. He also knew how hard it was to kill an Abrams.

"Straight back, Irina!" he yelled into his helmet mic. "Back to the tracks."

"Reload!"

They rocked when they went up and through the still-burning foundations of the destroyed frat house. He wanted to get behind another house, before the enemy could fire. They almost made it.

The incoming round hit them on the front of their glacis. For a brief moment, it sounded like the world's largest sledgehammer had been swung at them. Every sensor in front of him went down, clouded out by an expanding fireball that he couldn't see but knew was enveloping them. The temperature inside the tank rose precipitously as his gaze went over his most critical readouts. Their engine was still running, and most lights were still green. It was going to be a moment before his view screens reset, if they did at all.

"Go, Irina, back, back." It had to have been another HE round, he knew; and he suspected that he was up against an M1-A1, the first version that had been relegated off to National Guard units. It boasted a 105mm canon versus the 120mm that their M1-A2 carried.

"Everybody OK?"

"Gun's up!" Antwan yelled loud enough that he was sure he heard it through his helmet rather than the speakers built into it.

"Sight's working!" Cruz reported in from the gunner's seat. "Range finder is down!"

They'd been drilling as a team for a week, and none of them, himself included, could have held the jockstraps of his old tank crew. But he couldn't have been more pleased. They'd just shrugged off a hit from another tank and were still functioning.

They weren't going to need the range finder.

"Irina! Soon as we're behind the house, go around and then straight down into the field. Drive right up alongside it. Cruz! Wait to fire until you have them broadside."

Sam Hirai watched the Javelin missile fired by Gerry Baker streak right past the enemy tank, going over the top of its turret and across the field, until it impacted the side of a building that had already been hit by the artillery strike. Its explosion didn't do anything other than to cause a lot of small-arms fire from the trenches to be directed at Gerry's position.

He and Will Rodale were in the house next door to Baker's team, creeping along the floor. A very large part of him wanted to be back inside the Bradley that had dropped them off. He hadn't noticed any signs coming in, but from the pictures of girls in groups spread across the walls, he was guessing it was a sorority. Most of its windows had already been blown out by the artillery rounds, one of which had demolished the house on the far side of them. They had crawled and scooted along the floor until they were beneath the open window frame overlooking the Madison Bowl. He had a great view of the enemy tank, which had managed to shoot back after taking a hit from their own tank.

He propped the head of the missile over the window frame and had to come up on his knees to get a sight picture of the enemy through the Javelin CLU's range finder. He made certain he was in direct fire mode as he held the reticle against the side of the tank and pulled the trigger to lock in the targeting. Will slapped his shoulder, and he pulled the trigger again. There was always a pause. This time, it felt as if something had gone wrong. The infantry out there, hunkered down in their hastily dug trench, was just across the street; they were going to see him any . . .

The cacophonous POP of the launching charge was caught and reflected by the parlor room and its massive blown-out bay windows. The missile ignited outside the window just past the house's front porch, and shot over the heads of the defenders who had been firing at Baker's team. For them, there was no mistaking where the missile had come from.

Will tackled him to the floor just as the room came apart and automatic weapons fire ripped into and through the front of the house. He heard Will cry out as something tugged at his leg, then slammed into his shoulder. A loud explosion lit up the room, and his last thought was that he'd hit the tank.

"Fire!" Drew yelled moments after the second Javelin slammed into the enemy tank. His Bradley fired a TOW missile, and he prayed that they had the sixty-five yards needed in terms of minimum arming distance. They had it. He was watching through his view screen, whose external camera was mounted just outside his hatch. The TOW impacted low on the chassis of the tank between the two bands of tracks. When the fireball cleared, he could see the tank was missing most of its wheels and track on the near side and smoke, probably from the Javelin, was pouring out of its engine compartment.

"Go, Tommy! Finish him!" The tank wasn't going anywhere with one set of tracks destroyed, but he knew the crew inside and their gun could still be alive. No sooner had he spoken than the turret on the target tank starting spinning around towards his vehicle. Everything that made the Abrams such a formidable tank was working against him at the moment.

"Back! Back! Back!" he yelled into his mic. Just as they started to move, he caught a flash of movement as Salguero's tank shot out onto the field, its treads rooster-tailing turf and dirt as it scrambled for purchase.

"OK, slow down, Irina," Salguero ordered. He could see the target tank's gun, aimed 60 degrees away from them in the direction of Skirjanek's Bradley. That would be the last mistake he was going to allow them. His turret slewed as Cruz brought their cannon to bear in line with the side of the enemy's turret.

"Stop!" He waited for the tank to slide to a stop on the turf. Seventy tons of steel and depleted uranium had a lot of inertia. It seemed to take forever.

"Fire!"

He watched in satisfaction as the driver's and tank commanders' hatches blew skyward, riding a volcanic gout of fire. The hull of the tank itself appeared strangely whole as the occupants within were incinerated.

"That's a kill!" he radioed. "Move!" He did not want to be sitting alongside the beast when its ammunition blew.

"Forward, Irina!"

"Gypsy Team." Skirjanek's voice broke in. "My Bradleys, enter the bowl. Suppress all resistance. Tommy, go kill that other tank. It's got Bruce's team stopped. It's up ahead of you between the admin building and the big church."

"Copy, rolling!"

"Reload!" he yelled just as an enormous explosion from the destroyed tank rocked them. He placed a destination carat on the driver's screen. "Irina, get us there!" The sound of small-arms fire was pinging off his hull. He could understand the desire to shoot at them, but what part of tank did these idiots not understand?

Uwasi's first Javelin had managed to knock a track off the Abrams that had stopped Bruce's column cold. He'd fired from around the corner of the anthropology building at the tank that sat in the courtyard of St. Paul's Memorial Church, between the fancy-looking church and a large residence it shared a lot with. The tank had fired back a moment later and destroyed the Bradley directly behind him. He knew the only survivors from Naks's Bradley were going to be people who had managed to dismount before they had been hit. The Bradley was still burning, its ammo popping off within the crisped shell. Gunny "Captain" Bruce was yelling at him over the air to get elevation.

He grabbed the collar of the member of the troop who had been assigned to carry his reload, Wilson something, which had confused him, because he'd always thought Wilson was a surname. "Go." He turned the scared civilian toward the back side of the anthropology building. "Get inside, climb to the top floor."

He fairly threw the man forward and followed after. Once inside the building, they sprinted up the ancient wooden staircases. They'd just reached the landing of the third and top floor when a massive explosion north of them rattled through the building. Uwasi figured there wasn't a window left in any building within a quarter of a mile after Poy's artillery. The noise from the explosion and the fight at the far end of the bowl sounded like it was just outside.

He peeked out of a window and spotted Salguero's tank, a large Puerto Rican flag spray-painted on its front glacis, moving across the field towards them. Behind it was the flaming wreck of what had been the other enemy tank.

"Just what we need! He'll never stop talking about it!" he shouted. Wilson was down on one knee, holding the reload case of another Javelin, looking at him like he'd gone crazy.

"What are you talking about?"

"Salguero! We have to kill this tank ourselves!"

Wilson cringed as Skirjanek's Bradleys opened up in the distance with their M242s—the 25mm autocannon and TOW missiles could more than deal with anything the enemy had left, with the critical exception of the tank that lay one hundred yards away below them.

"Tree in the way! Come on." He pulled back from the window frame, ducked down, grabbed a handful of Wilson's BDUs at the shoulder, and fairly dragged the man across the wooden floors after him. It wasn't until they reached the classroom at the end of the hall that he found a break in the foliage that presented a clear shot.

"Get it ready!" he instructed as he backed off into the interior of the room and raised the CLU to his shoulder, aiming out the window. The sight picture brought a smile to his face. They were too close to fire in top-down mode—but from their elevated position, he had a direct line of sight to the top of the turret.

He dropped to one knee and turned the CLU over. "OK, let's reload. Hurry!" Salguero was going to drive up right behind that bastard and put a rod of depleted uranium up its ass while its attention was focused on Captain Bruce's Bradleys. He liked Salguero; the guy was a warrior, but he did not want to have to listen to the hothead talk about how he and his stupid tank had saved their asses. Gunny or Captain Bruce would understand.

He'd drilled with Wilson for the last two days. The guy had gotten to where he could ready a reload in the dark, but now, he cringed every time one of the colonel's Bradleys opened fire out in the bowl. The sound of the Bradley's 25mm autocannon was a very distinct, very fast POP, POP, POP. He didn't want to think about what the Bushmasters were doing to the enemy infantry. A TOW launched outside, its rocket engine sounding more like a humming whir in his head than the sustained whoosh of a Javelin. The explosion of its impact followed soon after, and he assumed another enemy Bradley had just died.

He clapped Wilson on the top of his head. "Hey, those are our people shooting; relax . . . breathe."

"Ready," Wilson breathed in a gush once he had the Javelin reload mounted to the CLU and the connections between the two secured.

He'd been watching closely. He shook his head and removed the rubber cap from the missile's nose.

"Jeez . . . sorry."

"'S OK, man. You're doing great." He breathed out, doing his best to calm his own nerves. "Get to the side of me."

He stood and locked on to the tank below. It was bringing its gun barrel around, elevated for a target well beneath them. He saw Salguero's tank at the edge of his vision, climbing out of the bowl onto Madison Lane. He waited for the thermal seeker to "find" the tank, and then switched the CLU over to its narrow field of view, which allowed for more precise targeting. He held the reticle over the center of the top of the turret and pulled the lock trigger. Two very long seconds later, the missile fired, ejected out of the tube by its booster and then igniting its flight motor a split second later.

He had a perfect view as the missile lanced down at an angle and struck the turret. The enemy tank exploded; the turret itself dislodged and almost popped off like he'd seen old Soviet T-72s do when he'd hit them in Syria. It was then he saw the bloom of fire from Salguero's tank gun come roiling out from behind the churchyard's manor house.

"Shit!"

Wilson popped his head up over the windowsill and then looked back at him. "You got it!"

"Yes, we did! You be sure to remember that!" He hoped Poy's drone had been recording the fight. Against what he knew would be Salguero's claim, he was going to need proof.

He watched as Captain Bruce's and Mason's Bradleys below them roared out from their cover and joined Skirjanek's forces in the mopping-up activity around the bowl. There were as many white flags waving out in the bowl as there were people moving. There were a lot more not moving.

Chapter 32

"What are we going to do with them?" Jason asked, looking over Skirjanek's shoulder at the shell-shocked enemy. Fewer than a hundred of them had survived to raise white flags. Those who had holed up inside the admin building were being escorted out under guard.

Skirjanek shook his head. "I don't think it should be up to us."

Jason knew who the colonel wanted to make that call. The civilians had started emerging from the dorms and classrooms within minutes of the firing having stopped and were already gathering around. Skirjanek was smart; he had just about every woman in his command acting as a community liaison officer at the moment.

Given the questions they were getting, it made sense. Some of these people had escaped from whatever hell they'd been living in and *had* considered Charlottesville a refuge. "Is your group safe for women? What about kids and old people? What if we don't want to stay?"

Jason gestured at the admin building. John, Ray, Pavel, and Pro were inside with a squad's worth of rifles, looking for survivors, two of them in particular. "Any sign of the two ringleaders?"

"Nothing yet." Skirjanek shook his head. "I'm really hoping they didn't survive. We have no idea how much support they might still have."

"I'm guessing a lot less than they had, before they started shooting their own people."

Skirjanek shrugged and offered him a grin. "We said the same thing about Saddam."

He and Farmer had been on the top floor of the architecture and design school building during most of the battle, on the half of the roof that was still standing. Their decision to hole up during the artillery salvo had been a wise one. They'd sniped at the defenders as best they could, and both had been shocked at how long most of them had continued the lost battle. Whether these people had continued to fight out of anger or some loyalty to Cooper, he didn't know. But he did not want Cooper added back into the mix.

"You know what I think . . ."

Skirjanek looked at him and nodded slowly before jerking a thumb behind him at the damaged building. "Same as me, I suspect. Between us, I've made sure Pavel does not let that woman come out of there alive. Not the kind of order I thought I'd ever give."

Jason nodded to himself. "Not the kind of world any of us ever thought we'd live in." He smiled. "Besides, it's Pavel. You didn't give him an order; you gave him permission."

"Doesn't make me feel any better."

Jason didn't answer the man. He knew Drew had made the adjustment to the end of the world; he wasn't worried that they'd convene some sort of court-martial. But he knew the type. Skirjanek was a career officer, a West Point grad, versed at a genetic level in the old-school warrior ethos rather than the bucket of "woke" bullshit that some officers seemed to have taken away from the place in the last twenty years. In Skirjanek's mind, dealing with civilians was a job for civilians, and that included meting out justice.

"I didn't want to distract you while you were out looking for Pro and then prepping for this," Skirjanek continued. "But I've been on the radio with Hoyt and Michelle the last two days. They're parked south of the city with supplies, waiting for word that it's safe to come in."

"Michelle made the trip?"

Skirjanek gave a chuckle. "She made Hoyt cut out the dash of a JLTV to fit her wheelchair in." Skirjanek paused and then smiled at him. "Rachel came down as well."

It was the best thing he could have heard. He grinned to himself. "Get Michelle among these civilians." He waved at the approaching crowds. "She's lived their story. They'll trust her."

Drew nodded at one of their Humvees that had come up after the fighting. "The group that made it to the lake on the far side of the golf course doesn't seem to be filtering back. Can you get out there, try to convince them it's safe? Take some of Reed's team with you, and don't take any chances. I think it needs somebody with a little more understanding than Captain Bruce is going to be able to find at the moment."

He'd seen the Bradley from John's column get taken out. "Who'd we lose?"

"It was Naks's Bradley." Skirjanek shook his head. "He'd kicked his dismounts, so it was just him and his crew. I'm sorry, but I don't know who they were beyond Henry Nako. I understand he'd been studying to get into law school before the virus, working at his parents' carpet store in Pittsburgh."

Jason felt a moment of shame; that was more than he knew about Naks, who had come south with him and Reed. He'd only known he was one of the guys who helped Daniel take the mall back. Somebody who had worked hard, never complained, never said much at all.

"I lost both my Javelin teams as well; Mr. Baker's and Sam Hirai's. Four more people who had no business doing what I asked them to do."

No one was a civilian anymore. Skirjanek was smart enough to come to that understanding himself. He didn't need to be told.

"Over here, sir!"

Pavel wondered if he would ever grow accustomed to being called "sir," by Americans no less. Flags and countries were a thing of the past. "Clan" he understood. When the colonel went on about the "them" and "us" that he was so certain the world would revolve around for the next century, Pavel heard only "tribe." The Volkovs, his father's family, was Cossack from as far back as things were remembered. These people were his tribe, his "host," and he had a place of importance here. There was nothing he would not do for their survival. Looking for survivors in the ruins of the enemy's headquarters made little sense to him. But he'd been given an order.

There were enough flashlights lighting the way that he had no issue in seeing past the pile of rubble that had almost blocked the basement hallway, and into the room beyond and its sole occupant. Not a room, he realized—a cell. The man had been handcuffed to a pipe above his blood-covered head. The injured man held another hand in front of his face as if to block the beams of light seeking him out.

"Leave me . . ." the man rasped when Pavel reached him.

As much as he wanted to say, "As you wish," and move on, he was almost certain this was General Marks. They'd circulated the pictures the scouts had come back with.

"Where is Lisa Cooper?"

"Wanted . . . my help." Marks almost seemed to be trying to laugh, but a gout of blood bubbled out of the man's nose, mixing with the mask of dust covering his face.

"Where is she?"

"Tunnels," the general almost shouted. "Steam tunnels . . ." A smile cracked the pale mask that was the general's face. "Lost."

"How many people does she have with her?"

"How many, here?" The man's eyes tried to flutter open but slammed shut against the cake of dirt covering him.

The man was delirious.

"Where did she go?"

The general was moving his head back and forth with great effort. "Lost . . ."

"Sir, we've got two bodies here," one of his men shouted from behind him after joining him in the room, carting a first-aid kit. "A soldier and a woman. Dark hair; it's not her."

He almost ordered the man and his medical kit back over the hill of rubble, but he focused on the general's handcuffs. Perhaps he'd tried to stop Cooper. What had the man said? "How many, here?"

He turned back and slapped the general. "There are two bodies here! A guard and a woman. How many went with her?"

The general's head shook, causing another mini avalanche of debris to cascade down his face. It took what seemed like an eternity for the general to realize he was conscious again, and he repeated the question.

Marks coughed. "Two here, just one . . . one with her."

Pavel backed away so that the medic could get to Marks. He bumped into Pro, who was already climbing back over the pile of rubble, out of the room. The young man was driven to find Cooper; he could understand that. They all could. They had searched the hallway approaching the general's cell on their way down, and there hadn't been any tunnels.

He grabbed the back of Pro's tunic and yanked the young man to the left side of the blockage. "This way!"

The footprints made in the thick layer of dust were easy to follow in the flashlight's beams. The two of them made it to the end of the hall, where they came to a heavy steel door. The door had been opened since the building had been hit, and there were no prints beyond.

"You will stay behind me; do you understand?"

"Alright, yeah." Pavel didn't believe him in the least. The teenager sounded almost excited.

Pavel gripped his flashlight in his left hand and held it against the bottom rail of his rifle. "Hold your torch like this."

Pro clicked his flashlight off and activated the one attached to the underside of his weapon. "I didn't break mine on a doorway last night."

"Fine." Pavel felt himself grin. "Save the other. We may be down here for some time."

There was a set of metal stairs leading down into a cinder-block subbasement. Large, insulated steam pipes passed through the room below them; the tunnel that carried them stretched in two directions. Even from the landing above, he could see the two sets of prints in the cone of light. One from a pair of boots, the other from a pointed pair of toes separated from a small heel. Beyond the clearly defined perimeter of light was absolute darkness.

*

Jason had been directed by one of Charlottesville's civilians, a woman named Sally, who had seemed far more concerned with the well-being and future of the other civilians than any of the surviving combatants. Reed and one of his men were in the back seat. Another Hummer, loaded down with water jugs, had followed behind them. It wasn't much of a lake; more of a really big, four-hole water hazard sitting at the back edge of the former golf course cum farm. The crowd gathered there under the shade of trees lining the water, some sitting on picnic benches, were very much armed and didn't look at all happy.

"I think you're up." Jason didn't take his eyes off the crowd through the windshield as he spoke to the woman in the seat next to him. "Please tell them they can trust us. If they want, we will just go away and leave them the water. We don't want any trouble."

He watched Sally approach the crowd, aware of his hands on the steering wheel and how much he wanted to drop them in his lap and get his hands on his Glock 17.

"Why we doing this, again?" Reed asked from the back seat.

"I think the colonel wants to deliver a message to everybody who's left. One message, one story; not have half a dozen different groups out there spinning what happened."

"Yeah . . . I'm not sure that's worth getting shot over."

Reed made a really good point. He watched the crowd as they gathered around Sally. It was fear and exhaustion that played on most of the faces, not rage. He couldn't blame them; they'd had to fight their own people to get off campus. They had little reason to trust anyone.

"See that big guy?" Reed slowly sat forward until he was almost hunched over between the two front seats. "Far left, next to the picnic table."

"Yeah," Jason intoned, looking with just his eyes.

"He was at Zion Crossroads with that Josh character, when they delivered Cooper's note."

"You sure?"

"Yeah, that's him."

Josh Keynes was another "somebody" they hadn't found yet. They'd hoped to find somebody to talk to who held some semblance of authority. That was the problem when you took down a police state or removed a dictator. Depending on the situation, either everyone claimed to be in charge, or no one did. These people were scared, and right now no-one was stepping forward. Jason was still watching the man when Reed clapped him in the shoulder. "Speech time."

Sally had turned back towards the vehicle and was waving at him to come forward.

"You too, Reed."

He made a point of slinging his gun around to his back and made sure Reed had done the same before walking over to face the crowd. There were thirty or forty people gathered who had been listening to Sally. The majority of those who had sought refuge here must have been satisfied with waiting to be told what to do. Jason could see hundreds of people stuffed back into the woods, waiting.

He pointed back at the other Humvee. "We brought water," he started. "Cooper and her minions shut off the water on campus sometime yesterday; people there have been pretty thirsty." There was a stirring in the crowd that he would have had to be blind to miss. Reed saw it as well and had already turned to wave their second vehicle forward.

"That's great," an older man spoke up. "We do appreciate it, but what happens to us now?"

Other questions sailed out of the crowd before he could answer the guy. As much as he wanted to strangle Skirjanek for sending him up here to deal with this shit, he let out a breath he didn't know he'd been holding. These people weren't going to shoot at them.

"One question at a time! Please. To answer the first question—you can do whatever you want. Charlottesville is yours. We have our own settlement up north. We don't want yours. We would like to have a neighbor we can trust. One that doesn't go out, attack, and kidnap other settlements."

. . . and on it went for almost an hour.

"Where'd you say your settlement is? Tysons Corner?" The young woman with a toddler on her hip stepped through to the front edge of the crowd. He did a double take; he'd seen this girl somewhere before.

"We used to be in Tysons," he replied, racking his memory. His brain was as tired as the rest of him. "We moved when Cooper sent her spies in, and we caught them. We figured out we were the next group on her list."

"You don't remember me, do you?"

"I'm sorry, miss, I don't." He almost answered otherwise, because he knew she looked familiar.

The girl turned her shoulders to address the crowd. "I don't know anything about this other bullshit he's spouting," she shouted. His hopes of having this go well took a nosedive. He glanced at the men he'd brought with him, and they all took the hint and stopped what they were doing to focus on the crowd.

"This man saved my baby's life, when he had every right to kill me and my Will. We attacked him, and tried to kill him. And he still helped us when he didn't have to. I say we can trust him."

Jason felt the tension go out of his shoulders as the crowd itself seemed to uncoil. He lifted a fist and pointed at the young mother, remembering. "The girl on the motorcycle? And your friend? Will?"

She smiled grimly and nodded once back at him. "They shot him yesterday, when we were trying to get here."

"I'm sorry" was all he could think to say. A lot of graves would need to be dug.

Trucks had been sent up to collect the people at the lake; several had already departed for the campus with a full load. Many of those headed back had already said they weren't going to stay, and planned to return to wherever they'd been when the forces of Charlottesville had found them. He knew the colonel had been counting on that. Skirjanek wanted a community of settlements, the more the better.

Jason could only think in terms of some sort of mutual defense agreement; he had his own community to worry about. Skirjanek was miles down the road and years ahead of that in his thinking. He was taking into account some form of mutual defense, sure, but he had ideas regarding a common military force in addition to localized militias, trade between the communities, and some sort of very loose legal framework. It seemed like a stretch to him at this point, but so far, these people at least seemed inclined to listen to what Skirjanek had to say—and they would likely listen to Michelle too. The relief column from Potomac was on campus. Skirjanek had radioed a few minutes ago and let him know they'd arrived safely.

"I thought for a second there, that young girl was going to nominate you as her baby daddy." Reed punched him lightly in the shoulder. "I was picturing myself the best man in some sort of postapocalyptic shotgun wedding."

Jason had to smile. "I knew I'd seen her before."

Reed had started to say something when Jason's radio squelched loudly. "Gypsy One—for Jason. Immediate. Gypsy One, Jason. Do you copy?"

"Shit . . ." Jason pulled the radio. "Jason, Gypsy One. I copy."

"Pavel and Pro are in the steam tunnels beneath the campus, in pursuit of target one. Get back here. We are finding access points under all the old buildings and putting teams down. We need to find Josh Keynes—ask the people up there if they know his twenty."

"On my way." He looked up; Reed was gone and halfway to the truckful of refugees.

"Reed, let's go!" He was about to leave without him when Reed jumped back down off the truck, leading the big guy he said he seen with Josh Keynes.

Reed didn't wait for the big guy to catch up with him. "This is Eric—he's a friend of this Josh character."

"If you have any idea where he is, tell us." Jason did his best to keep his emotions in check. "He's not in trouble; a lot of our friends owe him and Dr. Vance their lives. But we need to find him. He may know where Cooper is trying to get to in the tunnels."

"He isn't helping her, trust me," Eric replied. "He was going to hide out with the doc somewhere in the hospital. He knew Cooper would have both of them killed after she figured out they'd tricked her."

"Do you know *where* in the hospital?" Reed beat him to the question. The medical complex was massive; it was something like three hospitals and a med school all mixed together. Combined, it was nearly as large as the campus itself.

The man just shook his head. "I'm sorry. If I knew, I'd tell you."

"Shit!" Jason slammed his fist against the door of the Humvee.

"Did you mean she's in the steam tunnels? I helped run the power plant; the campus electrical grid runs underground, in places alongside the old steam system. I know some of them."

"Hop in." Jason slapped the rear door and was already sliding into his seat.

*

Chapter 33

Ray's small sector of the campus-wide search had him on the south edge of campus, not far from the stadium and a massive brick building labeled the Aquatic & Fitness Center. He turned into the parking loop that ran around the building and mashed on the brakes.

"What the hell?" Elliot was in the seat next to him. The colonel had paired him up with Elliot when assigning search areas. Skirjanek had been focused on finding Cooper, not to mention worried about Pavel and Pro; Ray figured he'd have to forgive the colonel for pairing him with the only other person in the Gypsies who had tried to kill him at one point.

Ray had been running from one thing or another since the virus had struck. He knew what a bug-out vehicle looked like; he'd daydreamed of such a thing not long ago. Parked adjacent to one of the twenty-foot-tall AC compressor units was a black SUV with a massive heavy-duty luggage rack covered in tied-down gear and equipment.

"What's that look like to you?"

"Sweet ride."

Elliot was a good Marine. He knew that because John, Farmer, and even Jason had told him so. Skirjanek was convinced Elliot was some kind of savant. Ray wasn't convinced; Elliot had the imagination of the box that held the proverbial rocks.

"That's a bug-out machine." Ray was sure of it.

"I'd go with something lower profile." Elliot waggled a hand back and forth. "Hey, wait a sec. You think this might be where she's trying to get to?"

Ray wanted to backhand a fist into Elliot's forehead.

He took a deep breath and counted to three. "I suppose it could be. Let's see if we can't find a nearby entrance to the tunnels."

"This is a fairly new building." Elliot pointed his muzzle at the fitness center. "But this close to the stadium, I'll bet there was an old building here before; most of the old buildings have those subbasements."

Ray almost did a double take at the Marine. He was starting to figure the kid out. You just had to get him focused on the right problem for his brain to work. Elliot was almost incapable of turning the page himself.

"Sounds right, let get inside."

The subbasement was there, all right. As near as he could tell in the flashlight- broken darkness, they were directly under the Olympic-sized swimming pool. They found the steam tunnel that came in from the north, made a 90-degree turn, and then ran off into a matching pitch-black tunnel to the east.

"Which way now?" Elliot whispered.

Ray had radioed in that they'd found a suspect bug-out vehicle. There would be someone else sitting on the SUV outside soon, if there wasn't already. Ray shook his head. "Neither, we'll wait. Kill your light."

He did the same and pulled his NVDs down over his eyes. Every team Skirjanek had detailed to the tunnels had been given a set. There wasn't any ambient light to work with, but the ghostly image was clear enough that he was hopeful he wouldn't shoot Elliot. Elliot, in the meantime, didn't have a set. He had a perfect excuse for accidentally shooting him.

*

"She took her shoes off," Pro whispered. The footprints had changed; the smaller of the pair now looked like bare feet. There were large patches of damp mud covering the concrete floors in places. Following the prints through those areas was easy. The dry patches always started off easily, but the footprints would soon disappear. When they came to a junction amid a patch with a dry floor, they had to try each tunnel that branched off until they picked up the footprints again. They'd gotten lucky at the first four-way junction they'd come to. They'd guessed right on their first try. At the most recent four-way junction, they'd spent the better part of an hour exploring down two tunnels until they'd been able to determine which way the quarry had gone.

The whole time, Pavel had been like a mute robot dog following a scent that only he could detect. Only Pro could see the tracks, too, and had felt he needed to say something. Pavel had been so quiet, for so long that he was beginning to wonder if the guy remembered he was behind him.

The Russian stopped in place and held his position for a good ten seconds before turning around to him. "Yes, she did," Pavel whispered as he stared at him, bringing a finger up to his lips.

OK, I got it. No talking . . . at all. Except he knew they weren't the only ones down here; he been hearing echoes of footsteps. There'd been a clanging slam of some sort of heavy door twenty minutes ago that could have been right next to them or a mile away in the tunnels. He knew Pavel had heard it, but he'd ignored it and hadn't even paused to listen.

He tapped at his ears while Pavel still had his flashlight, or "torch" as he called it, pointed at him, then made a walking motion with his fingers. Pavel just nodded and tapped his own ears, and then pointed down the tunnel in the direction they'd been headed. Pavel bent over next to him. "She is close."

"Which way?" Lisa whispered as quietly as she could. The tunnel they were in terminated at a T junction. Ben was just ahead of her, shining his flashlight at the massive steam pipes. There'd been a few at the previous junctions, that had been labeled with some sort of arcane system that she was sure made sense to the type of worker bees who put pipes together.

Ben's flashlight paused, shone down the right-hand tunnel. "I think this way is west."

"You said we were trying to get south." She tried and failed to keep the frustration out of her voice.

Ben's flashlight came back to the wall of concrete that blocked their current tunnel. "That isn't an option anymore, is it?" He sounded pissed off too. They both knew they weren't down here alone. Sound was the one thing that seemed to travel well down here. It wasn't like it needed to see where it was going, and it didn't care if it was lost.

"OK, let's go right."

She waited half a moment before following. She stepped on something hard and sharp, and tensed as she felt it push against, then pop through the pad of her right foot.

"Shit!" she cried out and slammed a hand over her mouth in time to stop what else had been forming on her tongue.

Ben was there in a second, a hand out, his palm ready to slam down against her face. "Put your damned shoes back on," he hissed at her, his face inches away from her own.

For the briefest of moments, she was worried more about Ben than the people looking for her. Then he was up and moving. She pulled out the piece of broken beer bottle and forced her shoes back on. By the time she was moving, Ben was thirty feet ahead of her in the tunnel, but seemed to have stopped and was waiting on her.

Ray had just sent Elliot back topside to check in. The radios were worthless down here. Elliot had been gone a few minutes when he heard a women's distinct cry of "shit." It was close, close enough that he couldn't tell which tunnel the voice had emanated from.

He looked down both tunnels from where he knelt, half leaning against a trio of large pipes. Neither of the yawning pits of blackness offered the slightest hint of a glow of light, and he couldn't figure how anybody would even try to move down here without a flashlight. Then he saw it. His night vision goggles picked up some ambient light leaking out of the tunnel to his right. Just enough to frame the interior walls.

Gotcha . . . He brought up his assault rifle and waited as the glow slowly grew a little brighter. He could almost see the dark outlines of the pipes in the tunnel itself, but he had to wonder if it was his imagination, knowing the pipes were there. Minutes crept by, long enough that he was aware of wanting to move his legs, which were starting to tingle with sleep.

A door slammed somewhere in the building above him. Elliot! He almost screamed in frustration. The tunnel he'd been watching went back to pitch black. Whatever light had been approaching was now gone. He was down to his ears, listening for the slightest whisper of a footfall to make its way out of the pitch-black tunnel.

There was a nothing for a minute or more, and then he heard movement, like fabric moving with a body. He brought his gun to his shoulder and aimed into the darkness of the tunnel, willing the night vision goggles to see something. A supernova of light exploded in the tunnel and burned through his eyes, lancing into head before the goggles dampened their electronic irises. A bright glow was seared into his brain, and it was all he could do to stay upright and pull the trigger blindly. His senses overloaded; he was only peripherally aware that he wasn't the only one shooting until several bullets slammed into him.

The shooting stopped as suddenly as it had started. She had been following Ben, hanging onto his belt in the pitch black, when he'd stopped and turned on his flashlight again. She caught a glimpse past Ben's hip of someone kneeling thirty feet away, aiming a gun at them, before she let go and threw herself to the ground. Ben's rifle fired on full automatic until she heard him grunt and the rifle clatter to the floor. The booming sound of the shots in the confined space was still bouncing around in her head. The echoes were loud enough that she couldn't be sure the shooting had stopped until she opened her eyes and saw Ben's flashlight lying on the floor, lighting up his unmoving body.

She got to the flashlight on her knees and oriented it down the hallway. There was a figure there, slumped against a big pipe, not moving. She shook Ben's body and let the beam travel up his torso. He didn't even look like he'd been hit until she got to his head. The way he was lying, facing away from her, she could tell most of the top of his skull was missing.

She scrabbled through his vest for another magazine and then picked up his gun. She stopped what she was doing as her nerves got to her, and she shined the flashlight back up the tunnel. The enemy soldier was still there, and hadn't moved any more than Ben had. She took a deep breath. Steven had shown her how to shoot and operate an assault rifle. He'd thought it was important, and she'd humored him, the whole time thinking that if it ever came to her defending herself, she had much better weapons to use than a gun. But not now—now she had to get out of this fucking tunnel!

She got the flashlight oriented along the barrel of the gun like she'd seen Ben do . . .

"Don't move!" She felt something hard push into her back. She didn't have to guess what it was.

"Throw the gun down and then turn around!"

She dropped the gun and flashlight. Flashlights behind her came on just as quickly. One was attached to a rifle inches from her face. Part of her was glad she'd been caught. If they'd just let her tell her side of the story, she could blame it all on Steven.

She turned around and was struck by the face looking back at her. It took a moment to process. Even with the harsh light in her face, she could tell it was just a kid, a teenager. She could almost make out the face of the person standing behind him, but the glare from the light at the end of the kid's gun was too much.

"Well . . . aren't you going to be the hero. You caught me."

"We aren't taking you prisoner." The kid spoke slow, like he was trying to control his voice. The barrel of his gun came up and centered on her forehead, inches away. "My friend is dead because of you."

"I'm sorry you think that, but we haven't done anything but defend ourselves."

"Pro . . ." A man's voice spoke softly from behind the glare of light. "You do not need to do this." The voice sounded strangely accented to her, but her ears were still ringing to the point she could barely hear at all. "This kind of justice is of the devil. I would save you these nightmares."

"Listen to him. He's right. I'm certain your colonel wants to hear my side of the story." She was frozen in fear. The kid's grip on his gun was something she could almost feel across the space between them. The end of the barrel was vibrating with tension in front of her face.

"I can't," the kid gritted out between clenched jaws.

A hand came around the teenager's shoulder and slowly pushed the barrel down and away from her. "Is better this way. You are good person, Pro. A good soldier."

Finally, somebody she could deal with. She was going to make it through this. She promised herself that these people would someday regret letting her live. She watched as the man stepped around the teenager. Her hope melted away in a panic as she took in his hard face and utterly remorseless eyes. The man crossed himself in some archaic gesture and then kissed his own fist. The cold eyes never left her own.

"My people have very old saying, from before the time of the tsars. 'God understands.'"

"What . . .! What are you talking about?" Just what she needed, some religious nut.

"It means, I don't have nightmares."

The man casually brought a handgun up to her forehead . . .

*

Chapter 34

Rachel pulled back from looking through the window of the hospital room and smiled at him. Jason had missed that smile.

"You're right." She almost giggled. "He's out cold. I would have thought he'd be out there helping Michelle."

Jason shook his head. "He knows what he's doing. The last thing these people need is an alliance shoved down their throats at gunpoint."

Ten minutes earlier, Skirjanek had walked into an empty room, and collapsed on the bed. He hadn't moved since. They'd all come to check on Ray. His body armor had stopped three rounds; his body had caught two. Dr. Vance had assured them that their friend was going to be fine once he woke up. Pro was still in there with him, waiting for him to wake up.

They'd found Dr. Vance and Josh Keynes waiting for them outside the hospital. The doctor had gone straight to work on the wounded. Josh had been delivered to Michelle by Skirjanek. The two of them were out on campus right now, trying to calm nerves and allay fears together.

"What about him?" Rachel pointed to the room across the hall where "General" Steven Marks lay, with IV tubes hanging above him and his head wrapped.

"I don't know," he admitted. "It's going to be up to the people here. We know he wasn't party to shooting his own people. I can't imagine they'd worry about healing him up to just run him out of town."

"The guy tried to infect you all."

Kyle looked at her and shook his head. "I know what I'd vote for, probably Skirjanek as well," he pointed down the hall to where the man had pretty much collapsed from exhaustion. "But we can't tell these people it's up to them and then make an exception for their General, who in his defense, was locked up by Cooper." Josh Keynes had seemed concerned enough over Marks's condition that Jason was willing to bet the former military man would find some forgiveness here. As far as Jason was concerned, the man could and should have dealt with Cooper himself. But as Skirjanek had pointed out to him, civilian control of the military wasn't any type of insurance that the civilian side wasn't going to go astray.

"And you, Captain Larsen?" Rachel danced back in front of him. "What does your future hold?"

"Well, I've got a teenager in there who's going to join the Marine Corps once things settle down. I've already told Skirjanek I'm heading back up to Potomac. I guess I'll take it from there to see what's next."

"You're not going to sign up with the Colonel and disappear?"

He reached out and grabbed her hand. "I'm not sure how to break this to you, but I've got someone waiting for me at home. I've heard from her, and she's even managed to get us a house that I haven't even seen yet."

"You're certain she'll take you back?" Rachel faced him, her face glowing. "I'd heard you almost abandoned the poor girl."

"A misunderstanding." He shook his head. "I'd been a coward, but I think she forgave me."

"How can you be so sure?"

He leaned down, kissed her, and held her tight. Suddenly, everything was alright. No virus, no fighting. It was just the two of them. He pulled back and smiled. "She seemed very accepting of my apology . . . enthusiastic even."

Rachel smiled and laid her head against his chest. "I love you, Jason."

"I love you too." They held each other for a long time in the quiet of the hallway.

"Jason?"

"Yeah?"

"Your earlier apology, and my enthusiasm, as you put it . . ."

He pulled back and smiled at her. "This hospital is almost empty. What say we find a room upstairs? I'd love to apologize again."

She patted his chest and smiled up at him. "That sounds nice, but I've asked for an appointment with Dr. Vance. Did you know she was trained as an obstetrician?"

***

Some notes –

As always, I hope you've enjoyed reading this story. If you have, please leave a review on Amazon. Reviews go a long way in determining the success of an individual book or the continuation of a series – and to be clear, publishing for Amazon or any modern publishing platform is working for an algorithm that eats reviews in order to survive. To the reader in Australia who sent me a glowing e-mail; when I mentioned that I would send my kids to his house to wash his car if he left the same review on Amazon – I did not know he was in Australia. The same goes for a recent reader in Texas. I really need to stop farming the kids out. Reviews are truly appreciated.

I set out writing "End of Summer" with the intent of producing something my wife would enjoy, and she likes post-apocalyptic stories. By the time I finished the book, I had a vision for a series that would follow Jason, Rachel and Pro into the future and I still do, albeit with a few more central characters added. The response to "End of Summer" has been beyond anything I could have imagined. I certainly didn't write the book knowing the world be soon be facing COVID-19. To those who think I was trying to somehow game our real pandemic, I'd suggest they check the publication date (August 2019).

As always you can sign up for my mailing list for future releases at www.smanderson-author.com -OR- you can follow me on www.facebook.com/SMAndersonauthor/ .

I won't apologize for not updating my web page or posting on Facebook as often as I probably should. My free time can only be spent once and I'd prefer to be writing (and yes, there will be a book 3 in this series). To be honest, I think social media is a mixed bag. It's as cool as it is absolutely, and horrifically inane. That said, I write books and I've been convinced of its necessity. What I do enjoy about social media. is meeting and talking to readers. Please feel free to drop me a line, I will answer. Best regards, Scott.

Printed in Dunstable, United Kingdom